HAPPY NEW YEAR

Also by Robert C Fleet

Thrillers:

Salt City
Heart of Stone

Fantasy:

White Horse, Dark Dragon
Last Mountain

HAPPY NEW YEAR

A

NOVEL

BY

ROBERT C. FLEET

RED FROG

HAPPY NEW YEAR

For information contact: redfrogmedia@gmail.com
Red Frog Publishing is a division of Red Frog Media
112 Harvard Ave. # 43 Claremont, CA 91711.

1   2   3   4   5   6   7   8   9   10

ISBN – 978-0-9850-276-4-3   ISBN - 0985027649

visit our website www.redfrogpublishing.com

A famous writer once wrote something to the effect that

"You have to lose your jewels when editing."

So, with that in mind, this book is dedicated to my editor, who wouldn't let me keep the sloppy sentences I fell In love with, but made me write a story.

HAPPY NEW YEAR

恭喜發財

INTRODUCTION

It started with a movie that didn't happen.

Having spent a little over a year in Saudi Arabia in the second half of the 1980s just before things blew up really bad in the Middle East, I came home with four unfinished novels, because there was nothing else to do there except eat, exercise, drink illegally, or – for me at least – read a lot and write a lot. Well, that wasn't too surprising since I was there as a scriptwriter, working with some of Hollywood's older castoffs, plus some brilliant young Saudis, male and female, who were more talented than the country or the job would allow, and mixing around with some high-falutin' Europeans, such as one of Jean-Luc Godard's editors – all of us drawn by the lure of romance, adventure and, really, money. And there was a lot of sand. And, adventure nil, there was nothing to do. And there was a proxy war between Iraq and Iran that the U.S., Saudi Arabia and Kuwait were semi-paying Saddam Hussein to fight and that those of us in the Eastern Province, on the Gulf, tried to ignore, despite the occasional body floating up on the beach from firefights in the Gulf.

Reading. Having discovered years before that most of the classic books were actually good once I wasn't in school and being graded on them, I am something of a sieve, sucking in almost everything. Of course there were limitations on availability, since censorship was fairly strong in the Kingdom, but expats are a canny lot and I inherited a boxload of paperbacks from the scriptwriter before me. I discovered lots of authors, styles and genres to avoid, but four new loves: Dick Francis and his tight horse-racing-themed mystery novellas (I go to the track once a year because of him), John le Carré for his grasp of humanity in the middle of all the geopolitical muck, Joseph Wambaugh for his chaotic, absurd and ultimately tragic books like *The Delta Star* (if I say "Magilla Gorilla" and "Our Lady of the Freeways" you'll know what I mean) – and even Jane Austen, who is really, really funny and I am glad that the *Jane Austen Omnibus* was the only thing I had to read for the month of October 1988. But, really, *Happy New Year* has nothing to do with all that (except for the last chapter, which you will figure out for yourself). What that year had to do with *Happy New Year* is that I came back from the Kingdom full of stories and ideas. For the next 5-6 years I couldn't put them down on paper fast enough.

But I love filmmaking and theater as much as I love writing in general, and I was exiled to the Kingdom after a particularly disastrous feature film adaptation of my novel *White Horse, Dark Dragon* aka *White Dragon* aka *Legend of the White Horse*, for which I ostensibly wrote the screenplay, with the finished production ending up in studio hell.

And so, despite an offer to stay in the Kingdom at twice my original salary, I returned to the U.S.A. in 1989 prepared to make a movie based on one of my screenplays that I was absolutely *assured* had funding secured.

Which it didn't.

Thirteen drafts and promised financier/producers later, it still didn't.

And then the massacre at Tien An Men Square happened and a couple of years later a financier put up money for an "American" movie on the subject. Full of inspiration I wrote it. We got the green light, we opened an office, hired actors, spent money and, three days before production was to start... were informed that the money had never actually been there. THAT was the auspicious start of *Happy New Year.*

But, as many writers will tell you, I had fallen in love with the story.

Not only that but, as a screenplay, I had been forced to make dozens of compromises between my imagination and the realities of the budget. (Plus the fact that you can't hear what the characters are thinking in a movie.) I was already deep into my novel-writing activities and I was fully aware of the difference between that and a movie script or stage play.

And I was angry.

Soooo, I wrote *Happy New Year* in a heat of anger, using the outline of the screenplay's plot to completely change the main characters and bring in Sam Williams from *Heart of Stone* and references to Mark Cornell from *Salt City.* I wasn't being clever: in my mind I had already joined the two together in a still-unfinished novel, *The Quiet Child,* and they had lives of their own that just seemed to fit with the storyline of *Happy New Year.*

Oh, for the record, I have always been interested in Asian themes – Japanese Studies was one of my majors in college – and the great Korean-moved-to-America-back-to-Korea actor Soon-Tek Oh I count as one of my best friends and major influences.

But, in the end, this is supposed to be a thriller with the genre taint of mystery and politics involved, so if you are in the mood for something with a slight edge and hopefully a little smarter than the norm, enjoy!

RCF 2013

COMEDY

They were all *pagliacci*. Clowns. That magical troupe of half-masked pratfall artists, crowded into two nondescript Citroen "Ugly Ducklings" and careening into the village square in chugging, gravel-churning hysteria. Had children been free from school this heat-choked Friday morning they would have assumed with natural ferocity that the circus had arrived.

There were no children to fill the piazza, however, and there was no circus, either. There were no clowns. There were, instead, five men and two women in rubber half-masks, with bright, liquid, determined eyes gleaming through the small eyeholes cut behind the comedia dell'arte noses, pinpricks of emotion beneath the arching, caricature brows. Their mouths were dry from anxiety, not from the heat of the late September morning. They had come to rob a bank.

A tense Coquette piloted the more crowded of the two Citroens, following a handsome Harlequin who showed distinct signs of aging around his temples. She looked nervously at the puny alleys spiraling off the piazza at odd angles, expecting at any moment to see a battalion of police vehicles spew out. But none did. Everything had been too well planned.

Yes, the Professor, dressed in his Harlequin costume this hot morning, had thought it out well. On Friday mornings the bastard-rich landowners filled the village bank with lira to dole out their penurious sums to their tenant farmers and village suppliers. Their money, not the bank's. And not the farmers' money. Not yet.

So Friday morning was the key time to take the money, before the foolish peasants would turn around and redeposit their undervalued efforts into the capitalist-manipulated bank. Or take the money out of the bank and spend it on useless goods that the rich stocked in their stores. Take the money before noon. For the Revolution.

The clowns' Citroens came to a stop near the village fountain, near - but not directly in front of - the decrepit bank's faded wooden doors. Coquette leaned forward in her seat as it was pushed up by a grinning Pantalone and a scowling Dottore exiting the rear seat of the Citroen. Il Capitano remained in the passenger front seat beside her, leaning forward as well, his overhanging rubber brow balancing well with his jutting, real-skin chin.

"You will wait here with the engine running?" he asked hoarsely, the thick Sicilian accent sounding a discord to Coquette's Northern ear.

"Si," she nodded. "That is what is planned."

"Si," Il Capitano shrugged in agreement, "but, maybe, you want to see... ?"

Coquette nodded and quickly stepped from the Citroen: she wanted to see, not to wait. The engine was running, she could return quickly – but she would see.

The Professor-as-Harlequin, his Citroen already abandoned by its two passengers, Ballerina and Pierrot, almost deserted his place behind the steering wheel at the sight of Coquette stepping out onto the street. *No!*, he thought sourly, once again surprised by the Italian blood's impetuosity. *She cannot – !*

But the Professor did not move. Timing was essential: to leave the car and stop Coquette would waste time. If everything worked well, she would return to her post after the robbery and pilot the getaway car without incident. But if he, too, were to throw planning to the wind and slow down the schedule, then there would be no chance for success. The Professor turned his eloquent Harlequin mask nose towards Coquette and stretched his bitter Tuscan smile beneath it. Inside the Brigade it had long been a rueful joke that he was a Borgia on his maternal side.

Coquette felt a shudder run though her body. She guided her delicate step away from the Professor's sardonic gaze and followed Il Capitano across the cobbled piazza. Soon she was between the broad shoulders of Dottore and

Pantalone, followed by Ballerina and Pierrot. The Professor would not steal her satisfaction with his morbid plan-making, she reasoned to her herself. The Professor could not argue with success.

The Professor, for his part, refused to care any longer: his stomach was already knotted in pain, there was no more room for another twist. He swallowed his adrenaline-driven fear almost physically and forced his hands to remain on the steering wheel. He would not move. He would not worry about this. The plan was still good. Timing was still essential. He would not wreck the plan.

The plan. Simple and direct: destroy capitalist institutions directly --- with minimum danger to the People.

The People. The Professor allowed his attention to regard the dust-poor square. The People had not yet responded to the Brigade's message. Ancient vineyards struggled against environmental reality on the hard hills beyond the village. The People let themselves be lost in a cycle of hard work and exploitation.

A weather-chipped pieta squatted under the shade of a solitary cypress in front of the church. The Professor involuntarily made a Sign-of-the-Cross, unembarrassed by the Catholic gesture that contradicted his agnostic beliefs. The People needed to know that someone other than an Institutional God cared about them. The Professor saw his troupe of clown bandits push into the bank. He wished Coquette had stayed at her post.

Pierrot was at his theatrical best bursting through the door.

La commedia comincia!" he cried, stamping his foot three times on the hardwood floor for effect, waving his Colt .45 revolver with a flourish. The others carried Uzis, small, ugly, practical instruments of death. Pierrot liked the feel of his "Wild West" six-shooter.

"I am Gary Cooper!" he laughed to the startled clerks and stooped grandmothers standing in the bank's small lobby. "Or maybe I am John Wayne!" He spun the pistol on his finger and pointed it with frightening directness at the assistant manager. "I wouldn' move if I were you," Pierrot drawled in English imitation of The Duke.

Then, straightening himself suddenly in a gesture of British prissiness, Pierrot added effetely: "Please – we shall make this as painless as possible. The Revolution needs your cooperation. After all: you *are* the People."

His entrance complete, Pierrot stepped aside to let his colleagues enter the arena with weapons drawn and assignments determined. "Stand next to me," he whispered to Coquette, whose tag-along impulse had brought her into the bank without a purpose. She obeyed without question, joining Pierrot in surveying the actions of their temporary hostages for signs of dangerous, unexpected movement. Of course, Pierrot had a weapon and Coquette did not, but she set a deep scowl upon her mouth and barked short, unnecessary orders to a pair of spinster sisters who were wetting their pants over by the Postal Window.

Once inside the bank, excitement crowded out fear for its share of the adrenaline rush. Il Capitano, Pantalone, Ballerina and Dottore found themselves automatically following the absent Professor's plan precisely: he had drilled them for weeks, knowing that they would need to work instinctively rather than with thought. Ballerina shook her long brown hair from in front of her mask's eyeholes and shoved past the shaking customers to face a window clerk directly.

"Fill this bag," she ordered in a hoarse voice. Beside her, Pantalone and Dottore made similar demands to the other two tellers. Their voices, too, sounded hoarse to her ears.

Il Capitano took his demand to the bank manager, a comfortably plump, middle-aged Roman who had remained seated behind his desk since the bandits' arrival. He did not rise until Il Capitano approached his desk. Il Capitano hated the Roman bank manager at once.

"I want you to open the safe and give me the Friday payroll!" Il Capitano ordered with terse, concise precision.

The Roman bank manager considered Il Capitano a moment and then nodded toward the tellers' windows, a faint smile bending his lips.

"Take that money," he said calmly. "It is not insured. It will hurt us more."

Il Capitano did not like Romans. He did not like Roman accents. He did not like being told what to do by more than one person.

"We are not here to negotiate!" he said strongly, his Sicilian accents grating across the Roman's words deliberately.

The bank manager refused to notice the insult. He cocked his head forward and offered an expression of mild admonition.

"But you do not want to take the money from *our* safe."

Il Capitano was not happy that his dangerous, threatening presence was having no apparent effect upon the Roman. He spat out an oath proscribing the Roman to perform an Oedipal sexual act, then commanded:

"Open the safe now! The Revolution wants all of your blood-stolen money!"

The bank manager uncocked his head and held out his hands in a demand for understanding.

"Pardon, Signore – but this is not our money. It is *Sicilian* money. Do you understand?"

Coquette noticed the guard first: the old man was lost in a deep sleep behind a chest-high potted plant decorated in atrocious pseudo-Etruscan style. He sat with his back wedged into the corner, his thin rump nestled deeply into a pillow he had obviously put upon the solid, straight-backed chair to act as a cushion. An ancient shotgun rested point-down into the worn carpet covering the lobby floor: it rose from between the guard's legs to provide a handrest for the old man's balance. The guard was waking up.

Coquette grabbed at Pierrot's free arm and pointed out the developing problem.

"The guard!" she whispered furtively, as if the hostage-customers with their arms raised did not have their eyes riveted on their captors' every move.

Pierrot swung his pistol with easy grace towards the old guard.

"Don't move, you old fascist," Pierrot laughed with an edge that carried itself into the guard's awakening consciousness.

"Io non sono Fascista," the old man muttered, hearing the words of accusation coming from a half-lifetime's disgrace earlier. "I'm no Fascist!" Still rubbing the sleep from his eyes, the guard stood up.

Pierrot, unlike Il Capitano, did not object to a dialogue with his prisoners.

"Sure you're a fascist!" he taunted, spinning the pistol on his finger once again. "Everyone who works for this institution of capitalist exploitation is a fascist." Pierrot added a grand wave of his free arm to implicate the entire building. He enjoyed the theatricality of the masks. He enjoyed the power of the gun.

"I am not a Fascist!" the old guard cried with a sudden, waking vehemence that startled Coquette.

"He could be dangerous," she nodded nervously to Pierrot.

"Dangerous? This old fascist *dangerous?*" Pierrot found himself shaking with suppressed laughter at the thought of the old turd caught sleeping behind the potted plant being considered dangerous. "The Revolution is dangerous! Fascists are not dangerous!"

"I AM NOT A FASCIST!"

The old man raised his ancient shotgun.

"Don't move, old man. I will kill you." Pierrot's voice was cold and dead. His finger tightened on the trigger of the pistol.

He and Coquette died in the blast from the shotgun.

Il Capitano heard the sound of his own gun, an Uzi, echo like a faraway rachet as his finger squeezed automatically on the trigger, a jerking reaction to the shotgun blast. The Roman bank manager's gesture of world weary supplication to the Sicilian revolutionary crumpled into a blank of surprise as his life disappeared under the barrage of close-cropped gunfire.

"IO NON SONO FASCISTA!"

Pantalone was the first to respond, diving to the floor even as the panic-stricken bank customers ran screaming like chickens in circles about the bank lobby. His half-mask twisted on his face, moving the eyeholes down to his cheekbones. Pantalone grabbed his head with his hands in fear. Above him, still standing at their respective tellers' windows, Dottore and Ballerina twisted around, looking wildly about for a target. They could not see the old guard – his shrunken body was hidden behind the giant vase – but his cracked voice screamed once again:

"IO NON SONO FASCISTA!"

The old man woke up fully now, realizing that he had to defend his name for his last chance at honor. Without thinking about the customers running in front of him – old friends, old neighbors, old enemies who had taunted him half a century before when they had betrayed Il Duce – he turned his ancient shotgun towards the two masked figures who were staring at him across the lobby. There was one barrel left to fire. He could not decide who to shoot. He pulled the trigger.

The old man would never know that he had killed the two spinster sisters. Her cry was short and the Professor's bullet found its way into the guard's head faster than the speed of sound.

Almost at once the screaming from the customers stopped. Not from any force of personality exerted by the Professor, standing in the doorway in place of the fallen Pierrot and Coquette. From simple lack of ability. They had been scared for too long. Their burst of panic was an explosion of emotion in normally dead lives. The loud burst of sound from the shotgun followed by the short crack of the weapon in the Professor's hand had been like a slap, waking them from their uncharacteristic hysteria. hey stood frozen in place again. No one yet realized they would feel even more emotional buffeting in the weeks to come. For this moment they were emptied.

The Professor looked at the cowering Pantalone hugging the floor. "Get up," he ordered in his classically-accented, university-clean Italian. His beaked Harlequin mask nose turned to point at Ballerina and Dottore. "Take the money bags."

Through the small eyeholes his pale green eyes searched the dark recesses of the room until he found Il Capitano far behind the counter, standing at a wooden desk deep within the administrative portion of the bank. "Have you opened the safe?" he demanded in a loud voice.

"IT IS THE MONEY OF MAFIOSI!" Il Capitano cried out in deep shock.

"It is the money of Revolution now," the Professor responded. "Take it." He allowed his eyes to check the clock: there were still five minutes. Then the Professor directed his eyes to look up, to see the vaulted, turn-of-the-century architecture that hovered over the bank lobby. He did not want to look down at the scuffed tile floor. He did not want to see the bodies lying there. He did not want to see Pierrot and Coquette, their masks repainted a sudden red. He did not want to see the old Fascist guard, grotesquely fallen back into his chair so that his death resembled sleep. He did not want to see the black-dressed spinster sisters lying head-to-head in awkward comfort. Or the surprised Roman bank manager still gesturing for the Sicilian Il Capitano to understand him.

The Profesor did not want to cry.

CHINESE CURSES

1989, by most accounts, was a crazy year.

1988 had been the year to give people hope. Almost a decade of attritious war had ended in the Middle East when Iraq was somehow persuaded to stop its aggressions on Iran. Hope: a truly powerful aphrodisiac. Costa Rica's president Oscar Arias had persuaded the Central American community of nations to adopt a tentative truce in their violent civil wars. Hope: better than religion to inspire great deeds. Yasser Arafat had acceded to Israel's twenty year demand for recognition – and forsworn terrorism to boot. Hope: dreams better than grim reality.

In China, where the economic revival policy of leader Deng Xiaoping was regarded as nothing less than miraculous by admiring capitalist world leaders, democratic reform was considered a done deal needing only the requisite motions of popular involvement. Palestinians in the Occupied Territories saw the direction of history and began the "intifada" – a children's and mothers' crusade to win world moral opinion and recapture their homeland from Israel by a means short of war. Hope.

In 1989 that hope was taken and transformed into the greatest revolution for peace of the century: the Cold War ended. Within twelve months Eastern Europe would be de facto a group of free nations. People – ordinary people, not students or soldiers or political activists – literally tore down the Berlin Wall peacefully – laughing, singing, playing in the crowd control water cannons until the police themselves joined in the celebration.

Arias' shaky peace plan worked so well in Central America that the Contras could return to Nicaragua, staging a nonviolent comeback that led to free elections by the Sandinistas and – a surprising year later – an even more surprising upset victory. The white South African government began to shake its head at its own mistakes and began the laborious process of releasing the world's most famous political prisoner, Nelson Mandela.

East Europeans began to realize that freedom meant being hungry and unemployed.

Palestinians and Israelis began to realize that neither side trusted the other – let alone themselves – well enough to engage in an honest dialogue: children died from rubber bullets and survivors of the Holocaust heard themselves described as killers of innocents.

Salvadoran priests and nuns discovered that military bullets still killed in the night, even if accompanied by words of conciliation.

Romanians threw out the dictator Nicolae Ceausescu —only to discover the dark horror of their own vengefulness in doing so.

Chinese students gathered at Tien An Men Square to demand liberty.

Liberty.

They built a quick-plaster statue to celebrate "liberty": the Goddess of Democracy. Brought her to Tien An Men Square, where emperors and their courtiers had paraded in glorious aristocratic cruelty for dynasties, where Mao Tse-Tung (or Zhe Dong as he is now called) marked the final "liberation" of China forty years earlier. Now the students were ready for a new liberation: the liberation of DEMOCRACY. Let's give a little song of praise for their efforts:

> Amazing Grace
>
> How sweet the sound
>
> That saved a wretch like me.
>
> I once was lost
>
> But now am found
>
> Was blind, but now I see.

Philippe had flocked to China with all the other little

French boys in '88. Here was the new excitement: learn some Chinese, set up the family connections in Beijing (not "Peking" anymore as his father kept mistakenly writing), live like kings for pennies on the black market exchange rate. A television was only a third the price as in Hong Kong, video tapes were always available from Shanghai, rock music of course was only a cassette away. *Had the Chinese heard of Milli Vanilli yet?*, Philippe wondered: two formidable black men from Germany and Jamaica with most excellent dreadlocks who sang so much better than those high-nosed American rockers (except for Madonna, bien sur, and maybe Lisa Hartmann).

Philippe, after a short summer of effort, spoke Chinese with passable finesse – and he met Fuong Lee. It was not easy to avoid noticing Fuong Lee on the campus: if he was not charismatic as an activist speaker, he was at least not dull. Philippe had quickly learned that most Chinese activists were long on lengthy, tedious dialectic and short on interesting, clear ideas. He avoided most of the activists as much as possible: Maman and Papa had armed him with instructions to cultivate mid-level members of the Communist bureaucracy who showed promise of advancement in key areas of the Import Control Offices. Philippe found these people to be as interested in his tapes and videos as he was. So was Fuong Lee.

That was how they met: at a government office discussing videos. Philippe had loaned his contact a new

Rambo video. Now - knowing it had been copied for some "private enterprise" pirating - he needed it back to pass on to another contact. But Fuong Lee was in the office and waiting for him. The *Rambo* video was in Fuong Lee's hand.

"I like *Rambo*," Fuong Lee said in perfect English.

"I like the *Rocky* movie better," Philippe answered in heavily-inflected English.

"You think a street fighter has a chance to win?" Fuong asked in Shanghai trader's pidgin.

"I like the trying," Philippe smiled back in the street Chinese he knew better than the literary Mandarin he was studying.

He was trapped, then, and he knew it immediately: Fuong Lee was Rocky in a political sense, a Chinese activist street fighter who saw success opening for an ambitious twenty-two year-old student at every opportunity. Philippe was an opportunity.

Philippe knew that, to a certain extent, Fuong Lee was using him: bringing the young Frenchman to student meetings, accompanying him to appointments with members of the government establishment. Fuong Lee encouraged Philippe to say a few words, then quickly stepped in and dominated the meeting, arranged a new appointment, solo, becoming always central to everything.

But Philippe liked being used thus. On his own, Philippe knew that he would never have become the center of anyone's attention. Even his contacts with government officials focussed on the merchandise Philippe held out as enticements, not on himself. With Fuong Lee, however, Philippe was thrust into prominence as the attention-grabber. Very soon, in fact before the year had closed-out, Philippe realized that he had become an essential part of Fuong Lee's credentials.

And he began to believe in Fuong Lee.

Fuong was never subtle. Short, pointed pleas for specific ideas characterized his speeches. "We have instruments of communication," he argued, "but we are not allowed to communicate. How can we bring about economic reform if we do not communicate?" It made sense to Philippe.

"The old guard hamper Chairman Deng's programs. They must be replaced by a new guard. We will support the new guard." That excited Philippe, particularly when Fuong put such an emphasis on the "we" that there was no question as to who was the new guard.

"Until we are free to support Chairman Deng as we see fit, there can be no Democracy!" Fuong proclaimed – and Philippe stood beside his friend, in love with the power they flirted with.

That love helped Philippe stay awake through the long, all-night sessions. The student movement was excruciatingly dull, Philippe had deduced that from afar long before he met Fuong. Joining his persuasive friend at the activists' planning sessions was an exercise in tedium. Each leader seemed intent upon delivering his own diatribe (*Are there no beautiful women leaders?*, Philippe wondered) – a lengthy agenda that harped upon the same magical words endlessly: Democracy. Liberty. Freedom.

"Liberté, égalité, fraternité!" Philippe muttered in mild derision one sunrise as he stumbled home to his apartment with Fuong Lee after yet another all-nighter.

"You are a fucking aristocrat?" Fuong returned the derision in his best street-Shanghai drawl, a character voice he slipped in and out of with frequency. But always with a smile, which kept people liking him. Which kept Philippe following him.

"No, I am a f-fuck-ing nouveau riche!" he slurred in French-Chinese response. "But we had our Revolution two hundred years ago and I am tired of textbook history."

Fuong Lee did not take too much offense at the reference: he was now living in Philippe's Western-style apartment, a decided improvement over his own student hole, and his opinion of the "riche," *nouveau* or *ancienne*, was not derogatory. But he liked his history.

"OK, fucking bourgeois: for you we will leave the textbooks behind."

They left all their textbooks behind that Spring of 1989, and conquered Tien An Men Square instead. Philippe stood at Fuong Lee's side as they did it. Everyday. The first demonstrations were more exciting than sex, danger hovering over every moment. Fuong was in his element here: quick minute-long speeches through a megaphone – hoisted atop Philippe's shoulders – then disappearing down into the growing crowds.

As the demonstrations grew larger, though, Fuong lost some of his earlier impact on the students, his place taken by the emboldened activists who needed long dozens of minutes to squawk their same limited ideas.

But Fuong Lee had found a new audience on the periphery of the demonstration. Two new audiences, in fact: the workers and the soldiers. To the students Fuong Lee was a well-spoken, if limited, speaker. They still believed in the Confucian mode, and if an educated leader was not capable of exhibiting his vocabulary and expertise *in extremis*, then he was perhaps not so educated as he needed to be (the students did, after all, have to stand behind their own constituency of tradition). So, gradually over the first few days, Fuong Lee left the students to be led by Wang Dan, Guo Haifeng and the others. He wanted to lead "the people."

With the workers first, and then the soldiers, Fuong Lee's short speeches fit in perfectly with their "I've-got-other-things-to-do-but-I'll-listen-for-a-minute" attitude. Somewhere during the first half-hundred such speeches, Fuong discovered that his "Shanghai character" made an even better impression upon the non-students. Quickly his speeches became more crowd-pleasing in their casual obscenities and pointed political jokes. This became a crucial turning point as the Tien An Men demonstrations grew into the Long Siege.

The Russian leader Mikhail Gorbachev was coming to meet with Chairman Deng. There was a very clearcut division between the new guard and the old in Deng's government. It was time for the students to take to the streets in force to settle the issue. In with the NEW! Out with the OLD!

In the middle of it all, Philippe received the greatest gift of all: a video camera sent by Maman. She and Papa had somewhat forgotten their erstwhile representative for the past half-year (Philippe often thought resentfully that they had forgotten him for the past half-life) – the camera was a conscience-relieving response to a request Philippe had made months earlier. Its arrival was fortuitous: everything was happening too fast for Philippe to remember. So he began to record the best moments.

A new reality emerged. From being Fuong's "Westerner," a witness over-the-shoulder to great events, Philippe now evolved into "The Eyes": Fuong's official eyes, watching the chaotic activities that Fuong was too much a part of to see himself. The Goddess of Democracy statue was built up over several days – in Philippe's camera memory Fuong could see it happen in minutes. The Procession of the

Goddess was headed by student leaders – Philippe saw only Fuong and the Goddess, dual symbols of the movement's evolving moral strength.

Philippe and Fuong began to separate. Fuong headed student groups that left the Square to negotiate with government representatives; he persuaded Army officers to encourage their troops to cheer the demonstrators. He needed his Eyes to watch over Tien An Men while he was gone. The Eyes was sent to roam through the demonstration, watching through a two-inch square the faces and voices demanding Liberty, Democracy, Freedom.

They started out sleeping in the Square, Fuong needing to be close to his movement, Philippe too exhausted to leave. Then, after the camera arrived, they stopped sleeping. Every night, at midnight, or later, Fuong would draw Philippe to some open patch on the dark plain of sleeping bodies and they squatted down next to one another. Philippe would attach an earphone to his camera, set the whole affair upon Fuong's shoulder, and play back the tiny eight millimeter cassette images of the day. Fuong sat there facing Philippe, his right eye pressed against the viewfinder, watching the playback on the tiny black-and-white monitor, waiting impatiently if the battery went dead and Philippe had to fumble in his pockets to find one with enough energy left to power the day's memories.

Philippe would watch it all play across Fuong's face. The left eye, screwed shut to aid the right eye see the viewfinder, would sometimes pop open when a particular image seized Fuong's heart. Philippe would ask what it was and, gradually, he began to anticipate the moments that would excite his friend. Within a week he had succeeded to the point where Fuong was exhausted from emotional involvement at the end of the two hour cassette. His Eyes had become too incisive.

"Go home and recharge your batteries," Fuong sighed on the restless edge of sleep that night, eyes failing to stay open. He smiled as his head bumped heavily on the stone pavement. "Sleep in your real, Western bed."

Philippe was gone, then, when the tanks rolled in. He slept very well as machine guns stuttered on the other side of the city. Fuong saw the soldiers rush in without his Eyes --- but he remembered the images well enough. He was lucky, though: Captain Du, with whom he had joked regularly for the past two weeks, shoved a rifle butt into Fuong's nose and broke it. The bloody mess obscured his face and the first rush of soldiers swept by his unconscious body lying on the sidewalk. Within hours Fuong's puffed-up face was unrecognizable, and he allowed himself to be swept into a garbage truck carrying refuse from the city, one of the last vehicles to exit before Beijing was closed off by the military. As Fuong nauseously sat among the rot and watched his movement die behind him, he tried to figure out what had happened. It took him days to realize that Chairman Deng had decided his sacred economic reforms did not need Democracy, Liberty and Freedom.

The video camera's batteries were already recharged when the Army began their roundup of student leaders. They knew, of course, where Fuong Lee really lived, and did not waste time looking for him at his assigned student quarters. Philippe woke with a start at the sound of the apartment door being kicked open. He had been dreaming in Chinese, and he could not for some reason remember any French, except for three, stupid textbook phrases: liberté, égalité, fraternité.

CROWN ROYAL

1990 was even more screwed-up than 1989.

No need, really, to think about all of the good things – and there were plenty. By 1990 so much of the promise of the earlier years was fulfilled that there was a glut of change from the old horrors. Then all of those changes began to transform themselves from miracles to annoying realities. East Germany and West Germany became one Germany and, oh, how easy it was to remember 1939 if you were a Pole! (And why not? The "democratic" leader of the dominant West G., Helmut Kohl, talked openly about rolling back the pre-War borders to take back a chunk of land. Never underestimate the historical amnesia of a once-and-future master race.)

It didn't pay to be a Lithuanian, either: not when thirty-five years of Western rhetoric about sovereign Baltic States is sacrificed to the convenience of post-Cold War Soviet buddies.

And so on.

A bit of a squeeze on Panamanian drug presidents who crossed their old CIA pals by not toeing-the-line deferentially enough – but their Columbian cartel drug chums figured out quickly that a little hot war on their own government would keep the hounds at bay for a while.

Looking around Chinatown in Los Angeles, you could see the home crowds muster up their support for the Tien An Men exiles: say nothing and keep a low profile lest Chairman Deng mess up their lucrative trade contacts. The Goddess of Democracy raised so high in Tien An Men the Spring before just couldn't be allowed into the Chinese New Year Parade. "Not pertinent to our theme" was the imminently practical explanation. The University of Southern California marching band, of course, fit in perfectly with the Sinic celebration.

That's getting ahead of the story, though, because before then – in fact before 1989 had faded out – a handsome young Chinese man began surfacing at small-scale rallies around the U.S.. He would pop up from the crowd, speak several short, effective phrases, then sink back into the crowd. He started off speaking only Chinese. English began to sprinkle into his phrases early on. By Fall he was making his sudden appearances at non-Chinese rallies. He looked a lot like Fuong Lee.

Jenny Luck thought about that as she applied the thick eyeliner to her shallow-set eyelids, working carefully in the cramped car seat to find the right combination of refracted light and reflection from the rearview mirror. There were beautiful eyes under the purple-smudged lids and, if the eyebrows seemed a mite too delicate set against the thick crust of rouge on her prominent cheeks, she would repair that with a heavy dose of eyebrow pencil in a moment. For now, still engaged in the dulling, repetitive task of preparing her face, Jenn revelled in the luxury of thinking about Fuong Lee instead of work.

She liked his face, had noticed it in the news coverage of Tien An Men the Spring before. Now she had recognized the fugitive dissident's face in the background crowd in a photograph taken at a recent demonstration in front of City Hall. He had spoken for a few moments, too, she read, but there were no pictures of that. The papers did not know who the quick-spoken Chinese speaker was - or did not care to find out. Jenny Luck did.

But that was on her time. Now was professional time. Or almost was. Almost time to step out onto Santa Monica Boulevard and compete with the pretty boys for attention. As soon as Sam was ready. Wouldn't be too smart to step out onto the streets without your Black Angel. Particularly for a hometown Chinese girl standing on the edge of a Russian neighborhood.

Jenn tried out the eye make-up with a quick succession of blinks: her eyelids didn't feel *too* sticky, so she would still be able to see.

And the first thing she saw was Sam staring with fierce anger at a public telephone half-a-block down the street.

Trying to call Marie, Jenn thought with a jealousy-tinged annoyance that gnawed at the edges of her immediate professional preoccupation. She noticed with alarm that the barrel of her pistol was peeping out through her open handbag. She shoved it back into a pile of tissues and snapped the bag shut in a quick, one-handed movement, her eyes back on Sam.

Sam was fruitlessly jamming a coin into the pay phone, then pounding at the side of the otherwise faultless-appearing machine when the money became stuck halfway in. He needed to call Marie, Jenn knew, and though she begrudged him the time, she also knew that until Sam made his call he would not be there by her side. Then he would be *her* Black Angel 100%. But not until then.

Santa Monica Boulevard on a September Friday night at seven o'clock.

The newspapers said that summer had ended three days ago, Jenn remembered. Too bad nobody told the weather: it had been 105 degrees on the street that afternoon and, even though the earlier sunset now had the sky glowing orange-red in the smoggy haze, the temperature was still pushing ninety. She stepped on the accelerator and let the engine idle a little higher to push the car's sluggish air conditioner into action. It was a technique guaranteed to use up gas quickly in the already-gluttonous Caddy, but it wasn't Jenn's money. And Sam wouldn't mind coming back to a cool haven after his phone-searching jog over the hothouse sidewalks.

Jenn let her screechingly short skirt ride up even higher as the A/C shot a spout of cool dampness across her lap. Closer, but still across the boulevard, Sam was emerging from a Mexican grill-cum-gay bar, his dark face flushed almost to pure blackness by an obviously failed effort to find a working and/or free public phone inside the place. He wouldn't push his weight around, not so near The Business, so his 205 pounds of thirty-six year old muscle were left to charge from the grey shadows of the grill and out onto the monoxide-hot sidewalk in another burst of wasted anger.

We live on too much emotion, Jenn thought idly. *We should chill out more.* They wouldn't, of course, but Jenn had read somewhere that just saying things like that out loud helped "acknowledge" the situation and relieve some of the stress. She'd told that to Sam and he had just smiled.

Right now he wasn't smiling. He was standing twenty yards away, holding the mutilated receiver to the public phone nearest to the Cad, back where his odyssey had begun. Jenn decided that Sam had given too much attention to Marie already and stepped out of the car. Three passing cars of jerk-offs praised her with loud catcalls before she remembered to lower her skirt. Sam saw her, though. Time to start the night's work.

No, it was too late.

Sam was not particularly into drugs, but in his position it was not good business to turn away the small-time dealers who worked the streets. He was standing too near the freeside alley to beg off on account of exposure. He tried, and the dealer simply arched a dripping nose in the general direction of Jenn and sniffed:

"Let the yella whore wait. Maybe she'll pick up some money while you're spenin' yours."

Jenn reached into the Cad and cut the engine, grabbing out her handbag before closing the self-locking doors. She leaned back against the hand-buffed gloss finish and pouted. Sam smiled his professional smile. "That's what we here for, baby!" he called out with a wave, following the dealer into the alley. Jenn could see that he was mad as hell at not getting through to Marie.

The alley smelled like the worst stench of greasy fast food from the hamburger shack that fronted it, combined with rich, thick cabbage odors from the Russian-Jewish immigrants whose apartment house backed it. Sam, whose tastes ran the gamut from Detroit soul food, through German schnitzel, French crepes and Jenn's Cantonese delights, didn't mind the Russian food smells, but gagged at the old grease burning in a cloud coming from the wooden screen door of the hamburger shack. Sam knew without a doubt that the dealer would step into that door. He even wagered a small bet with himself on it. He won his bet.

Sam hadn't planned on carrying cash that night, just a couple of hundred for show, nothing for heavy exchange. This was a new block, he was the new face, Jenn the new bod. At the same time, Sam wanted the dealer to know that

that *they* - he and his lady - were not interested in chump change deals. He waved away the rock cocaine with a gesture that carried over more than a little of his accumulated impatience.

"Powder, man."

"You said you don't got no money."

"I see, I like, I buy tomorrow."

"'S not fuckin' Bloomindale's! I'm not gonna set up a display counter for your ev'ryday convenience!"

"Set up for *your* convenience, then, Mister ex-Noriega," Sam said, covering the dealer's exit from the back door and letting the smaller man see that the black pimp was carrying. But Sam was a diplomat.

"You got nothing to lose: we here, you show. Time already spent."

Time was what Jenn had plenty of at the moment: she was not about to step away from the security of the Cadillac without Sam keeping an eye on her. And she knew that Sam was counting on her keeping an eye on him.

She could see him now in vague reflections against the metal freezer door just inside the hamburger shack back entrance. The dealer's voice carried out to the street in an unintelligible stream of complaint. If the stuff was good, Jenn expected Sam to mollify the crud's greed with a sample purchase.

The fruit seller had probably been a big man when he was young.

As he pushed the orange-filled grocery cart into the alley entrance Jenn could see that the heavy forearms had once carried thick muscles. Probably an old construction worker. Definitely a Russian.

It was odd to see anyone other than a Mexican selling fruit on the streets, Jenn thought. The old fruit seller probably owned three shops and had a hundred thousand in undeclared profits hidden in his apartment, she decided. The "poor fruit seller" business was probably to keep the IRS off his case. The Russian Jews emigrated from the Soviet Union, but they never trusted the American government. Well, why should they? It was only because they were Jewish that the U.S. had taken most of them in: they were pawns and they knew it. Anyway, selling black market produce was a whole lot more honest than dealing drugs or running a savings and loan. Jenn was only annoyed that the man had decided to set up shop near the alley. She could not see Sam without appearing obvious.

"Ostav menia, nie snimay!" The shrill voice blasted out from a third floor apartment window. Jenn recognized the woman's accent as from somewhere in southern Russia, but could barely make out the words: Don't take my picture!

"Nie vehodi v moyu kuchnyu! - Stay out of my kitchen!" Sofia added with a vehement shake of her head at Boris. The stupid man, she muttered to herself and the steaming pot of borscht. Couldn't he see that she looked a mess? Couldn't he see and that there was no room for *one* person in this God-abandoned little kitchen, let alone *two*! Especially him and his brother's camera!

"I just wanted to take a picture to send to Lenya in Novograd," Boris protested, "to show them what we have."

"We don't have much of a kitchen," Sofia grumbled. "You want to show them that we don't have much of a kitchen?"

"*They* don't have an apartment," Boris answered sullenly, leaning against the kitchen door and idly scratching his son Mischa's head. *Mischa is allowed in the kitchen*, was what he was really thinking, *why not me?* Boris could not help feeling jealous of the attention Sofia had taken from him and given to Mischa since the boy was born two years ago. Two years! Just after they arrived in Los Angeles. They didn't have an apartment then, either, and Sofia had thought *this* apartment and *this* kitchen too big for wonder. It didn't seem small at all for the first couple of months. Boris let Mischa crawl past him and wander into the living room.

Three floors below, on the sidewalk, Yevgeny looked at the heavily made-up Chinese prostitute who leaned against the Cadillac only ten feet across from his grocery cart fruit stand. With an effort he suppressed an urge to impress her. Instead he picked up two large oranges and remembered that once his balls had been that big and that he had known a Tartar woman twice or three dozen times during the War.

Then he tossed the Chinese prostitute one of the oranges without warning.

"Hey, old man! What're you doing!" she yelled at him, deftly catching the orange with a reflexive action faster than Yevgeny had expected.

"I would have give you a grapefruit like your bootiful breasts, but I don't have any!" he smiled back. Ohhh, he wished he were forty again. Or even sixty. This being old held too many disappointments in oneself. All he had left was charm. At least the Chinese girl was laughing.

Oh, Jesus!, Jenn found herself laughing, quietly pleased at the harmless come-on from the old fruit seller – and at the very delicious-looking orange he had thrown her. A real Israeli blood orange from Jaffa. The scent caressed her nostrils and made her mouth water. It was still too hot today, and the small sections would each be so succulently juicy. And then there would be orange peel under her fingernails. And her lipstick would smear. *Oh God, you are cruel!*, she thought.

The whiny voice in the alley doorway crooned, "It's good. I told ya it's good. I'm showin' ya it's good. So tell me it's good to make me feel good."

Sam looked down at the little dealer and remembered for the thousandth time why little dealers stayed little: they liked their product too much. Truth to tell (and Sam could without even trying the stuff), the dealer's cocaine was such low-grade crap that Sam would look more like a chump if he bought it than if he passed. But this was the first day. A Black Angel had to make his mark on a new territory quick. Or maybe push the stakes up fast with this doper.

"Sure it's good – if you're from hunger. My lady 'n I ain't from hunger. We want finer things."

Up in the third floor apartment, while his parents jabbered and ignored him, little Mischa saw the beautiful opportunity of freedom and it inspired him to new heights of accomplishment: he rose to his feet and walked!

"I am thinking, Boris, that maybe Lenya and - what's her name?"

"Marfa."

Sofia let her soft arm squeeze into Boris' side. "Marfa and Lenya, maybe they will like to see our kitchen." Sofia's large, cowlike eyes half-closed with satisfaction: in a photograph, with no one in it, this kitchen would look *huge*. And Marfa and Lenya did not even *have* an apartment!

Mischa saw the open door to the balcony as yet another chance to test his growing powers. He had seen TV. He *knew*.

It was Jenn's angle, leaning back against the Caddy, that let her see what Mischa was up to first.

"Oh, hell -" she muttered, swallowing the words.

Mischa put his tiny hands atop the railing and pulled: he had done this many times in his crib bed.

Sam could take the dealer's bad breath no longer. He raised his face away and looked up, seeing –

"Oh, damn."

Mischa pulled himself up to the top of the rail and teetered gloriously: first walking and now the world!

Yevgeny was disappointed: the pretty whore was looking over his head. Perhaps a pigeon was about to crap on him? He looked up defensively.

"Oh, fuck" he said in pure, Mother-tongue Russian.

Mischa drew himself up to his full thirty-inch height and thrust out his arms.

Sofia began to gulp uncontrollably as she looked past Boris' shoulder to the balcony rail.

"Miii–scchhaa!" she croaked.

"SUPERMAN!" Mischa cried.

"POLICE! OUT OF THE WAY!!!" Sam and Jenn shouted in near-perfect unison.

And it *is* true: real life happens in slow motion when a crisis occurs.

Mischa knew the beauty of perfect flight, winging down the three stories with arms spread and heart happy, while Jenn was absolutely certain that an eternity of time and an infinity of distance separated her from the fruit-filled grocery cart that lay under the falling boy's trajectory. She shed her stiletto heels even as she ran, but even that was too slow.

Sam seemed to perform complete leg splits as he bounded through the back door and across to the cart in three leaps, smashing his foot down on the soft hood of the tiny Honda Civic parked in-between and using it as a springboard to launch himself up towards the child.

Yevgeny felt the Chinese girl shove him back fiercely away from his cart and wished that his once-taut stomach muscles had not long since turned to jelly.

Sofia stood screaming into Boris' ear at the kitchen door, and Boris wondered what had just happened.

It ended not with a bang, nor a whimper.

Just a splunch.

Caught in mid-air and ten feet above the ground by Sgt. Sam Williams of the LAPD, Superman Mischa ended his first flight in an ungraceful but highly liquid descent into the fruit-laden grocery cart, an impact of such squishing significance that orange juice was said to have run freely like the River Volga (or so Yevgeny reported on his Loss Statement to the California state Franchise Tax Board). Jenn, smacked out of the way by a flailing black arm, saw pieces of the once-desired Jaffa orange cling stickily to her arms, legs, leather skirt and easily-stained silk halter. She also saw a two-bit drug dealer run frantically down the street, disappearing into a crowd, where he would no doubt inform colleagues and casual customers alike about the true identity of the new black pimp and his Chinese whore.

There was, at least, silence from the baby.

But not silence from his mother.

Within seconds the dazed tranquility of Sam and Jenn was disturbed by Sofia's repeated mantra cry of "Mischa! Mischa! Mischa!" in tumbling syllables of hysterical emotions falling down upon their heads. She leaned precariously over the edge of the balcony, giving Jenn a momentary heart attack that her partner would soon be squashed by the plump Russian matka.

Although Sam was still sighing with relief atop the sinking pile of squashed citrus, Jenn shoved the cart a few yards out from under the balcony. The object of his mother's cries, Mischa, stood on Sam's heaving stomach and squealed with delight at this new trip.

"Jenn?" The voice was weak with expected disappointment.

"Um-hmm?" Jenn felt the same growing sense of dismay.

"Is there any chance that our cover is still good?"

Jenn looked over at the back door to the hamburger shack. It stood flung open, a crowd of kitchen short-order help looking out at the fruity chaos.

"No, Sam." She pulled a pathetically small tissue from her hand bag and held it out to her erstwhile ex-Black Angel. "Here."

"Mischa! Mischa! Mischa!"

Just about then the sound of Sofia's grating voice inspired Jenn to thoughts of violence, and she fingered the pistol still hidden in her handbag. Her fingertips also brushed across her police badge. Professional sang-froid got the better of her.

"The baby is OK.!" she shouted up to Sofia in clear, university-trained Russian.

But a Russian mother was not to be mollified by any smooth-talking official.

"How can he be OK?" she moaned for all the neighbors to hear of her misery. "He has fallen three stories! He is hurt!"

"I said he is OK!" Jenn called up with growing peevishness. "Listen to me!"

"He cannot be OK!" Sofia began to feed upon her delicious emotions. "You are lying to me!"

"I – said – he – was – $O – K$!" Jenn's annoyance chopped up the words into small Russian epithets. Then, grabbing the child off Sam's belly and holding him up, she cried out in English: "I'll damn well show you: HE'S OK!

Sofia said nothing for a moment, and Jenn allowed herself to considered the matter settled. It was a premature hope. Sofia whined down to the cabbage-grease scented alley in English:

"It is too far to see. Can you bring him up?"

Jenn lost her temper, releasing simultaneous curses in English, Russian and Mandarin that ended with the virulent promise: "Can I bring him *up*!? Oh, you're damn right I'll bring him *up*!"

Holding Mischa at arm's length, she whisked away from the grocery cart. Sam could hear Jenn's complaints echo though the tiled hallways, mingled with the baby's delighted laughter, as the two disappeared into the apartment building. "I'm going to damn well give as many citations for child neglect that I can think of! Bring him up! What does that cow think we are, a lifesaving babysitter service!?

The complaints died away with the distance traveled, leaving Sam to survey the wreckage of his pimp clothes. There was a piece of fruit lodged inside an indelicate crevice of his anatomy. Removal required an even more indelicate hand movement. Sam stopped in mid-reach at the sound of chuckling. The old Russian fruit seller was watching him.

"No, no," Yevgeny shook his head, "don't stop. I am learning your new way to make orange juice." Even though he smiled as he said this, the old man could not help surveying the mess in combined fascinations of dismay and delight. Now to have the black pimp-turned-policeman performing comic acts was an unexpected dessert of pleasure.

Yevgeny thought of how he would embellish the details for his bored grandson ("I threw my fruit cart under the child, to cushion his fall if the police failed –"), then began to notice that there were several perfectly good oranges lying about the sidewalk. The old man felt his stout knees protest as he bent down and began picking them up, stuffing the oranges inside his shirt – they had skins, people could peel them! – when an attempt at reaching a whole orange rolled under the cart brought him face-to-face with a handful of cash held by a white-palmed hand.

"Here," Sam said, thrusting out a small wad of juice-soaked dollar bills.

"Nyet!" Yevgeny answered gruffly. Feigning offense, he forgot to speak English as he added: "I don't want money for this."

Sam understood the gesture, but needed to thank the man.

"I'm sorry, I don't speak Russian. Do you speak English?"

Yevgeny had never spoken politely with an official before, particularly not with the black officials at Immigration. But this black policeman was speaking politely to him – and Yevgeny knew he was a hero, to boot. Yevgeny was amazed.

"I don't expect you black persons to speak Russian, but the Chinese lady does?"

"Yeah." Sam could not say why, but he was suddenly embarrassed. "She studied a lot. I – I don't speak any languages." He held out the handful of money again. "You helped me. I messed up your fruit."

Yevgeny shoved away the small-beans money dismissively.

"It's a stupid world."

Then he saw something he wouldn't have expected: the black policeman squatted down and began picking up oranges from the street – and he was shaking. Though Yevgeny had never had enough imagination to be terribly frightened himself – once, in the War, but never over others' safety – he recognized the policeman's problem: he had been scared.

"Hey, you, policeman -"

Sam did not look up: he needed to keep moving.

"M'name's Williams, sir. Sergeant Sam Williams. The lady's Detective Jenny Luck."

"You don't have to do that, Sergeant Sam."

"I don't have to do a lot of things, sir. That's why I do 'em."

Yevgeny looked at the powerfully-built black man on his hands and knees and thought of himself. The black man had been more strong ten years before, the old man could tell. *But never as strong as I was*, Yevgeny thought proudly.

"How old are you, Sergeant Sam?"

Sam swept the last decent-looking fruit survivors into the remains of his sports coat. "Whatcha want to know for?"

"I want to know if you are old enough to have a drink."

Sam dumped the pile of oranges into the grocery cart. He shook the coat more than was necessary to cover up the quaking feeling in his arms. But he saw that the fruit seller noticed.

"I *need* to have a drink, sir," Sam tried to smile, "but you see that I am too young to go into a bar by myself."

Yevgeny spit between his teeth, a gesture he had perfected in Odessa dockyards half-a-century earlier. "Is that so?" he said craftily. "Maybe I know somebody who owns a bar."

"I can't -"

"I'll even buy you a drink – just one. Don't drink like a fish because it's free."

Sam did not refuse.

The old man turned and began to walk away from the grocery cart, to be stopped by a gesture from Sam.

"Uh, what about the fruit?"

Yevgeny calculated the actual loss versus the tax loss, noted the profit, and resumed walking away from the cart.

"They're always stealing from me. Let them steal this. I want a drink."

Sam had no further objections, noting that the grocery cart had a better chance of making it back to the Hughes Market down the street if it was abandoned than if it remained in the old man's custody. He started to followed the ex-fruit seller, then remembered Jenn.

As if on cue, Sam heard her powerful, barracks-trained voice collide with Sofia's lowing Russian protests from somewhere within the room behind the third-floor balcony that had so recently been Superman Mischa's launching pad.

They were too far away for Sam to make out the words – or perhaps Jenn was speaking in Russian – but the general intent was clear. Sam wondered whether Jenn had learned her curses on the street or in university study. Whatever the case, he knew from experience that his partner was just getting her second wind. He had time for a quick disappearing act. Besides, she had the car keys.

Tino was proud of his accomplishments as busboy at the Moscow Nights, especially at times like these. The night manager, Nadia, was somewhere buying last minute supplies before the evening customers started streaming in, and the new bartender hadn't shown up yet. Now Tino was in charge. Two beers down the bar, a Courvoisier over at the window table – and polishing the glasses just like he belonged in charge of the bar. Just keep all of them refilled and Nadia would be happy. When the dirty (did he smell like oranges?) black pimp walked in, Tino even knew the routine: the Moscow Nights did not cater to such clientele.

"We're no open yet for you," he said with less of a sneer than he had intended. On a closer look the stinking black pimp looked dangerous. You never knew.

"Don't fart so loud, Tino, you'll scare away a dollar drink!"

Yevgeny pushed into the Moscow Nights behind Sam and gathered immediately that his night manager, Nadia, was A.W.O.L. He was proud of the little busboy for following through with policy, though. Still, he did not want the Sergeant Sam to know it was his bar: you never knew if this government official talked to the tax people.

"*My brother* owns this place," he said more to Tino than to the policeman he was rushing up to the bar. "This Tino boy is Affirmative Action: *my brother* hires wetback Mexicans so we don't get Russian relatives asking for jobs. You know what we call Russians coming here? Vacuum cleaners – they want to suck up all our money!"

Tino never could follow the elaborate sentences of the owner, and he began to wonder if an immigration sting wasn't being set-up on him.

"Mister Yevgeny?" he gulped, wishing he had not positioned himself behind the bar. Where was Nadia?

Yevgeny slapped Sam with a heavy paw across the back. "My police hero here needs a drink. I am buying for him: I don't want him to shit in his pants!"

Sam stretched his lips into a pained resemblance of a smile: he did not expect to find any fellow cops in the place, but he could not afford to have his on-duty presence advertised. And he couldn't leave. His hands would not stop shaking.

The old man was preoccupied with the busboy.

"Give me strong Russian drink, Tino," he said with belabored precision that underscored his failure to realize that the Mexican spoke better English than he. "Vodka – or stronger: champagne and vodka. No water. No agua, comprende?"

Tino unsteadily poured two shots of vodka and reached deeply into the undercounter refrigerator for Mister Yevgeny's private champagne. "Si," he answered, looking nervously at the door. The old man mocked his fears.

"Our friend here is ready to bolt at the first sign of La Migra," he explained to Sam. "You are not Immigration, are you?"

"No, sir."

"No, *Yevgeny*. You are drinking my drink."

"Yevgeny."

They held their glasses together. The gentle clinking of glass against glass belied their attempted bonhommie. Yevgeny held his glass away from Sam's and asked him quietly:

"You did not have to help me. No rules said you had to?"

"No rules said I had to."

Yevgeny saw his black poetic youth.

"Too bad your hands are not steady, Sergeant Sam. Drink."

The old man raised the long thin glass to his lips and poured the sparkling combination of grape and grain down his throat. Sam, after a moment's observation for technique, did the same. He felt the warm explosive reaction spreading out along his chest even as the last drops trickled onto his tongue. The old man's hand cuffed his left ear a second later.

Sam felt his head nearly rip off, then instinctively ducked his shoulder protectively as the fruit seller's huge left hand came rushing in at the other side of his head.

"Hey, old man, what the fu–!" His words were driven out with most of his breath by a two-handed shove to his diaphragm.

At that instant Sam was certain that he was going to die of asphyxiation. That was all he could get his mind to concentrate on. But somewhere in the reaches of his con-sciousness a button was pushed that caused him to lower his head and charge into the strong old man's huge stom-ach, ramming deeply through the rolls of fat and finding the memory of a muscle hiding in the center. It did not cause the fruit seller to fall over backwards, but he *did* stagger back a half-dozen steps, heaving huge breaths and smiling wickedly.

"Come on, black hero!" Yevgeny shouted in incom-pre-hensible Russian. To Sam his words were like a bullfighter's taunts to a dying, spear-pricked bull. He charged again any-way.

Yevgeny struck at the bulleting black head and then grabbed with a bear hug at the policeman's arms. Sam let his knees go soft and dropped under the deadly hug. He then angled a hefty shoulder of his own into the fruit seller's groin. The old man's several layers of blubber protected him from the major impact, but this time Sam found enough breath – and instinct – to use his leverage advantage. He twisted at the waist, straightened his legs, and hurled Yevgeny over his shoulder. The big man came down on the carpeted floor with a dull crash. His flailing legs cracked into two bar stools and sent them tumbling to louder effect. To Sam's horror, the old man sat up almost immediately, apparently unaffected by the leaden fall.

"Yob tvoyu mach!" Yevgeny cried proudly, pointing at Sam. "Your hands they are not shaking anymore!" He turned to the busboy, who was still standing behind the bar in paralyzed rabbit-fear. "Tino, one more drink for me. Nothing for Sergeant Sam: he's got to go back to work."

PAX ROMANA

The villa had been a youth hostel for twenty years. Now it was abandoned, waiting for a Japanese or Libyan investment group to buy it at below market value and convert its low, tiled structure into a plaster motel. The tall parallel rows of cypresses twisting up the road from Florence to the top of the hill still cast magnificent shadows at all times of the day except noon.

The villa still recalled the casual elegance of the last century when it had been built from a model of richer majesty designed a century before. But the plumbing had never worked well when it was new, as the Contessa had noted for five decades before "donating" it gladly to her entrepreneurial hippie great-grandchildren in 1964. And age had not improved the structure's ventilation problems in the summer, nor its damp exposure to northern winds during the winter. The Contessa had not minded leaving the villa at all - memories included – to conclude her destined existence in the old-age home known as Nice.

The electrical wiring had always been well-designed, though. There was even a separate, gasoline-driven generator built into a hillside bunker to compensate for the often-irresponsible government power supply. It was that generator supplying the power now, obviating any need to contact the official power bureaucracies. The water, too, could run off of hand pumps. All of the comforts of modern life: indoor toilets and lightbulbs. No one knew they were there.

Of course, *five* people knew about the villa. But they were all present. Modesta Rivan and her producer, Paolo Servetti, had driven with a staff cameraman and a soundman to three different hotels as they were given the incomplete pieces of information that eventually directed them to the villa. No one knew they had come here – but that was Modesta Rivan's style. She would obtain her interview at any cost, following whatever ground rules were necessary. Paolo was glad they were no longer in Beirut.

Modesta, for her part, wished that she was in Rome. There were too many television stations in Italy now, and one needed to be in the center in order to keep an eye on the shifting administrations. And finances. She and Paolo were still smarting from the bankruptcy last winter of their station – and the paycheck that had suddenly become insolvent. True, she had been able to take "Modesta Rivan Talks" to a rival station within hours of the news, but the bankruptcy had cut into her negotiating position. If she had been in Rome negotiating, "Modesta Rivan Talks" would have switched to Studio CineParma two weeks earlier and with double its current budget.

Still, sitting across from her subject, Modesta wanted to be no other place at the moment. This interview had been almost impossible to arrange, and she had expected to be sitting in the back room of some smelly apartment, crowded into a dark closet with her cameraman leaning over her shoulder in a futile attempt to tape some decent footage. The villa was a bonus. Stripped of furniture – except for the two large chairs they would interview in – the villa had been made ready for her with forethought. It would be a classy shoot: just the right amount of Spartan elegance set against a backdrop of Florentine hills.

"Modesta, we need the intro."

Modesta turned towards the voice, but there was no camera next to it.

"Paolo, the camera is not on me."

"Just your voice for right now: we will intercut with the titles."

She nodded, then began: "For Italian Television Studio CineParma, this is Modesta Rivan." The soundman - Modesta could not remember his name, but knew he had three children and a Vespa motor scooter – came up to Modesta and twisted the connection on her lapel microphone, stepping over the several coils of cable the cameraman had flung about the floor between the half-dozen lighting instruments positioned about the room. "Please repeat," the soundman whispered, listening intently on his earphones.

"For Italian Television Studio CineParma, this is Modesta Rivan."

A brief smile of pride crossed the soundman's face, replaced immediately by concentration. "You will sound perfect," he said, walking gingerly back to his instrument console.

Paolo stepped between the two chairs, followed by the cameraman, Gianni.

"We will shoot the master first, Modesta, then your close-ups, then his. Standard order."

There was a throat-clearing cough from the occupant of the other chair. Despite the fact that the lights had been set up to put him in deep silhouette, his jade-green eyes very clearly conveyed their message to Modesta.

"There will be no retakes, Paolo. Start with a wide shot on us both, then zoom-in on him. Keep the camera on *him*: we'll intercut my close-ups later."

"They won't match," Paolo protested.

Modesta flashed her sweet, dictatorial smile. "You are a genius, Paolo. You will make them match."

Paolo moved away from his prima donna and guided Gianni to his position, inventing a new shooting design on the spot. Modesta turned her smile towards the silhouette.

"We won't have to reshoot anything," she said reassuringly to the nervous amateur.

"We wouldn't," was the confident reply. Modesta was vaguely disconcerted: Paolo had allowed Gianni to arrange the lights too well – she could see her subject's eyes, but not his lips. The eyes were important, but the lips were where . . . where she could tell if she had control.

"I want some music," she was told.

"It will interfere with our sound."

"It will give us a 'sound track'," he said with ingenuous firmness, pushing the button to the small Walkman tape player in his pocket. Thin sound spiraled delicately from the soft rubber headphones also tucked in his pocket, easing its way into the lapel microphone he had let them attach to his coat. Modesta could not even hear the music. The soundman could. He squeezed his eyebrows together in surprise at the first notes, then smiled in recognition. Pink Floyd. He looked up at Modesta's subject with a wary respect – did the man know what he was doing?

"One, two, three –" the silhouette spoke. "Are we in sync?"

The soundman needed only a minor adjustment of his dials. He smiled, wondering *whose* interview this was to be. A nervous energy began to fill the room.

Modesta knew whose interview it was *supposed* to be. She took command at once.

"Yes —" *what* was the soundman's name again? "— we are in sync." She turned her head towards the now-placed camera. "Paolo, Gianni, I begin."

Paolo nodded agreement. Modesta saw Gianni's finger tighten on the camera's Record trigger. She turned back to face the silhouette.

"We will tape my introduction later," she explained with irritated brevity. Then, on a breath of air, her "interview" voice became heavy with intelligent concern as she asked:

"You are called 'The Professor.' Why?"

I am called many things, the man inside the silhouette thought, most of them obscene. "I went to university," he answered aloud. "I have a doctorate. Two, if you count – " the silhouette's hand emerged from the darkness to catch a shaft of spotlight in a wave of dismissal, "– but you can't."

Gianni knew that, despite Paolo's instructions, if he left Modesta out of the picture for too long she would throw a shit fit. He zoomed-in to a complimentary over-the-shoulder of the silhouette that left their star in attractive profile as she asked her next questions.

"And for twenty years you are with the Red Brigade?"

"Fifteen. I – entered – the service of Communism late – after –"

Paolo imagined the cutaway close-up of Modesta they would insert this evening at the studio: she would be listening intently –

"– after too many years of seeing poverty inspired by Capitalism... greed."

– Modesta should nod in "understanding" here.

The silhouette shifted in his seat, and Gianni had to zoom-in past Modesta's profile in order to keep his dark outline in the frame.

"This is all cliché, of course." A rueful chuckle emanated from the silhoutte. "We will look at it better: I was angry and not patient."

The soundman had to admire the way The Professor metered his words to the rhythm of the music: it was a beautiful, pre-edited propaganda sound bite.

"But you have stolen from the Mafiosa: this makes you a mercenary, does it not?" Modesta's inflection was deferential, impossible to take offense at without appearing irrational. She was excellent at picking a subject's weakness and politely scratching at it.

"No, I am a terrorist," The Professor's eyes smiled with an almost matter-of-fact pride, savoring the word. "Only: I am efficient."

He knew the argument by heart, had fought for the dialectic in a hundred meetings.

"Mercenaries fight wars, wars kill a lot of people. That is inefficient." He held his breath a moment, then let it out with the question:

"You see?"

Modesta had not expected The Professor to make this justification in the interview. Her notes were useless at this point. "Efficient terrorism?" she asked, needing to buy time to prepare an alternative line of questioning.

"Thank you, I needed a cue." The Professor's eyes smiled again. "YES! Because the philosophical implications of terrorism *require* efficiency! Cut off the limb with gangrene, don't kill the entire body!"

The soundman noted a sudden change in the silhouette's voice: a moment earlier he had sounded almost relaxed, enjoying the center. Now the Professor spoke with a slower deliberation:

"And now I would bring to terrorism 'high technology'. A bomb in a public toilet is better than a raging continental war, but the public usually misses the message, blaming the 'mad bomber' - as you journalists call him - for the murder of innocents..." He let the phrase trail off, incomplete.

Modesta took his murmuring silence for weakness. "And you would say differently," she asked with just the right hint of critical disapproval.

The Professor disappointed her. "No, I agree," the silhouette nodded with the same degree of disapproval she had exhibited. "I want only specific targets attacked, not bystanders. I want to strike fear into the hearts of the *Powerful*. What are the Powerful anyway? They hide behind the bodies of the masses! Not any more: with skilled craftsmen guiding the hand of terrorism, the cancer is cut out, but the *limb*, yes, even the *limb* is spared!"

"But, pardon me, Professor, but what ideal can this be for? Whose side—"

The Profesor did not let her finish: he knew the question and he did not have an answer yet. But he knew the beginning. He could never forget the beginning. There were too many beginnings.

"I've spent almost two decades... underground... How many true believers left?" Modesta could see the Professor's eyes looking to her for understanding. "Nobody is naive anymore," he whispered with a desperate intimacy that did not elude the lapel microphone. The silhouette's next words were clear and strong:

"Ten thousand people die from chemical 'mistakes' in India and the U.S. chemical lords pay off the families at one thousand dollars a body." His voice changed to a parody of gee-whiz Americana. "Oh, boy!" he exclaimed.

Modesta's voice stepped into his soundtrack: "Then you were—"

The Professore cut her off with a rapid spit of words.

"And when there were no family left? When a blind grandmother had five thousand American dollars and no one of her family left to touch? And they *drive* their gas-drinking Detroit limousines! And they *go* to their American churches!"

"But–"

"They do!"

"Yes."

The silhouette had leaned so far forward in his seat that he was virtually standing on the balls of his feet, an animal ready to spring forward. Now he flopped back onto the heavy wooden chair in bitter triumph.

"Yes," he echoed her agreement with finality.

Gianni did not catch the moment, but Modesta's look of intent was true now. She listened to the silence.

"You are a beautiful woman," the Professor said with simple audacity.

Modesta smiled "delicately" – perhaps the camera had zoomed-out to catch her expressions again? - but she also felt true pleasure at the compliment.

The Professor let the seconds tick by, until the woman's smile became a blush under his concentrated stare. She was ready to speak, shifting her eyes uncomfortably to the sheaf of notes in her hand. He did not let her.

"We were like stars, you know. Rock and roll stars." Even the Professor had to smile now at the memories of naive popularity. "We played 'heavy metal'."

Heavy metal. Punk. New Wave. Professor. Harlequin.

–Does she understand what I mean? Does she understand *why* I mean?

"You are living underground for years, but you have agreed to this interview: you are not afraid you will be followed? Afraid we will betray you?"

A good question, the Professor thought, *it deserves a good answer. It is time to end the interview anyway, I have said my three speeches.* He smiled the response, a smile that he knew she could not see in his silhouetted disguise – except in his eyes.

"Do you think you are seeing my face? I will not look like this in two hours."

"So you are not afraid?"

"And as for betrayal –" He raised the automatic pistol from his lap. Did they think he would come unarmed? It glistened in the spotlight, a negative contrast to his still-dark form.

"No," his smile hardened, "I do not trust you."

Gianni saw the weapon swing in his direction. He did not waste concern for the safety of the camera but fell to the floor at once. The tripod was cracked with the first shot, and the camera fell to the ground with the next two. Miraculously it was still running, and Gianni was to receive an award later that year for his camerawork. At the moment he was joining the others in cries that combined the words "Christ!" "Shit!" and "Run!" with equally reverent urgency.

Paolo, rather inaccurately to Gianni's later recollection, screamed to Modesta: "He's shooting at ME!"

Modesta, for her part, remained rooted in her chair. The camera did not record her expressions, lying as it did on the floor. But to television audiences see her only as the camera did, from the waist-down, she appeared to be bravely facing the gun-wielding lower body of the terrorist who stood in an obvious position of dominance – a dominance which silenced the voices. (For the television presentation the soundman deftly edited their cries of terror into a few brave exclamations of alarm.)

Then the Professore spoke coldly the words that were never broadcast:

"You have your fun with your interview and this 'spy' secrecy. Do you feel the piss running down your legs, the shit filling your pants? That is fear.

"This is my life. I do not respect you."

He shot out the camera then, the interview concluded.

Stupid Monday

Sam considered murder a viable alternative, but discarded the idea in favor of torture.

I love this, he thought, *I love sitting here. I love waiting here. I love the fact that this is on my own time. I just fucking love starting the week off like this.*

"All rise."

I just fucking love it.

The judge delayed his appearance for a dramatic second, then stopped in the doorway for another long moment of effect. He nodded myopically at his well-groomed, snappily uniformed bailiff, and the middled-aged officer-of-the-court began his worn spiel with a smart crispness.

"This session of the –" he spoke with a slight Hispanic musicality that complimented his well-shaped moustache and slightly full sideburns, "– is now in session, the Honorable Johnstone Burns presiding –" He did not, apparently, need to pause for breath before launching into his next paragraph of instructions.

"The instructions for behavior in the court are these –"

It had started with a rumored cockfight, which later became clarified into a dogfight. A two a.m. Sunday morning special event for the bloodsport-loving element of the ethnic community. Actually it was to be a mixed-ethnic soiree, which allowed Sam and Jenn to capitalize on it from a couple of directions. It would be a fine opportunity to see which upstanding members of their constituencies were privately bankrolling such a "harmless" gambling activity.

No busts were planned from their side: the dogfight was on unincorporated county land and so fell into Sheriff's Department jurisdiction. In fact it was a tip from some friendlies over there that had cued-in the Task Force. There would be a bust, then, but the black pimp and his Chinese whore were to be pulled in with the rest of the crowd – by arrangement. They would even have a second charge thrown down on them: cruelty to animals. Sam and Jenn were going to bring their own fighting dog.

The ideal dog, everyone knew, was a pit bull. Yessss, a lot of friendly pit bulls hanging around on a moment's notice. Well, the second choice (admittedly on the lame side, but no one said the pimp was supposed to be crackling smart) was a fierce-eyed, cow-hearted German Shepherd K-9 officer named Snappy. Snappy had originally been trained for crowd-control security duties, but, despite an appropriately menacing demeanor, the rookie dog officer seemed to consider pigeons more threatening than humans and was constantly ignoring his (obviously unintelligent) human colleagues who failed to perceive the feathered threat. Snappy was about to become a K-9 Academy washout when his true talent was uncovered.

Drugs.

Cocaine, heroin, marijuana – Snappy had a nose that zeroed-in on the full range of illegal substances. The ability was discovered quite by accident when, at what was to be his final day of evaluation in the field, Snappy started to nip at the rear pocket of an unfortunate striking hotel worker in Century City. The pocket was full of what was later analyzed to be rock cocaine – although only small crumbs were all that remained, and those were brushed off of Snappy's whiskers. He liked the taste.

A career and an addict were born.

Snappy was now a full-fledged K-9 Officer in his third year of service to the Department – and a flower child of the dog world. His human partners had learned to restrain the dog enough to retain needed evidence, but it was quickly recognized that Officer Snappy's performance level was directly related to his desire for immediate gratification. Pavlov would have understood. Snappy needed a buzz.

Well, he was safe.

That was what counted to Sam and Jenn, neither of whom could confess to a liking for the usual run of hungry-eyed K-9s. As the set-up was arranged, they were treated to a quick introductory afternoon with Snappy, and then "the leash was passed on to the Ethnic Task Force per temporary transfer request."

"– All persons in attendance in Judge Burns' courtroom will conduct themselves with proper respect to the rules of decorum. These rules include the following: –"

Sam nodded familiarly to a vaguely recognizable acquaintance: was the dude a cop or a baddie? Jenn was sitting three floors down drinking coffee and reading another one of her Russian novels. She would remember.

"No smoking of cigarettes, pipes or cigars. Failure to adhere to these rules will result in a charge of contempt."

Russian novels! Better to read up on the Criminal Code for the Lieutenant's exam. Sam slid down on the wooden seat and tried to make himself believe it was an easy chair. He spread the thick reference book across his knees.

"No gum chewing, tobacco chewing or snuff. Failure to adhere to these rules will result in a charge of contempt. No reading, –"

Damn! Sam shut the Criminal Code book with a muffled snap. The bailiff raised a practised eyebrow.

"– or magazines. Failure to adhere to these rules will result in a charge of contempt."

They had borrowed a car from Vice: Jenn pointed out with acumen that K-9 patrol cars always stunk and why should they mess up their own Task Force vehicle and, anyway, they were supposed to be undercover and *needed* one of Vice's impounded pimpmobiles. The stinking part of the argument was the most persuasive (to Sam, who agreed *not* to explain this aspect of life to the Vice lieutenant), and Snappy found himself enjoying the night ensconced in the back seat of a convertible Caddy, the breeze blowing across his moist nose in a most satisfactory fashion. He was mellow. The night was warm. The world was good.

The world was not so good.

Sam pulled the Cadillac up to a smooth stop at the red light. They were only a few short blocks from their destination. He could have made the light easily, but he wanted to be seen. Jenn couldn't flirt the Vice lieutenant into giving them the pimpmobile often, so this would be the big First Impression that people would have to talk about. There were a few righteous dudes over on the corner watching. Jenn gave them a look to hunger for.

Sam did not see the danger. He did not see the birds.

Snappy did.

Correctly speaking, Officer Snappy's eyes were deceiving him: there were not pigeons sitting in the display window of the Aguas Calientes All-Night Bodega and Eggroll Deli. They *were* a pair of bored cockatoos who amused themselves by imitating every sound they heard *except* the sound of human speech. The green one particularly liked to "bark." His turquoise partner and sometimes-lover contented herself with cooing like the dirty pigeon birds that sometimes tried to share the roost they were chained to and steal the cockatoos' food. Both were trying to perfect their lame imitations of a cat's meow when the Cadillac stopped at the intersection outside the Aguas Calientes. Sensing a failing performance, the less-talented half of the team resorted to her tried-and-true repertoire.

"Mew, mew!" cried Big Green.

"Cooroo, cooroo!" cried Lover Girl.

"Shut - Up!" cried Ify, the night manager who loved them, but.

He was too late.

With an heroic leap that ripped the door handle his leash was attached to from its leather-lined door, Snappy charged the terrorist fowl, howling his intentions to bring them to swift justice. Sam wondered if he had just bitten off the tip of his tongue in his shocked first reaction to the thousand decibel roar in his ear. Jenn's eyes lost their Asian slant for a moment in wide-eyed surprise. The Caddy rocked from the aftershock of being the two-hundred pound dog's launching pad.

The reality of bringing Snappy to heel was less difficult than the first daunting seconds would have indicated. Approaching the cockatoo impressionists at breakneck speed, Snappy was brought up short by an impromptu chorus of "Rowrf, rowrf!" from Big Green and the sudden, disturbing discovery that the hated, heinous, hideous pigeons - had - *disappeared!*

Jenn caught Snappy easily then, attracting his attention with a gentle whistle and a hand clap that brought the dog running to where she now stood on the curb. Meanwhile Sam parked the Cadillac. It was then that Jerry Jerk, Officer of Last Resort, appeared.

"All persons cited must appear in person before this court. Failure to do so will result in a charge of contempt and a bench warrant will be issued."

Sam idly (and boredly) watched each of the suited attorneys reassure their (alternately worried, concerned, curious, too-stupid-to-care) clients that this was only a first step. The case would be assigned to another judge, not this lemon-sucked face of a calendar organizer.

"No talking in court. Violation will result in —"

Sam flicked the ticket back and forth between his fingers. Well, a good pimp stuck up for his girls. They took away my Cad, took away my dawg – don't get to take away my wimmin. Let 'em all see me here. Judge'll look at my papers, see it's all a mistake and...

See that it was *Jenn's* name was on the ticket!

Actually, Sam did not blame the blueshirt for showing up and hassling them: that's what the two undercover cops were dressed up for and that was the blushirt's job. People crowded around the pimp and his lady and laughed when the white cop started calling them down – not because of their obvious profession --- but because of the city's leash laws!

"Dawg's ona leash, ocifer," Sam drawled, calling attention to the obvious. "Damn thing's still trailin' parta my auto-mo-bile!" Sam was careful to be polite to the blueshirt, but as a supposed pimp-with-pride he had to make his points as a Dude With Something Of An Attitude or their cover would be weakened.

"Yeah, leash," the blueshirt said with disappointment. He couldn't really deny that he caught them *trying* to control the animal, even if momentarily unsuccessful. Then he saw it.

Or didn't see it.

That's what was missing – it.

The license.

Taking off Snappy's dog license had not been a matter

of ill-considered whimsy. In fact, they had nearly forgotten about his I.D. tags until the Vice lieutenant asked Jenn how she expected to explain owning an LAPD K-9. Thanking him for catching the oversight (and moving fast so that the Vice lieutenant would not put the same two-and-two together they had about dogs and car smells), Jenn removed the tags. She still had them. In her purse. In her locker. In the station.

Knowing that pimps hated to have their product line taken out of service, the blueshirt purposely signed off the ticket to the prostitute. *Let her spend an hour down in a courthouse line*, the blueshirt thought with a laugh – if she ever shows, of course. You never knew: these pimps and their kind were pretty particular about keeping their wheels registered and fully insured, maybe they felt the same way about their "dawgs."

Sam still didn't hold it against the blueshirt too much. They made their dogfight, had a story to tell, and got busted with the crowd by the Sheriff's Deputies. Contacts were made that night and, who could tell?, maybe one or two would pay off later.

"Get up to court!"

Jenn looked up from her book, annoyed. It was hard enough trying to sort out the Cyrillic letters and assorted Russian phonemes in the middle of a coffee shop. What was Sam doing here now?

"C'mon, Sam: you lost the draw, *you're* supposed to sit in court and let me read my book in peace."

"Idiot judge playing God. Since it's your name on the ticket he won't let me plead and pay. You're facing a contempt charge and a bench warrant. I don't know if he's called your name again yet. Let's go!"

Screw the Russians. Jenn threw down a handful of change for the tip and followed Sam at a heel-clattering pace up three floors to the courtroom.

No, it was not the blueshirt Sam resented, it was the *law*.

Quietly, and without wearing the pimp persona, Sam and Jenn had stopped by the Court Clerk's office to present their evidence that the dog identified in the ticket, Hell Hound (well, in front of the sidewalk crowd "Snappy" had not seemed an appropriate name for a pimp's killer dog), was in fact an undercover K-9 Officer who was legitimately and validly licensed. Simple.

"Wait in line please."

They could not show their badges. Some faces in the line were from the dogfight.

An hour.

"Fine for unlicensed dog is one hundred fifty dollars."

"He has a license. Here." Sam showed the photocopy of Snappy's police registration. The clerk did not look at it.

"Here," she said, rubber stamping a small form and handing it across the counter.

Sam was almost out of the Clerk's office before he realized that the ticket had not been canceled. This time he had no qualms about jumping to the head of the line.

"What's this? I showed you the dog's license!"

"Not my decision. You want to pay, fine's a hundred and fifty dollars. You don't want to pay, plead Not Guilty in court. That's your date."

That was that.

Sam knew an Assistant District Attorney, of course, who could fix the ticket for Jenn. Hell, Jenn knew a couple herself. But a dog ticket?! Friendship favors weren't for wasting on bad jokes like this. And a quick check with the Captain assured them that paying the fine would *not* be considered a legitimate item for reimbursement. Annual budget time, of course. Nor would ignoring the ticket be acceptable: the Department frowned upon their officers descending to the level of common scofflaw.

Besides, the dog had a license, didn't it? Waste another hour in court, show the judge, save a hundred-and-fifty – oh, and remember: this is on your *own* time.

"Jennifer Luck."

"Here, your Honor."

A whole Monday morning wasted.

"How do you plead?"

Over in a minute.

"Not guilty, your Honor. Here's proof that the dog is licensed."

No time to get some sleep before going on-shift at four.

"Save it for trial, Miss Luck. You're scheduled for three weeks from this date, October eighth, Room 297. Be there at nine a.m. Sharp."

GAME SHOW

The image of their feet appeared first on the screen, in distorted black-and-white.

"Can't we get a simple, clear, image?" the Colonel demanded.

The First Technician looked up at his superior with the empty eyes of a shi-tzu puppy. The Colonel repeated the question in Cantonese.

The First Technician apologized with a sympathetic shrug: "*Buxing* – Not possible."

The Colonel once again cursed a government bureaucracy that could not invest in decent surveillance equipment. He cursed to himself, of course, leaving his lips untouched by even a hint of remonstrance.

Besides, what was the use? It was all *buxing* – not possible in China. The Colonel knew that a fantastic, high-definition Japanese video system and television were sitting in his commander's living room – but that was not "official." Large screen, too, not a decade-old twelve-inch monitor left by an American trade delegation in 1982. Not a dying-tubed anachronism whose picture curved at the edges and gave the viewer a headache after five minutes.

The Colonel blinked his eyes for the dozenth time and wondered for the thousandth time since picking up the French boy whether he should haul in his own television and connect it to the system. Watching the boy eight hours a day, it could save his eyes. But – once in, never out – the Colonel knew that he wasn't going to take a chance on having some higher-up see a decent television in the office and then requisition it to his personal "official" use. Better to keep the headaches, they made it easier to hate the pathetic kid.

The monitor showed three pairs of feet: two booted, one sandaled – the surveillance camera had not picked up any faces as they shambled down the long hallway.

The Colonel made a written note to advise the building maintenance sergeant *once again* to readjust the hall camera: perhaps the sergeant would get the message finally and maybe buy back some of the screws and other hardware he had sold on the black market so that the building he was supposedly responsible for could utilize at least a few of the supplies it reputedly stored in inventory. Maybe a few screws? Maybe the sergeant needed a transfer to the Tibetan Occupation? No, the Colonel was a realist: the Tibetan Occupation units were too poor to survive the sergeant's quartermastering "talents"–

half of the Army would freeze to death after he'd sold off their coal and blankets to the fat administrators and generals who would protect him from prosecution. Ah, for another Cultural Revolution!, when a smart young cadre could call up a little mob violence to wreak his private revenges.

Anyway, the Colonel noted, the three pairs of feet were almost to the end of the hall. Back to work. He flipped his attention to another equally antiquated security monitor and switched it on.

Interrogation Room #7 was revealed after a tenuous moment of decision on the monitor's part whether to work or not. The surveillance camera set-up here had not become misaligned: the image was focussed correctly and (within the expected limitations) clearly. The Colonel turned up the Audio dial under the monitor and heard the shuffling feet approach #7's closed door. He wanted to check that everything was in place before they entered.

#7 was a spare, functional place – not intentionally sinister, but effectively so in its utilitarian, impersonal nakedness. The Colonel no longer even noticed those characteristics, however. His attention was on the furniture. In the center of the room a horseshoe arrangement had been prepared. There was only a single chair, set in the middle of the horseshoe. A small television (new!) sat on top of a video player on the middle table. The Colonel breathed a sigh of relief at the sight of the two machines: they had been special requisitions because the boy's camera used France's SECAM video system, not compatible with China's PAL standard. The Colonel was tired of waiting. It was time to get rid of the French boy.

The sound of footsteps stopped.

"Go in." The Colonel heard the soldier's voice clearly from the hall monitor, muffled through the #7 monitor: the solid security door discouraged sound waves.

Philippe had never been in this room before, although the door looked like the dozen others he had entered regularly for the past half-year. His first glance was to look for people, for the conversation he needed – but the room was unoccupied. He stood uncertainly between the two Chinese soldiers and did not enter the room. Where were the people who would talk to him? Had they taken him to this room just to be alone again? Oh, Mon Dieu!, Philippe was losing his hold on the Chinese language, he had not spoken to anyone for so long!

"Qu'est-que c'est? Je ne comprend pas."

"And the guards do not understand French, Philippe."

The voice came from a small speaker set over the doorway. Philippe had to lean into the room to see it. "But we both speak English," the Colonel's voice continued. "Come in."

The voice was not threatening. Rather, it was paternal: understanding, yet firm. In response, Philippe took another tentative step into the room. The door was closed behind him.

Am I alone again?, Philippe thought. He looked up at the small speaker for further commands.

Nothing.

The Colonel watched Philippe stand alone just inside the doorway, see the lone chair in the middle of the horseshoe of tables, then hesitantly shuffle over to it. He waited for Philippe to sit. It was a five minute wait. Philippe was losing his conception of time.

The Colonel pushed the "Remote Zoom" button and prayed a small, recidivist, Taoist good luck chant for the equipment to work. It did, and - the Taoist gods were generous to the Party today - the zoom-in was still focussed on Philippe. Good. The Colonel did not want to be in the picture. He left his aide, a competent major, to oversee the monitors and left the surveillance room. Philippe did not move from his chair in the two some-odd minutes it took the Colonel to reach Interrogation Room #7.

This would be the Colonel's twenty-eighth session with Philippe. He could have reached this step much earlier, but nothing was ever ready: from higher-level policy decisions to dirt-level space procurement. After the Tien An Men incident, there had been a thousand dissidents to discipline and punish; the interrogation rooms were still booked solid for two months. The French boy was an oddity – either a major inconvenience or a potential opportunity – the policy-makers had not decided which. So the Colonel had been delayed.

When the Colonel entered the room Philippe jerked his head in attracted reaction. The Colonel was not visible on the monitor. Whatever unseen gesture the Colonel made, it kept Philippe in his seat. The Colonel's uniformed body crossed between the French boy and the surveillance camera, but it was too close to distinguish beyond a that of a quick, passing blur. Philippe's head and eyes followed the moving figure.

The young man began to speak –

– then hesitated.

The Colonel turned on the television and video player. He inserted a video cassette he had been carrying into the player. Waiting for the first image to appear, he looked over at Philippe: although dressed in prison garb, the boy did not look unwell. This was important to the Colonel.

"Watch, Philippe," he said before turning his attention back to setting the proper volume level on the television.

It was Tien An Men Square. Philippe and Fuong Lee's Tien An Men, edited from the hours of eight millimeter cassettes that Fuong's "Eyes," Philippe, had recorded.

Philippe had never had a SECAM system television in China to watch the tapes on – he and Fuong had always watched playback on the tiny camera monitor. In black-and-white. These images were much larger – shakier than Philippe remembered – and in color. In color. Philippe may have lived the events in color, but he shared them with

Fuong in small, monochrome intimacies. The images he saw now were unreal. Fantasies of how rich they believed their student rebellion to be. Philippe began to think that he was watching a movie of the event. But where was he? In this Hollywood version there was no partner for Fuong Lee. The Eyes was absent, Fuong had no Eyes. Philippe closed his own eyes: these were not his memories.

"Let me plasy something new, Philippe." Philippe kept his eyes closed, hearing the Colonel's hands opening and closing a video deck. "Something not from your camera,"

"I lost my friends – I lost my eyes – when I fled Beijing!" Fuong's voice was clear and strong – and in English!

Philippe opened his eyes quickly and caught the brief glimpse of Fuong Lee finishing his sentence, then disappearing into a crowd of Americans standing in front an old, poorly designed building called "City Hall – City of Los Angeles."

The video image jumped abruptly. Suddenly it was a different day and a different place. There was a new crowd. The camera jumped from face to face – until Fuong Lee jumped out.

"We had a revolution for Democracy – and now it is gone!"

Then Fuong Lee disappeared again. The screen went blank, the colors of Fuong Lee's face replaced by grey, electrical "snow."

The Colonel turned down the volume level, but left the video playing.

"There is another moment with Fuong Lee, Philippe, but I want to talk to you first. We have not treated you badly these months, have we?"

"No." Philippe would have given the same answer even if it had not been the truth.

"We could not. You are here on a scholarship, an excellent student of Communist ideals." This was untrue - the scholarship was a sham and Philippe's credentials had been paper excuses to bring a Western currency-carrying student into the country. But the Colonel had worked for several sessions to instill in Philippe an undeserved sense of accomplishment. "We respect your ideals."

He waited until the image of Fuong Lee would once again flash onto the screen – there was no sound this time –then he added:

"We respect Fuong Lee's ideals."

On the screen Fuong Lee was seen to be speaking more comfortably in English now, and he was describing in strong terms the massacres on Tien An Men Square. The Colonel had found it convenient to lose that portion of the audio when editing the tape.

Philippe trusted the Colonel as someone who had not threatened him or treated him badly for the past six months, but he could not fully believe such an expression of admiration for his friend.

"You respect Fuong Lee?"

The Colonel looked at the young Frenchman with a sincere directness.

"Yes."

Philippe lowered his eyes.

"Look at me, Philippe. Look at me."

The boy obeyed the gentle-voiced command.

"You understand that the tragedy of Tien An Men was that the students were not acting for themselves." Philippe *would* understand it that way because, as a non-witness to the massacres, he had been receptive to the Colonel's allusive explanations for months, "They were pawns in a power struggle. Their side - *our* side - lost."

It was the Colonel's turn now to lower his eyes, to make an admission. He raised his eyes again and smiled with wry familiarity.

"Bien sûr, Philippe: *our* side."

The Colonel stood up with an impatient gesture of impotence. He spoke rapidly to himself, virtually ignoring Philippe. "*Our* side! The students were not alone – but we were all too weak then. Too weak! Do you know what that means, Philippe? It means we have to make alliances - that takes time – consolidate our positions – time, again! – Tien

An Men, the students," the Colonel was grabbing ideas from the air, pulling Philippe with him, "– too soon!"

"We had the city on our side!" Philippe protested. "Several cities!"

"We needed the entire country!" the Colonel countered. "And we were growing in strength. We *are* growing in strength. Now. Right now! We need young voices such as Fuong Lee's to rejoin us."

"He is my friend." Philippe said the words without hesitation. He had denied knowing Fuong Lee at his first interrogation.

But the Colonel understood. "I know he is," he said with sympathy, "and you are lonesome without his friendship."

He turned his back on the boy to hide his own emotions, using the need to change video cassettes in the player as an excuse.

"Watch this, Philippe, and when you are finished, you can return to your room."

The blur of the Colonel's quick-stepping body crossed between Philippe and the surveillance camera again as the young man turned his attention to the television. He was still excited from his conversation with the Colonel. He did not notice the sound of the door opening and closing behind him: the ripe, carefree accents of the woman on the screen had suddenly grabbed his full attention.

"Bonjour, Philippe, mon fils!"

"Maman!

The Colonel rushed into the surveillance room.

"Zoom-out!" he commanded the major, "I want to see the video as he reacts to it."

The camera was still focussed-in on Philippe's face for too many seconds, however - the Remote Zoom button needed to be punched several times before it activated - and the Colonel heard only the petulant pouty tones of the woman's voice, self-indulgent cadences that babbled a clear, underlying intention: that *she* was the true "sufferer" from being separated from her son. Philippe's face registered only empty disbelief.

"My lovely son," she mewed, "how are you? Joyeux Noël! You do not write, as you never do! I am so lucky that you have friends in the government who send me letters about you: your success with our contacts is such a pleasure. I am so proud of you."

The camera finally zoomed-out to take in the entire room, leaving Philippe a small, immobile figure in the middle of the wide space.

"As you can see, I have a new car: it is a Renault, and I love it! When you return for vacation, I *may* let you borrow it — but do not count on it!

"I am so busy, if you can understand..."

Day and Night
Sunrise, Sunset

Well, yes, it was a format just about the same as the five other market leaders in the Los Angeles area:

"Good Morning again from K-C-A-T, The CAT!"

And if the format didn't work out and produce higher ratings by the next fiscal quarter, then they'd scrap it and try a Classic Oldies formula.

"The city's finest in hard rockin', easy talkin' radio."

Or E-Z Listening.

"It's nine-thirty and time for a brief news update –"

Keep the commuters listening.

"– followed by Officer Millie Wendell with a traffic report."

Sam stopped by the closed door where Millie would be reading "her" traffic report into a telephone hookup with

KCAT. The department was giving out traffic reports faster to the public than they were to their own patrols. The Task Force Units had to hit the Chinatown/Downtown section of Sunset Boulevard: it wouldn't hurt to get there without a traffic hassle, Sam reasoned. He tapped on the door then stuck his head in without invitation.

Millie shook her head and showed him the faxed report from Traffic Central: it was twenty minutes old. Millie – "Fast Track Millie" – had no new insights to offer on the three Sig Alerts that had already tied up the Pasadena-Harbor Freeway link and two far-flung sections of the Santa Ana and Ventura Freeways. Sam and Jenn would have to take overland roads for an hour before being in the clear.

Sam was ticked off by the delay to the day's schedule. Not that they were on patrol, but they had places to be.

The fax machine in the next room – *Millie's* fax machine during traffic report hours – began to hum its dull messaging chords. Sam gave the machine a passing glance:

TO ALL DEPARTMENTS:

INTERSTATE BULLETIN

It wasn't for Millie, hmm, hmm, hmm. But who really cared?, Sam shrugged, leaving his curiosity on hold. If it was important enough, or meant for the Task Force, then a copy would end up on his or Jenn's desk. Probably both. And copies were easier to read than the greasy-mud fax "originals."

The bulletin, in fact, was nothing special – a routine Federal request for information. Fishing.

TO ALL DEPARTMENTS: INTERSTATE BULLETIN

NAME: FUONG LEE

OCCUPATION: STUDENT/REFUGEE STATUS

AGE: 21

ETHNIC: CHINESE NATIONAL

DISTINGUISHING MARKS: NONE

WEIGHT/HEIGHT: UNKNOWN (AVERAGE)

REMARKS: PERSON ENTERED U.S. ON STUDENT STATUS, CONSIDERED POLITICAL REFUGEE. WHEREABOUTS IMPORTANT TO DIPLOMATIC RELATIONS. NOTIFY FEDERAL OFFICIAL HOTLINE.

There was the usual grimy photograph accompanying the bulletin, nothing remarkable. Nothing vaguely capturing the charismatic effect Fuong Lee had on his listeners. Just a Chinese face.

Fast Track Millie pulled it off of the fax machine, making her way past the information to the next set of traffic reports – her last set of the morning – setting the bulletin on a pile of similar fishing expeditions incoming from federal and local law officials across the country. If there was anything odd about this request Millie was too busy with her own concerns to notice: the Chief had commented favorably upon her reading a few days ago, he was considering moving Officer Wendell into the television traffic report slot. Important concerns.

Millie settled back into her own office and turned down the volume on the radio she had set to Blast level when running out to pick up the traffic report fax. This was her monitor of the program.

"– On the international scene, it is not a Merry Christmas shaping up for the President as party leaders from both sides of Congress were critical today when it was revealed that the military embargo on mainland China, invoked after the Tien An Men massacre last Spring, was lifted in less than thirty days by Executive Order. –"

Millie had heard these same news reports eight times this morning, they never changed. They were at least a half day behind the headlines on the *L.A. Times* that occupied an important position under her coffee cup and its accompanying plastic cup of orange juice and Winchell's doughnut (crumbs). No mention on the radio news of the front page photo in the times: National Security Advisor Brent Scowcroft making a smiling dinner toast to his Chinese hosts.

"– White House Spokesman Marlin Fitzwater indicated that the President did not consider the matter to be a major issue, despite the fact that documents have surfaced linking his brother to lucrative trade deals with China. –"

Thank goodness there were no reports on the White House dog today, Millie sighed. The jerky deejay, Charlie Wow – "WOW THE K-CAT!" the bus billboards advertised – *loved* to segue from "and that's the scam on Millie the dog. Now here's our very *own* (honk!): Millie the Cop!" Yeah, it would be great if the chief transferred her to the TV Patrol.

"– In sports, another sad day for local fans as victory is lost in the final few seconds of overtime. Details after this message. –"

Millie took a quick sip of her orange juice: her slot was just after Sports.

The fax on Fuong Lee, as it happened, did not sit too long in the Incoming slush pile.

Crime was slow that day, a gift from the cloud gods who understood that nobody in Los Angeles knew what to do when it rained, criminals and erratic drivers alike. The clerical staff used the lull as an opportunity to attack the backlog of papers crammed into miscellaneous corners around the station.

No one had much intention of actually *doing* something with the various documents gathered together. No. The essence of a professional clerical was in knowing how to pass on the real work to someone else while imparting an impression of businesslike perception to one's superiors.

In this case the Fuong Lee bulletin, being recent, was still near the top of the incoming pile and so was processed among the first. As Sgt. Sam Williams had foreseen, the bulletin ended up on his desk, albeit a half week earlier than expected. Coming back from a fruitless day weaving among downtown traffic obstacles, he and Det. Jenny Luck discovered a fresh pile of pointless Inter-Department Memos and vaguely directed bulletins distributed evenly between their desks, all bearing faint resemblances to Task Force affairs.

Sam did not bother to read the Fuong Lee bulletin. Seeing the Chinese face he tossed it over to Jenn's desk in exchange for two black-faced bulletins from her direction. It was not fair, of course: there were more blacks than Chinese on the Fed lookout lists. Sam didn't bother to worry it, though. He slid the bulletins into his "Get To" drawer and remembered his promise to himself: white guys and Republicans were the only crooks he'd help the Feds catch. It wasn't a policy he said out loud.

Jenn had her own "Get To" file for Asians in which she intended to lodge the bulletin for an indefinite gestation period, but she made the mistake of looking at the photo before dropping it in the already-overflowing drawer.

Fuong Lee.

She had not seen a photo of him for two-three months, not since late summer, when police crowd surveillance photos of the Chinese demonstrations had landed copies on her desk. This photograph was probably from Fuong Lee's visa, a quick, unflattering Hong Kong job that reflected only the haggard look of a refugee who had spent the past two weeks in hiding. He still wore the dirty T-shirt he'd had on the last night at Tien An Men Square, dried-brown spots of blood from his broken nose staining the cloth despite repeated hand-washings. His nose was still slightly swollen as well, and his haircut was the bad, pseudo-60s style that the student dissidents wore in Beijing.

Fuong Lee did not look like that anymore, Jenn knew. The LAPD photos from September showed a confident young man, dressed comfortably in an American mode and - though still lean and wary - definitely not reminiscent of a just-escaped rabbit. No one would recognize Fuong Lee from the Federal bulletin. Jenn didn't bother to read it thoroughly, but did shift the bulletin over to her "Stars" folder, to join her earlier scrapbook clippings.

"Hi, Marie. Crappy day 'cause of the weather. Need to catch up on paperwork and legwork. Be home late. Sorry... Real sorry. See you tonight."

Jenn vaguely heard the brief message Sam was leaving on his telephone answering machine, noting only the "catch up – home late" passages. God, the man was loyal *and* honest with his wife! Most cops would just breeze home whenever. Most wives learned to live with the inconsideration – or left.

Jenn looked at her "Stars" file and amended her previous thought, changing "wives" to "spouses": it worked both ways. Jimmy Luck had been an awfully good husband, except that he was married to a cop. When he and Jennifer Xu met they were both students at UCLA and International

Relations majors on the track to State Department careers. Jimmy, *Doctor* James now, had minored in Poly Sci, while Jenn had taken a liking to Sociology. Marriage in their senior year had worked well considering both came from second-generation families that pretended to be modern but harbored "traditional" tendencies.

Then came the Grad School/Job Necessity conflict. Both had scored well on the State Department exams. The waiting list for openings was a two year minimum. Graduate school was de rigeur, but so was income – and Jenn beat out Jimmy in finding a high-paying position quickly: her Sociology degree and female *and* Asian minority status, combined with an off-the-chart application test score, qualified her for an immediate position in the Los Angeles Police Department. Blah-blah-blah. Two years of work and grad study. Blah-blah-blah. Jimmy kept her sane. She could leave the job at any moment. Blah-blah.

Martin Cordez.

He was thirty years old and had not even finished high school. Some rumors – and Jenn had seen the reports to confirm the rumors – placed Martin Cordez at the center of some ugly drug traffic business a decade earlier. But he had changed. Everyone knew he had changed. The *LAPD* even believed he had changed – and Martin Cordez was now heading a tough anti-gang movement in East L.A. that challenged people's imaginations with its bold program of confronting the gangs eye-to-eye for control of the neighborhoods. He called it "Stop The Street War." Two attempts on Martin Cordez' life convinced the Mayor's Special Council on Youth that the man needed protection.

It was funny how easily a little make-up, bad hair styling and night light could make a Chinese grad student/policewoman look like a Mexican *chica* cruising through the streets.

Martin Cordez had protested when he first learned there would be a police unit shadowing him. Jenn never learned if he relaxed his opposition before or after he recognized her as one of his protectors.

They met the first time in public – on the streets while he was making his rounds setting up a neighborhood anti-gang effort – and both Martin and Jenn treated the encounter as if she was a street girl joining his cause. The Department liked the arrangement, it allowed them to have an officer near Cordez without open exposure.

She went to bed with Martin four days later.

Professionally, the Cordez assignment was a major success for the young patrolwoman, a stepping stone to making Detective grade and permanent transfer to the Task Force. Jenn never told Jimmy about Martin and it was the first of many lies.

For Martin Cordez the Stop The Street War program was also a stepping stone: he "sold" it to a city agency and advanced into the political mainstream with a full portfolio of accomplishment, a portfolio that he continued to expand. Jenn met him occasionally, but he had "arrived" now, and she missed some of the desperate urgency of his earlier missionary zeal.

"You ready to go, Jenn – a bite to eat while working?" Sam was snapping on his waist holster. The small service revolver looked ridiculously small attached to his large frame.

"Yeah. You miss Marie again?"

"I'll call her while we eat. Korean barbecue?"

It wasn't Martin Cordez that killed Jenn's marriage to Jimmy Luck. It wasn't even the time with Councilman Lorenz or the African National Congress organizer (strangely enough, she'd met him at a UCLA grad seminar, *not* through the LAPD). Maybe it was the fact that she stopped leaving Jimmy messages. Not like Sam and Marie.

"Kamsahamnida!"

Sam grinned the Korean gratitude at the waitress as she laid thin strips of raw beef across a small, open-flame grill in the center of their table. Jenn's nose wrinkled with pleasure at the rising spice-filled smoke. She particularly appreciated the accompanying sizzle that shivered the meat.

"See," she chided her partner, "you can speak something other than English!"

"Yeah," Sam answered, "McMasters taught me to say 'Please,' 'Thank you' and 'Where's the bathroom?' wherever I goes."

"Smart man," Jenn manipulated her chopsticks to turn over a few of the more bronzed pieces of beef. "It took me four years of college to figure that out."

Sam was busy shuffling around the meat on his side of the grill. "Smart about some things, slow about others." His eyes winced a brief, pained memory.

The meat was almost ready to start popping into a mouth.

"School teacher?" Jenn asked politely, her attention more focussed on her empty stomach.

"Army sergeant. Dead."

"Viet Nam?" Jenn knew Sam had been over there.

"Bank robbery. In Germany."

The incongruity forced Jenn to think of her second preoccupation of the moment: the glass of brandy-and-soda in her left hand.

"It's a stupid world," she said, raising the glass in ironic toast to a dead man she never knew.

"I've heard that before," Sam agreed, matching her in the quickness with which they downed their drinks. But his partner was faster in snatching up her chopsticks and picking out the most-ready pieces of grilled beef.

Sam felt the heady exhilaration of the brandy caress his empty stomach. He signalled to the waitress to bring two more. The bill was already creeping to the seventy dollar mark, but Jenn had offered to cover it. He gingerly plucked up a piece of beef and let it cool.

"So, Detective Luck: why does a single, divorced policewoman agree to pay for such a lavish meal as this?"

Jenn was famished: if drinking made Sam pensive, it made her hungry. "Two reasons," she said around mouthfuls of the juicy meat strips. "First, desperation – I need to brown nose my immediate superior, a black dude named Sergeant Samuel Williams. Second – and this is most important – I am able to pay for this little to-do because I received a very nice alimony check today from a sonuvabitch who could afford to pay twice as much."

That was the real reason their marriage broke up, of course: the simple fact that Jimmy had found money-scented charm in the daughter of a rich Hong Kong banker needing a family connection with U.S. citizenship.

"To bitter memories!" Sam offered the toast this time.

"And bygone spouses!

Jenn beat out Sam this time, but he finally built up a momentum of attack on the beef, sliding his emptied glass across the table to join the four others he and Jenn had earlier assembled. Jenn added hers to make it an even six, then tried to stand up.

"Need to visit the little girls' roo– ohh!"

Sam caught her with a strong, not-much-steadier hand. "Here," he said, rising for better balance. It was a mistake, his borderline sobriety unprepared to handle a sudden change in altitude. With a jolt to his spine Sam fell back onto the bench seat, pulling Jenn down next to him.

"Oooh," she moaned, feeling her bladder protest the shock. "Maybe we should have saved the brandy for after the food!"

"You're young," Sam advised. "You won't feel a thing."

"And you – ?"

"I'll hurt like hell – and you'll have to live with it."

Oh, yeah, the Chinatown stakeout for TV, Jenn remembered, the reason they had worked late plan-making in the first place.

"I won't translate for you," she threatened with a sullen petulance that was simultaneously betrayed by her hand squeezing on his knee.

"You won't have to." Sam's strong features assumed an angry, exaggerated scowl. "I'll just look at the locals with my hungover eyes, growl three times, and they'll understand everything I want. It worked in Viet Nam. It works in El Centro."

"Buuut – will – it work – on syndicated television?" Jenn found her voice turning silly-sounding, a high-pitch twang replacing her usual controlled meter.

"Television!" Sam made a dismissive gesture. "They look at this face and they figure I know what I'm talking about.

Shit, girl!" Sam fell into his Detroit persona. " I said 'shit': it work on my review committee – I gonna be Lieutenant next month, you see. We talkin' 'Streetwise' with a cap'tal 'S' here!"

Jenn's hand squeezed tighter, kneading the thigh muscles that were broader than her hand could hold.

"It didn't hurt, you know," Jesus!, she was whispering and it kept going high-pitched at the end, "it – did not – hurt that you practically memorized the civil and criminal code."

Nope. Didn't hurt."

"So, Mister Good Memory, remember me when you're Chief of Police."

Sam let his muscles relax and his leg respond to the heat from Jenn's leg. "You forget we in El Lay, China Girl," he said, a serious thought penetrating the jive-joke accent. "If I expec' a be Chief a Police, I expec' a be Mayor!"

Jenn leaned her chin on Sam's shoulder.

"Remember me *then*."

"Will you sleep with me *then*?" Sam heard himself ask the question from the distance of an observer.

Jenn closed her eyes, letting the dizziness of the brandy make her own voice a distant sound. She needed to let it speak for her. The voice would still be in control.

"When you stop being in love with your wife," the voice said.

An Episode For Sweeps Week

"It's all Yin and Yang, you see: the forces of good, that's us, we're Yins (or is it Yangs?), against the forces of bad, which should be the Yangs. I picked this up at night classes over at City College. We were talking about Kierkegaard, see, and the point is, even though he was talking about a leap of faith, he was *really* talking about sex! You see, he –"

"Here."

"I don't like Chinese tea."

"– Kierkegaard, the philosopher, he was dumped by this woman when he was young, and he spent the rest of his life trying to figure out why. 'God,' he was saying in all those books –"

"It's hot."

"Coffee is hot."

" 'God, why did you let her dump *me*?!' Wild, isn't it?"

Detective Sergeant Sam Williams didn't think it was 'wild,' nor did Detective Jenny Luck – and their lack of enthusiasm created a chasm of silence when Patrolman Rodney Sinclair finally paused long enough to come up for air. After an awkward moment of unbalance, when Sam and Jenn finally realized that their uniformed support officer had stopped talking, the gap was filled by a new pair of voices:

"This is a pretty dull angle," the director complained, leaning over his cameraman's shoulder to kibitz on the set-up.

"Whatta ya want? It's a police stakeout, it's what they're giving us!" The cameraman *knew* what the director wanted – to put his hands on the camera and do the set-up himself – but that was against union rules.

"Yeah," the director agreed with desultory gracelessness, shooting a sharp look over at Sam, "this is what they're giving us – but will it play on prime time?"

It did not matter what the cameraman intended to say: Officer Sinclair had caught his breath and retraced his train of thought.

"So with Kierkegaard, like with most people, God didn't answer him. So Kierkegaard figured out he had to have a 'leap of faith' in God in order to understand why the girl dumped him."

"Sinclair." Sam's eyes were closed.

"You can call me 'Rodney'." He was taller than Sam, blacker, and the director kept wishing the LAPD had had the smarts enough to realize that *Police Files U.S.A.* needed at least *one* white face on the stakeout team.

"Sinclair —" Sam *refused* to open his eyes until Jenn took that stinking Chinese tea away from under his nose, "we're going to be staked out here for the next twelve hours — or until the booguys decide to make their little extortion visit. Shut up until then, please."

Sam's ill humor made its point: to everyone. Rodney moved away from the grim detective sergeant to join the cameraman, who was busily rechecking a nonexistent loose connection, and then hover over the director, who suddenly found a need to consult his notes. Jenn, grimmer than Sam, forced the styrofoam cup of tea even closer to his face.

"Get it away from me, Jenn!"

"When you drink it. It will make you feel better."

"The smell makes me feel like vomiting right now."

"That's the herbal medicines in the tea. It will make you feel better."

Jenn said "It will make you feel better" with every futile offering she had made to Sam this morning: the aspirins, the bromides, a vile-tasting Thai candy that was called "Tiger"-something. Now this Chinese tea crap. Sam knew what he needed: he needed not to drink two brandies on an empty stomach and four brandies after dinner. He knew that last night. He did not even *like* drinking that much and he had told Jenn so. But she was only twenty-eight and hardly felt the after-effects. Now she was acting Oriental Healing Woman on him. Shit on that!

"Excuse me, Sergeant Williams," the director broke in on Sam's indulgent self-pity, "I need some additional information for our narrative."

Sam opened his eyes now because his eyelids felt uncomfortable: his contact lenses were slipping around behind his eyeballs. He blinked twice and found himself staring at the video camera. The chunky director encased in silk jacket with the logo "NEW THIS FALL: *POLICE FILES U.S.A.!*" emblazoned across it was standing over the cameraman's shoulder.

"Yes – ?" The director had introduced himself earlier, along with the cameraman, but Sam hadn't been listening to the names.

"On this stakeout – is it an old Tong gang, or just a bunch of street thugs?"

Sam smiled sarcastically.

"Ask Detective Luck, she's the expert – or, at the very least, she's Chinese."

Sam saw the video camera swing around to catch Jenn muttering with exasperation: "Tongs! There aren't any–"

"Try not to look directly at the camera. Look just to the side, at me."

The director's crisp, impersonal command caught Jenn off-guard. Momentarily disoriented and slightly intimidated, she began to speak stiffly in semi-officialese:

"In the Task force, we monitor activities throughout ethnic immigrant communities, Chinatown in this case, although Little Nam is also nearby..."

Sam leaned back on his carton and watched respectfully as Jenn went through the department-approved speeches they had gone over the night before.

As stakeouts went, this one was not too uncomfortable: they had built a "wall" of cardboard cartons behind the store owner's cash register – he normally used the area for storage, so it was dry and relatively large – and there was ready access to a bathroom and munchies. Jenn had persuaded the PR people that there was really *no space* in this "dirty, cramped little hole" for one of them to tag along.

So, with one blueshirt for tactical support and the camera having an easy peek through the carton wall, it looked like the makings of a clean operation. If the baddies decided to show – and Sam figured they might since the Task Force was working on a solid tip – then this little show-and-tell would mean certain lieutenanthood by summer. And Jenn could be a lady sergeant! Wow, almost enough to forget being sick to one's stomach!

"– We received word from sources that a small group recently arrived from Hong Kong has begun extorting payments from local merchants. We persuaded the owner of this store, a victim, to let us stake out the extortionists the next time they were expected."

The RING–RING–RING of the bell alerted them to the entrance of the three people. Sam felt his muscles stiffen, then immediately relax into a ready tension.

"Cut the camera!" the director whispered in panic to the already-moving cameraman, "Get it in place! No, just swing it! Now! Now!"

It was fortunate that the arrivees were customers, greeted by the storekeeper, Ching Kung, with a loudness that covered up some of the more insistent of the director's cinematic commands.

"Teenagers," he explained to the old ladies buying amazingly large amounts of noodles and canned lichees and dropping them into seemingly bottomless plastic carrybags. "Teenagers" was a good enough explanation for them: they all had a grandson or a nephew who spoke only English and roughhoused in the backrooms instead of helping with the family businesses. The old women each exchanged with Mr.

Kung a sorry story about how the Vietnamese were taking over Chinatown by working *harder* than their own children, then arrived at the mutual conclusion that they should all be sent back to North Viet Nam where they belonged – except for Mr. Nguyen up the block, of course, who offered very good buys on beef, much better than those bloodsucking newcomers from Hong Kong who drove all the prices up.

After a long, pointless argument on the nature of proper white-balance versus getting-the-shot, the director and the cameraman each made a secret vow to never to work together again, then noticed that their best strategy was to have the camera set-up on a tripod. This accomplished – to a chorus of Officer Sinclair's myriad questions – they sat back on cartons next to Sam and Jenn and waited.

And waited.

The thudding beat of the music reached them first. Bass notes pierced through the cardboard wall, dancing through their bodies before they were even conscious of the accompanying music that filtered into the store moments later. The booguys had arrived, each masked like the Lone Ranger.

There was, of course, the same RING–RING–RINGing doorbell to announce the three masked youths' entrance that had ushered in the old ladies hours before. It had been a slow morning, and there'd been few such announcements since. This time the bells were lost in the deafening roar coming from a boombox portable music factory carried by the caboose-end member of the entering trio. If nothing else, they were not trying to disguise their arrival.

Behind the carton wall the chaos was considerably more controlled than it had been earlier. Or perhaps it was the loud music muffling the cameraman's shuffling movements and the director's hectoring commands.

In front of the wall Ching Kung stood by his cash register, feeling a familiar indigestion take possession of his bowels. He did not know which he feared more: the threat of danger, or the possibility of embarrassing himself.

Sam and Jenn had assumed their ready positions automatically, each one pressed close to the carton wall, one eye pressed to a carefully pre-selected peephole.

"We need to get them in the shot, standing in ambush!" the director whispered frantically to his cameraman.

"Shut – up!" Sam mouthed with silent vehemence.

The three Lone Rangers were taking their time walking down the long grocery aisle. Boombox started to close the front door, but was stopped by a shake of the head from the apparent leader, who thrust his hands into his oversized pants pockets and spoke with an accent of East London Cockney condescension.

"Need the air, luv – and th'exit."

"What should *I* do?"

Sam turned his attention from the bickering television

people to Rodney. The uniformed patrolman *should* have been edging around the building and making his way to cover the front entrance. Instead, he was standing in the middle of the small storage area, looking like a clumsy giant made all of arms and legs.

With a pointing head gesture Sam indicated to Jenn to take over the patrolman's role.

Nodding agreement, Jenn started to step towards the closed back door when the boombox music suddenly cut off. It was too late to leave, the creak of opening the back door would alert the Lone Rangers.

A growing sense of despair seeped into Sam's consciousness, undercutting the urgency of the moment. He turned to the eager patrolman and counseled with soundless lip movements: "Be – ready!"

Rodney whipped out his nightstick like a sword and assumed a ridiculous, semi-crouched, wide-legged stance. Sam's misgivings were fueled by a contribution of comisery from Jenn as she shook her head at the patrolman's "preparedness."

Finally ready for business, Cockney led the Lone Rangers in a swagger down the aisle to face Ching Kung across the checkout counter.

"Allo, luv," he grinned his greeting to the silent store owner, his Chinese features only slightly obscured by the black mask. "Got the tidy bit for us this week?"

It wasn't just for the television show that the Task Force had advised Mr. Kung to refuse: they needed the extortionists to make specific threats. The storekeeper shook his head 'no' to Cockney – who feigned an elaborate disappointment in response.

"What's 'at? I see no *green*? Oi, luvs," Cockney turned his back on the grocer to address his fellow Rangers, " 'e's forgot why 'e hired us!"

Sam gritted his teeth. These punks were good, they were saying the wrong words: you couldn't win an extortion conviction on an employee-employer dispute, no matter how obnoxious the demand sounded.

Cockney indicated a glass jar on a chest-high shelf.

"See that, luvs?" he said to the Lone Rangers, then turned to Ching Kung and nodded to the same glass jar. "See that, Missa Kung? There's a fly on the food: *un*-hy-gen-ic!"

Suddenly, hands still in his pockets, Cockney lashed out a foot and smashed the glass jar, sending its contents spilling around the floor. The wiry masked man turned back to the storekeeper and shrugged his shoulders for understanding.

"Remember, now? We're pest specialists. Oi, here's another little fingy flyin' on the food!"

His foot whip-kicked with precision to destroy a jar from a higher shelf.

"And another!"

A still higher kick!

Cockney spun around in delight to face his two partners.

"Luvs: we come all a way from Hong Kong a help this man wif his pest problem –" he whirled back to face Ching Kung, " – it's expensive comin' all a way from Hong Kong!"

The threat had been clear. Jenn squeezed her face tightly against her peephole.

"Say – the – words," she whispered to herself.

Cockney leaned his face closely into Ching Kung's. That is to say, he was in full close-up for the *Police Files U.S.A.* camera.

"You gotta *pay* us for our service or we'll find a LOT more flies, right, luvs?!"

Without bothering to look back, Cockney knew from the routine that Boombox was nodding his masked agreement – and that the third Lone Ranger was pulling out his (illegal but dramatically effective) switchblade knife for display.

This was it!

"Now!" Sam mouthed to Jenn, and the two began to pull out their service revolvers with slow and careful precision.

Behind them Rodney, his perceptions heightened by the ether of tension in the air, realized that the bust was coming next. He saw the plainclothes detectives pull their guns and decided to do the same.

He forgot that he was still holding his nightstick.

Rodney did not even think about the nightstick as he opened his fingers to unsnap his holster. The resonant wooden baton clanged on the concrete floor with a loud, teeth-grating solidity that reverberated through the store before it fell into a steady tattoo of clacks settling into a dead standstill. It was heard.

Sam did not need to speak a word of Chinese to understand the gist of Cockney's next comment: "IT'S A SET-UP!" Cockney cried in Cantonese, pulling his hands from his pants pockets and hightailing it past his surprised colleagues towards the open entrance door.

Sam and Jenn were only a half-second slower in their reactions, each cutting around the carton wall barrier that separated them from the main body of the store.

But their pursuit was almost aborted from the start. With a commanding roar born from six months on Traffic Control, Rodney understood that action was called for:

"POLICE! FREEEEEEEEZE!" he cried, charging *through* the wall of cardboard cartons! His huge body shattered the light receptacles into bunches of flying debris, knocking Sam and Jenn into the side shelves of the grocery store. Ching Kung fell under his counter and decided to stay there.

Cockney did not consider it a viable option to turn around and witness the chaos behind him. Sprinting through the front door in imitation of lightening, he only noted in passing that his colleagues Switchblade and Boombox had much slower reflexes than he had thought.

Police Files U.S.A. had found a master team: the director and cameraman successfully avoided serious damage from Rodney's flying wall charge and stumbled in upright positions behind him through the debris, capturing the action for home viewers with a wrenching accuracy that would leave many of the audience motion sick. Sam was already struggling to his feet before the two remaining Lone Ranger shakedown thugs finally woke up and decided to turn tail. By that time Jenn had shed her shoes and was leg-pumping a sprint down a parallel aisle – while Rodney succeeded in kicking the grocer as he plowed past.

For whatever reason, Boombox did not release his magnum-sized sonic device, and Switchblade made it through the front door ahead of him with two steps to spare. Boombox had worse luck: jamming his radio against the door, he was suddenly stopped short. In later account of the incident to the Public Defender, he was unclear whether he had stunned himself – or had the wind knocked out of him by the Chinese policewoman who slammed up into the thug from behind with her fists jamming.

Less than seven seconds had elapsed.

Sam rushed past Jenn and her prisoner. Rodney followed several steps and scant seconds behind.

By the time Sam burst through the door into the blinding daylight, Cockney had already made it straightaway half across the street and Switchblade had cut right down the sidewalk. It was a typical winter day in Los Angeles: warm, bright and disorienting. Sam wanted the little Cockney fucker that was the leader of the punk extortion trio for himself. He pointed with his arm towards the fleeing Switchblade and saw from the corner of his eye that Rodney was doing something right.

Given another two hundred yards, Sam probably would have caught Cockney, despite the fact that the kung-footed thug had flung off his Lone Ranger mask and was becoming increasingly difficult to distinguish from the crowds of holiday season shoppers crowding the sidewalks. Cockney realized that he was losing ground, too. When he saw the motorcycle stopping for a red light, he did not waste precious time in internal debate: he grabbed the surprised rider by the arm and yanked.

"GET OFF 'N WALK, LUV!" Cockney bellowed, his command stirring some instinctual urge to obey in the rider, who instantly found himself stumbling awkwardly away from his own motorcycle. Sam could only run with futile desperation towards the spot as Cockney hopped onto the running motorcycle and sped off, oblivious to the red light and fender-scraping closeness to death with which he flirted.

Sam felt his gums ache and taste of salt with exertion, but he forced himself to continue running and U-turned his body back towards the store. He would help Rodney in the pursuit of the third Lone Ranger, Switchblade, who had yet to discard his mask and was running away from the store a full block down the street from where Sam had lost Cockney.

"Freeze! Stop! Put down the knife! Stop it, I said. FREEZE!" Rodney cried in distant, dogged, pursuit of the extortionist. He was more than half the distance closer than Sam, but losing ground fast.

"Freeze! Stop! I said STOP! Police! POLICE!"

Between Rodney and Sam, the *Police Files U.S.A.* jacket of the director bobbed dramatically, exhorting his panting cameraman to run faster, not miss a shot, "Try to zoom-in, don't lose the shot, we're falling behind, you fuck!, we're falling behind, gimme the camera, I don't care about the goddamn union rules, GIMME THE GOD'M CAMERA YOU SHIT!"

Switchblade held on to his open knife with talismanic hope: this was his guiding star, cling to it, this had always been his power, cling to it. His lungs burned, but the adrenaline pumping through his legs would not let him slow down.

"Stop–running–this–is–the–police!"

The black cop would not stop shouting! Switchblade twisted his body to the right and dashed through a car-filled alley more to escape the noise coming from the uniformed policeman chasing him than as part of a strategic decision. He was already to the end of the alley and bursting onto the open space of Phoenix Shopping Plaza before Rodney turned into the alley.

Yevgeny liked Chinatown: it reminded him of a Kirghiz street market he had explored in 1948, only with more beautiful junk to offer and less of value. He liked Asian women. He did not say this to his grandson. He told his grandson they were shopping for cheap radios to send to Russia and sell for twice their worth. His grandson was a little smartass going to Hebrew school and learning computers as a hobby. His grandson had no sense of romance.

Yevgeny was disappointed that there were so few people out shopping this afternoon. So few Asian women today. He had sent his grandson into a martial arts equipment store, then leaned against a good-luck Buddha shrine.

When Yevgeny heard the faint voice shouting something about "freezing" his first thought was: December is too *late* in the year to be selling ice cream on the streets in Los Angeles. (Moscow was another matter. There you had to sell the *flavor*, not the chill – winter was too long.) Yevgeny turned to see who was such a stupid street vendor.

He saw his friend Sergeant Sam instead.

From Yevgeny's point-of-view, Sergeant Sam was third in line behind a frantically running young Chinese man wearing a small black mask followed by a frantically yelling tall black man wearing a police uniform. From Sam's perspective, he had just passed the bickering *Police Files* team and was fast catching-up to Rodney – Switchblade was in distant sight.

"Freeze, I said! This is the police! Stop running!" At last a complete version of Rodney's nonstop harangue weakly reached Yevgeny's hearing and the immigrant fruitseller understood the odd procession coming his way. Well, it was a boring day. He could stop a small Chinese thief any day.

Phoenix Plaza is wide at many points – and narrow at others. Switchblade knew he had plenty of room to escape around the Buddha Shrine.

Until the fat old man stepped out with clear intention of blocking his way.

Rodney saw the development clearly – and he did not want a civilian involved.

"GET OUT OF THE WAY!" he shouted, changing his panting chase chant, "GET – OUT OF WAY!"

Yevgeny heard him, but what did the policeman know? This was a small Chinese, Yevgeny could catch him with one arm!

"Look out, old man!" Switchblade cursed in Cantonese, finding his legs becoming less controllable by the moment. He aimed for a gap between the old round eyes and the Buddha Shrine. Instead Switchblade was snapped to a standstill by a sudden jerk on his left arm. The old man was holding him!

Yevgeny smiled. The Chinese was easy to catch: he might be slippery, though. Yevgeny pushed his bulky torso into the masked thief to discourage further forward progress.

The knife slid into his abdomen easily. Too easily. Switchblade was uncertain whether or not he had actually pierced the old man's flesh, fearing the point had only torn his jacket and was dangling in empty air. The round eyes was still holding onto his arm! Switchblade pulled his knife back and jammed it into Yevgeny a second time.

The *Police Files* camera caught the murder to imperfect effect: they were too far distant to see the grey surprise enter Yevgeny's eyes. The director, handling the camera now, was not worried. The shot would justify his taking over before the union review board. With a steady hand he followed the sequence of events: Switchblade pushed aside the old man and resumed running, the uniformed cop and the plainclothesman ran up to the fallen body together.

"I've got the old man," Sam said with a rush, falling to his knees to grab Yevgeny's head. It would be a minute more before he would recognize the Russian fruit vendor.

Yevgeny was unable to comprehend the reason why his body was shaking so uncontrollably. Every muscle in his strong frame fought to deny the draining power of the gaping ulcer in his solar plexus. His Sergeant Sam was putting his black face next to him. Recognition flowed into the dark eyes just as Yevgeny came to a sudden realization.

"You –" Yevgeny was disappointed that his rich voice sounded so weak, "are maybe bad luck." Ooh! This pain from such an idiot for no reason! "Stupid world!" Yevgeny cried angrily.

Then he forgot his pain. He was dead.

"YOU FUCKER!"

Rodney's cry had changed from one of command to that of pure anger. He wanted – he *willed* – the fleeing murderer to stop, realizing with every jack hammered shove into the pavement that the fugitive had a fifty pound, hundred yard advantage that was growing steadily.

"STOP, YOU FUCK–"

He swallowed air in painful gulps.

"YOU FUCK–"

The director had his shot of the dying victim/concerned cop. He leapt up to follow the chase.

"FUCK–"

They were almost out of the narrow band of streets comprising Chinatown, skipping through half-filled parking lots and industrial side streets.

Despite his relatively recent arrival in Los Angeles, Switchblade had been quick in learning the geography of his new territory, at least in terms of the Chinese environs: China-town, Monterey Park, border areas of downtown. Nothing was as complicated as Hong Kong had been – which was a disadvantage at the moment: the fugitive murderer could not simply turn down a hodgepodge-created side street and disappear.

But he knew that north of Chinatown the remains of once-vast railroad yards crisscrossed a warehouse area. To make it there would probably ensure escape.

To make it there, one had to cross an open space where a dozen side streets emptied onto a plain of old train tracks. Switchblade did not doubt that he could outrun the slowing black policeman over the flats.

Fuong Lee liked the area in that it was close enough to Chinatown for him to blend in – and still not a real part of the energy-sucking Chinese community. He had been crowded so much of his life. The usually empty railroad tracks were one of his favorite thinking spots. Occasionally a train would lumber by, its crew carefully on the lookout for drunks on the tracks and cars speeding out of nowhere. *Where would I be going now?*, Fuong Lee would always think, not without a pang of envy.

Today he was not stopping by the area to look at trains – Fuong Lee knew that none would be going by at this mid-day hour – but simply taking his quickly-purchased groceries back to the loft quarters he had arranged through fourth parties. He passed the lone car parked on the periphery of the open space and remarked only that this was the fifth time or so he had seen the bland-faced warehouse clerk sitting there eating his brown bag lunch and reading a newspaper. *Is this a kindred spirit waiting for the trains?*, Fuong laughed to himself.

He saw the masked man suddenly appear at the far end of the tracks.

"You fuck–"

The accusation flew weakly behind the running man. Something metallic flashed in his hand. He was running with obvious effort, and the effort was rewarding him with less speed than he expected. The black policeman appeared at the far end of the tracks moments later.

"FUCK–"

His was the voice crying out. A policeman. Fuong Lee's first instinct was to hide away from any police. He did not follow his instinct. He was fascinated by the chase.

Switchblade had underestimated the endurance of the black policeman – and his own nervous wasting of energy. Instead of having a major lead on his pursuer, Switchblade could only manage to maintain his original hundred yard advantage over the dogged cop.

"FUCK–"

Fuck yourself!, Switchblade thought frantically: the black policeman's threats were scaring the shit out of him!

"FUCK–"

Switchblade saw the car across the open space and immediately decided on a course of action inspired by Cockney's earlier success: a quick steal and an easy escape.

Rodney saw what the escaping murderer was planning to do, too. Despite his best efforts, though, he could not make himself run any faster. The fugitive would be at the car a full half-minute ahead of him.

Henry Glanz was not aware of the slapping feet on the pavement until the man was almost at his car.

"OUT OF CAR!"

"What?!" Henry's thoughts were still intent on his newspaper, trying to find his wife's horoscope, supposedly on page C7.

"OUT OF CAR!" The screaming masked man grabbed at the door handle.

"I – ?"

Switchblade had only moments: he pulled the car door violently open.

Henry lifted the pistol from his lap and pulled the trigger.

In later trying to remember for himself, Rodney compared the two killings he had witnessed that day. In the first one, the old man had hardly seemed aware that he was being murdered, life was so strong in him that it came as a surprise that he was suddenly dying.

There was no surprise for Switchblade, he was dead immediately.

The hole in his heart was small – it was, after all, only a .38 caliber bullet – but Switchblade's life was over the instant it happened. Henry had time to look at the gun in his hand and wonder what exactly had happened. By the time he looked up, the man he had shot was lying on the ground. Through his open car door Henry could see a tall black uniformed policeman standing stock still fifty yards away, staring at him. A moment later the policeman seemed to have floated up to the car, but Henry had not noticed him moving.

"Who *are* you?" Rodney asked slowly.

Henry could not remember his name. "I – I was just having lunch, I like to read, he didn't look nice, I –" Henry had nothing else to say.

Rodney thought about the words.

"He didn't look nice."

It is doubtful whether Henry heard the whine of the approaching sirens, but Rodney did, and became immediately conscious of the people about to show up. He looked behind – no one yet – then at Switchblade's body, then at Henry.

"Get out of here," Rodney said quietly.

"Well, I –" Henry held out his gun.

"It's a No Parking Zone," Rodney heard his voice start to crack. "Get outta here!"

Henry Glanz was conditioned to obey the law. Without another word he fumbled-on the car's ignition and drove off. It was only then that Rodney saw the Chinese man standing over on the sidewalk, mute witness to the scene. With a defeated sag of his shoulders, Rodney raised his arm at the bystander and commanded wearily:

"Don't move. They're gonna need to talk to you."

Fuong Lee did not want to be a witness.

"I don't speak English," he said in primitive Cantonese with a stupid smile plastered across his face. He started shuffling away. "No Engelish."

It was too late: Sergeant Williams had arrived, followed by the *Police Files* camera team.

"Stay here," Rodney made a firm gesture with his arm that left no room for mixed interpretation.

It turned out to be an excellent segment, selected for Sweeps Week by the syndicator in order to garner *Police Files U.S.A.* top ratings for its time slot. All of the elements of episodic drama were there: a quiet, routine stakeout, sudden eruption of violence, a murder – and the murderer brought to swift, fitting justice. The director turned the camera back over to his cameraman as he fitted the final pieces of the story together on the spot.

"Patrolman Sinclair had downed the murderer, who apparently attempted to attack him with the knife he had used to kill (find out the victim's name) only minutes before. An official inquiry was held: there was some question about the caliber of bullet found in the body, but – as Police Files U.S.A. has recorded – it was what the cops on the beat calls a 'clean kill'."

They used some footage of the Chinese bystander, but since the syndicator did not like subtitles, they edited him down to a few quick shots.

"We were unable to establish whether this man actually *saw* the incident, as he does not speak English."

That was a partial untruth, the director knew, but the Chinese bitch policewoman refused to translate. He was pretty certain she was lying, but he put in her official statement:

"Task Force investigators already on the scene discovered that the man had not witnessed the event."

What the hell if she *was* lying – this was syndication, not the news.

Fuong Lee listened carefully while the police and ambulances circled around the black policeman and his body. He learned that the body was Chinese. He learned that there was some question about how the black policeman killed him. The refugee dissident learned that there were two police without uniforms – another black man and a Chinese woman — who came up to the uniformed policeman and counseled him. Apparently they suggested that he basically not answer questions, but let his superiors draw their own conclusions. When the major confusion subsided, the two plainclothes police came up to Fuong Lee.

"I hear you don't speak English," Jenn said to the reluctant witness in sarcastic, colloquial Cantonese. "We know the basic story: what do *you* say?"

Fuong Lee looked warily at Sam and Jenn, then answered in clear (but guarded) English:

"I saw... what the policeman says... happened."

The two detectives looked uncomfortably at one another. This was the answer they wanted to hear, but... Sam began speaking to a nearby wall:

"Not that it matters, but the man who was shot had just killed an old man."

Fuong Lee twisted his lips in a smile of commiseration.

"Not that it matters."

Jenn shot the next questions at him in rapid Mandarin, matching Fuong Lee point-for-point in accent and inflection. She was angry and she knew why.

"Where are you from?"

"Texas."

"Why are you here?"

"For the air."

"Do you have a name?"

"A very bad one."

"For the record – ?"

"Elvis Chang."

WHAT IS THE MOON?

"La luna!"

The words were uttering in full, reverent awe: an appreciation of the round, perfect orb hanging in the middle of the jet black sky.

"La luna bella!"

The old man sat back in his chair and uttered another exclamation of admiration to the moon. His bottle of Chianti sat (still half full!) on the small circle of tabletop before him, his large glass was (still!) half-filled next to the bottle, the night was (still half!) warm despite the Christmastime chill of winter. This was a beautiful night! This was a magnificent night! And –if this was not *the* best Chianti, and not *the* best café in Taranto – then it was still (more than half!) as good as the best street cafés in Roma and Napoli because *here*, in Taranto – on the heel of the boot! – in Taranto the moon smiled down in her fullness with such a beatific glow!

She had to be shared.

The old man (maybe, perhaps, inspired by a little drunkenness - but only a little!) saw the quiet young man sitting at the table next to him and grabbed at his sleeve.

"Mi scusi, Signore – "

"Eh?" The Professor woke from his open-eyed sleep, quietly startled. He had not been aware that he was sleeping. He never slept anymore, there was too much pressure.

The old man nearly fell from his chair, pointing with enthusiasm.

"La luna!"

The Professor could not bring his thoughts to focus on the old man's excitement.

"Si," he answered without interest.

"No! No 'si'!" the old man cried urgently, pulling harder on the younger man's sleeve. "La *luna*!" The old man *had* to share this beauty!

"Prego," The Professor tried to remove the old man's hand gently, but was not successful. "Signore!" he added with stern command, his pale green eyes turning a hard jade for the moment. The old man let his fingers loosen with disappointment and tried to plead:

"La luna, che bella!"

The Professor felt the caressing rhythms of the old man's Southern accents wrap themselves around this simple paean to the moon. His own Tuscany produced hard,

German-influenced sentiments, precision married to romance. He looked at the old man and shook his head. It was time to make his telephone call – again.

The Professor rose from his seat, rummaged in his coat pocket, and pulled out a handful of thousand-lira notes. He held them out to the old man: let the lunatic drink some decent grappa.

The old man shoved the Professor's hand away.

"No, no lira – la luna!"

He was at it again, pointing to the full moon with a passion. The Professor stood with the handful of lira notes extended for a moment, then dropped them back into his pocket with a shrug: the old man was crazy, of course. He turned to step away from his small table. The telephone call. And then maybe some sleep. He doubted it, but maybe some sleep.

The old man had read the Professor's eyes.

"No, Io no pazzo!" he cried as the young man with the greying hair turned away from him. "I am *not* crazy!"

The Professor shrugged: it was not worth the emotional involvement.

"O.K."

"You think I am crazy!"

"Non." The Professor needed to get away from the street tables and into the café.

"You think I am crazy!" The old man ran behind the

young man and grabbed both his arms. He was surprised by the immediate violence with which the Professor flung him off.

The Professor, his arms upraised, threw them even wider open in exasperation. "Be crazy!" he cried, then disappeared into the warm interior of the cafe.

But the old man was not to let it lie without the last word. He stomped his foot in anger and curved his fingers into devil's horns pointing at the departing young man's back.

"I *curse* you –" he said with shaky strength, "I am not crazy: it is a beautiful moon!" The old man raised a furious fist at the white, empty hole in the black sky. "Damn beautiful moon!"

It could be a damn beautiful moon, a damn beautiful sun – or a damn *ugly* anything! for all the Professor cared at the moment. A chill was inside of him and the rush of warm air that hit once inside the café did nothing to abate his interior shivering.

This was his third time making this call in as many nights. His third night of waiting for someone to answer – to come to his next night's waiting place. His third night, day, night, day, night, day without sleep. He could not sleep. If there was no answer tonight, he would have to leave Taranto for the temporary haven of the next "safe house" – which, of course, was no longer safe anymore.

Had they ever been safe?

It did not matter now, for *now* was what mattered, and *now* he could only use the pre-ordained safe houses for a few hours' restless lying on a bed, wondering about the people who accepted him without question when he arrived at their doors, unannounced. Would they betray him in an hour, or four hours – or ever? So many were honest and loyal, still, but who could tell? There need only be one to plant the doubt, and there had been more than three this past year of 1989. Not even the whole year, really, just these last few months, when the world had started to fall apart.

The Professor had never been a Stalinist – he was too wide-eyed to be doctrinaire in religion *or* in politics. But if his core of belief had not been shaken by the grim realities of the gulags and other fascist horrors – if the *ideals* still made sense despite the contradictions of history – why should there be any major undermining of faith now that the Soviet empire was democratizing?

Were the poor suddenly rich? Had capitalism suddenly spawned a noncompetitive concern for the People's welfare? It was not over!

The café owner did not know the Professor, but five years ago his son did. The owner had been asked by his son to let anyone who identified themself properly to use his telephone, no questions asked. And the owner, refusing to ask *any* questions, did not know that his son had lost the faith of his political radicalism upon graduation from university – and the offer of a middle management position with Fiat.

He was writing inventory numbers on a tally sheet when the Professor approached the old black telephone on the bar counter: the customer had already identified himself an hour ago, asking if some expected call had come in earlier in the evening. No calls for the customer (from the north, yes? Milanese, or –)

"Prego?" the visiting associate from his son asked, lifting up the receiver.

"Si," the owner nodded, carrying his tallies to the far end of the counter, nearer to where Luchese carried on his regular complaint about the lack of art in Italian cinema since Sophia and Gina turned old. Stupid ass! If Luchese ever *paid* for a cinema ticket he would see that Italy was still fully represented. The owner listened to Luchese's droning complaints well assured that they obscured overhearing the visitor's call: the owner did not want to be *asked* questions, either.

The Professor dialed the number with practiced hands: the number went back many years. Almost to the beginning. His fingers remembered automatically. It had rarely been used so often without response – except a decade earlier when they'd shot the Pope.

Ptoo! The Professor mentally spit out the memory with distaste every time he thought of it.

Why had they arranged to shoot Il Papa? The idea was an idiocy that the Brigade had rejected without debate.

True, the Vatican was worse than a capitalist institution of oppression: it was a *feudal* dinosaur. OK, so the Polish Pope wasn't docile like Pius, or simple like John, or cold and distant like the intellectual Paul. (The Professor had admired *him*: beneath the dull facade, Paul was a revolutionary trying to pull the Church into the 20th Century). And, yes, this reactionary Wojtyła had successfully undercut the courageous Liberation Theology priests fighting fascism in the Latin Americas. But the real reason for the assassination attempt?

The Professor had known the *real* reason as soon as he heard the proposal: the Soviet Union's General Secretary, Leonid Brezhnev hated Pope John Paul II. The Russian feared the Pole on purely nationalistic, non-Internationale terms.

The Professor did not need confirmation of the Brigade's dismissal of the proposition: there were some symbols in Italy that were too sacred to touch, and even the most simpleminded cadre could tell the Russians that Il Papa was one of those icons. Besides, Euro-Communism was on the rise; Berlinguer was only steps away from power in Rome; in France Mitterand had been forced to use the Party as allies to form a coalition victory. These were not radical enough steps for the Brigade, but they were important inroads.

Then the Russians had gone and clumsily recruited a fanatic Turk – using the heavy-handed Bulgarians as the conduit!

The Professor remembered the smell of chaos that had invaded the Brigade when rumors of their involvement with the crime began to sour so many of their "haute" supporters. There was no escaping fact. The Brigade was compromised. Cells had been used. The policy of "no questions, no danger" had been exploited to slide the Turk into Rome via the pipe-line established in concert with Palestinians and French cadres.

The Professor had had his first experience with calling the number to no avail then.

He had assumed responsibility for damage control and he needed the Russians' cooperation. Instead – dammit, he remembered *this* well – they had dawdled, letting him, letting the *Brigade* hang for days! The reassuring voice he had spoken with so often before was now silent. Then it was replaced: by a careful voice, a voice that betrayed doubt.

Later, when the damaged was assessed irreparable and new structures created, the voice had become seductive: literally *feminine*. She spoke Italian and Russian with equal fluidity, and her inflections were a teasing provocation in both languages.

The Professor had become Harlequin-the-Bandit then, to his own mind at least. The intellectual dialectic was unnecessary now, because she believed in them – in him. Argument was minimum, she asked the favors. Justification was nil, she held out the promised fruits for the grabbing. "Evangelina," the Professor-as-Harlequin took to calling her in his playful moments of imagination. There were few enough of those to stand out in his memory. "Evangelina, is your apple so sweet?" he allowed himself to ask her once, but she had missed the joke and he realized that her proffered cornucopia of delights was too professionally considered to be real. He wondered if Evangelina's would still be the voice he would hear. He wondered if the telephone would be answered *this* night, finally.

It was a complicated call to make from this part of Italy: telephone service on the heel of the boot was notoriously inconsistent. The Professor dialed the first two numerals three dozen times before the busy signal from the central exchange cleared and allowed him to finish the sequence. He glanced at his watch: it was still within the acceptable half hour.

One ring.

Two rings.

"Hallo?" The voice was shrill: a housewife's annoyed interruption of a late dinner, probably with a crying child in the bedroom, angry that Mama had abandoned him to feed Papa.

"We are in need of our friends' support," the Professor began, his mouth dry with apprehension, although his Italian was telemarketing-smooth. "Charitable donations are tax deductible and will be accompanied by a signed receipt. Am I speaking with the lady of the house?"

"We don't need to get your tax deductions," the woman said irritably and hung up.

They had answered his call!

The Professor put down the receiver and looked at the black telephone with unwanted relief. One part of him had wanted them to never answer, to be lost forever, perhaps destroyed by the internal security police. Then he would be alone with a reason.

But he did not want to be alone.

The Professor felt an untoward gratitude for the telephone surge within him. They had answered! He wanted to stand there and stare at the black instrument, regarding the mechanical totem with reverence, until they called back, but that would have been unacceptable.

Instead he went into the filthy closet the owner had labelled a WC and relieved his bowels in a long, inconvenient attack of nature. Did he have a fever? Three days without regular sleep had given the Professor a headache, it would not be unexpected if revisionist bacteria decided to attempt a coup. He laughed quietly to himself in the dank, fetid water closet: his intestines squirmed spasmodically but could still see humor in the dialectic.

He returned to the bar and was drinking a Compari at the counter when the telephone rang. The owner answered, giving the name of the café, then held out the receiver:

"You are the telephone salesman?"

"It is a profession," the Professor apologized. He left the owner a salesman-sized tip under the Compari. "Pronto," he said into the receiver.

"Hallo." It was the woman's voice again, this time unannoyed. Evangelina. She waited for him to repeat his sales pitch.

"We are in need of our friends' support."

Evangelina did not answer at once. When she did speak it was with cool disinterest.

"I will speak Russian – because you understand it and I want to be precise."

"Da. Ya slushaiyu," the Professor let the words carry as much righteous indignation as "Yes, I am listening" could convey without slipping into melodramatics. He added: "I have been waiting for several days for our friends to be 'precise'."

Evangelina ignored the implied criticism: she would be *very* precise.

"We can no longer be 'friends': our status is too different, we have drifted apart." She sounded so very like a matron casting off her gigolo.

The Professor's answer was to plead.

"We have been like your family," he heard himself say with uncontrollable dismay that the note in his voice played perfectly to the gigolo's part. "We need one another."

"No..." Evangelina hesitated. The words had struck a chord. "Our hearts and heads are different now."

"We *believe* the same things!" The Professor spoke to her unseen eyes.

"Before we grew up, maybe," Evangelina's voice assumed an air of nostalgic superiority, "but you are still–"

"Don't –"

There was more than pleading in the Professor's voice, there was threat. It gave cause for Evangelina to hesitate again. "Don't make me beg."

"No, I won't..." Professor could hear her fingers cover the mouthpiece; she was speaking with someone else. He knew that he would never speak with Evangelina again. Or this number.

She removed her fingers from the mouthpiece to offer quietly: "I will give your name to friends."

This was it. A table scrap from an embarrassed relative. The Professor could not restrain his sarcasm.

"This is the end result of your 'perestroika', your 'glasnost'? It is prostitution."

"It is capitalism," Evangelina answered with little apparent regret, cutting off the connection.

Despite an overwhelming realization of failure, the Professor felt surprisingly clearheaded as he replaced the telephone receiver to its cradle. There. It was over.

No more indecision.

No more foggy hopes.

Evangelina had been courageously open with him, he realized, and he felt a pang of regret at having repaid her candor with such ill grace. She was the messenger, of course, not the decision-maker. He had never known – would never know – what *her* thoughts were, what *her* decisions might have been.

Not entirely true. Evangelina could have refused to answer his call – it was obvious she had debated the issue for three days, had called in a supervisor for instructions, had pressured someone to display the minimum honour of making a clean break.

The Professor had no illusions: the Russians were closing shop. They would continue their own network, of course, but employed in subtler games than the Brigade's open endeavors. With a smile of nostalgia he wondered: What now did Evangelina think of herself after the "layoffs"?

The Professor nodded his cursory thanks to the café owner he would never see again. It was acknowledged with an equally cursory nod that was more to the Compari tip than to the departing "friend of my son." The Professor stepped out into the growing chill of the early winter night.

He paused just outside the door, to enjoy the last hints of warmth from within before pulling his jacket tight and walking away into the stone-cooling streets.

The old man was still at his small table, the bottle of Chianti now a bare millimeter of memory, the drinker sleeping awkwardly in the wooden chair, chin on chest.

Not snoring, though. The Professor appreciated the small courtesy of the pensionaire in somehow learning to spare the world his cacophonous snorts of breath. So many other of the old drunkards did not think of the People's comfort.

The Professor smiled once again and again and again at his failure to maintain a puritan view of the dialectic.

He looked up at the sky and found the old man's moon, grown small now in its flight to the top of the sky. Small and cold and far away.

"La luna..." he whispered melodically.

Christmas passed. New Year, too. And with the conclusion of the holiday season the airport rush had slowed to its usual winter slump, starting 1990 off to the same rocky fiscal quarter for the airlines that every year buffeted them with.

The Tom Bradley International Terminal at LAX was no exception, and the security cameras passed over empty hallways more than they did full ones. Even when the jumbo air cruisers arrived they were only fifty percent or less occupied. Philippe, then, held a solitary position in the camera's frame for several seconds as he entered the Baggage Claim area before passing through the U.S. Customs check. Immigration and DEA agents watched this area with particular care since passengers from Thailand, particularly Western students, were prone to carry "investment bricks" of heroin for a supposed easy sale to L.A. middlemen. But there was nothing extraordinary or even interesting about the young Frenchman. His appearance seemed about par for the course for passengers from such a long flight: tired and, perhaps, a bit uncomfortable with his own skin.

DAMN TUESDAY

It's my turn, I can't complain.

Damn.

Besides, it's my name on the ticket.

Double damn!

Jenn laughed sarcastically to herself at the quaint, outmoded obscenity, a relic from her mother. "Double damn" was Mom's strongest epithet, reserved for moments in the kitchen when (she thought) no one was around, said often enough to ensure it's being heard by everyone in the family. When Emily Xu said "Double damn" in the kitchen it was a cue for all concerned to put on a particularly somber face and hope that the storm brewing inside her would pass. *I wonder what she'd feel about some of the fucking, shitty, scumbag words I've learned on the force?*, Jenn thought.

She'd feel a hell of a lot more *relieved* if she used them, that's for sure: Momma Xu was one uptight, semi-traditional lady.

Semi-traditional – that was the key problem, Jenn decided, letting her attention wander around the half-deserted courtroom. If Mom would be all traditional Chinese, or all American Chinese, then maybe she would.... Curse like a truck driver or live like a dowager empress? Jenn smiled at the picture of either image:

"Getcher feet off the fuckin' furniture ya boozin' asshole!"

"It pleases us, Xu Hsiao (Dad), to have our breakfast brought in to our chamber."

It was even more fun trying to imagine Dad's reaction to either "New Woman" version of Emily Xu.

Attorneys were starting to wander into the courtroom now, less concerned about the morning's start time than the early-arriving central players in the whole proceedings, the defendants.

"Jennifer? Jenny Luck?!" The Encino accents were the giveaway: Jenn turned in her seat to see Nancy Wong, Attorney at Law, Order of the Coif, advancing with predatory familiarity.

"JENNY!" Nancy screamed enthusiastically, raising a horde of nervous glances from the defendants and nary an eyebrow among the courtroom professionals.

"Hi, Nancy," Jenn answered at a considerably more toned-down decibel level.

"You look *great*, Jenn!" Nancy cried, stopping in

mid-air kiss to lean back on a stiletto heel and review her *good* friend's ensemble.

Jenn had to suppress a snotty comment, because she had deliberately come to court dressed exactly like she hated to be dressed: in a tailored business suit, wearing a fluffy secretary-tie and pulling her hair back into an executive-style, sprayed-down chignon. Her makeup was of a thickness that administrative managers found attractive. She would have worn glasses if her eyes didn't ache from the unnecessary magnification. In other words, Jenn looked exactly like Nancy. (Except, she thanked Christian and Chinese gods, she did not share Nancy's ham-thick thighs.)

"So, Nancy, how's life with the D.A.'s office?" Jenn asked.

"*You* know!" Nancy said, shrugging elaborately and holding out for Jenn's admiration a foot-wide pile of manilla folders she carried with effort. "*You* guys keep giving them to us and we keep prosecuting 'em – it's a really bitchin' load."

Jenn stepped closer to Nancy and emphasized in a low voice: "I would appreciate you not telling everyone in the courtroom what I do, Nanc, some of the people here –" she added a conspiratorial smile she knew Nancy would appreciate, "– you know – sometimes I work undercover..."

She let the last word hang in the air as an implication that would speak for itself.

"Oh!" Nancy said to the world. "Then I better not talk

to you *here!*" She was physically incapable of speaking in anything other than exclamations.

"No, better not."

Nancy turned away from Jenn with painstaking disassociation and continued down the aisle toward the City Attorney's table.

She was almost there when an inspired thought hit her consciousness, causing her to spin on her heel.

"Say 'Hi' to your Mom for me, OK, Jenn!" Nancy shouted across the room, then "forgot" again who Jenn was and turned back to her colleagues.

"I – am – *ready!*" she cried, plopping her files down on the table and throwing her arms wide.

It would have been ridiculous if she weren't effective. Nancy Wong had an almost-perfect conviction rate. Jenn thought Nancy was a schmuck but had no choice except to respect her.

I hope she doesn't have *my* case in that file, Jenn prayed silently, she'll fight me into a corner and I'll be lucky to retain my badge. Nancy's primal-urge/D.A.-aggressiveness maybe wasn't that bad, but to have her beating down would still be embarrassing – and all because of a dog.

Jenn gracefully scooped in her skirt and sat down on the padded auditorium seat, reflecting on the ingratitude of justice. First the stupid dog ticket in the first place, then the idiot know-nothing court clerk, followed by a hard-nosed blind prelim judge. OK, so Sam and Jenn were being hard-nosed about this, too, refusing to take the easy way out and split the hundred-and-fifty fine.

But we're *innocent!*, Jenn screamed silently.

Innocent. With documents to prove it.

Simple.

So – ?

So, the first judge schedules a hearing for October with a second judge, the second judge has too many cases so he shifts some to a third judge in November, the third judge calls in sick and reschedules the entire day into January 1990. So, here we are. So, here I sit. So – you're wasting my free Tuesday for Christ's sake let's get going!

One bright spot: Despite Nancy's flawed abilities at discretion, Jenn did not really fear being recognized.

She had dressed up Nancy-like for a purpose – few of her street "colleagues" would recognize the Century City-plastic Asian businesswoman as the same earthy Chinese whore belonging to the black pimp Sam-Ray. (Sam liked the little addition to his name, saying that a good pimp had to have a few extra syllables to throw around. Sam was becoming increasingly full of shit.)

Even when she was in her comfortable "non-street" police plainclothes Jenn presented a distinctly different look than her hooker persona. Or maybe it was just the fact that, except for other Asians, most whites, blacks and Hispanics

couldn't tell one yellow girl from another. A racist general-
ization, to be sure, but Jenn and Sam's success on the Task
Force the past two years had proven the stereotype. Oh, who
cares?!, Jenn thought with disgust, her head reeling from the
old problem of trying to decide if her sensibilities were becoming coarsened or not.

So what *do* you care about, Ms. Luck?

Not cheating on my partner.

That, maybe, was not the clearest articulation of her
internal discomfort, but Jenn knew that it was a start. Sam
was sitting at hearings all this week, telling everything he
knew about Patrolman Rodney Sinclair and the righteous
kill. Sergeant Sam Williams was upright and stood by his
people. Detective Luck was not first on the scene, he was.
He took the flack, she got the positive PR from the TV show.

He didn't know that "Elvis Chang" was Fuong Lee.

Sam was no virgin about all this, Jenn knew *that* well
enough. But she also knew that she had held back some
potentially important information from her partner. Why?

Oh, I *know* why: he's Fuong Lee, the hotshot hero of
Tien An Men Square, and I believe in that sort of... bull.

But why did I hold back on telling Sam?

I have to tell Sam.

The full complement of Assistant District Attorneys
had made their appearance, finally. Across the short space

separating the prosecution and defense tables, the Public Defenders were still lining up. Any privates today?, Jenn wondered idly. Burroughs, Menendez, Deane: she recognized all of the P.D.s, nobody else appeared to be showing. None of today's defendants could afford to pay an attorney. A good day for the legal system.

Tom Deane had been the last of the Defense lineup trailing in. Jenn knew *him* well enough – and not particularly on an adversarial basis. Big boned, meaty and full-bearded, Tom Deane came down from his inherited villa (read: old tract house) in the foothills of Alta Loma to put in two days a week pro bono for the Legal Aid Society.

And to defend causes he believed in.

This, alone, should have been enough to give Jenn the same feelings of repugnance towards the liberal-leaning Deane that most cops shared. Jenn wasn't most cops. She was educated. She was a woman. She was Asian. She had loved Martin Cordez.

Tom Deane had defended Martin Cordez.

Jenn saw Tom talk with Martin almost every day for the three months she'd been assigned to protect the social activist. She heard the defendant talk with his lawyer almost every night she slept with Martin. The charges were civil charges, fronted by a group of "concerned businessmen," but motivated by a local political leader who wanted his increasingly-popular competition to be harassed to distraction and pumped dry financially by the lawsuit. Martin Cordez was still new at the power games played by the straight world back then: his political activism was on the street level, real and untainted by favors owed yet. Just as Jenn was drawn to the raw integrity of Martin's endeavor, Tom Deane was attracted by the blank slate.

"Maybe this time," he had confessed to Jenn once when he realized she did not share the typical cop-antagonism toward his efforts, "maybe Marty can grow up to do something without carrying a lot of baggage." Tom Deane hated baggage. Jenn understood that. More than anything liberal or conservative or whatever, Tom respected *integrity* of motivation. Martin Cordez had integrity of motivation, Tom judged, so he deserved to be represented by Tom Deane.

Tom didn't represent "Marty" anymore, and Jenn didn't sleep with Martin anymore, but *Mr.* Martin Cordez was successful and no one could argue with his accomplishments and what he had done for the city.

"Hi, Tom," Jenn silently mouthed the greeting when one of his stray glances recognized her. Tom nodded and smiled back.

"Shhh!" Nancy shushed loudly across the two tabletops. "She could be *undercover*, Tom!"

Tom hated Nancy. She beat him too often. He secretly believed she conspired to take only open-and-shut cases in order to build up an impressive track record, but he disapproved of gossip and so refrained from publicizing his opinion.

Ten-fifteen. The judge was over an hour late starting the day's session. Jenn knew the morning would be long when she saw the judge pooke her head out and call in one of the Assistant D.A.s to the his chambers for a private conference, instructing sharply, "I want to see all of the evidence, counselor." Right now, Jenn figured, there was one sweating prosecutor trying desperately to salvage a case that probably suffered from an overabundance of: A. Insufficient evidence, B. Inadmissible evidence, C. Tainted evidence, or D. All of the above.

She let her eyes wander to Tom again. He usually picked out interesting cases for himself. Any colorful defendants sitting in the wings?

No, not today, Jenn realized. Tom was asking the bailiff if there had been any messages for him, had anybody called, had *anybody* said *anything* about a "Lawrence Wanger"? The bailiff shook his head "no" so many times and with such fluidity that Jenn worried for a moment that it would unscrew and fall off. Looks like Tom Deane has got himself a No-Show today, Jenn tsk-tsked her tongue. Bench warrant time.

The judge entered without display.

"All rise," the bailiff called out lethargically.

Everyone stood.

"Thanks," said the judge, sat down and dove right in to business. The D.A.s and P.D.s were apparently used to the this: they plopped back into their seats without instruction. The public did likewise.

"City versus McDorman?" The judge did not look up from her computer-generated list of cases.

"The Prosecution is ready, your honor!" Nancy chirped proudly.

The judge was uninterested.

"Defense?"

"Defense requests a continuation, your honor."

They haggled over validity of the delay, discussed new dates, and were on to the next case before Nancy had closed her folder on the first.

"City versus Roseman?"

"The Prosecution is ready on that one, too, your honor!"

There has to be a spring in her butt, Jenn decided, watching Nancy pop down and up so quickly.

The defense attorney was ready on that one, the judge said fine, and each of them – judge, prosecutor and defense – threw their City v. Roseman files over to the side. On to the next case.

Nancy popped up and down a few more times, then began sharing the caseloads with her two male co-workers.

Over on the Defense side, Tom Deane watched as his fellow defenders shuffled through their files to answer the judge's questions –an angry bench warrant was issued for a bail-skipping Driving Under the Influence – and Tom shot worried glances at his wristwatch again and again. There were only a few files on the table in front of him, all held together by a giant rubber band. Some – one was miss – ing...

"City versus Wanger?"

"The Prosecution is ready!" Nancy was hungry for action.

"Defense?"

Tom put his hands upon the table and used them as a brace to raise himself to his feet. It was an impressive movement, indicating a grave concern.

"Your honor, I am going to have to ask for a continuation," he said with some thought.

Nancy objected: "Your honor this has been the third continuation!"

The judge looked severely at Tom.

"I am inclined to deny your motion for continuation, counsellor. This case has had adequate time for preparation. There is no valid reason to consider further delay."

Sure there is, thought Jenn with a chuckle: his client didn't show!

"I agree, your honor, and I am only asking for a delay until this afternoon. I've just received a message from the defendant that his plane has been closed-in at San Francisco due to fog. The defendant," he used his voice to raise a figurative finger and cut off Nancy's intended objection, "resides in San Francisco."

Jenn sat up in her seat, shaking her head to clear her thoughts. There was no messenger – ? – Tom was lying!

"Your honor, the Prosecution is ready to try this case now!" Nancy was adamant.

Did anybody else notice? The attorneys at both tables were nose deep in their files. Only Nancy and Tom exhibited interest in the case, and Nancy was objecting again. The judge decided against her argument.

"Case continued until this afternoon." A disinterested eye towards Tom. "I will *see* your client then, counsel?"

"Of course, your honor."

Jenn caught Tom's attention as he turned away from the Defense table and started out of the courtroom. She made a gesture that she wanted to talk. He did not go to her, but waited by the rear door.

"Nice to see you, Jenn, but make it fast. I'm in a hurry." Unlike Nancy Wong, Tom Deane's version of a whisper could only be heard from a few inches away.

"Where you going?"

"San Francisco – to get a client." There was almost a twinkle of innocence in his eye.

"– versus Luck?"

"The Prosecution is –"

Jenn turned back toward the bench in time to hear the judge call her in turn.

"Defense?"

"Ready, your honor – here's proof of the dog license."

"What?" The judge had been looking at the Defense table. "This is about a dog?"

The Assistant D.A. – *not* Nancy, thankfully – looked as confused as the judge. He opened his manilla file. It was empty. He had left the papers on his desk.

"Actually, your honor: I don't know. I am afraid I have to apologize. The Prosecution is not ready at this time due to insufficient evi–" The young barrister knew he was facing a dismissal of the case. He groped for salvation, grasped, and found a winning excuse.

"Due to the fact that the defendant has not presented her alleged document to the District Attorney's office, we have had insufficient time to evaluate the evidence."

"All right, look at it," the judge said with finality, moving her finger down to the next case on the list.

"Case continued."

ELVIS LIVES
ON VIDEOTAPE

Sam had made his call to Marie and now returned to the car.

"Well, well, well," he said, resuming the conversation where it had left off.

"Did Marie have anything to say?" She never did, but Jenn wanted to change the subject.

"Well, well, well."

"OK, Sam, I know you're pissed."

Jenn was behind the wheel, as usual when they were undercover. Sam continued to stare sightlessly at the passing scenery.

"Well, well, well."

"Stop your British prig imitation and say something."

"Well, well—"

"Cut it, Sam!"

Jenn turned the steering wheel gently, despite her state of agitation, and guided the car into a red No Parking or Standing Zone. There was no use trying to pretend they would get any work done until it was over.

Sam did not display any particular awareness that they had come to a stop. Jenn waited for him to speak, hoping that he would not launch into another chorus of wells.

He didn't say "well."

He said:

"Elvis Chang."

Chinatown in Los Angeles is bigger than New York's Chinatown. There the public face of Chinatown is reduced to a scroungy block of Mott Street and a few adjacent corners. The true Chinatown in New York exists in the seeping blocks of old buildings, warehouses and apartments that crawl between the river and Mott Street, where real life goes on away from the face of tourism and the official eye. Los Angeles' Chinatown has its back streets and private life, too, but the public face is broader than its East Coast relative's. It played much better on a video camcorder.

"Narration Number One: I am in what is called China-town now —" The words rumbled by in smooth, educated French, which passersby took to be the mumblings of a rich, drunken college student.

"I didn't hide it from you, Sam, I told you." Jenn knew her tone was too insistent.

"Well, well—"

"Don't. Please."

Jenn reached around and retrieved her briefcase from the back seat. She rummaged among the file folders, finally pulling out the crappy fax bulletin on Fuong Lee. "Here." She held it out to Sam.

"Um," Sam bit his lower lip, trying to recognize the Elvis Chang he had met briefly two weeks earlier in the blurred face staring out from the fax.

Some people are disappointed by L.A.'s Chinatown: it looks so... so... so Southern Californian. Sure, there are a bunch of pagoda roofs plopped on top of gas stations and restaurants, but it's mainly wide streets and characterless post-War architecture. (Architecture? It was hard to imagine an architect putting his efforts into so much of the bland structural design.) One wanted to see Hong Kong's dark alleys re-created – New York had succeeded in this aspect somewhat, but, then, New York had its own dark creepiness stamped on *every* ethnic neighborhood. One wanted to see the teeming masses of Chinese that characterized Shanghai or Peking (here it was still OK to use the old spelling).

"– recording for orientation... for memory." Philippe did not remove his right eye from the camcorder's viewfinder. He had perfected the technique of walking with both eyes open at Tien An Men Square. The skill had come back easily in the first minutes of his walk. "With no contacts yet, I will do –"

Jenn restarted the car, debating whether to turn on the A/C or not: it was eighty degrees outside. She opted instead to drive with the window open. Sam kept his pane of glass closed tight and continued staring at the Fuong Lee photo.

"Want to tell the federales?" Jenn asked, knowing that the question had to be addressed.

Sam did not answer immediately. When he did, it was with another question.

"Did you see this bulletin before we met him?"

"Yes," Jenn wouldn't lie to her partner, adding hastily: "I didn't pay it much attention, though. I recognized him before the bulletin."

They were still in the deep Hispanic section of Sunset Boulevard, near Elysian Park, just below Dodger Stadium. No ball games in January. Traffic was heavy for mid-afternoon, but they would hit the left on Hill street in a few minutes, into the heart of Chinatown.

She asked again – it mattered to her:

"Want to tell the federales?"

"– as I have always done: memorize the places, not the names."

Philippe found the sound of his own voice soothing, calming the excitement that burst in on his imagination through the camera. Truly, the camera: his open left eye, which saw the peripheral world the camera eye excluded, did not register the images as real. "Place du Pigalle, Les Halles, Tien An Men..." These places were memory images totally different from the sunshiny reality of this new Chinatown. So many cars – even the curiosity of a Chinese woman driving a black man – but none of the intense crowding of vehicles and people of La Rive Gauche near Rue St. Jacques.

"I can say what I want, I will edit."

"No, I don't want to tell the federales, Jenn."

Sam looked at his partner for the first time since she had told him about Fuong Lee. "You could have told *me*."

"I did."

"Then."

"It – wasn't the right moment."

Sam nodded in grudging agreement with that judgement call: Rodney's righteous kill of the switchblade murderer had been a bureaucratic nightmare from the first.

"And I didn't know he would lie."

And I really expected him to call me, Jenn said to her own thoughts. She had left "Elvis Chang" her official card, offered the requisite confidentiality, and made no mention of the federal bulletin. Fuong Lee should have trusted her.

He should have *wanted* to talk to her. She was Chinese. She was educated. They could talk.

Philippe had lost track of the afternoon. The small red light indicating "Low Battery" was flashing insistently in the corner of the viewfinder screen – and this was his spare battery, the original long since drained out. He needed to see so *much*, though! To put so much into words for the Colonel who trusted him.

"It is my hope to find Fuong Lee soon, but I am to expect two others who will help me."

Sam had found the .38 caliber target pistol a half block away from the shooting, lying on the nearby railroad tracks. It was scuffed and the barrel bent, obviously thrown from a moving vehicle. Without even trying to guess, as soon as Sam read Ballistics' report on the Chinatown takedown, he'd known that this was the gun. Rodney had admitted it to him at once, more uneasy with being portrayed as a hero than with the crime of letting the unknown shooter go.

And Sam told Jenn.

And Jenn had only then told Sam about Fuong Lee.

So... Rodney was in shit and Jenn was in shit and Sam had the choice of staying clean or stepping in with both feet.

"No, I don't want to tell the federales," Sam said, wondering whether he could explain this to Marie over the telephone: Jenn was his partner, he had to trust her instinct.

"I want to see if his address is any good. Call him Elvis Chang or Fuong Lee or Old Mother Hubbard."

And Sam said to himself in unspoken words, to see if the tainted witness, Elvis/Fuong Whatever (*if* he could be found), would still back up Rodney's story – plus verify the additional "detail" that Rodney had made up of wrestling with the switchblade murderer over a stolen pistol, which had gone off smack into the murderer's gut.

Could he tell Marie about covering up for a decent cop as well?

"...Yeah... check out the address..."

"Any reason *why* the address should be good?" Jenn asked with a sarcastically rueful smile. The smile was a mask: inside she was quietly happy with Sam, knew she had been righteous in confiding in him, realistic in expecting Fuong Lee to have lied to her.

"Maybe 'Elvis Chang' doesn't care who knows where he lives." It was a shot in the dark, but something in the Chinese man's face had told Sam that Fuong Lee believed he had gotten away with his deception – again.

It would be dark soon. Philippe had been standing too long in one spot. He was growing cold: the extending shadows from the buildings carried in them the cold from the mountains that hovered over this corner of the city, defeating the extra-warm day with ease. The camcorder's batteries were so low now that he dared not attempt to record anything, yet he kept the viewfinder pressed to his eye and planned out shots for tomorrow. Fuong Lee would see Chinatown through his "Eyes" when they met. Philippe knew he would be pleased.

The Chinese face popped in front of the lens, filling the viewfinder frame. Without thought, Philippe muttered a polite "Excuse me, please, you're in my way" in Mandarin – but the face did not move. Philippe remembered where he was. He repeated the request in heavily accented English. The face still did not move. It smiled.

"'Allo, Frog!" Cockney could see his own reflection in the small lens circle. It was a distorted image but, to his mind, damn good looking. "Missed you at the airport."

IN THE VINEYARDS OF
THE JOLLY GREEN GIANT

Grapes.

Lots of Grapes.

Small, round, dark, plump – grapes.

Maybe a thousand on this vine alone.

Or so it seemed – set against the backdrop of withered vines and neglected fields that marked this newest addition to Prospero i Domenicci's residential real estate holdings. As the crisply painted sign so boldly announced to the passing motorists who sped by at one hundred fifty kilometers per hour, *this* was to be the new heaven for seven hundred lucky families.

And only twenty minutes from Roma!

Well, maybe that was stretching things a little: the advertising firms should have written "20 minutes from the border of Rome's most outflung suburb – *if* there is no traffic on the highway, which, by the way, we have been promised on good account that there *will* be an exit built *directly* to our development." But that phrase was too unwieldy for effective marketing, and so it was edited a bit for space considerations.

But Prospero knew, when he made Domenicci arrange the purchase through his uncle's bank, that there were seven thousand families in Rome – not just the advertised seven hundred – seven *thousand* who were hungry for their own homes and were not afraid to leave the city to get one.

It had not always been like this. When Prospero was a boy, only farmers and peasant merchants lived outside of the city. He knew. He had fled from the vineyards to the comforts of Rome's twenty-four living and crowded anonymity. Oh, and yes, the rich had their villas – but they maintained their city homes as well.

Almost four decades of American movies had changed that heady faith in urban supremacy. Now every mother's child with a television set was familiar with the suburban housing tract where E.T. visited earth – and wasn't *Knots Landing* an accessible version of J.R.'s lifestyle in *Dallas*? The French had picked up on this shift in attitudes first, building upper-middle-class villages outside of Paris in the early 1980s that were quickly snatched up. And the French did not even *like* Americans!

In Italy, actually, there were more excuses for creating a planned suburb than in France. The Italian world did not have a Gallic tradition that revolved around only one city as the center of all national culture. Plus, the underground economy of undeclared income – which was a national tradition – had created the need for thousands of entrepreneurs to look to outlying villages for warehousing and industrial space. Prospero i Domenicci, perhaps, were casting their nets out a little farther than the prudent developer would, but they were not alone in joining the party.

They *were* behind schedule, however. A (*not* unexpected) lethargy on the part of the regional transportation bureau had delayed the promised highway exit. In consequence, Domenicci's uncle's bank exhibited a (very *un*expected) reluctance to finalize the construction portion of the loan until potential customers passing on the nearby highway could actually stop to buy a home. So, Prospero i Domenicci, each to his own respective domain, were currently exploring channels in government and banking circles, seeking the best bargain of whom to bribe in order to break the impasse.

Leaving grapes, lots of grapes, flourishing on one vine, while the rest of the vines dried-up in lingering death.

One wondered, if one was passing on the highway, if that was a farmer or a trespasser standing in the middle of the failed vineyard?

From the safe distance of a moving car, one could not tell. It was impossible to become involved in the man's situation. All that one could see before speeding by – unless impelled by a whimsical desire to crane one's neck uncomfortably – was a small figure with his hands in his pockets and his feet planted wide apart, squinting against the sun.

And then, of course, one lost track of the man in the rows-upon-rows of scraggly vines that formed neatly vertical, horizontal and diagonal patterns. The neglected plants were long past needing water.

But their roots were deep. Prospero i Domenicci would have to make their earth-moving machines dig deep to tear the vines out, smooth them over, forget them.

"When you've lost the passage, when you've lost the game," Harry hummed the old Country & Western moss-gatherer with passionate melodic interest as he wondered which of the many dirt tracks to turn down. "When you've lost the home you live in, And nothing's quite the same –"

"Harry" wasn't his real name, of course, but he'd always liked it, and used it as much as possible for "visiting." There was a small Fiat parked at the far edge of the next field.

"You got to ride a road to anywhere –" He saw the man standing in the center of the vineyard next. "You've got to just get in a car –" Yep, this was it.

"Your destiny is waiting there, It may be very far –"

"You can turn on the camera now," Harry broke his singing to point out the solitary figure to his backseat passenger.

"There's our boy."

He started singing to himself again. "You don't know where you're going to –" Actually, Harry did.

"You don't know where you've been –" From Rome, of course.

"Brothers of the wilderness, Lost in –" Harry liked the image, "– the wind."

No wind today. Still. Quiet.

"Lost in the wind."

The big American car grumbled heavily over the un-used-for-years cart tracks, the General Motors' shock absorbers taking the jouncing ride with workmanlike good will. The camera image was fairly steady, given the conditions.

"I'm not opening the window," Harry advised his passenger. He did not turn his head to see if the comment was acknowledged. He explained anyway: "The Professor might see you." There was a pleasant twang to Harry's speech. Midwest. Harry liked to think it was a tough, John Wayne-type voice. Most listeners thought of Henry Fonda in one of his meeker moments.

"He'll see me when you open the door," Harry's Security Second noted.

"Not through tinted windows he won't."

"You think he doesn't know I'm here?"

"I think," Harry didn't really think about this at all,

he *knew* from experience, "he'll figure someone is here — but he won't know for certain so he can't say I violated the conditions of the meeting."

Yeah, that was one interpretation.

"And he can't know for certain if we got him covered with a rifle or not." That was the more important interpretation.

"What about *him*? Whose he gonna have with him? What're they gonna have? Guns? Bombs?" The Security Second was ill-at-ease. Unlike Harry, he preferred *never* having contact with "the help."

Harry looked across the field with as much concentration as the uneven track would allow him to take his eyes from the task of driving.

"Too difficult to tell from here. Why don't you use the zoom to check it out close?"

"Can't. Too far away. Our guy's about at the range limit. He's not moving at all, y'know."

"I noticed," Harry said. That's what interested him anyway, the guy standing in the middle of nowhere. He wasn't a bolter, that's for sure. "Better stop here, anyway," he reassured the passenger, smoothly braking the eight-cylinder Chevrolet beauty. Harry loved his American car. It was a bitch to park in Europe, though.

"How's the voice?"

"Tinny, like always, but clear."

"Buono," Harry twanged a businesslike smile as he opened his door with an apparent casualness that continued to obscure the back seat passenger from any outside eyes. His business suit was comfortably constructed of wool to keep him cooled from the low-impact Italian sun and warmed from any winter chill in the air. It was a God-beautiful day that was only increased by the desolate vineyards surrounding them.

Harry took a hundred or so long, easy strides away from the car and stopped another ten steps short of The Professor. Il Professore. Harlequin. Harry figured he'd seen the man in a dozen different surveillance photos over the last couple of years. Sort of nice to see him live.

"Bongiorno, Professore." Harry dropped his own hands into his pants pockets in imitation of The Professor. It was not an aggressive posture, not defensive. Merely comfortable.

"Bongiorno."

"Parla Inglese?" Harry knew for certain The Professor had been in the U.S. three times since 1980.

"Si."

"OK. Non parlo Italiano molto bene –"

"But you speak Italian good enough," The Professor smiled with a nod of compliment.

"Just good enough," Harry corrected him with a nod

accepting the compliment. He could see The Professor's pale green eyes darken as they focussed in on Harry's tie tack. His microphone. Time to play it straight.

"I didn't come alone." Harry kept his back to the car.

"Nor did I."

From the middle of the vineyard, Harry could see the small Fiat clearly. The driver's side rear window of the two-door car was open a crack. A gun barrel protruded through the crack. Automatic.

"Israeli? You don't buy Russian?"

"Quality," The Professor answered.

Harry thought about the concept of evident threat versus implied threat. He recalled the military specs on the Israeli weapon. It was a close up number.

"Too far away: from this range he would have to be an excellent marksman, or hit us both."

The green eyes were palely smiling.

"Well, you know, one or the other."

Harry understood why they had never captured The Professor. Well, it was good the times had changed.

"Our mutual friends said that you were open to new friends, new financing."

The Professor turned his back on Harry, stepped over to the brittle branches of a sky-reaching vine and brushed his hand across the top. There was a vaguely musical twang from the vibrating twigs. He turned his attention to the ruined field.

"I am not from this part of Italy."

Harry was used to the necessary courting ritual – they were all like brokenhearted young girls getting over a jock ex-boyfriend. "No?" he asked with apparent interest. Was this the third or fourth seduction scene he'd played recently?

"My part is green, wet. Winter snows from the Alps. Summer, spring, autumn."

"Old friends, new friends," Harry cut to the point; this operation was short on time.

"Old friends, *true* friends." The Professor was prepared to speak pointedly as well. "Our Russian lady is wrong: I am not looking for new friends – there are still those countries that believe in ideals."

Harry wanted to put this small-timer straight: "You are European, not Chinese."

"Eh!" The Professor threw up his arm derisively – or was it defensively? "I did not desert the cause."

Harry cut him off.

"Fine. Sure. OK. All right." This guy wasn't going to split, and was too intelligent to play the New Lovers game with. To the point. "You agreed to the general details of the arrangement, didn't you?"

The Professor did not respond at once, then nodded 'yes.'

Harry felt generous and decided against pressing the point. Besides, there was no advantage in having his new employee eat crow. "Let's go over specifics," he said with a significant drop in emotional level. They were two colleagues now, discussing their profession. "The Beijing government wants a certain 'Fuong Lee' to return to the mainland."

"Return him, then."

"We want to avoid a diplomatic embarrassment. He came in as a refugee: if we return him, we're bastards; if he denounces us and returns publicly, we're fools."

The Professor smiled sympathetically at Harry.

"We won't discuss the 'bastard' part. Is he very inclined to denounce you and return publicly?"

Harry knew the Fuong Lee file by heart. He knew every one of his operation case files by heart; he kept no written records if he could avoid it. "Fuong Lee denounces us with extreme... regularity. But I think he's grown fond of American hamburgers."

"All the world loves McDonald's."

"Yeah, well let him get 'em in Beijing." Harry said this without any overt animosity towards the subject, adding the silent coda: and let him eat them quietly. "Persuade Fuong Lee, however necessary, to return to the mainland. He's keeping a very low profile, so Beijing has enlisted a friend of his to get you close to him."

"And how do *you* help me persuade this Fuong Lee?"

"We don't. *We* are not involved –" Harry maybe agreed with Fuong Lee, but it didn't matter, "– but we're not an obstacle, either."

"Clean hands, eh? You should be a Roman, they have that tradition." The Professor pulled his own hands from his deep pants pockets now at last. They were finely-shaped hands, long and well-formed. There was a callous from writing on the middle finger of each hand. He was ambidextrous.

Harry let the comment pass, kept his hands still pocketed, kicked at the dry, dusty soil.

"My father grew up on land like this: Dustbowl Oklahoma. Didn't give him a thing back." He wanted to give The Professor something personal. "And he lost a leg somewhere about a hundred miles from here. Freeing Italy from the Nazis and the Fascists." Harry always felt he had a little more control over his operatives when they saw him as a human being, a face, a heart. "Small world, eh?"

The Professor nodded. Harry had more business to attend to.

"You won't be staying in the U.S."

The Professor understood the concern.

"I have no reason to."

That settled without conflict, Harry went on to the next detail. "Here." He held out a small booklet.

The Professor looked at the item warily.

"What is it?"

"A passport. Documents that will get you across borders: you *are* a wanted man." Harry said this with a matter-of-fact authority that was surprised by The Professor's own matter-of-fact step back from the document.

"Do you think that I will *trust* you?" he smiled in parody of the American's homespun geniality.

"We are working together –"

The parody dropped into intensity; The Professor took another step back. In the rear seat of the Chevrolet, the camera recorded the rejection and captured every lightly accented word perfectly.

"I will not let you have *any* control over me. I will come into your Fortress Americana when I want to, and leave when I want to. You think that *you* shake hands with the Devil – I think *I* shake the Devil's hand!"

"You are alone–"

"I am not alone!" The Professor pointed to his Fiat, "I have never been alone! I am a part of history, one of many: we are inevitable."

For all his intensity, The Professor was not angry. He was never fully angry, and that, he felt, was his internal flaw: he always saw himself ever-so-obliquely from the outside, even in his passions. He could not lose himself in his passions as he so fervently wished.

"Why do you hate us?" Harry asked with his most naive, ingenuous tone of voice. He wanted to know. He always asked that.

The Professor knew his own answer, which was separate from the dialectic. He did not care for dialectics in the middle of this field.

"Because you walk the earth as if you know the answer to everything – so confident, so ready to try, so full – as if you can do anything."

"We can't, you know. We have our own world of doubts and weaknesses."

"I know that now. I started hating you before I did."

The Professor turned and started to walk away from Harry, making a direct line for his Fiat. He stopped abruptly in mid-step, in mid-thought, and turned his head to look back at the American.

"You are going to America, too?"

Harry relaxed his shoulders; he had his operative.

"I am the monitor on this operation."

The Professor savored the word.

"'Monitor'..." he purred, then suddenly clapped his hands together enthusiastically. "Success!" he cried, letting his Italian blood bring the hands high into the air with a flourish.

The camera recorded Harry and The Professor walking in opposite directions. The Italian was singing a Verdi aria with discordant enthusiasm. The American was silent, letting his thoughts progress to the next steps of the operation. The camera caught Harry at a highly unflattering angle from under the chin as he approached the car door.

"Turn it off," Harry commanded his Security Second before opening the door.

The Professor loved Verdi. Not as music, but as songs from a childhood that heard Verdi's operas as a part of everyday life. Rock and roll was art, but Verdi was in the back of one's heart always. As he crawled into the tiny Fiat, The Professor sang even louder for the benefit of the watching American. With nonchalant skill, he shielded the back seat from view as he undid the Israeli-made automatic weapon from its propped-up position in the crack of the rear window. That done, he settled into the driver's seat and watched the Chevrolet lumber off. It looked incongruously in place among the ruined field's gnarled rows of vines.

"I wonder if he was alone, too?" he asked himself aloud.

The Fiat started with only a little effort – an improvement over its performance earlier in the chilly morning.

"No," The Professor shook his head in answer to the question. "He could not have been alone: the Americans have a much bigger Overhead budget."

OH WHERE, OH WHERE CAN FUONG LEE BE?

Philippe did not like the smart-mouthed man from Hong Kong – and Cockney, for his part, didn't care.

"We're 'ere to 'elp one anover," he explained to Philippe with an oppressive degree of insolent pedantry. "I'm 'elpin' you ta get aroun' Chinatown 'ere, an' you're 'elpin' me ta make a pretty tidy."

"A pretty tidy" – Philippe resented having to associate with the mercenary Cockney. It caused him to worry about the unknown third member of their team who would be arriving later. Was everyone so cynical?

About Fuong Lee Philippe found his emotions jumping spastically to extremes. He wanted to see Fuong so badly, for the past – and for the present.

Philippe's afternoon alone on the streets of Chinatown had uncovered three handbills stapled to telephone poles that each bore the unique imprint of his friend's conception. Fuong's definitive, strong personality blared out from the weather-abused pieces of paper even before Philippe had laboriously read the Chinese and English texts to find his friend's signature at the bottom.

They were not recent handbills, though. Philippe could derive from them no indication of Fuong's current whereabouts. But their style and substance – particularly the *style* – reassured Philippe that the Colonel had not been mistaken in his assessment of Fuong Lee's talent to inspire. More than anything, now, Philippe wanted to rejoin Fuong.

And bring his friend back to where he would be most effective.

Philippe did not waste time trying to explain any of these feelings to Cockney. Within their first half-hour of awkward association Philippe came to the disgusted conclusion that his "guide" was a reactionary thug, enlisted in all probability because his neutral ignorance of politics was presumably preferable to the problems that would have been encountered in trying to recruit an idealist.

As Philippe readily understood, the politics he was to embark upon with Fuong Lee were delicate and subtle matters, matters demanding a mental discipline that most idealists did not possess, requiring a period of adjustment that history did not have the luxury to extend at the present time. Philippe had been lucky. The Colonel had taken a personal interest in him. The two could so easily have missed one another, the Western student lost in the rush of events.

As always when thinking of the Colonel, Philippe felt a blush of confusion. Maman and Papa he loved – that was his duty – but did they love him in return? The Colonel made no pretenses of filial affection, yet it was obvious that he respected the young Frenchman. *Did I ever really fear the Colonel?*, Philippe thought more than once, embarrassed by his earlier foolishness. It was only inevitable that they should have met: had the Tien An Men demonstrations never happened, Fuong Lee and the Colonel would have most certainly found one another – and Philippe would have been with them.

Tien An Men. The Colonel was cruelly candid in explaining how the demonstrations had ended. Although Philippe had seen nothing with his own eyes, the Colonel's bitter recounting of the radicals' eruption into violence –and the reactive military "solution" it produced – had been horrifying in its vividness. It was no wonder that Fuong Lee had run away: the extreme elements of both sides were too dangerous to trust. And it was no mystery why the Colonel wanted Fuong back: the process of–

"Right, luv, the daydream's over for now. Let's get on." Cockney had less patience than they had given him credit for: he was bored with the stupid Frog and wanted to find the Fuong Lee chappie as soon as possible. Maybe even before their precious "Professor" showed up. That would be the best show, of course: find Fuong Lee before that Professor got to L.A., get the bugger where need be, and split the payment with no one.

The problem, of course, was that Cockney had no idea where to get Fuong Lee *to* once he was found. The friend of a friend of a friend that had gotten him this gig had no idea; the Frog what brought the down payment didn't even seem to *know* the idea; and Cockney himself didn't want to go to a lot of work until he could be certain of a proper payoff. The Professor-Wallah knew who to contact, when and why, so that was that.

Plus there was the fact that they had to *find* Fuong Lee in the first place.

Cockney figured that if the boss boys had bothered to tell *him* who they were after he might have put out some words of wonder and produced the precious prey prior to the Frog's arrival. Nope, that was too simple. Only the Frog knew who they had to find, and with him speaking decent Chinese and all, Cockney had little chance of finding their fish solo. (Even if he did, Cockney reasoned with an instinct-inspired suspicion, it was abundantly clear that the Frogman was intended to make the initial contact. Whoever "they" were – and Cockney did not have any overriding curiosity to confirm his suspicions – keeping the waters muddy concerning their plans seemed to share equal status with their desire to find Fuong Fucking Lee.)

Relations might have been better between Philippe and Cockney if The Professor was with them. Unknown to either young man, the "leader" of the team was not scheduled to show up for a day. Perhaps even later: Cockney's instructions were unspecific and Philippe had been advised that The Professor would contact them directly with the time and place of his arrival.

In the meantime the two reluctant "colleagues" accomplished less than they probably would have done if each had started his seeking out alone. Chinese New Year was soon to be upon Chinatown, uncles and aunts were scurrying in from their suburbs to buy appropriate holiday decorations, and the search found the streets clogged with extra faces.

Tim Ma had seen the foreigner wandering around Phoenix Plaza earlier in the day. Not a lot of interest was engendered by the Frenchman – until Tim heard him speaking Chinese in the dim sum shop a couple of hours later. It was highly accented Cantonese – the French guy spoke with a Mandarin accent? – but the words were more surprising than his facility with the language:

"I am looking for my friend, Fuong Lee."

Tim Ma glanced up from his textbook at this and listened more intently. There was a brief exchange between the Frenchman and the shop owner. The owner *knew* of Fuong Lee as an annoyance, but did not have personal acquaintance. Then the Frenchman bought a steamed pork roll and left the shop without further comment.

"The Frenchman was my 'eyes'," Tim had heard Fuong Lee say once, "I need eyes like that again." But Fuong Lee never elaborated on the theme, and seemed unfocussed when asked how the French student in Beijing had contributed to his efforts.

"Well, at least he had a comfortable bed I could bring a girl to, not living with Mommy and Daddy like everyone here," Fuong Lee had joked mockingly, passing on to a different subject with his usual rapid-fire decisiveness.

Fuong Lee doesn't understand, Tim thought defensively, remembering words he did not think to say at the time. What Fuong Lee never *tried* to understand (and this ticked off Tim, even though he wouldn't say it out loud) was that here, in America, Chinese parents tried to be more Chinese than Confucius. *We're stuck with a lot of the old ways*, Tai thought resentfully (particularly when remembering how he had to always agree with his stupid grandfather), and maybe a little Mao-like housecleaning wouldn't hurt. Well, Tim knew, he's never say *that* in public right now: Mao was about third place down on the Chinese-American shit list, behind only Deng Xiaopeng this year and anything Japanese.

"ONLY FIVE MORE SHOPPING DAYS TILL CHINESE NEW YEAR!!!" The sign glowed in luminous English letters. Philippe stationed himself beneath it for hours – to Cockney's annoyance – asking every group of likely-looking Chinese college students the same question:

"I am looking for my friend, Fuong Lee. Have you seen him?"

Tim Ma found the Frenchman stationed there twice more during the afternoon as he went on his shopping rounds for the Chinese New Year. He did not talk directly, but listened-in for any more information. There was none. "Have you seen Fuong Lee?" No, Tim Ma had not. But he might. In two days. Fuong Lee had promised to show up at one of their planning sessions for the New Year's protest. Fuong Lee knew when and where. No one else ever would.

"Only five more shopping days till Chinese New Year, Sam: be sure to take out your checkbook and buy yourself a good astrological forecast!" Jenn's voice carried undertones of the slightly singsong happy sarcasm she always felt when on a stakeout.

An enjoyable cynicism always accompanied Jenn during the long hours of waiting. *Will we, or won't we?* It was another one of the things she had never been able to explain to her ex. She'd tried. Jimmy'd given her the same blank stare as when she had tried to explain why asparagus tasted good.

"Kung Hay Fat Choy – *Hap*-py New Year! C'mon Elvis Fuong Lee Chang: Come – Home." Sam's enthusiasm for the joys of a stakeout were considerably less than his partner's, but his interest, as always, never flagged.

That was Sam's strength: his concentration. As they sat alongside the railroad tracks that amble incongruously through the border of Chinatown and the warehouses of North Spring Street, the several hours' intrinsic boredom never interfered with his attention on the half-employed factory that stood dark and seemingly empty a half-block down Elmyra. They had arrived before sundown, in time to mingle with the twenty-five non-union textile workers who emerged from a ground floor sewing shop hollowed out of the once-large remains of a hundred-person enterprise. Jenn put a sag to her shoulders and easily resembled the tired women milling about the front entrance. There she read the building directory and established that the top two floors were subdivided into four living lofts each. So far "Elvis Chang" had not lied: the address – #2-B – was residential.

With no name on the directory, of course.

In fact, the living loft arrangements for the building were probably less-than-registered with the Zoning Board: there were *no* names next to the loft identification numbers. Officially, these could just be divisions – offices, maybe – of the failing textile firm. Most certainly none of the tenants would be filing for the California State Renter's Credit on their tax forms come April.

Jenn had not gone up to 2-B. There was no telling, during the daylight hours, whether the tenant was in. If, in fact, that tenant *was* "Elvis" – and if he was out – Sam and Jenn both agreed that they did not want to alert Elvis Chang, or his neighbors, to the fact that someone was waiting for him. This seach was all informal for the time being. Very informal. *So damn informal,* thought Sam, *that we don't even begin to put in for overtime on this little Fools' School of Police Stakeouting.* Better to wait until dark, let the occupant of 2-B turn on the lights, *then* pay the visit.

Concentration. That was what McMasters had taught Sam. What was it: eighteen, nineteen years ago? It took only a second to dart a swift glance down at the palm-sized electronic chessboard on his lap, then his eyes were back up at the window. Every move Sam worked out in his imagination, allowing his eyes to stay riveted to the building facade.

It was a handsome building, actually, barring the smog-blackened bricks that distracted from the classic Art Nouveau doors and window frames. Knight to Queen's Bishop Four.

Sam did not need to look down at the board: he had learned the simple keys by touch. He listened with secret pleasure as the chessboard's clock ticked away the seconds before responding to Sam's move. It wasn't enough anymore to beat the small computer – he could do that on Beginner and Novice levels without effort – but to make the computer *think* for forty seconds, maybe even two minutes, at Expert level!

"You know, Sergeant, every time that little toy of yours bleeps my reception is crapped up." Jenn had plugged her own timekiller – a pocket television – into the car's cigarette lighter. She was trying to finagle an electronics-whiz cousin from Taiwan into rigging up the car for cable reception. So far he had been unsuccessful.

It was nine-fifty p.m. now, and the lights in 2-B's window still looked in upon a deep darkness. Jenn felt obliged to voice the hourly Official Doubt:

"It could be a wrong address."

"Could be," Sam agreed. "You wanna go in?"

"Wellll... I'd like to see the end of the show."

"Police dedication."

"I like to think so."

Sam pushed the Pause button on his pocket computer, saving the game for twenty minutes. He planned on being back in five.

"If you can hold down the fort and tear one eye away from the screen, I'll go visit a little boy's room."

"Yo." Jenn was feeling macho: she'd spent the weekend with her parents and had had to endure another forty-eight hours of their silent disappointment at her failure to remain a sweet, achievement-oriented little daughter of Hsiao and Emily Xu.

Sam left the car and turned his head away from the loft on Elmyra street with a casual disinterest. He did not expect Fuong Lee to be "lurking in the shadows" wary of surveillance, but there was not enough traffic on the street to disguise their stakeout very well. It was, in fact, a pretty half-assed set-up, but Sam wasn't going to jeopardize it anyway by out-and-out staring at the loft when he was standing on the street.

Besides, Sam had long before understood, just because the stakeout wasn't set-up to ideal standards didn't mean it was not going to *work*. Life was idiotic enough to prove a point like *that* more than once. Like the old Russian guy said: it's a stupid world.

"It's a stupid world."

The words came rushing down on Sam with a vehemence made even more violent by his attempts to ignore them for the past two weeks. He needed to talk to Marie. Shit, he knew he was going to call up Marie even before he made up the lame excuse to Jenn about answering the call of nature. There was a pay phone past the next streetlight. Sam had noted it earlier when Jenn was mingling with the textile workers. He could still see the loft from there.

The lights to 2-B were still out. Come – Home, Fuong Lee.

Sam fumbled with the telephone receiver, cursing once again the genius engineer who devised the short metal cords on pay phones that stopped a foot shy of a reasonably tall man's ear. Why did they do it? To stop vandals from ripping-off the receivers? *Nothing* stopped them. To save money? Five cents a foot of cord, c'mon?!, well, maybe *times* millions of pay phones – OK, some sense, But still! Sam leaned down and hugged the receiver to his ear.

He knew his Calling Card account number by heart – he had to, he'd lost his card a month after receiving it. The city was getting so divided up, though, that what used to be an easy ten cent, seven digit call was now zero (let the operator know) – three digit area code (it's only over the hill!) – seven digit number (normal) – one ring for the operator – wait (will it be a beep or a real voice: a beep) – fourteen digit account number – "Thank you for using Pacific Bell" the recorded voice says with lifeless warmth - ring (for home).

Ring.

Ring (no one will be home).

Ring (the answering machine should kick in now–)

"Hello, no one's home right now," Marie had recorded the message years ago, the tape was sounding scratchy with use, "but if you leave your name, telephone number, and a brief message – " It was a voice-activated shut-off, but why tell the salesmen? "– we'll get back to you at the earliest convenience." Sam had asked Marie to leave off their name and telephone number: anyone calling should know who they wanted.

Beep.

Sam said nothing.

Beep.

The answering machine disconnected. The insistent hum of the dial tone rushed out of the receiver. Some people hated busy signals. Sam hated the taunting chord of the dial tone. He dialed the sequence of numbers again, listened to the recorded operator, waited out the recorded Marie.

Beep.

"Hello, Marie," Sam spoke with the vague formality he always unconsciously assumed when speaking to answering machines, "I am sorry I am late again tonight, but it is work."

Sam waited for the familiar, imagined objection, then answered:

"I know: it is always work."

He waited now for the courage to tell Marie, then found it:

"But I have to work tonight because I keep having dreams about that old man I told you about last week, the fruit vendor, who died. I don't want to think about him anymore. It is easier not to think when I'm working, and if I'm home I'm boring you, girl, with this thinking. He was a Russian. Chinese New Year is coming in only five days. Did I ever take you to a Chinese New Year's celebration? I don't think so, but..."

You had to remember not to wait too long, or the answering machine would click off the connection.

"...maybe when we were dating – that was a long time ago, yeah? This old dude was *funny*! He's the one what give me the almost cracked rib, remember? That was a few months ago. He died so fast I think he was surprised. Will I be surprised when I die? I don't want to be. I want to be ready. For what..."

What would she say if she were listening right now –

Beep.

Sam looked at the telephone with surprise: his eyes had been closed. The dial tone drilled out at him. He'd waited too long, the connection was cut. He couldn't leave the message like that.

Numbers, wait, numbers, recorded operator, recorded Marie –

"I'm sorry, I'm thinking about it, yeah? Boring you again. I can't think alone, it seems. I'd eat a bullet, I think, but never if I could think out loud with someone else. Marie, I'm sorry. I shouldn't say these things. Marie. I should say your name more. Marie.

"Marie.

"That sound better than what I am thinking. Marie."

This time he could stop talking. And wait.

Beep.

He would never hang up on Marie.

ELVIS LIVES
LIVE

There was a light in the window of 2-B, 4025 Elmyra Street, Los Angeles, California 90012.

There was a silhouette moving about within #2-B. Occasionally that silhouette stepped close enough to one of the interior light sources to reveal a familiar face.

Elvis Chang was home.

Sam reset his portable electronic chessboard to Save the Current Game.

"What do you think the odds are that if we knock on the front door 'Elvis' is gonna split?"

"Awfully good." Jenn had already stowed her pocket television in the double-locked car glove compartment. Sam was gone by the time she reopened it, slid his game in and locked the compartment again. Jenn made sure the car doors were locked - both she and Sam had keys - then walked without haste to the building's front entrance. She made no apparent attempt to deaden the sound of her approach. To a casual (or observant) onlooker, Jenny Luck was just another office girl probably visiting an artist boyfriend in one of the building's lofts – maybe she even slept there herself when there was no work to go to the following day.

The entrance was supposed to have a locked security door, opened only by a buzzer from within. That was the theory. The status quo that had evolved over the recent years since its half-conversion to living lofts and the establishment of an exquisitely low standard of building maintenance was for each tenant to install his own metal security door inside, each loft a private bastion. The halls were No Man's Land.

The doorbell to 2-B was unpleasantly intrusive. Fuong Lee had never heard it used in practice, in fact, and he did not recognized the source of the tripping noise for the first second. By the second second the arrival at his door was announcing herself:

"This is the police. We'd like to speak with you."

It was a muffled voice, the metal door swallowing nearly all of the coherence. Jenn repeated her introduction in Mandarin.

"This is the police. We would like to speak with you."

She could not hear Fuong Lee stumbling rapidly away from the front door, across a wide empty space, towards an Art Nouveau twelve-foot high window with a red FIRE

EXIT sign to the side of it. Jenn knew the window existed, though.

Fuong Lee stopped his escape from the front door in mid-step: there was a black man standing on the fire escape landing outside his window.

Sam opened the window effortlessly.

"Why don't you let Detective Luck in, Elvis?" Sam stepped in through the opened window warily, his eyes on the aborted escapee. "And, later tonight, you might want to repair this window lock: it's broken."

Fuong Lee did not move at once, the full impact of his situation making its effect felt as he began to recognize the black man entering his loft as one of the police who had questioned him about the street killing a few weeks earlier. His name was... Sergeant Samuel Williams. No need to remember, though: that was the name on the I.D. the black man held out. The female voice outside the front door was probably the Chinese policewoman.

"Let's go, Elvis – let my partner in." Sam shut the window behind him and indicated his instructions with a nod of his head. Fuong Lee nodded acquiescence and turned towards the front door.

Sergeant Williams had called him "Elvis" – Williams, the police officials, did not know. But the Chinese policewoman did, she had called him by his real name when they first met. In Mandarin, though, not English. Not for the others to understand. The woman could be an ally, then. A possibility. Fuong Lee had recognized the signals at their earlier meeting.

He had always felt comfortable with the heavy bolts that secured the front door of his loft. The loft itself was a donation from a complicated network of supporters. Fuong Lee had complicated the network himself: he did not want to be easily found. Once found, he did not want to be easily reached. The solid steel door with its iron bolts would keep people out. He'd failed to consider that his escape route was also a way in. He would remember the lesson if these police gave him the opportunity.

Jenn recognized "Elvis Chang" as Fuong Lee the second he opened the door. If there had been any secondary doubts earlier, a hope that her memory had played a trick on her, the face above the black oversized sweatshirt played those thoughts false: Fuong Lee looked even more appealingly intense than his "Stars" file indicated.

"Elvis Chang?" Jenn held out her I.D. and badge as she asked the question.

Fuong Lee tilted his head toward the interior of the loft. "Come in," he said.

"No," Jenn drawled with a smile, her experience of the past three years overpowering her admiration for the refugee leader, "I think I'll just wait here till you take a few steps back into the room."

"You think I will try to run?"

"I think I am wearing high heels and don't want to find out." Jenn wasn't, but she wanted him to look down: Fuong Lee would see a pair of beautiful legs and low-heeled running shoes. Either way he interpreted it, he would get the right picture.

Fuong Lee stepped back from the front door and into the center of the loft. Sam noted that, after an initial impression of roominess, the space was rather dismal, definitely well-within the "student-artiste" mode of mismatched furniture and half-finished renovation. Like his partner, Sam mentally compared the reality of the face he was seeing with the smeared fax photo in the Federal bulletin on Fuong Lee. Since the suspect's attention was on Jenn, Sam decided to fuck the mental jazz and look at the fax for real. Yep, Elvis Chang was their boy.

Jenn waited until Fuong Lee was safely distant from the front door, then stepped inside and shut it behind her.

"I am waiting for you to talk, Detective Luck," Fuong Lee said in Mandarin with musical sincerity.

Jenn did not want to shut out her partner: Sam was sticking his neck out for her as it was.

"I think Sergeant Williams has some questions to ask you," she answered in English, adding sarcastically, "Elvis."

Fuong Lee knew from her tone that he was caught, but he would not respond. He could not ignore the black policeman, though: Sam was holding the fax photo of Fuong Lee in front of his face like a mask.

"So I asked him, I said 'What is your name?' 'A stupid name,' he said. 'For the record –' I said. 'Elvis Chang,' he answered."

Sam lowered his "mask."

"Hmmm – Not that we believed you at the time, but one has to ask the question: 'Why?'"

Fuong Lee hesitated. He was unfamiliar with American government tactics. Should I act afraid? Should I bluster? He looked over at the woman: she had not responded to him yet, but she did not look closed. Were they *that* subtle? He opted for simplicity.

"Why tell you a false name? You are the police."

"Well, yes," Sam agreed. Jenn could almost physically see him adopt his baldly fake naive-sarcastic persona. "We established that we are the police at our first little get together, at which time – I must take note – one rather high-profiled Chinese refugee neglected to identify himself."

As if in response, Fuong Lee repeated:

"You are the police."

"Detective Luck," Sam turned to Jenn in mock appeal, "I don't recall repetition being a major characteristic of Chinese culture." Sam's mocking smile hardened as he turned back to Fuong Lee, "Let me try phrasing the question differently. Why didn't you tell us your real name, kid?"

Fuong Lee weighed his options. There were some. Maybe the killing he had witnessed was as straightforward as it seemed.

He needed to find out.

"You are the police – not federal government?"

"Ahhh," said Jenn, understanding immediately.

"Yesss," Sam hissed, a beat behind in comprehension, a step quicker in follow-up: "No, Mr. Elvis Fuong Lee Chang, we're not related to the federal government and –" with a nod to his partner, "– speaking for myself, I don't want to give a dog's damn about politics. It's screwed up enough around here as it is."

Jenn stepped in quickly at her cue: "Which doesn't make us any happier about having you lie to us."

They were flippant, too flippant for Fuong Lee to follow their shifting attitudes. His base instinct in sizing up relationships, though, was sending him no warning signals. The refugee dissident began to feel that he could trust these two on the basis of their simple loyalties. He had to test their reaction.

"You knew I was lying."

No response.

"Lying to agree with you... about your colleague's... 'action'... and the other man with the gun."

Sam sent the signals to Jenn: *We're here because you recognized him and didn't say anything to me. Answer him.*

"It was a different kind of lie," Jenn said.

"And now your federal government wants me –"

Jenn cut him off: "Wants to know *where* you are. There's a difference."

Fuong Lee liked the fact that it was the woman talking.

"Do they know now – from you?"

Jenn could not answer that, it had to be from Sam.

"We have a certain amount of discretion in our record-keeping," her partner said noncommittally, "I want to know *why*, though: why you hide, why they look for you?"

Fuong Lee had not known there was an official lookout for him by the U.S. government. He had suspected it, though, and this confirmation seemed a relief. Why?

He walked over to the FIRE EXIT window. Behind him, Fuong Lee felt the two police officers tense, but he opened the window anyway. The fresh air still smelled of the nearby Amtrak railroad engines, but it was cool enough to trick his body into feeling refreshed by the breeze. Fuong Lee knew he could not outrun the black man. He would not even consider trying.

"I saw a picture in the newspaper last month of your National Security Advisor shaking hands with a man in my country who ordered the execution of a hundred of my friends. Your President lifted the military embargo a month after the Tien An Men massacre – I believe he has relatives with certain business contracts? – and he has vetoed legislation that would prevent refugees like myself from being forced back to China.

"So you ask: Why are they looking for me? Why am I hiding? I do not think I am a stupid person. I do not want to walk into a hangman's noose."

Jenn gave a version of the same advice she had once offered Martin Cordez – with the same half-hearted belief in its validity:

"You make speeches and agitate for movements against those things happening: you could just lie low, ignore the politics and they will ignore you."

Fuong Lee smiled a most excellent smile of rueful folly.

"Maybe I *am* a stupid person."

Jenn answered in Mandarin.

"But," she needed to know, "if you keep a high profile, you can do more – and you can be safe from any government?"

Sam began to look at the furniture, to examine the handbills that stood in small stacks atop a long cafeteria-style table pushed against an unpainted wall. Fuong Lee answered Jenn with sincerity. There was no reason to lie to her. He was happy that she spoke Mandarin: its twelve-tone beauty and allusiveness conveyed his feelings with direct impact.

"I can be safe," he agreed, "but my friends cannot. There are pressures on everyone who sides against the Beijing government. Too much money has been invested there. Too many people *here* have set up relatives in business *there*. The people who help me – what we represent – we threaten their personal lives."

That was the speech, now for the meaning. For the woman to understand.

"It is better for me to be alone."

He wanted so much for her to understand.

"Let those who help me do so anonymously," Fuong Lee rushed on, the words tumbling from his lips, almost without calculation. "We will build up support from those who do not have a personal connection to China, from those who can afford to have the courage to act morally."

Jenn could not help thinking of Jimmy Luck even as she thought of believing in Fuong Lee. "You despise the Chinese here, then, and the U.S. government?"

Fuong Lee would not answer that question: he could tell the woman did not need him to. Instead, he smiled with resignation and brought the black policeman back into the conversation by speaking in English again:

"As I just told you, it is safer to be alone. The problem is, I don't like being lonely." He waved his arms in a gesture of belated introduction to the barren loft. "I would like nothing better than to forget all politics – and I hate giving up."

Sam barked a soft laugh.

"Yeah, well, join the police department: you'll enjoy the frustration."

Jenn recognized her partner's cue. It was time to leave. It was all in Sam's hands now anyway, really: how to handle Fuong Lee, how to handle the feds, how to handle Rodney's Review Board on the shooting. Sam might as well close down the interview now as anytime, Jenn thought, or she would go on talking to Fuong Lee until morning. This was it, then, in all probability. She and Sam made departure movements toward the front door. Sam stopped with his hand on the doorknob, the door still closed.

"You splitting this place as soon as we leave?" he asked, tracing a chess move with the index finger of his free hand across a checkerboard poster that cried out in blood-red letters: WE ARE PAWNS!

"Normally that would be advisable," Fuong Lee answered. "What do you suggest?"

Sam bent down and picked up a piece of two-by-four wood scrap that was lying by the entrance, a doorstop apparently, judging by the gouges along its side from where the heavy metal door had dug in when trying to swing closed. He carried the chunk of wood over to the FIRE EXIT window, closed the window, and jammed the wood behind the frame, effectively "locking it."

"*Should* you leave?" Sam said, standing back to admire

his handiwork, "That's a question of whether or not you like the neighborhood."

His next remark was addressed to Jenn, even though his eyes were directly locked into Fuong Lee's.

"Nobody knows you're here."

FOUR CORNERS

Take a road map and head north from downtown Los Angeles on the Harbor Freeway, the One-Ten. You'll pass Chinatown on the right, but you won't see anything except an exit sign: Chinatown is down in a gully and you'll be heading uphill. You'll pass the exit for Dodger Stadium on the left, and you won't see that landmark, either: a couple of brush-overgrown hills stand between the highway and the Stadium. Beautiful traffic foul-ups during baseball season when the team has a good year.

You'll be traveling over a natural pass through the hills, man-widened in the 1930s to accommodate the innovative Pasadena Freeway that branches off on the down side of the slope.

Three loomingly tall tunnels carve through some earth that was a little too rock-solid to cut away. The tunnels boast attractive structural lines and a pre-WWII belief that public architecture should have an intrinsic beauty. They are blackened now by the few billion cars that have painted a thousand coats of exhaust fumes across their facade in the past five decades. But you probably won't notice that, since every time you enter a tunnel half-a-dozen idiots will honk their horns and smile inanely at their own cleverness, oblivious to the fact that they have driven the nearby drivers another digit up on the urban stress scale.

If the Pasadena Freeway flowing seamlessly out of the Harbor Freeway displays the attributes of a well-planned endeavor, the entrance to the much-later-constructed Golden State Freeway, Interstate 5, delivers ample proof of improvisation.

Somewhere between the first and second tunnels, if you are paying attention to road signs instead of looking out for your own neck on the winding highway, you will see an exit sign indicating that the LEFT LANE ONLY will give you access to the Golden State Freeway. At forty-to-seventy miles per hour (let's not kid ourselves about speed limits), you will attempt to persuade your way into a left lane already filled bumper-to-bumper with seasoned commuters who don't wait for the advice of a road sign. You will probably make it if you remember the cardinal rule of California freeway driving: never signal your intentions.

Once in the left lane, prepare for a thrill as you test your reflexes and brake pads by suddenly decelerating to ten miles per hour in order to execute a near-ninety degree left hand turn onto the cliffside exit road, noting all the while that your experienced I-5 veterans dive into the same hazardous, curving deathtrap with existential grace and a heavy accelerator foot. These battle-hardened drivers exhibit little patience for life-loving interlopers on their concrete range.

But the I-5 once arrived at is a modern beauty, multi-laned and speed-inducingly straight.

Soon you will be flying through the San Fernando Valley – *The* Valley – with little enough to engage your attention beyond the occasional Highway Patrol sharks out hunting their random prey. Avoid driving a brightly-colored automobile, a low-slung classic, or anything else that looks like it costs more than you can afford multiplied by three and they will probably ignore you. It is a proven fact that an anonymous, grey Honda Civic can tool along at seventy, while a red Fierro will get zapped at sixty-five. SUPPORT YOUR LOCAL POLICE bumper stickers don't help much, but BORN TO ROCK and DIE YOUNG, LIVE HARD will do you in. It is advised that you switch your radio to a Classical Music station immediately upon being pulled over.

Just about the time you are leaving The Valley you will see great torrents of water tumbling down the hills on your right. These are part of the famous California aqueduct system, and provide an easy demonstration of how over fifty percent of the state's water brought down from the rainy north is lost into the air through evaporation. You will notice that you are straining speedily up some low mountains – and that the freeway shows signs of anticipating a schizophrenic split. Don't worry. In another few miles the signs will sort themselves out. Turn right onto the Antelope Valley Highway, #14.

Into the Mojave Desert.

It may look pretty built up now, and at night the blinking streetlights spread out to a limitless horizon more numerous than the stars, but those sights are deceptive. Hop out of your car and try to walk to that nearby house over on the next ridge and the hundred degree-plus temperature will combine with the crumbling earth and heat-glimmering rocks to make it an ordeal. If you make it. Better to stay in your tin can and hurtle safely past the fading dangers of the desert.

Of course, in mid-winter, the desert can be devastatingly cold. A clean cold, devoid of frills. There are few trees to shed leaves and tell the world that it is the dead season. No dormant fields of brittle grass wave in the cold wind. Tumbleweeds cross the highway in the winter less frequently than they do in September. It's just cold. Snow stands on the peaks that rim the desert – and you can see them clearly – hundreds of miles away.

Be forewarned: in the summer some of those same mountains seem to be still covered with snow. Its a fake. Salt.

Or borax. Some places the desert stinks with raw chemicals lying exposed on the ground, scraped into piles by hardluck blue collar workers who can't find jobs with the military on one of the half-dozen bases that claimed huge chunks of the Mojave.

Edwards Air Force Base is the most famous: Chuck Yeager jet jockeys, sound barrier breaking Stealth fighters, space shuttle landings, Jet Propulsion Laboratory. But there's more than Edwards hiding out in the desert. The Navy has its Weapons Center up at China Lake, the Marines took over Twenty-Nine Palms, and any recreational pilots thinking of flying randomly over this arid real estate had best plan on being buzzed by bored, scrambling khaki flyboys more than once.

Heading north up the 14, you'll pass Palmdale, then Lan-caster, then signs for Edwards AFB, then – finally – you *leave* Los Angeles County just before arriving at the elaborate junction town known as Mojave.

It is interesting that in this entire great desert only one town laid claim to the desert's name. And such a pitiful example of a town at that. Tehachapi forty-five minutes away has a main street, at least, plus a Christian Church with a bell tower and a maximum security prison. Mojave has a lot of railroad tracks and truck-stop motels – and a very strong sense of self-satisfied understanding that you had *better* stop here if you are thinking of going much deeper into the desert because here, in Mojave, we are *it*. Gas, food, lodging, water.

Take their advice, buy them here. Then turn east on Highway 58 and pass on.

It used to be called Four Corners. Newer maps represent a developer's influence most probably with the *nom du place* "Kramer Junction."

Four Corners describes it better. Here Highway 58 crosses east-west with the north-south running Highway 395. Both are two-lane asphalt jobbies, straight and practical and possessed of so few frills that a heavy wind can obscure their existence with dirty sand in a matter of minutes. These highways run between unimportant places, but possess an integrity of function that is impressive in itself. Not many vehicles travel 395 and 58, but those that do *need* to. They carry in supplies that keep some people alive, and carry out goods that – while small in demand – can only be produced from the earth *here*.

In the middle of nowhere.

There is a small grocery store on the southwest corner of the intersection. A temporary Mexican pottery stand has been sitting on the northwest corner for years. A gas station fills the southeast corner and, in asymmetrical fashion, a small motel sits behind the gas station while the northeast corner of the highway intersection-Kramer Junction-Four Corners stands empty witness to the flat desert beyond.

There are always several automobiles parked in Four Corners, ninety percent transient. A large Capri with tinted windows stood at a catty-corner to the grocery store, it's motor running to keep the air conditioner humming at low power. Southern California was having a record-breaking warm, dry winter and, even though the desert night would dip below freezing, the noon sunlight was its usual merciless self. With the windows up it would have been over ninety inside the Capri without air conditioning.

And Harry did not want to roll down the windows.

"OK, they're here. Lights, camera, action! – That's how you all do it out here in California, right?"

Harry's Surveillance Second did not bother to respond as he flicked on the video camera from the back seat of the Capri: he was always hearing stupid Hollywood jokes from the Monitors they sent in from out-of-state. He had a steady hand, and the image barely wiggled when Harry put the Capri into gear and slowly drove across the uneven gravel parking area towards the gas station. He played with the zoom button and focussed-in on the small Accord stopped next to the Self-Service pumps.

A Chinese man had just stepped out of the Accord and was looking uncertainly at a pump.

Harry pulled up to the opposite side of the same pump and jumped out of the Capri.

"Pay before or after?" he hollered out to an attendant who had yet to move his butt away from the small television he had blaring next to the cash register inside the station.

"After!" was the distant, disinterested reply.

"Thanks!" Harry called back with a disproportionate heartiness. He pulled out the nozzle, flipped on the connect lever, and handed the primed-and-ready nozzle over to the Chinaman.

"Here y'are, pal. I'm using Extra."

The Chinaman, a wide-faced example of pseudo-Japanese businessman's fashion, accepted the nozzle with a neutral nod and began pumping Unleaded Regular into the Accord. He watched the price meter carefully.

Harry's enthusiasm was unaffected.

"I really like California," he said to his fellow road warrior, "reminds me of parts of Italy."

Harry was more interested in recounting his travel adventures than in pumping gas; he slopped liquid down the side of the Capri as he put the nozzle into the fuel line.

"Met an interesting fella a few days ago: called himself a 'travel agent'. Specializes in livestock. His motto, he said, is 'Bring 'em back alive!' " Harry laughed with genuine pleasure, adding:

"Anybody'd be happy making travel plans with him, I think."

The Chinese businessman offered another neutral nod, then turned his attention to cutting off the gas flow at precisely ten dollars. That accomplished, he replaced the nozzle on the pump, screwed tight the Accord's gas cap, and stepped into the station to pay the attendant in cash.

The Surveillance Second's camera caught the transaction barely – the contrast between the exterior sunshine and the shadowy interior light was too extreme – but was more successful in capturing the face of the Chinaman as he returned to his car and drove away. The license plate number was in perfect focus. The Surveillance Second had it radioed in before Harry returned from paying the attendant for the Capri's gas.

"Here's the receipt," Harry said, handing the slip of paper back to the Surveillance Second.

He watched the Chinese businessman drive temperately away toward Barstow in the east.

Good, Harry thought, *he goes east, we can take the direct route south back to L.A., down the 395.* You can snap it up to a hundred with nobody watching on the 395.

Harry took a last look at the departing Accord and shook his head sadly.

"Russians used to be more fun," he sighed to himself.

COMPROMISE FRIDAY

In the end, the City Attorney's office agreed to settle.

Sam accompanied Jenn this time, the two agreeing that their individual efforts had met with enough bad luck to put a definite bogey on the Officer Snappy Ticket Affair, Besides, they had both wasted enough time to equal the one hundred and fifty dollar fine. They would give the system one final shot and if there was *another* continuation then they would pay the damn fine and count themselves suckers.

Their plan hit an immediate snag.

"Two thousand three hundred and fifty-eight dollars," the anonymous voice informed Sam when he called up the Court Clerk's office to see who to make the check out to if they failed to clear the ticket this time.

Seated across from Sam at her desk, Jenn began to choke upon her lunch of microwaved ramen noodles. "Court costs!" she sputtered. "We forgot about court costs!"

Indeed they had, as the voice proceeded to explain to Sam: the municipal court system did not look kindly upon citizens protesting a ticket and then losing interest in the affair.

"But what about civil rights?" Sam protested. "We've got the right to go to trial if we're innocent."

"But if you pay the fine you're saying you're guilty. The computer here shows you've used up – let's see – *three* days of the court's time. Plus the City Attorney's office has been working on the case."

Sam listened with a sense of defeat.

"Yeah... sure... good-bye."

"Don't you want to know how to make out the check, sir?"

"I'm sure they'll tell me if I lose."

"I'm sure they will, sir."

So Sergeant Samuel Williams and Detective Jennifer Luck sat outside the D.A.'s office at their scheduled interview time with a feeling of dread. Nothing had gone right so far, why should this so-obvious-it's-ridiculous meeting be any different?

"You wasted our time with *this?*" the Assistant D.A. assigned to their case yelled.

"It was not our choice," Jenn replied, seeing that Sam was in no mood to answer diplomatically.

"Why didn't you just get somebody here to fix it?" the A.D.A. yelled again. "Jeez, you cops're doing it all the time!"

"Call – it – integrity," Sam said through clenched teeth. "We thought – we were – *innocent*." He began clipping his words. Jenn worried that he was going to explode.

"Innocent – shit! This has gone on for months, now it's on our *records*! Now *we* gotta take the fall!"

"Just – cancel – the ticket," Sam suggested tersely.

"No way, Jose," the A.D.A. replied. He was balding and kept looking at the top of his head reflected in the plate glass covering his law school diploma, which was nailed into the wall behind Jenn. "You know how much the city's spent on this case so far?"

"Two thousand – three hundred – fifty-eight – dollars," Sam said.

A brief pause for surprise.

"Yeah. Plus my time today. Do you know what that means?"

Neither Sam nor Jenn knew what that meant.

"We've got to plea bargain."

Perhaps if maintaining a healthy line of communications with the District Attorney's office was not important... Perhaps if the Assistant D. A. could not have made their life on the force a political nightmare... Perhaps if Sam was not going up for Lieutenant and Jenn for Sergeant soon, then, perhaps...

Well, *then* perhaps the Officer Snappy Ticket Affair might have gone down in police annals as the first justified killing of a prosecutor by an enraged citizenry.

As it was, Sam merely promised himself to find out the man's license number and make sure his car was towed some day soon. Meanwhile, and Jenn negotiated the settlement.

The offered terms were Machiavellian: The officers agreed – *agreed* – to admit to an "obstruction of justice" by failing to identify themselves and the offending dog to the ticketing officer. The District Attorney's office, thus absolved from blame, would then recommend that the ticket charge be dropped in light of mitigating circumstances (i.e. maintaining a plainclothes cover). Case closed.

Not enough, Jenn objected – and here the aforementioned potential promotions entered into the negotiation.

"Prior to walking into our next courtroom," Jenn insisted, "we want two signed letters of recommendation from the D.A.'s office to our Station Commander."

"I'll write them right now," the Assistant D.A. said quickly, recognizing a bargain when he saw one.

"*You're* not good enough," Sam objected, agreeing immediately with his partner's line of reasoning – and feeling more than a little bloodthirsty. "We want the District Attorney himself to sign the letters."

The A.D.A. blanched.

"The whole purpose of this – agreement – is to *avoid* having some of us on the line look bad in front of Hiram," he explained in a *we're-all-in-this-together-aren't-we?* tone of supplication. "If I take this up to the ninth floor" – the District Attorney's sanctum sanctorum – "that's not going to make a good impression, is it?"

Sam and Jenn had to agree with the reasoning, if not with the A.D.A. himself.

After a few moments' spirited haggling, the "on the line" Assistant District Attorney disappeared from his office and returned five minutes later with letters of recommendation signed by his immediate supervisor, who carried a little more weight and was also one of the "All-in-this-together" boys.

None of which prevented Sam and Jenn them from having to make another appearance in court to enter the plea bargain.

So this is Justice, Jenn mused for the millionth time as she sat next to Sam in the courtroom waiting for their case to be called. Plea bargaining was no sudden revelation – she had been through dozens of such sessions with felons brought into the Prosecutor's office – it was just a little ridiculous in this case. Is this how Justice works?

"I don't believe in Justice!" she had spit out angrily at Tom Deane one day after he was unexpectedly defeated in fighting off a Temporary Restraining Order put on Martin Cordez. Tom had been fooled into thinking that a judge would listen closely and be able to discern the true from the false.

"People can lie and get what they want: there's no such thing as Justice." Jenn said bitterly, more upset than Martin, who turned around the next day and successfully promoted the T.R.O. as a moral victory to his supporters.

"Maybe..." Tom chewed at the edges of his moustache – it was always growing scraggly by the end of the week – and shook his head with disbelief once again. "Or maybe I just wasn't smart enough this time."

"You're smart, Tom. It just doesn't work."

"No," Tom answered with a singular conviction. "I was probably too stupid. I became a lawyer because I believe in Justice. I just have to approach this case smart enough to prove it to you that it works."

He had, at least, proved to Jenn that he was smart enough to *make* it work. Sometimes.

And Fuong Lee?

Jenn did not want to think about him. Something ached. She would rather think about Justice for the one million and first time. She could not stop thinking about Fuong Lee.

Jenn leaned closer to Sam for comfort. Sam did nothing in response, but his presence was comfort enough. He was her partner, there was comfort in that thought.

There was no comfort in Sam's thoughts. As they sat in the courtroom waiting he saw familiar faces sitting nearby. They did not recognize him, and they had no reason to. A grey-suited attorney, a thin young Hispanic in his late teens, a thicker-bodied older version of the young man wearing a spider tattoo on his neck, and a dark-eyed woman of middle years who looked to be from Aztec stock and wore a bewildered expression.

"How many times did you hit him with the bat?" Grey Suit had asked an hour earlier over his cup of decaf coffee. He slid his notebook away from the cup: the outdoor table was unsteady, he did not want his notes to be splashed.

"Nine, maybe a dozen times," Thin Chest answered diffidently, his eyes focussed on his knees.

Sam was drinking espresso at the next table, waiting for their appointed court hour and looking at the halls of justice gleaming appropriately across the street. He hated being in courtrooms and would wait until the last minute.

"I need to know for certain," he overheard Grey Suit insist.

"Why, man?" Spider Neck objected, pointing at Thin chest. "He wasted the chollo – nine times, twel' times – it don't matter now: the dude stayed wasted." Spider Neck could not removed a trace of approval from his voice.

"If he hit the alleged victim under ten times, then it was impulsive – if he did it more than ten times it shows premeditation."

"Yeah – ?"

"Self Defense versus Assault. Probation versus two-to-ten in Folsom."

"Oh, then Geraldo hit him nine times, right, Mom?"

"Como?"

Spider Neck patiently explained to his Indian mother why young tin-chested Geraldo was so quick-tempered that he beat the dude senseless by accident – yes? – if the judge asked her about Geraldo, he was impulsive, yes?

"Si," Geraldo's Mother agreed uncertainly.

Spider Neck turned to Grey Suit with another pressing concern. "It's no problem about the other two times?" he asked with businesslike solemnity.

"The previous assault charges against young Geraldo here are in a different jurisdiction and involve other people. They have no bearing on this hearing."

"Oh."

Oh. Sam watched now as Grey Suit led Geraldo past the bailiff and back into the judge's chambers. A prosecutor followed. Today was settlement day, the bailiff had advised the police officers, everything would be settled behind closed doors.

It was quiet in the courtroom, the assembled attorneys quietly whispering among themselves, the various defendants too self-conscious to say anything beyond a nervous comment or two. The court reporter laughed gently at a joke the bailiff told her, then went behind a small desk and turned on a radio. The Beach Boys were caught in mid-harmony and "Good Vibrations" drifted gently around the room. Officer Snappy's case would be called next.

Jenn dozed next to Sam's shoulder. Spider Neck bounced his head rhythmically to the music's back beat two rows ahead. Officer Snappy's erroneous ticket would soon be plea bargained out of existence, and on the other side of two inches of oak door Geraldo haltingly lied his way to temporary freedom.

DRIVEN TO TEARS

In the not too distant past, Los Angeles County was forced to look to the east and set a permanent border with the next community of interests, San Bernardino County. The ensuing political wrangle ignored natural geography, cut a couple of towns in half, and ended up with both counties holding on to patches of real estate within the other's territory.

It was not an even swap. Los Angeles County held the more powerful sway of influence up in the California state capitol. A cursory reading of both counties' maps tells the whole story: airfields and water reservoirs miles within the border of San Berdoo are still a part of the big L.A. – which sacrificed valuable scrublands to its neighbor in return. As a result, the thriving Ontario Airport sends its revenues to the benefit of distant communities, while its S.B.Co. namesake town is stuck with the traffic jams and subsidiary road upkeep expenses.

A whole string of small airports still service the private plane traffic in the name of Los Angeles County. Cable Airport is one of them. Philippe and Cockney sat in the coffee shop that squatted under the control tower at this outpost of Angelino hegemony. They had not spoken to one another for two hours.

This silence brought them to the attention of the coffee shop's senior waitress. Normally, and this was a normal day, the customers in her shop were talkative: private airplane owners tended to be excited about their flying machines and that omnipresent god of flying, The Weather. Pilots would talk for hours about flying conditions, reworking flight plans on the basis of half-hourly weather reports, seeking out other pilots' experienced advice on where the best tail winds could be found, tracing new routes on their maps ("just in case"). Or discussing mechanical problems with the airport's resident aviation mechanics. The senior waitress' heart went out to the mightily patient guys over in the hangars who had to listen to the repeated and repeated and *repeated* worried jabber and opinions from a clientele that probably could not change a tire on their own *car*, let alone diagnose a "flutter" in the aileron.

Or they were passengers waiting to fly off with a pilot friend, hiding their excitement and worry behind a facade of busy talk.

Or they were waiting for someone to arrive, talking about anything other than The One Fear that every relative of a private pilot secretly felt.

Or whatever – they *talked.*

The white boy sat sullenly before a homemade cinnamon roll. The senior waitress had heated it up for him when the two first arrived (which was midafternoon, she remembered, because she had just come on shift and would be there until closing). The Asian guy smiled and looked around with a confident attitude, but he did not talk either – except to order another piece of blueberry pie à la mode every half hour.

One thing was certain, the senior waitress had no difficulty in observing, the two did not like each other *at all.* They would most probably tip crappy as well.

Although the white kid – was he Mexican? He didn't look it, but he had an accent when he ordered the cinnamon roll – was the more downfaced of the two, he appeared to be intensely attentive to every plane that flew in. You could see him rousing himself from his sulking stupor at the sound imagined or real, of every propeller buzzing into Cable.

The Chinese guy – he was funny-talking, too – was caught up in his tablemate's alertness at first, but the ensuing hours of apparent disappointment dulled his interest. He steadfastly refused to respond to any new landings, and the white kid's intermittent enthusiasm was greeted with a mocking smile.

"'E said fife o' the clock, luv," the Chinaman announced sarcastically to the ceiling more than once, always adding an alliterative "fuckin' Frog face" quietly enough so that only his partner – and the frequently passing senior waitress – could be disturbed by the words.

They were not pleasant customers, and the senior waitress wished she had given the window booths to her junior colleague instead of losing one-sixth of her table space on those two.

Philippe left the cafe at five o'clock promptly: even if Cockney *needed* to finish his precious third or fourth dessert, Philippe would not remain sitting any longer, especially opposite the Chinese reactionary.

The young Frenchman clutched his camcorder case desperately in his fingers, quickly unfastening the snap as soon as he was out in the cooling late afternoon air – and away from Cockney. He needed to record, to talk to the tape, to say what he felt and interpreted. Without interruption. Without some "ordure" – this garbage from Hong Kong – looking over his shoulder and strumming his "My, my, my!" tunes at every important observation Philippe had to make.

Please, Philippe prayed to a desperate inner self, *let this "Professor" be the honest man this Chinese is not.*

He guided the camcorder in a steady panning shot across the airfield, capturing the rows of small airplanes, open hangars and the small, extremely functional airport tower itself.

The control tower was not tall, but its smooth lines rose confidently out of the stone-and-mortar architecture below it, reminding Philippe of the small chateaux that dotted the Loire Valley, once the castle keeps of minor lords protecting their feudal dairyfields and vineyards. Had the Cable Airport control tower formerly been the strong beacon for pre-War pilots barnstorming across California?

A range of mountains loomed only short miles behind, but Philippe had difficulty reconciling the airfield's solitary American West ambience with the plains of suburban housing tracts stretched out into the valley below. He had that problem with all of this Los Angeles. Everywhere Philippe went he was surrounded by a city and then, just as always, a small mountain would jut up through the houses and office buildings, raw and so sparsely uninhabited as to appear wild. Not a hill. Not a "site for future development." A fullscale mountain. Here, to the immediate north, against the warm (almost hot) sun of the receding day there stood a white-crusted peak bouncing freezing drafts of wind off its near-treeless flanks.

For some reason Philippe found it almost as important to understand this geography as it was to grasp the people who lived here. Much as he loved his camcorder, he knew that it was inadequate for the task. The vision was too big, too... Not complex, actually, but simple. Too large and *simple* to hold in a camera.

The buzzing sound grew insistently louder.

This would be The Professor's airplane. It would have to be.

It would have to be.

It was a Trans-County Charter twin-engine Cherokee. These identifications were clearly marked along the airplane's exterior along with a Federal Aviation Administration identification number. Beyond that Philippe had no idea what type of airplane it was. Three airplanes had arrived since five, but Philippe knew that this was it. The Professor had arranged two identifications: one with Philippe and one with Cockney. Philippe's was the initials TCCC2.

TCCC2. This had meant nothing to Philippe until he had spent the afternoon watching airplanes. Gradually he had come to understand the uncomplicated code. *Trans-County Charter Cherokee* airplane, *2* engines. He had not told Cockney about his difficulty in understanding The Professor's message. Philippe would tell the Chinese thug nothing.

Cockney wanted to kick the little French dick in the asshole. He had told the Frog the time and place, now the effin' fag was playing screw-you games. *Ah, well, m'luv,* he told himself, letting nothing worry him with too much grief, the bleedin' Professor would be here whether or not the Frog cooperated, bringin' some more of the pretty tidy. *An', m'luv, they need me. Even if they don't think so, they need me.*

And now the Frog was pointing his little camera with more than minimal interest at the charter plane that had just dropped in. Face lit up like a sun, it was. Cockney rose from the table with a patient grace and brought the check over to the coffee shop cash register. No need to leave more than a five percent tip, the waitress hadn't had to do anything for them.

The Trans-County Charter floated in from Palm Springs with hurried elegance: the pilot knew that there would be a full load of business passengers to Burbank trying to skip over the rush hour freeway traffic. With little deference to leisure, he tooled the twin-engine Cherokee off the short runway and taxied around the airstrip speedily to stop almost at the doorstep of the control tower. His three passengers were advised to unfasten their seatbelts before he had come to a complete stop, and the pilot was out of the plane before the propellers had stopped chopping. He skipped under the plane and had his wheel blocks in place even as the three commuters crawled out of the Cherokee, voicing their cursory thanks and goodbyes.

Philippe had framed the Cherokee wide in his view-finder and now was having trouble distinguishing the faces of the departing passengers. They all looked so – normal. Which...?

"O.K. Philippe, luv. Enough a the movies for the 'ome telly."

Cockney had stuck his tête stupide in front of the lens again.

"But I need to record!" Philippe protested.

"I'm finkin' the gen'lman we're about ta meet won't like." His voice carried a singsonging admonition.

"He won't care," The Professor said dryly.

The Professor saw his first recorded impression later that evening when the young Frenchman played back his hours of tedious videotapes. He looked different, as he knew he would. Nothing radical – glasses, a hair shade, a moustache – all simply a different style. The Professor would not be casually recognized, but, if anything, he was now dressed rather obviously to attract notice, his crimson pullover sweater attracting most eyes away from his face.

"Gor! Whyn't you advertise for attention?!" Cockney commented as soon as they met.

The Professor turned an evaluating eye on the Asian. He had already recognized his two contacts from inside the airplane's window.

"I want them to look," he explained carefully, his English precise and unforced. "And they will remember a man in a bright red pullover – which can be shed as easily as their memories."

Professor's faded green eyes impressed Philippe as the most intelligent he had ever seen. The color did not come across on the camcorder's black-and-white viewfinder monitor, but the later playback displayed the shade perfectly. Philippe wondered if Cockney understood that he was being reprimanded.

Cockney didn't.

"Good idea," he shrugged with grudging acceptance, "I'll 'ave ta try it."

Professor smiled. "It works." He then turned his attention to Philippe. "Now stop the little machine."

Philippe began to protest, for The Professor *had* to understand: "But I have to – Ow!"

Cockney had grabbed his wrist at a pressure point, forcing Philippe to release his grasp on the camcorder.

"I believe the gen'lman don't want it."

Philippe opened his eyes from the pain to find his video camera in Cockney's possession. He turned his face in mute appeal to The Professor.

He did not find immediate solace. Professor had been watching their squabble with a different interest. He spoke first to Cockney:

"*You* are not, then, the person who knows this Fuong Lee?"

"Local talent, guv, knowin' the wicked ways a Chinatown. Philippe 'ere's our guide to Fuong Lee."

The green eyes turned on Philippe.

"You have located him?"

Philippe answered with wounded pride.

"I have let people know who I am. They will let Fuong Lee know. We will find each other –" he shot a superior, possessive look at Cockney, "– alone."

Professor saw the immature face with its open appeal for empathy. He gave it.

"Of course," his smile to Philippe was very sympathetic, "you are his friend and he is frightened. You will persuade him to return to where he is needed?"

Mollified, Philippe confided readily in the older man: "Fuong Lee has always been very strong, very stubborn. If he is afraid, then I... I don't know."

"You will do what is best for Fuong Lee and," The Professor had made this type of speech to a score of new recruits, it had been easy to believe once, "our ideals. We will be here to help him escape America when he needs to."

Cockney was tired of being ignored, even if only for a minute.

"Well, we free sound like a buncha jolly Red conspirators, don't we?" His intrusion had broken The Professor's spell. The Professor decided to confirm his hold on the young Frenchman at a later meeting where the noisy Chinese would not be in attendance. The noisy Chinese was talking again. It was hard to understand him.

"Gotchyer car right 'ere, guv, Philippeboy 'n me drove up in it: bland 'n boring like they asked."

The Cable Airport parking lot, like the runway, ran up to the door of the cafe. Cockney led them a few short paces away from the cafe's entrance to a small, four-door Chevrolet Chevette, circa 1978. It's maroon paint was unscratched, but faded to a dull, unpolished sheen.

The Professor stood away from the car as Cockney slid in behind the steering wheel. Cockney's action, like all of his physical movements, gave evidence of a controlled grace. Even the sarcastic tilt of his head was relaxed. Seeing the Professor's hesitation, Cockney popped his head out the window.

"Problem, guv?"

"I am evaluating: you, the car."

"An' – ?"

"If the tires are good, I am content with both."

Cockney did not know why but, like Philippe, he wanted this man's approval. "They said get new tires, guv. You got 'em."

"Good."

"But the car 'as no pickup, guv. We'll never speed away wif this."

Professor waved Philippe into the back seat, taking the passenger front seat for himself. "I want an anonymous vehicle. I want everything quiet and – anonymous. If we have to 'speed away,' then we've failed."

Then, abruptly, but without aggression: "How much did you pay?"

Cockney did not miss a beat answering: "Three thousand dollars."

The Professor ran his forefinger across the cracked vinyl dashboard. "How much did they *give* you to buy such a car?"

"Three thousand," Cockney smiled in confident conspiracy. "An' I even 'ad ta bargain 'em down a bit."

Later that night, after his handholding session with Philippe, The Professor would pull from his toiletry bag a plastic handled, steel-reinforced hairbrush. From his jacket pocket he would take a palm-sized metal cigarette lighter. Various other pieces of odd, hardened plastic would be scrounged from his shoulder bag. And they would all fit together to make an unattractive, functional automatic pistol, bought (almost) over-the-counter in Berlin. Virtually invisible to the international airport x-rays and metal detectors. The Professor did not think it would be necessary for Fuong Lee. He did not have the same confidence in Cockney.

They settled in to the Chevette and Cockney began driving with elaborate care. ("It's a grandmum's car, guv. Don't wanna give it a 'eart attack.") They were still within sight of Cable Airport when Philippe leaned forward and uttered a plaintive whisper into The Professor's ear coupled with a subtle show-and-tell of the camcorder that did not fall into Cockney's rear view mirror sightline.

"Can I? While we drive?"

Professor assumed the paternal role he knew would be necessary to nurse Philippe through the next few days.

"Please, record," He nodded politely, adding a turn of the head to face Cockney. "I want him to record this trip."

"I'm the legs 'n 'ands, guv: you're the mind." Cockney flexed his fingers on the steering wheel with the coiled control of an eagle's claw. He was wearing leather driving gloves because they, well, they *felt* good even when wrapped around such a crappy plastic steering wheel. He turned off the small suburban lane towards the more heavily travelled access road to the freeway.

"Don't go this way, please," The Professor corrected.

"It's the way to the freeway," Cockney protested. It was also the only way he knew to get back to Chinatown, the way he had come out to the airport.

The Professor had memorized the road map of Southern California. "I want to stay near the mountains," he said simply, then proceeded to give Cockney a series of uncomplicated directions that accomplished his aim. There had been a full day to memorize the road map. Another day to memorize the detail map of Chinatown. Then detailed schematics of the Los Angeles water system. A hiking map for the Elysian Park hills that abutted Chinatown. Three coffee table picture books about the area. Although he lacked certain important specifics, The Professor knew the general area better than Cockney.

That had always been one of his talents, this ability to delve into a project with the researcher's thoroughness. The trip from Italy had been made with the same attention to detail. A jet to Greece, then to Berlin. By car to Frankfurt, then fly to Toronto. A drive into the United States via Niagara Falls – then on wings to Mexico City. If the Americans had expected to monitor his suspected entrance into the States, they would be put off by the sudden exit. A bus ride to Matamoros, a walk across the border to Brownsville. To Dallas-Phoenix-Palm Springs-Cable Airport. Nothing clandestine. A businessman with a terrible travel agent.

They were passing a sprawling tribute to American television: a monolithic mall painted in the pastel greens and pinks made popular by a defunct police action series called *Miami Vice*. The Professor had watched the television show on a trip to New York in 1984. He had liked the music and the style. They were dated now, though. Six years and outmoded. He wondered if the owners of this retail Nineveh would change its colors when a new fashion dominated the media.

Maps do not show the unexpected facial tics of the land.

Against the late afternoon glow of sunshine that bounced off the mountains, The Professor saw two giant white breasts loom unexpectedly above the trees that lined their route. Arrow Highway. A wonderfully evocative name for Europeans. Arrow. The luminous mammary glands evolved into a huge tent set in the middle of a small college, the University of La Verne. Knowing that the protrusions were tent poles did not alter the mental image: The Professor found the canvas tits attractive.

They hit the approach to the Foothill Freeway as the sun melted down to the horizon behind downtown Los Angeles, thirty miles distant. The rush hour smog gave the orange light an additional golden burnish. El Dorado. The Professor could not help but begin to feel excited. The emotion conveyed itself to Cockney, who had never seen the city from a distance before.

Philippe saw only The Professor, his face reflected in the window against which his shoulder pressed. Within minutes the sunset's illumination had died to a recurring memory, leaving only an outline of The Professor's face in reflection, seen only because of the dim green glare from the dashboard lights. More often, The Professor's head was silhouetted by the harsh beams of oncoming traffic headlights.

Cockney felt like talking again.

"I wenta Miami last year. Christmas, right? Where you bein' last Christmas, Philippe?"

"...Beijing," was the reluctant answer.

"An' you , Professor?"

"Ethiopia."

"What th' 'ell you doin' *there*?"

"Looking for the Queen of Sheba."

And guns. The last shipment. Through Libya. Then a

delay, and a trip down to Chad. Over the Sudan. To Ethiopia.

A cement factory, covered with small spotlights, gleamed like a science fiction fantasy across a kilometer-wide dried plain of crushed rock sweeping out from the freeway.

"I am the Queen of Sheba," she had said, staring down at him from the guardpost on the mountain trail.

She was old, and spoke Italian from the Occupation days of Il Duce. Who had bothered to teach a black Jewess Italian? Had she been beautiful?

The black Jewess moved her shrivelled arms deftly in and out of the small fire, rearranging scarce wood, as she made a tinned-beef stew for the four guards who manned the post.

"The Queen of Sheba," she explained, "she was the Queen of Ethiopia, too, before she threw her love to the King of Israel. I am sorry the stew is so dry, there is no water."

Here there is no thunder
Only heat.
Only heat and hunger
And crying voices shout soundlessly for attention
Beseeching from a thousand and one photo stands
Magazine cover perfect
With their swollen child bellies
Mother eyes
Large, round

Forgettable in the hundreds in which they appear.
Pawns.
Who remembers pawns?
No one when the heat continues
Without th-th-thunder
Wind to skirt about your ankles
Squint your eyes against the pain
Without thought to profiles and worry lines a
and age creases.
If you should live so long.
Watching the mountains
In your sleep.
But dreams just won't turn off like a TV set.
— Just didn't want to watch
a documentary tonight.
Not again.
It is too hot.
There is no thunder
Only heat.

The beer refinery on the left of the freeway glowed under its night lights, a dozen flags snapping in the dusk wind, emitting steam like a devil's building.

"Almost 'ome," Cockney crowed as they topped the next rise, and the skyline of the downtown was now a sparkle of heaven-reaching lights from which the long line of red taillights/ white headlights stretched out down the hill below.

Jenn took the unexpected night off as an omen of good luck. The beginning of the Chinese New Year. She couldn't face her parents' boring patronage tonight. Tomorrow afternoon's dinner would be enough. She needed to be in Chinatown.

Hill Street. Broadway. Spring Street. The decorations were up. Tomorrow's parade would bring out the old dragons Jenn had been frightened of at the age of five when her older brother, Ron, pushed her into the green one's monstrous face.

Elmyra Street. 4025. The light was on in 2-B.

Chinatown looked as The Professor had imagined it. Spring Street. Hill Street. Broadway. He tried not to look at the homeless shivering on the outskirts. Even in Chinatown.

Philippe was asleep in the back seat, the camcorder cradled heavily in a listless hand on his lap. Cockney glanced over at The Professor with respect: at his instruction they had crisscrossed Chinatown for two hours, over every street, past every store, bank, restaurant, apartment building. One more time past the electronics store with its display of a dozen televisions all beaming the same channel. Open late tonight for holiday shopping. A demonstration in South Africa on the news.

Fuong Lee opened the door. He was not afraid of Jenn this time.

"I did not think you would be here."

"It is a night for relaxation," he answered. "If I am with

them, they will be tense. Better to stay at home."

"Alone?"

"I do not tell anyone where I live."

"Here?"

"Please."

Cockney pulled the Chevette to a stop in front of the electronics store display. The Professor stepped out onto the sidewalk and walked closer to the televisions. He was separated from them by a wall of glass and the metal grill that had just been pulled down in front of the storefront. The televisions were still playing. No sound could be heard on the street. The South African demonstration, black faces calling for basic freedom, was replaced by another image.

Panama.

The Professor watched the U.S. invaders continue to "mop up" in the wake of their three week-old invasion. Brown faces looking at shave-headed white soldiers walking through them at gunpoint. (*Even the black soldiers looked white,* The Professor thought. *Am I the only one who sees that?*) A flag-draped coffin is brought out of a military cargo plane.

Professor closed his eyes.

They were there together for the purpose of lovemaking, their other differences were too great for them to be coy about it.

Jenn undressed first, but it was cold in the loft and she could not control her shivering. Fuong Lee put a blanket around her naked shoulders. He was used to the cold. He began to undress slowly.

He found himself unconsciously comparing the policewoman with the Goddess of Democracy who stared out at him from the poster across the room. Both stood draped in folds of material, both were admired: the Goddess by the throngs of demonstrators at her feet, this woman in this room by his single, lone self. She allowed him to show his homage by embracing him within the folds of the warming blanket.

Jenn wanted to do it all slowly, to come only at the last moment before exhaustion. Then to sleep: no conversation, no thoughts. If he could be gone when she awoke, or sleep until she left. Not to think of the reality.

Fuong Lee found her stronger than he had expected, but that was good. If she had been weak then her oldness would have been pathetic. Four years, five years – did it matter? Not tonight. But one thought.

Do I taste delicious fire in her mouth because she has power, because she can betray me?

They held one another's faces in the ancient ritual of dark examination, close enough to share a breath, trembling from the cold air and the hardness of loins. Her hands helped and he entered her. Fuong Lee closed his eyes.

Jenn raised her eyes from his face and stared at the Goddess of Democracy for a moment longer, felt the emotion wash out thought, then closed her eyes.

She was crying.

A Lie By Mutual Consent

Chinese New Year means nothing outside of China-town, and evening classes at Marti Community College went on as scheduled.

The State of California's extensive educational system had created a number of pocket community colleges, two year institutions offering an Associate's Degree in a limited number of Liberal Arts fields, plus an array of "color" classes designed to bring in some additional revenue from non-students seeking to understand the mysteries of computer operation, basic business math and home flower decorating.

Sam never thought less of a community college for its trash courses: he had picked up his Police Science credentials at Marti and he knew the academic courses were no breeze.

Marti Community College had once been a high school,

back at the turn of the century when graduating with a secondary level degree was in itself an accomplishment. The campus – despite some permanent dedications to the high school icons of football, homecoming queens and The Prom – was more reminiscent of a university atmosphere than many of the state's community colleges that had been built from scratch. The trees were tall and spreading, seventy years old, the grass lawns were pre-sod, abundant in some patches and worn to hard earth by impromptu student trailblazing in others. Sam had read once of an architect who refused to design sidewalks into his community plans. The architect would wait until a month after the buildings were occupied and then have sidewalks constructed where people crossed naturally, not where design theory said they *should* walk.

Sam had met Marie at Marti.

She still taught there. Not Police Science, but Sociology – another course of study he had found helpful in prepping for the promotion exams. Not the exams per se, but the oral review that was an equally important part of the department's advancement process.

Sam did not like school, had never liked studying, but a few people along the way kicked it into his head that a lot of life would be more interesting and understandable if you went to the trouble to see what other people thought about it. Was it McMasters with his crap chess that Sam had become addicted to? Or maybe Mark Cornell, another pre-force encounter. They'd split in '81, never the twain to...

But Mark Cornell had been a confessed "professional" student for a dozen years until just before he and Sam linked up for a couple of bad years. Not that Mark was bad, or that he and Sam had crossed the line or anything like that. Just a couple of guys caught in some sleaze times trying to figure things out.

Cornell liked to read, read all the time. Very thick, heavy books. Sam thought they were the dullest things this side of a self-righteous heaven.

Still, over two years with little else to do for recreation (how did we live without portable electronics?) led Sam to reading a little and listening a lot. And, much as he'd liked Mark, Sam wanted to hear the other side of Mark's stories. So he started looking into things that they had talked about. And other things. Then Marie started talking to him one night in the campus cafeteria and there were more things to look into.

"Too many sociologists and not enough connections."

That was the reason Marie had given him to explain her long stay at Marti.

Besides, she always added, "I have tenure, the most valuable asset a state college instructor can have. I would practically have to rape a dead body in front of the Board of Regents to lose my job."

Well, state cutbacks in the education budget had somewhat shaken that article of faith – despite a much ballyhooed

Lottery designed (so it advertised) to raise revenues earmarked for education – but the net result was that Marie clung more than ever to her position at Marti for the vague security if offered. As long as the campus itself remained open.

A late booking had left Sam and Jenn checking off-shift two hours into the evening.

It was a routine booking, not even Task Force business, but they'd made the mistake of being the senior officers nearby and offering to hold onto the suspect until a Vice unit showed up. Vice never showed, gallivanting off to their own new shift biz. It was an annoyance, but not particularly onerous. (Ha! "Onerous." *A word for Cornell to hear me use*, thought Sam.)

Jenn had muttered words about a Chinese New Year's dinner with her folks the following day. Sam declined the invite to join her. Knowing that Jenn was dreading the event (and that her parents figured they were sleeping together), it did not promise to be a fine example of Asian culture.

So the Task Force partners had parted for the day, each their own way, not expecting to see one another until four the next afternoon when they'd start the new timeclock week on swing shift.

Even though traffic out to Marti Community College in the San Gabriel Valley had not been bad, Sam made no attempt to rush since he knew Marie's class had already started before he left the station. He could have made it there by mid-session break, but he wanted more than a rushed ten minutes while a crowd of students hovered nearby. He stopped at a McDonald's opposite the campus parking entrance and consumed a nutritious dinner of generous proportion (two all-beef patties, special sauce, lettuce, cheese, pickles, onion on a sesame seed bun), then drove across the street, parked, and found his waiting spot. He had waited here a thousand nights, even though it was over a year since the last time.

The Social Sciences building was generously proportioned to offset its narrow depth with a wide facade of grey stone. The arching entrance that centered the facade was approached by a flight of brick stairs. An anachronism in earthquake-conscious Southern California, it nevertheless always boasted a contingent of students sprinkled up and down its comfortable steps, leaning against the heavy rail or plopped theatrically in staggered groups upon the cold bricks themselves. On winter nights the sitters were in a minority, even when the lush bushes surrounding the building still hugged the warm daytime air.

Sam's position, as always, was against the eucalyptus tree that faced the entrance. Its shedding bark was an occasional danger, but tonight it appeared determined to maintain all of its epidermal layers intact. The smell was overpowering and drove out the highway exhaust fumes from Sam's oxygen-starved blood system. He slid his back down the trunk until he was squatting almost like the montagnards had shown him in 'Nam.

Without intending to, he fell into a light doze, awakened equally by the sound of the exiting students and the dull aching in his knees. You jerk, Sam's joints complained, the montagnards are five feet tall, tops – what're you: six feet-two?

Nine-thirty, classes out. The first rush was one of multitudes: eighteen year-olds with the energy to still go out dancing vied with tired mothers needing to return to their homes quickly before the baby sitters charged for another hour. Hungry businessmen found themselves back in the real world after a three hour respite. Everyone struggled to adjust their eyes to the darkness without slowing their pace.

The next large group of departees were the talkers, groups of excited students arguing, repeating, wondering aloud about what they had just heard. This group walked slower, but Sam had to keep his attention focussed, because hurried instructors liked to slip out with this crowd. Was Marie among them?

She appeared at the entrance surrounded by the last wave of departees: the questioners. It was a slow-moving series of small groups, each instructor attracting a cluster of students, each student with the most pressing of intellectual concerns.

"– the assignment is your responsibility –" Marie saw Sam as he approached the bottom step, "– but I can help you with a topic." She often found herself looking at the bottom step even when she knew Sam would not be there.

"Don't worry," Marie advised. She had not expected to see him tonight. "Hello, Sam."

"Hi, Marie."

Another student had an equally pressing homework question. Sam moved up a step closer.

"Did you see the class?" Marie asked him, cutting off another student's third repetition of the already-answered homework question.

"No." A familiar smile. "I was late – as always."

"Don't *worry*," Marie said (with, perhaps, too much emphasis) to the remaining students. She stepped down to Sam and, an effective defense against further questioning, linked her arm into his with familiarity. The two walked down the reminder of the stairs together, with Marie repeating to her departing students: "Don't worry."

"You could, maybe, use that advice yourself," Sam said carefully. They were alone now.

Marie pointed with her free arm: "My car is over –"

"– in faculty parking. I know. I used my police I.D. to get past Security and park in the red zone next to you."

"I'm always hoping they'll ticket the idiots who park in the red zone."

"I'll turn myself in tomorrow. Let's cut across the grass."

"My shoes'll get wet," Marie protested.

"Mine, too, but I need a break from pavement."

The parking lot was only a hundred feet away.

"How was the class?" Sam could not think of anything else to say, so he fell back on the reliable, safe question.

"Tough. You couldn't use your old notes."

"How come?"

Marie smiled wickedly. "Outdated."

"Outdated?! It's not a subject that changes that much! It's only been –"

"Six years," Marie finished the sentence. They were walking among cars now. "Six years since your assistant professor/new wife gave you her precious Master's Degree notes."

"Well, maybe..." Sam's car was nearer than Marie's. They walked past it.

"Maybe seven years?" Marie's voice had an edge to it, a re-monstrance for years wasted, "I could be remembering wrong."

Sam's words came out hesitantly: "I want to talk about that..."

Marie pulled her face close to Sam's with a sudden ferocity, cheek to cheek. She could not look him in the face.

"No! *Don't* talk about things, Sam. Then I'll be afraid. Make meaningless phrases. Tell me about where you park. –Don't tell me a single, not a *single* thing about what you really think. Don't make me afraid, Sam. Don't make me think about what you do, about what could happen to you.

"Don't.

"Don't."

Neither one had slept. Jenn had not escaped. The unaggressively rowdy gang of teenagers at the end of the street set off their firecracker string to the accompaniment of childlike cries of laughter.

"Kung Wu Shin Shi," Fuong Lee said from his perch on the windowsill.

"Happy New Year to you, too," Jenn agreed. They had both abandoned the bed. She wrapped herself securely in a blanket and burrowed deeply into the beanbag chair that constituted the pride of the loft's furniture deployment.

Fuong Lee turned way from the street to smile at her.

"One day too soon, of course."

Jenn offered the expected compliment.

"We could repeat the performance to get it on the right day."

"No –" Fuong Lee continued smiling. They both felt the need to smile. "I will be on the streets tomorrow night. And, I think you too, yes?"

Jenn searched around on the floor for the tea cup she had deposited there moments earlier. Finding it, she lifted the cup in a mock toast:

"Here's to the Task Force: may our flag fly high on

Chinese New Year!" She downed the still-warm liquid for comfort, adding: "Or at least higher than the Goddess of Democracy will stand tomorrow."

Fuong Lee was mildly surprised.

"You know, then? The other man said you do not follow politics in Chinatown."

Jenn rose from the uncomfortable beanbag chair and shuffled across the wood floor to the Goddess of Democracy poster. The floor was cold under her bare feet.

"Sam likes to keep things simple: he always fails. He knows he always fails." Why did she respect Sam for that?

Jenn turned away from the Goddess and faced Fuong Lee across the distance of the loft. Jimmy Luck had been his age when they were married. Martin Cordez had been Jenn's age now when they met. The gangs still plagued East Los Angeles. Would Fuong Lee be more successful than Martin? His face had the same look of determination, even though so young. Or was it Martin's instinct for personal survival she saw there? Could one separate the accomplishments from the reasons?

"We heard about your little brouhaha" – Jenn liked that word, it could not be translated into Chinese – "over the Goddess of Democracy: A copy was made here in L.A., the foreign students want it in the New Year's Parade, the Chinatown Chamber of Commerce said – and here I quote – 'It does not fit into our theme this year.'"

"Pressure from the mainland." Fuong Lee said this without resentment.

"They say there is no pressure."

Again without resentment: "It would be very difficult for them to say in public that they are afraid."

He said nothing more for a moment, but Jenn observed that there was an inner dialogue going on behind his eyes. After another brief moment of consideration, Fuong Lee continued:

"So *we* will tell them they are afraid in public."

"How?" Jenn's professional curiosity was piqued, though she masked it by an equally professional veneer of cynicism. "Your pamphlets and corner speeches hardly can compete with a marching dragon and a hundred little costumed mandarins parading down Chinatown."

"True –" Fuong Lee fell into the Shanghai street accents that so readily conveyed his pragmatism, "that's why we chose the Beauty Pageant: beautiful girls in America are, I think, more popular than politics, yes?"

Jenn laughed at the absurd ambition.

"You're going to get the new Miss Chinatown to give a speech?!"

Fuong Lee smiled wryly. "Maybe *I* will give the speech: she will just stand there being beautiful – in front of the television cameras."

Jenn realized that she had been enthralled by the bold simplicity of the concept – and ignoring her other responsibility. "Ohhh," she sighed, "I don't want to hear any of this!"

There had still been an edge of humour in Jenn's voice – but Fuong Lee caught on also to the note of threat. His next words were suddenly serious.

"Please, *don't* hear anything I have just said."

Jenn's response was suddenly serious as well.

"I don't."

The teenagers had lit another string of firecrackers, then another, the two sets crackling away in counterpointed stutters of celebration. Jenn joined Fuong Lee at the window sill. He was partially dressed now, but shivering. She threw the blanket over his head and they both sat there in the artificial darkness. Her legs were cold now, until she slid them next to Fuong Lee's.

"Little political hero: if you wanted to be a bastard you could have a big blackmail on me tonight."

Fuong Lee brought her cold hands down between his thighs, warming them.

"No. Not tonight, Lady Jenn. I'm tired of being alone tonight."

Sam set the needle onto the record by feel in the half-light. Santana's "Caravanserai" album, old and scratched. *Did they reissue it on CD yet?*, Sam wondered. The cricket sounds were beginning to disappearing in the static slush. But the guitar was still singing clear. No words yet, not for the first twenty minutes. Where was the tape? Yeah, here. Sam slid the miniaturized cassette into the answering machine and pushed the Playback button.

"Hello, this is for Mr. or Mrs. Williams. Would you like to explore the mountains of Canada? Or the undersea caves of the Red Sea? You can, with a subscription to Traveler's Digest. I'll call back at a more convenient time to give you the details of this exciting opportunity."

Play it Carlos – no words! – only guitar.

"Hello, Sam Williams? Please call Diane King at 303-337-1444. You can call collect. It's a personal business matter."

"Personal business" – the catchphrase of the collections agencies. Diane King could wait forever.

"Hello, Marie. I am sorry I am late again tonight, but it is work."

Where is that stupid – Oh, yeah, over by the mantel.

"I know, it is always work."

Chinese New Year's Eve and no place to go. Sam traced his forefinger over the rectangular borders of the two frames: the wedding photo and the document. THE document.

"But I have to work tonight because I keep having dreams about that old man I told you about last week, the fruit vendor, who died. I don't want to think about him anymore. It is easier not to think when I'm working, and if I'm home I'm boring you, girl, with this thinking. He was a Russian. Chinese New Year is coming in only five days. Did I ever take you to a Chinese New Year's celebration? I don't think so, but..."

Marie looked damned good in the official wedding portrait. Sam felt that he looked too stiff himself. The ace bandage wrapping over the cracked rib the mugger had given him while working undercover the week before.

"...maybe when we were dating – that was a long time ago, yeah? This old Russian dude was *funny*! He's the one what gave me the almost cracked rib, remember?"

A lot of cracked ribs. Never shot a man, though. Marie never talked about either subject.

"That was a few months ago, the ribs. Bought me a drink, too. He died so fast I think he was surprised. Will I be surprised when I die? I don't want to be. I want to be ready. For what..."

This was where he forgot to talk and the answering machine clicked off for half a minute. Sam stepped away from the framed divorce decree and went over to the stereo so that the music could almost drown out his voice when it came back on. If the neighbors complained, hey!, it's fucking Chinese New Year's Eve! Ease up!

"I'm sorry, I'm thinking about it, yeah? Boring you again. I can't think alone, it seems. I'd eat a bullet, I think, but never if I could think out loud with someone else. Marie, I'm sorry. I shouldn't say these things. Marie. I should say your name more. Marie.

"Marie.

"That sounds better than what I am thinking.

"Marie."

EGGROLLS
IN THE EVENING

Ryzhaya was not surprised by the telephone call, only upset.

They take me for granted so casually now, she thought, brushing a heavy lock of red hair back from her eyes. Her stomach ached from nervousness. She had heard about changes coming. Maybe if they had not called so soon.

Ryzhaya put her makeup on carefully: now that she was a redhead again her color balance was too delicate for errors. *They* expected *me to be waiting!*, she shook her head furiously, *and I was!*

Would the money be decent at least? She doubted it and, besides, it was never a question of money. Money was for mundane considerations like eating and paying the rent. If she could have done what she had done for free, she would have. *But nothing is free in America*, Ryzhaya sighed, a*nd so my patriotism must have a price.*

But, then, the price had never been too high.

Back in 1978, when she sat in the Displaced Persons halfway camp in Italy, her Russian citizenship stripped away, soon to be replaced by an Israeli passport based upon the luck of having a Jewish grandmother, Ryzhaya had been content with the first offer: a small bookstore in Los Angeles in return for allowing certain American sympathizers to leave documents inside books she would later ship to Tel Aviv.

"Will this hurt the fucking Communists?" was the only question she had asked, still smarting from the inglorious cold shoulder she had received from her supposed friends once she announced her intention to immigrate. Jealous bastards!

The bookstore was a hole: to supplement her income, Ryzhaya had been forced to clean houses in the mornings before opening. This hurt her pride, and when the American FBI man walked in one day and began talking to Ryzhaya about her Israeli patrons she felt no qualms about being completely open with him – the Americans owned Israel, didn't they?

Soon she was able to forego the housecleaning in return for recording every document that was left inside her books. The FBI man asked her not to tell the Israelis and Ryzhaya asked him if he thought she was an idiot.

Then, in 1981, the Americans began a new game. The FBI man introduced another man – *not* FBI – who asked her to become friendly with Russian émigrés who seemed, well, maybe not as ready to embrace America and its ideals as they should.

Ryzhaya immediately protested in defense of her own patriotism. The new American sympathized accordingly.

"Don't you ever suspect me!" she warned him. "I am suffering here for your country, and I will suffer more to meet these fucking Communists if you tell me to!"

The new American understood completely. He helped Ryzhaya to expand her business to include a small restaurant where it would be easier to talk to the lying traitors.

1984. The Olympics were coming to L.A. It had been three years since Ryzhaya had let her "true" sympathies be cautiously known and, as anticipated, she was finally approached by the Soviet professionals.

Whatever else the Americans had expected from the U.S.S.R. Olympics team, they could count on it being used as an opportunity by the KGB. Ryzhaya was extremely valuable to her American friends then, so valuable that she almost forgot her Israeli patrons.

Until an unpleasant little Jew showed up wearing a University of Haifa sweatshirt and asking uncomfortable questions about how the small enterprise her Israeli patrons had set her up in had grown so large.

"Because I'm a fucking Jew businesswoman!" Ryzhaya roared at him in Russian.

Then, because she did not speak Hebrew and he only minimal Russian, Ryzhaya had caught herself in time and explained the expansion more calmly, providing a reasonable excuse that had seemingly placated the inquiring little asshole.

Ryzhaya never knew who was the more disappointed when the Soviets pulled out of the 1984 Olympics, the sports fans or the KGB. Most certainly her several contacts had planned on using the event to build a long-term network to supplant the aging radicals from the 1930s who had gone underground in the 1950s. Despite hysterical accusations in the press of intended Soviet disruptions of the Games themselves, Ryzhaya only heard more subtle plans: her Russians were sports addicts themselves, they wanted to see who won, too.

A few stayed behind when Soviet participation in the Los Angeles Olympics went bust. They visited Ryzhaya's restaurant frequently. The Jewish sympathizers continued to "lose" their papers inside her bookstore. Ryzhaya's income was from a comfortable number of sources now: Israelis, bookstore, FBI, restaurant, her new American friends and her newer KGB associates. She felt incredibly patriotic.

Then it fell apart.

Whether it was from stupidity or planned purpose, Ryzhaya never knew entirely.

A series of scandals hit California when a slow thinking FBI agent with a hard-on for blond Slavic women got himself tied-in with a couple of freelance Russian amateurs. Unsurprisingly, they were caught trying to pass on low-level "secrets" directly to the Soviet Consulate in San Francisco. Suddenly Ryzhaya's FBI man wanted no contact with any Russians, including patriots like herself.

Then Gorbachev came to power in Moscow and her KGB colleagues felt a new budget crunch.

The KGB drastically curtailed their activities. Ryzhaya had almost nothing to give her non-FBI American friends beyond a few Defense workers trying to peddle unessential schematics related to the Stealth fighter plane. By 1987 they withdrew their funding for the restaurant. Ryzhaya had to close it in 1988 when anti-Communist feelings among *every* faction of the Russian émigré community (that fucking Gorbachev had made capitalism stylish even among the leftists!) landed her at year-end with a deficit ledger.

The roof fell on her head in 1989: the Americans began prosecuting *Israelis* as spies!

Ryzhaya's FBI man had been transferred to somewhere in Wyoming, and her Israeli patrons (smarting from some documented "shipments" that led them to suspect her discretion) withdrew their financial support from the bookstore. Under pressure from strangers at the FBI, Ryzhaya talked more than she had ever talked before – but no one cared to listen. The bookstore closed in bankruptcy.

Then Ryzhaya was hit with an IRS bill for twelve thousand dollars in back taxes.

And then Harry began showing up.

Harry. Ryzhaya knew that wasn't his name by the self-satisfied way in which he informed her that it was.

"Harry" had no number to contact, no address to reach, no drop box, middleman or identification. But he was government, Ryzhaya knew that. Harry cleared away her tax bill with a "collection deferred until further notice" document that he held in his hands – and over her head. He had her do ridiculous things: take a letter to this man, drive that man to the airport, creating – Ryzhaya came to recognize – yet another "identity" for her.

"Who are the fucking Communists now?" Ryzhaya demanded once, and Harry had replied with a reasonable smile, "Maybe our friends – we'll see."

Ryzhaya had not liked that answer, nor had she liked the fact that Harry's version of remuneration for her efforts was a vague reference to "putting it on your account" and some very pitiful per diems to cover gasoline and meals. She was going to have to go back to cleaning houses pretty soon if things didn't improve!

Now Harry wanted her tonight.

Fine. Sure. Don't call for two months then show up right at the top of the new year 1990. Ryzhaya brushed her hair angrily, slipped on a light coat against the cooling evening and stalked out of her condominium apartment. *At least I paid for this*, she consoled herself as she waited for Harry on the sidewalk, thinking nostalgically of the BMW she had been forced to sell last summer.

Philippe was recording it all on videotape.

The Professor watched with amusement as Harry entered the Chinese restaurant with an attractive, red-haired woman, saw the camera, then executed an immediate about-face to stand outside in the street. The Professor's American "monitor" was obviously displeased by the young Frenchman's hobby.

It almost made up for the discomfort The Professor felt at being so thoroughly recorded. But Philippe needed to play with his camera, he'd made that abundantly clear to his new-found mentor during their conversation earlier. "C'est necessaire," he had repeated emphatically, "necessaire!" So this camera was Philippe's totem – The Professor would respect it for the duration (and success) of their association.

He knew that these recordings would complicate his life afterwards, but The Professor felt only a vague connection with any plans for the future. He could not concentrate very far ahead. Four, five days had been the extent of his projections last week. Now he was finding it difficult to think beyond tomorrow.

Outside on the sidewalk, safe from the identifying eye of the video camera, Harry was engaged in a heavy argument with the woman, her angry head shakings as fiery as her hair.

"I'm not going on the Italian's camera, Ryzhaya. The Pro-fessor saw me, he knows you're with me. Make the ar-rangements: you're the local contact."

"Yes, Harry!" her accent was heavy, "and I can to destroy my cover just like you if I walk in!"

"You're the local contact."

"I can to be of no use to you, Harry, if I am recorded."

"You're the local contact."

Harry's mantra of repeated identification was not reas-suring. Ryzhaya recognized the implications: Harry would not jeopardize himself, she was expendable after this opera-tion.

If I am disposable, Ryzhaya calculated frantically while continuing her verbal barrage of objection to Harry, *how do I protect myself when Harry is gone? Who are my friends?*

"You're the local contact."

Ryzhaya bowed to the inevitable: she needed to find an advantage, if there was any, from the Italian.

Her first objective was to remove the camera as much as possible.

Philippe was taping The Professor again, trying to cap-ture the trust he felt for the man in a profile shot. Happily,

Cockney was somewhere out on the streets. The young Frenchman was surprised when the red-haired woman whispered in his ear:

"I am thinking, dear boy, that you should go to another table."

Philippe had not quite translated what she said into a meaningful phrase when The Professor nodded to him seriously.

"Do as the woman asks, Philippe."

Reluctantly, but with puppy-dog obedience, Philippe left his mentor and sat at an empty table across the small dining room. As soon as he sat down, the camcorder was on his shoulder, taping The Professor in action. The woman purposely hunched her shoulders and let her hair fall across her face, but a zoom-in caught her features with clarity more than once. Philippe's interest was in The Professor, though – Fuong Lee would need to know him – and he soon zoomed-out to embrace the two conversants in the balanced give-and-take of their discussion.

"Where is the Chinese?"

The Professor recognized her accent and spoke in Ryzhaya's native tongue:

"Before I answer your questions I want to know why I am talking to a Russian again?"

With unconcealed impatience Ryzhaya responded also in Russian: "I am *not* your mother-fucking Russian anymore

— they took that away — and I am also not connected with your new friends."

Ryzhaya's thoughts raced ahead to her own self-preservation: *Who are these "new friends"?* Harry had coached her to use the phrase. *Who am I tangling the trail to protect?*

She continued speaking to the Italian: "Anyone seeing us speak together will not draw any correct conclusions. Again: where is the Chinese?"

Oh what the fuck!, Ryzhaya thought, *What are the "correct conclusions"?* Harry had given her only a question to ask, a document to give, and an option to tender.

Ryzhaya's unspoken inquiry was not a question The Professor was asking himself. With a sigh of acceptance he *knew* what impression the red-haired woman was to meant to convey: that he was working for the Soviets. The cheating never stopped. He switched to English.

"There is a man who will perhaps meet Fuong Lee tomorrow afternoon. We will introduce that man to Philippe tonight."

"And you will persuade the Chinese then?"

She doesn't know what she's talking about, The Professor realized.

"No," he smiled. "I will 'persuade' him in the dark."

Ryzhaya tried to see an advantage in the luminous jade-hard eyes. "Here —" she said with a rush, sliding over the flimsy piece of paper that Harry had given her, "you will use this diagram to help Fuong Lee escape. Someone will be waiting there every night for the next three nights from midnight to six a.m."

The Professor opened the delicate folds of tracing paper to find the schematics for the underground water disposal system: the Americans had accepted the superiority of his proposal.

"Good," he said simply, folding the paper tightly and dropping a spoonful of hot tea upon it. The tissue paper stretched and withered under the moisture. The water disposal system: a choice of a dozen entrances leading to a hundred exits, only one known to both he and Harry.

And if he decided not to trust Harry, then there were ninety-nine alternatives. Harry *had* to trust The Professor. There was no reciprocality.

Their conversation was almost ended. Ryzhaya needed to find an advantage from the Italian. She had nothing to offer herself: she decided to claim Harry's last missive as her own. The Italian would owe *her*.

"Do you need an incentive?" she asked with an apparent personal concern for his interests.

The Italian disappointed her.

"No, I do not want more money."

But, then, that had not been the intended offer.

"Better than money."

The Professor allowed a question to enter his eyes. Ryzhaya answered it:

"Life."

"That is a generous offer. You are, perhaps, really *Eve*?"

He was not responding correctly. Ryzhaya hurriedly explained Harry's circular message, hoping that its import would raise her status in the Italian's unblinking, hooded eyes.

"Your incentive to 'persuade' Fuong Lee to return to China is that, if you fail, two governments (I do not know which) have decided that... he is better off dead."

She was receiving no response. Ryzhaya stood up, adding in Russian:

"You might want to remember that, if things become too difficult for you. You don't have to try *too* hard to persuade him."

She left the restaurant, almost bumping into the two young Chinese men entering as she did so.

So that is it then, The Professor stared hard at his fake lacquer chopstick, *I am now paid to murder*.

Philippe kept his camcorder focused tightly on the impassive face of The Professor. The familiar aggravation of Cockney's leering face lurching into the frame was not a major surprise. Cockney's companion was: Philippe had seen him earlier in the day, maybe even talked to him.

Cockney was talking to him now, making his introductions for the benefit of Philippe's camera like an MC on stage:

"Tai, m'luv," he said to his reluctant partner, "'ere's a fella what I thinks your Fuong Lee will wanta meet: an old mate from Tien An Men Square himself!" Cockney bowed sarcastically to the camera.

"Philippe, meet Tai Ma."

PLANNING
FOR TOMORROW

After Jenn left, Fuong Lee made three telephone calls from the pay phone down on the street.

Oscar How wondered why he ever listened to his son Charlie.

"Dad!" Charlie had whined yesterday, forgetting (as he almost always did) to make even a courtesy gesture to Chinese culture by adding any respectful honorifics. "C'mon, *please*, Dad. I gotta do my part!"

"Do your part and work in the store!" Oscar had shot back in Cantonese. Charlie shrank back from that.

His father snorted: Yeah, sure! The kid couldn't string together two words of formal thank-yous in his ancestral language, but he knew every word that threatened his comfortable butt.

Oscar groaned inwardly at how cliché their family discussions had become. We're the sitcom family of the future, he rebuked himself, first it was the white Nelsons, then the black Jeffersons, now the yellow Hows. And every one gets a stupid son!

"Dad, I need your *permission*."

Maybe, Oscar thought, *I wouldn't mind Charlie speaking only English if he didn't sound like a Valley Guy from Glendale.* (OK, so the Hows *lived* in Glendale, he conceded – but the *store* was still in Chinatown! That's where our roots are. OK, again, so maybe our roots in California go back a hundred and fifty years – no reason to forget Chinese. OK, so maybe we never could read Chinese even in China, still...)

Still, Oscar consoled himself, Charlie, stupid Charlie, knew more about modern-day China than his father, or his grandfather, or even his *great*-grandfather ever could begin to consider.

"About the meeting, Dad..."

My boy Charlie's only stupid when I think about him running the family business: he knows more about Computer Science than I know about the price of wholesale textiles – and that's my business!

"You're not bringing in any workers for the store today anyway."

"It's New Year, Charlie. Who'd come in?"

"That's my point, Dad: you don't need it and I got

some friends who have to meet sort of in private."

"What sort of 'private'? You're not gambling?!" Oscar's cousin made a fortune fronting gambling rooms, but he paid a second fortune in protection, and a third fortune in buying respectability. Oscar did not want any part of that, no matter how many children he had to put through college.

"No, Dad, no gambling. Just... talking. You're going to the parade, aren't you?"

"Yes."

"Just talking, that's all."

"What time? I can drop off the keys."

"Sort of all day. Could I have the keys now?"

"Here –" a reflexive toss of the key and a sudden thought: "What do you mean 'all day'?"

"Some of the guys, well, *one* of the guys, really, we really want to talk to him a lot and he, sort of, didn't really tell us if he was really coming or when, really, just sort of said to Tai that maybe he'd come there if we were there. In the empty store."

"*Really* definite plans, Charlie," Oscar could not restrain his good-natured contempt for the logic of his very own Val-Guy. "And you're just asking me this this morning?"

"He only called Tai last night about sort of coming here."

Charlie sat rigidly upright on the bundled tack of silk bolting. Sharon was pissed off at Tai and, no matter how right she was, Charlie was glad she wasn't yelling at him with the same vehemence. Even if Sharon was the best looker on Spring Street, she was a bitch when was ragging on a guy.

"You're a stupid *ass*, Tai," Sharon mixed her Cantonese and English adjectives freely; the insults stung even more that way. "I don't care *what* your butt-brain thinks!"

Tai and Sharon could have been sitting at the long, rectangular cutting table – the chairs Charlie had brought in from his Dad's office were comfortable – but the two verbal combatants remained standing. They had remained standing since Tai arrived bringing the French kid with him.

"We don't even know if Fuong Lee will show up here today," Tai said defensively. "And, look: I didn't bring the Hong Kong guy, okay?! O – K?!"

"You shouldn't have brought *him*!" Sharon asserted with an aggressive jerk of her head pointing towards the office where Charlie and Tai had unceremoniously taken the French visitor in question and locked him in.

Tai knew he had made a mistake bringing a stranger without asking Fuong Lee beforehand. But the guy from Hong Kong had been so funny at first – sounded super-Britsh, y'know – and then so insistent! And this French student really seemed to know Fuong Lee. Besides, this paranoia was OK for some people, but Tai wasn't hiding his beliefs from anybody.

"You listening to me, Tai? What's the sense of security if you go and–"

"Yeah, yeah, yeah!" he shot back with annoyance at Sharon, tired of her tirade. "Of course *you* know better. Tits and ass really make a bold political statement!"

"They can."

Perhaps if the words had come from Sharon – or the reticent Charlie – the three would have erupted into a new round of argument, instead of dropping into the uncomfortable silence that followed the simple statement's utterance.

But it was Fuong Lee who said the words.

It was Fuong Lee – not Sharon, or Charlie, or any other student – who was standing in the doorway watching them argue with not-necessarily-humorous bemusement.

He stepped into the storeroom and spoke directly to Tai Ma in his most raucous Shanghai street slang:

"Melons and sauce sell it all. At least that's what they say in American advertising." Then he added in English for Charlie's benefit:

For Sharon's benefit:

To instruct:

"Sex Sells: Cars, Alcohol... Politics? – I think 'yes'."

Fuong Lee turned his charismatic charms on Sharon

and asked respectfully in Mandarin: "Are you ready for tonight?"

Sharon dropped her eyes and answered in a delicately slurred Mandarin, "Yes, szer-fu."

"Lee Fuong," he corrected her respectful honorific with reserved familiarity.

She thanked him for the honor with the trace of a smile.

"Then, Sharon," he continued, "if the judges are in-tel-ligent observers of beauty, you will be the reigning Miss Chinatown who stands by my side tonight."

Sharon felt gratified by the compliment, but proudly answered: "Five others have agreed to stand by you – if they win."

"Thank you!" Fuong Lee said grandly to the storeroom at large, breaking into a relaxed English that embraced all three comfortably with his shared concerns. "The Goddess of Democracy has to have *some* good luck on her side finally: I am tired of losing!"

But his spell could not override his followers' anxiety. Fuong Lee quickly noted the lack of shared group enthusiasm.

"Sharon? Tai? You were arguing – why?"

Tai (to his credit, Sharon noted) did not duck taking responsibility for his actions.

"I've – brought someone to see you," he said hesitantly,

but without fear.

Fuong Lee growled a quick Shanghai curse of disdain before catching himself. "I don't let *you* know where I live," he said with taut-jawed annoyance, "why do you think I want *others* finding me!?"

"Because he was with you at Tien An Men Square. You shared his room."

"Only one..."

The anger had not dripped from Fuong Lee's emotions as he began to realize:

Philippe – ?

"He speaks Chinese even if he is French."

Philippe!

The others could see the look of conquest fire into Fuong Lee's eyes.

"Where is he?" Fuong Lee demanded, looking at the bolts of cloth Charlie sat upon as if they were hiding a Frenchman. "Philippe!" he called out.

"Lee Fuong," Sharon attempted to suggest in Mandarin, "maybe it is not a good idea –"

"Ridiculous," Fuong Lee was laughing with anticipated delight, charging around the storeroom, looking.

"– he is coming from the mainland –"

"Philippe is The Eyes!" He must be in the office, of

course! Fuong Lee charged past the Americans. "He is my Eyes!"

The office door was bolted shut with a small combination lock.

"Is he in there?" Fuong Lee demanded.

"Hey, Philippe!" he called through the door as Charlie rushed to twist out the three-digit combination.

"Hurry up!" Fuong Lee demanded.

Charlie had the lock off in record time, though it was almost ripped out of his fingers by Fuong Lee's swinging the door wide.

The young French student stood nervously in the middle of the small, cramped office. There were no chairs, Charlie had pulled those out to the storeroom.

The overwhelming exuberance of Fuong Lee disappeared on the instant.

Both Philippe and Fuong Lee were caught up in the experience of a phenomenon usually reserved for their elders, the gap between nostalgia-inflated memory – and experience. In their eight months apart each boy had raised his missing friend to a height impossible to reach. Philippe would not have been surprised if Fuong Lee had brought his own personal burst of sunshine into the room. And, in return, Fuong Lee had expectations of hearing the cheers of a thousand supporters usher forth from the Frenchman's mouth. Neither one could live up to the expectation.

And yet...

And yet, there was...

Philippe saw the well-remembered confidence and inner strength radiate from Fuong Lee as he burst into the office. The other Chinese students behind this leader were so weak in comparison. So obviously without his vision. Followers.

For his part, Fuong Lee once again felt the dependence of the young Westerner. The video camera, Fuong Lee's omnipresent "Eyese," was curled familiarly in Philippe's hand. The Frenchman's face carried unreserved, unquestioning, unharassing respect – and love.

These emotional realities washed over both of them with a power that was stronger than their ill-conceived nostalgias.

The two boys jumped into each others arms, whooping disgracefully in the pure, unembarrassed joy of seeing one another safe, alive, here!, now! They performed an impromptu, ecstatic war dance of survivors' victory for the benefit of the astonished Sharon, Charlie and Tai, who had never seen Fuong Lee react with any but the most controlled emotional response. (Even when he was impassioned, some had noted, Fuong Lee's fever was self-willed and intricately precise.) The Colonel would have been gratified by the abandon with which Fuong Lee threw away his months-long discipline of caution at the sight of his old friend.

Perhaps, thought The Professor as he observed the students during the remainder of the afternoon, this is what Philippe's "understanding" Colonel had counted upon: the impulsive buoyancy of youth.

Fuong Lee led his followers in a mad charge through Chinatown that day, suddenly filled with an overwhelming confidence of success that he had not felt since the heady days prior to Tien An Men. Better than that, he felt invulnerable. He walked openly down the streets this day – and no one stopped him! The Chinatown parade assembled, marched, and disintegrated into its corner celebrations of the New Year – and Fuong Lee began his assault on the citizens' complacency with an open contempt for interference.

The Professor enjoyed the performance's manifestations: they reminded him of the '60s foolishness that had been so much fun to play.

Fuong Lee kissed Sharon good-bye and sent her off to join the other beauty contestants, then led his stalwart mini-band (duly recorded by Philippe's camera) on an aggressive poster-plastering sortie. A "Buy American – In Chinatown" poster was messily obscured by a baker's dozen of stapled-on handbills demanding:

WHY

NO GODDESS OF DEMOCRACY

IN CHINATOWN?

Careful not to disrupt the Parade per se, Fuong Lee col-orfully engaged small groups of bystanders in ribald derisions of the Chinatown Chamber of Commerce –

"Hey, I understand their lack of balls in standing up to the Beijing pricks."

– He criticized the Chinatown elders in colorful Shanghai epithetical "Confucianisms" mixed with hellfire student English. Always with a sense of knowing when to quit, holding his impromptu audiences in a sure grip.

And playing for the camera, his Eyes. Philippe.

Tired of watching the ineffective shenanigans, The Pro-fessor left surveillance to Cockney, returning to the previous night's restaurant to enjoy a bowl of their shark-fin soup. It was impossible to find such soup in Italy. Not enough Chinese. Except, perhaps, in Milan – good Chinese food there. Who knew why?

The early-setting winter sun brought darkness down on the streets at six. Philippe was still breathless from this non-stop reunion with his old friend. He had not yet had time to talk to Fuong Lee about the Colonel and the Colonel's trust in the self-exiled student leader. Or about The Professor, a man of decision, like Fuong Lee himself. Or about Cockney.

Cockney came to Philippe's thoughts with a sudden jolt when they met face-to-face on the corner of Broadway and Alpine Street.

Fuong Lee was leading them past a children's show of dragons and drums, through a small crowd of recent Hong Kong immigrants. The young people were dancing a hip-hop to black music on the street. Cockney was there, dancing with total immersion in the movement – until he saw Philippe.

He turned and smiled, then ignored the Frenchman in favor of his beautiful skirted-to-the-crotch partner. The message was delivered.

CONTEST

"Kung Hay Fat Choy! Happy New Year, Miss Chinatown! LET THE CONTEST BEGIN!"

Sam watched the Asian meat market with a jaundiced eye. Literally. The infection had set in sometime overnight while he slept uneasily. Except for the fact that it was too early in the year to take a medical leave, Sgt. Sam Williams would have signed-in for shift and signed-out sick with the same flourish of his pen.

There was also the fact that his partner had asked him to stay on duty.

"I've got to go to Chinatown tonight," Jenn said, "You're my partner. I don't want to go with a stranger."

"Don't go, then," Sam had answered uncooperatively, remembering the Collections message on his answering machine and knowing that he could not afford to take the night off anyway. But he persisted peevishly, "We both don't go. It's basically an elaborate security detail in Chinatown tonight. We've got real crimes to investigate."

"I've got to."

"Why?"

Jenn explained. Sam was her partner, she could trust him.

Now Sam knew why.

The knowledge did not make him feel any better.

Now Sam was with Jenn at the Miss Chinatown contest. Watching the obsequious Master of Ceremonies expand his overblown introduction to fulfill the expectations of the local-station-and-Public-Access-cable television cameras taping the concert did not improve his view of the world, either. At least Jenn had picked an observation post at the back of the theater; Sam could yawn with comfortable frequency without incurring angry glares for his rudeness.

Too bad the aisle door had to slam into his back with regularity.

"Hey!" The newest entrant pushed harder than previous late arrivals had. Sam felt the brass door handle dig into his kidneys. "Sergeant Williams! Detective Luck! Howareya?!"

It was Patrolman Rodney Sinclair. Sam's evening was complete.

"On duty," was Sam's terse reply, trying to focus his infection-clouded right eye on the current swimsuit-clad beauty gliding down the runway. Legs up to her armpits. Wow.

"On duty?" The uniformed patrolman spoke a fraction too loudly for the situation. "You mean they give you plainclothes routine security details, too?"

Sam saw Jenn's neck tense up.

Should I tell Rodney why we're really here?, he considered. *He owes us... No. I don't want to owe* him.

"You know," Sam explained with an apparently relaxed smile, "all the fun can't go to the rank-and-file."

Jenn's neck untensed. She nodded her gratitude.

Rodney was purviewing the contest with his own criterion for success. He particularly liked smiles. There were lots and lots of smiles up on the runway. Rodney engaged in a moment of private fantasy, which he shared with the detectives.

"Well, if the ladies get rowdy, I'll go up there and start with the handcuffs."

"Eh," Sam would not betray Jenn, but he could not let a fellow officer walk into a situation unprepared, "they may." Jenn looked at Sam with surprise.

"Huh?" Rodney's disbelief was generic.

"Some 'rumor' of a disruption. Outside."

"Whaaat?! Jesus, now I have to go make rounds! Why didn't they send more guys and tell us in advance?!" Rodney stomped out of the theater grumbling about the unfairness of having to miss the beauty contest because nobody in administration could talk to the cop on the street.

Jenn relaxed once more, understanding that Sam was not hanging her out to dry. She had confided in her partner again – and he had come through.

"You know, I'm listening to Rodney and I'm asking the same questions he is, too," Sam's voice was quietly directed to her ear. It was so smoothly polite that Jenn knew he was intensely angry. "Questions like: why didn't we inform anybody else?"

"*We're* here. We'll keep things from getting out of hand." She could not look at Sam.

"You *want* it to happen, don't you?"

"Some things have to be said, Sam!"

"Yeah." The word fell with deadly finality. "Well, I know you want to believe it."

There was an edge of defeat to Sam's voice that was new. It startled Jenn to the point of looking directly back at her partner despite her own discomfort with the situation she had placed them both in.

Sam did not see her. He was staring blankly at the colorful stage, where a trio of smiling "Empresses" were finishing a cutsy-slick song. "Do I have time to go call Marie?" he asked upon noticing that Jenn was watching him and not the stage.

"Until they announce the winner."

"I'll be back in plenty of time."

His kidneys ached. The different waters filtering through his system in the past five days had strained the organ's tolerance to its limit. The Professor had known that the last two glasses of water would send him to the water closet again, but he needed to wash the taste from his mouth. The taste would not go away. His own bile was judging him.

I have to call The Professor. The *ordure* from Hong Kong is following me – I have to call The Professor. Fuong Lee will not like the *ordure* from Hong Kong. I have to call The Professor.

"Come on, Philippe!" Fuong Lee's animated speech had captivated a new crowd of young people, he wanted his Eyes to record it.

"I need to make a telephone call."

Disappointment. A moment of searching. "Over there!" Fuong Lee shouted, pointing at the pagoda-roofed tourist attraction of a pay telephone box. Then he forgot Philippe for the immediate priority of his new potential followers.

The formica-topped table was polished with lemon oil after every customer. It gleamed with a luster more deep than the imitation lacquer wooden screens behind each table booth. The Professor was careful not to spill a drop of soup onto the flawless sheen. Machine-made, with more perfection than any hand could match, he mused. Look at the little flecks of fool's gold sprinkled in among the red swirls and black undercoat. Marred by an insensitive knife's scratching down into the surface over here. And over there. Perfection is a very transitory condition.

The telephone next to the front counter began to ring. No one was at the cash register. The owner had explained:

"Everyone call in sick today. Sick as hell! I see them in the Parade! I cook myself today and you have the best food in Chinatown!"

Actually, no. The Professor would have to disappoint the owner if he was asked point-blank about the quality of the meal: the food had been better last night when made by the regular cook.

The telephone rang for the fourth time, and the owner rushed out through the swinging kitchen doors to capture the unknown caller before he hung up.

The soup was passable, though.

The owner looked frantically around the sparsely occupied dining room – his fried won tons were already sizzling in oil – which one of the customers looked like he taught at a university?

"I have a call for a professor!?" he called out, giving up. He put the telephone receiver next to the cash register and scurried back into the kitchen. The won tons were beginning to burn and the smell slipped out the doors as he opened them. "For the professor!" he called out over his retreating shoulder.

The Professor continued to eat his soup carefully as he let his eyes wander over the other patrons' reaction to this announcement. When he was certain that no one was watching to see who answered the call, he wiped his spoon, placed it beside the bowl, and leaned across the short aisle to pick up the receiver.

Philippe's voice hit his ear with a blast, crying his complaints over the street noise behind him. He listened to Philippe with the faux respect expected of a so-called "sympathetic ear."

The Professor understood Philippe's fears regarding Cockney's likely impression on Fuong Lee. He listened with interest to the young man's jumbled endorsement of his friend's activities that day, and he approved of the fact that the Colonel's respected French emissary had had the discretion to restrain his impulse to blurt everything out to the talented student dissident as long as so many others were around.

"I would suggest, Philippe, that you not discuss your innovative proposal to Fuong Lee yet, then."

"But I have to tell Fuong about how important he is to China!" Philippe was worried: Fuong Lee was talking to a new group, he needed to record it!

"Tell him, then." The Professor put a challenging edge to his voice. "Go ahead. *Tell* Fuong Lee about the Colonel and myself in front of the Americans." Now he added a bitter ruefulness to his tone. "Then see what they do... They may look Chinese, but you will see with whose ears they listen to your words." It was overwrought rhetoric and The Professor knew it.

It worked on Philippe and The Professor knew that, too.

"I... will wait until you think it is right," the boy stuttered, wishing he could be next to, share, Fuong Lee's confidence at this moment. Or be with The Professor. Everyone was so *certain*.

"I will trust *your* instincts," he heard The Professor reassure.

He could not, of course, see the certainty in The Professor's eyes that, now, Philippe would say *nothing*, would act merely as the beacon to guide them to some time and place where Fuong Lee would be found – without a surrounding crowd. Some abductors preferred the anonymity of the crowd. The Professor did not. People might be hurt – someone always was – but the damage could be kept minimal if the abduction was timed well. Fuong Lee might be wary, but today his guard was down. Would his antennae be alert again tomorrow?

"Stay with Fuong Lee, Philippe. When the right time comes, you will talk and I will be there to help him escape."

Tonight.

ALLEY OOP

Rodney had always liked Asian girls. It wasn't a color thing, or an eye thing or any of the easy things everyone always put two and two together to figure out it meant. Rodney just liked the way they were altogether.

Not that he ever talked to Asian girls. Just enjoyed the fantasy. Standing at the back of the theater watching the Miss Chinatown contest was pretty much of a fantasy fulfillment.

Walking around and around the outside of the theater at almost ten on a winter's night was pretty much of a fantasy damper.

Nobody milling around in front of the theater – not counting the two Teamsters driving trucks for competing television stations. Left side of the building – OK. Back alley...

"Hi, son, whatcha doing?"

Tai realized that he must have been daydreaming. He was completely surprised by the appearance of the tall black policeman.

"Umm, just waiting around. My cousin's inside."

Probably the truth, Rodney calculated. Any disrupters would barge in in a larger group. Better to check anyway.

"What's your name?"

Tai was afraid. If his parents found out about this...

"Ma," he heard himself saying before he had time to catch himself. "*Charles* Ma!" he corrected the error immediately.

Rodney smiled: people always became nervous near cops. This kid was probably double-parked around the corner and figuring he was going to get a ticket. Not yet. Got to keep an eye out for demonstrators first.

"What's your cousin's name, Chuck?"

"She – Sharon." Hey, she'd be on TV anyway, everybody'd know her name.

Rodney recognized the name.

"Sharon Ma?" Eyes to kill, even from a hundred feet back in the theater.

"Y–yeah."

"Your cousin's a front runner, Chuck. Wish her luck." *Maybe, just maybe, I'll slide on back here after the contest*, thought Rodney, talk to maybe the new Miss Chinatown. After all, I'm a friend of her cousin.

The Chevette was not parked far from the theater, but The Professor wanted it at hand.

He also wanted Cockney out of his face for a few minutes. The Professor didn't need Cockney anymore. Didn't want him. Not too close, anyway.

Because he knew where Fuong Lee would be at a few minutes past ten this evening: standing near the backstage door preparing to disrupt the Miss Chinatown contest. There would not be many people around him – except for Philippe. There would not be a better time to "persuade" Fuong Lee. But not with Cockney around. The Professor sent his Hong Kong assistant over to the parking lot to fetch the Chevette.

A squat Laughing Buddha sat on the sidewalk corner, gathering pennies and nickels tossed into his lap for New Year's good luck.

Reflexively The Professor started to bless himself: in the orange street light, from the rear, the fat, hunched shoulders momentarily fooled him into seeing the back silhouette of a crude pietà. Madonna and dying Son. The Professor checked his gesture in the middle of the cross, then, remembering the real church he had visited earlier in the day deliberately resumed the act of blessing himself. This Buddha had more intrinsic God in him than the bright, spacious, unmysterious church The Professor had entered. There had been no shadows, no dark corners illuminated by cheap paraffin candles, where flickering lights made statues smile and gave God a place to hide. What was the use of religion if not for the mystery? There was certainly no hope in the Church.

The Professor turned a hard eye to Cockney in time to prevent the Chinese thug from honking the car horn to announce his arrival. *Different styles here,* he thought, and The Professor allowed himself to be reassured by the uncomfortable gouge of the pistol he had tucked into his waistband at the small of his back. He had worked with people he distrusted before. This time there was more anxiety than before, though: The Professor had never felt like one of *them* before.

"We will drive slowly around the theater until we see Philippe arrive with his friend," he instructed carefully, "and then we will introduce ourselves to Fuong Lee."

Philippe was excited: soon he would be joining Fuong Lee on the stage in this most audacious of political acts. This would be his record, as even now it was.

"Ni how bai how!" Fuong called out to the silhouette standing in front of the metal stage door marked with a huge "No Entry" sign painted in bright red letters. "How are you?" he repeated for the benefit of the camcorder.

Tai Ma and Charlie How stepped more conveniently into the light to answer:

"Hun haow!" they cried out in the broadly exaggerated style of Chinese audience approval. "Very good!"

The images of Fuong Lee and Charlie bounced wildly in the viewfinder as Philippe hurried to keep pace with their excited, skipping run towards the theater's backstage entrance. Tai stood in the background as a steady point of reference, clapping his hands in anticipated fun. Fuong almost cartoon skidded to a stop in the alleyway, turning to face the video camera directly:

"OK, Philippe, now you can use your camera for real: I want you to record our 'visit' to Miss Chinatown." He turned away from the camera. "Have they announced the winner yet?"

"Any minute," Tai assured him, slapping Charlie on the shoulder with a hopping excitement. Charlie, as always, said almost nothing, but his face glowed with the same spark of adrenaline-fueled energy.

None of them paid any attention as the Chevette drove quietly around the corner and stopped at the mouth of the alley. Their attention was focussed solely on the metal Exit door.

"The door is closed, Tai," Fuong Lee was observing with displeasure. "Locked."

"I paid a guy backstage to open it when they announce the winner. Said I was bringing flowers."

"And if he forgets?"

"All he does is sit back next to the door. I gave him twenty bucks. He'll wait for me to knock." Tai Ma pressed his ear against the sound-absorbing door.

Philippe heard the cars doors shut behind him, but it signified nothing. He did not notice the new arrivals until he saw Fuong Lee jerk his head frantically towards the mouth of the alley. Then Philippe followed the direction with his own erratic camera movement.

The Professor was standing near the Chevette. The merde from Hong Kong was with him, sitting in the driver's seat.

"Let us put down the camera now, Philippe," The Professor said quietly, almost too quietly for the camcorder's microphone to pick up. He walked over to Philippe and gently took the camera out of his hands, placing it on the flat, closed top of a garbage dumpster. He did not think to push any of the buttons, and so the machine continued to transcribe its electronic impulses.

"It is time for introductions."

In the two dimensional world of the video camera, turned suddenly ninety degrees on its side, Tai Ma and Charlie How stood mute bystanders watching the approach of the Europeans to Fuong Lee. In the viewfinder The Professor and Philippe appeared to be walking down from out of the sky and into a horizontal world, where the dissident refugee lay on his back looking up at them. The disjointed perspective did not altogether differ from that of Fuong Lee at the moment.

"Philippe?" he appealed to his follower for explanation.

The Professor, too, turned his eyes to the young Frenchman.

Philippe, now the center of both his idols' attentions,

felt suddenly shy. An anxious wish thrust itself into his thoughts: *If only the Colonel were here!* He grabbed at the thought in sullen desperation.

"Philippe." Fuong Lee spoke with patient strength.

The Professor listened to his tone of intuitive authority with approval. *The Chinese is good*, he thought objectively. Perhaps Philippe's patrons understand that as well. The Professor's eyes did not waver in their focus on his young colleague.

Philippe saw that he must answer, must explain. What were the words again? How to say it?

"Fuong Lee..." His voice was weak, he cursed himself, not strong and persuasive as it should be! "I want you to come back to China."

It came out as a demand.

Philippe did not want it to come out as a demand.

"AND THE WINNER IS – SHARON MA!"

Sam watched the most attractive girl on the stage clasp her head in her hands in the classic surprise pose of beauty contests. *Do they rehearse that?*, he mused, closing his infected right eye and focussing on the almost-crowned new queen with his overworked left. He leaned his head close to Jenn's and asked with vague mockery:

"Do I close both eyes now, partner?"

Jenn's eyes darted to the curtain screening off the wings

315

of the stage. Through the pumped up amplification of the pit orchestra she strained to hear the expected backstage shouts that would be a likely prelude to the demonstrators' entrance onto the stage.

Behind her, Rodney nodded his approval at the judges' selection. Then he slipped back out of the theater: he had only nipped in to see who won. Now he could stroll slowly around the outside again and visit his "friend" Chuck Ma. It was nice to know the cousin of a beauty queen.

Sam whispered to Jenn: "Well, Officer-most-likely-not-to-receive-the-Chief's-Award-for-Riot-Control? When the fun begins, do we stand here, twiddle our thumbs, turn a blind eye, or – ? Or – ? I'm waiting to know..."

"Give him his one minute for the cameras, Sam. He's earned that. Tien An Men earned him that."

Sam turned to face his partner: her face was etched with lines of anxiety. "You've got a way with telling the simple truth sometimes, Chinese lady."

"You are not serious, Philippe." Fuong Lee was neither angry nor accusing – just strong.

Philippe felt himself hesitate yet again. He looked to The Professor for support, but began speaking before he could read the message in the older man's eyes:

You have brought us to Fuong Lee, Philippe, don't you realize what you have done?

"I am serious! They – we – need you as a spokesman there, where you can help the liberal forces for democratic communism inside the government."

Fuong Lee was embarrassed by Philippe's naiveté.

"I hope to change things from here," he answered in the pedantic tones of a minister correcting an errant child.

"'Men in exile feed on dreams of hope,'" The Professor observed, dropping his hands into his pockets, the signal for Cockney to leave the car and join him.

Rodney saw the Chinese kid step out of the Chevette and disappear into the backstage alley. At least he figured it was a kid: these Chinese were always looking years younger than they really were. But the car was blocking the alley, a definite ticketing offense. Rodney did not feel like giving offense tonight, not with Miss Chinatown's cousin waiting by the backstage entrance. He turned away from the alley and headed out on a reverse round of the theater. No tickets for now. Give 'em a few minutes. If it was still there in five minutes, then too bad.

Sharon felt divided loyalties.

Despite her purest intentions, the new Miss Chinatown felt proud of the honor. The cheesy crown looked magnificently regal in the spotlights, accompanied by a roar of applause as it was placed on her head. The Queen's Walk down the runway was just beginning, and she felt the crowd's approval start to immerse her in its warmth. Where was Fuong Lee?

If he waits too long, Sharon thought pathetically beneath her glowing smile, *if he waits too long it will break my heart to lose this title!* Without intending to give away the surprise, she turned her head towards the wings – there was no one rushing towards her from backstage. Where was Fuong Lee?

"There's nothing happening," Jenn said with disbelief.

Sam's attention was on Miss Chinatown: her face, too, echoed Jenn's concern. If the demonstration goes bust, if there's some violence...

"It was supposed to happen now," his partner explained, starting to walk down the wall aisle towards the stage. "Something's wrong."

Sam, immediately behind her, shared the intuition.

Fuong Lee knew who was controlling Philippe. His accusation was directed at The Professor.

"You are feeding him lies," he announced in defense of his friend.

The Professor shrugged: he had not yet *had* to lie to Philippe.

Fuong Lee turned again to the young Frenchman.

"Philippe: I cannot go back. I can never go back."

"You have to, Fuong!" Philippe was near tears. "You can't betray us!"

"And – maybe – they will not betray *you*, Mr. Lee."

The Professor's comment shocked Fuong Lee in its bald objectivity.

"I have no promise," The Professor continued, "I only think logic. You are talented. They should use you. I will never say you resist."

And that was the end of his speech. Fuong Lee would never know if the European had more to say. His own followers had finally found their tongues.

"Get out of here," Tai spat in Philippe's direction. Abandoning his position by the door, he pulled Charlie with him to stand in front of The Professor and Cockney. "Get out of here!"

Fuong Lee touched Tai's arm – "Don't" – but was shaken off.

"No!" Tai angrily shouted, pointing at Philippe, "I'm sorry, Fuong Lee, he can be your friend, but he's trouble now. We lost our friends, we lost our country – he can't talk about betrayal! They can't talk to us!"

"Philippe was at Tien An Men with me," Fuong Lee said in bitter remonstrance, "you were sitting in your American living rooms watching TV."

"You know what I mean: we are Chinese, he's–"

Cockney was bored.

"Forgive me for interruptin' the dialectics, like, but I'm not gettin' paid by the hour here." He said it loudly and

319

disruptively, with a respectful bow to The Professor, "Am I, Professor?".

"No, you're not," The Professor agreed. There would be no useful discussion from this point.

"Right. 'At's wha I thought. HEEYAA!" With sudden, concentrated violence Cockney whip-kicked his foot into Tai Ma's chin, sending the outraged defender of Fuong Lee reeling backwards.

An instant later the quiet Charlie How found himself doubled over and gasping for air on the ground, the impacted target of a reverse kick into his stomach.

Cockney began bouncing on the balls of his feet, his hands upraised to chest level in an open-palmed boxer stance, his extremities filled with happy adrenalin.

"I quite like this," he smiled to The Professor, "I really do. I think I've found my modus vivendi."

Then, with savage accuracy, Cockney skipped over to Tai Ma, who was making a struggling attempt to return to his feet,   and viciously knifed a foot into the young man's ribs. Several darting kicks followed, suspending Tai Ma momentarily in the air from the blow of each impact, until Cockney let up and his victim fell to the ground senseless.

The Professor found that he could watch this quick, almost bloodless violence impassively – he had no liking for the two spoiled American boys – but, standing next to him, Philippe could not restrain an expression of horror from crossing his features. He almost cheered when the hapless Charlie charged from behind and plowed his head into Cockney's kidneys.

If Charlie had ever known how to fight seriously, or been frightened enough to run from the alley, he might have stood a chance of survival. Instead, looking down at the tumble of limbs that Cockney presented after the heavy blow from Charlie's head butt, the merchant's son looked to Fuong Lee for further directions. He panted heavily and wobbled unsteadily on his feet. He waited too long. Then, seeing that Fuong Lee was as paralyzed with indecision as he, Charlie turned again to face the Hong Kong thug and began a ragged attack.

Cockney needed a few moments to regain his breath, but he did not lose his poise now that he was aware of the threat. Charlie attacked with poor technique fueled by hot emotions – Cockney retreated with tactical finesse. Within seconds he had defused the young American's energy. Then he began to counterattack.

This time The Professor winced.

"Growl!" Cockney taunted, raising his hands to slap away Charlie's wild blows in an angry parody of a bad Kung Fu flick. "Ohh!" he cried, "Bruce Lee is comin' for me! Rowll!" he roared like a mock tiger, beginning to bounce again, slapping Charlie across the face with one hand every time he blocked a blow with the other. "Oi! Watch out, Bruce, I'm a dragon now, I'm a dragon now!"

It was a game now for Cockney, and Charlie saw too late that he needed to run away, to escape the alley, if he was to help Fuong Lee or save himself. Cockney did not let him.

"Stay on your feet, luv!" he cried, springing in front of his woozy opponent every time Charlie made a move towards the mouth of the alley. Cockney began "whipping" the young man's head with his hands – until Charlie covered his face defensively, crying in pain.

"Sorry, luv, no quarter given." Cockney was cold-eyed behind the sarcasm.

Then he blasted Charlie with a series of blows intended to inflict pain and, finally, mercifully, laid him flat.

Cockney stood over Charlie for several seconds, bouncing lightly on his toes. Unlike in the movies, he knew that these two people at his feet would not rise up again. If they were still breathing now, it was only from reflex action. They would not be in a few minutes. He had never killed anyone directly before. The adrenalin still pumped through his arteries and veins, making the blood vessels pop up near the surface of the skin. Cockney felt strong and powerful. It was a great feeling.

Fuong Lee wondered why the revulsion he felt was objective and not personal. He looked at Philippe standing next to the European, tears flushing in streams down his face. The European's face looked to Fuong Lee's imagination as one that had just suffered a sincere disappointment. The expression did not seem in keeping with the situation.

The Professor willed himself into action.

"Come along," he announced.

Cockney snapped out of his reverie.

"Right." Without a glance back at the bodies he rushed over to the Chevette and climbed into the driver's seat.

"Philippe." The Professor was still understanding, he did not upbraid the messenger for failing to convince the dissident leader.

Philippe nodded. Lost in the situation, he stepped over to the dumpster and retrieved his camcorder, without thinking he put the viewfinder up to his right eye. In the safe black and white world framed there he found Fuong Lee looking at The Professor.

"Do I have a choice." Fuong's words were not a question. He allowed the European to lead him over to the maroon car.

The stagehand mumbled. Jenn hated mumbling. Sam hated not understanding a word they were saying even when the stagehand did not mumble.

He hated uncertainty, also, and there was a lot of uncertainty about this whole situation.

"Are you sure they just didn't get cold feet?" he demanded of his partner, blinking his infected eye uncontrollably and trying to find a volume level that could compete with the blaring pit band without calling attention to the fact that two police officers were unsuccessfully searching for "missing" demonstrators backstage.

"I don't know, I... don't." The stagehand mumbled again and hurried off to hide behind the cyclorama and get as far away from the Exit door as possible. He fingered the money in his pocket and wondered if it had been worth the possibility of losing his job. *I hope those kids keep their mouths shut!*, he worried, *I did*. He knew that nobody would believe he had accepted their explanation at face value. Sure, it was the face on a twenty dollar bill he had accepted, but it was still unquestioning trust in the younger generation. Nobody trusted anybody anymore!

Despite the increasingly deteriorating condition of his eyesight, Sam had not missed the covert glances the retreating stagehand had cast over at his deserted post by the Exit. He wanted one parting shot at Jenn before he acted on his hunch, though:

"I think we will talk about conflict of interest when this night is over, Detective." The rueful smile and use of rank identification did not ease Jenn's distressed peace of mind.

"Let's try behind the hall," Sam added, indicating the door.

Damn, the car was still there!

Rodney pulled out his ticketing book with a sharp

gesture of annoyance. *I gave 'em five minutes, now they got-ta pay,* he thought regretfully, certain that this would put a damper on his relationship with the cousin of the New Miss Chinatown. He began writing the license number onto the ticket, still standing under the illumination of a street light at the corner of the theater.

As Rodney looked up from describing the car – Chevette, maroon – he saw that the car was filling up. It was a mixed group: two Chinese, two whites. The apparent host of the group was ushering the others in.

"Hold it right there, mister!"

The Professor was surprised: Rodney's Traffic Control-trained voice echoed forcefully down the half block of back street. But, The Professor noted with relief, the black policeman was not at an angle where he could see the whole alley – and the two bodies.

Yet.

"I saw this car parked here," Rodney called out, finishing up his vehicle description, "nobody was loading, and it's not a Loading Zone anyway."

The Professor had no worries about the ticket, or the car being identified – it would not exist by tomorrow anyway – but he did not want further incident. He began to walk towards the policeman.

"I will come–"

"Wait right there," Rodney cut him off. "I'm comin':

I wanta check those headlights, taillights and brake lights." *Might as well do it all*, he thought, wiping wistful hopes of a conversation with Miss Chinatown from his mind.

The Professor stopped at the Chevette's rear bumper, letting his shoulders sag. There was no hope, then: the advancing policeman would very shortly see the two fallen Chinese. The Professor looked up at the sky.

It was a full moon again. So soon?

It was a radiant moon.

"La luna..."

The policeman was only meters away: any moment he would see the carnage in the alley. The Professor let his right hand slide under his waistband and edge its way behind his back. He began walking towards the black man. What a beautiful moon.

"La bella luna..."

Rodney did not like civilians leaving their cars. "I told you just to stay put, mister."

"Che bella luna..."

The dude sounded foreign. "Just wait for me and –"

"Che pazza bella luna..."

"– I'll give you your ticket."

"Che pazza bella luna..."

The pistol was in The Professor's hand and its small

caliber explosion made only a tiny crack into the night air as he shot the black policeman. Rodney's eyes opened wide in surprise and sudden, silent death.

The Professor could not look at the body. He raised his eyes again.

"Che pazza bella luna."

What a beautiful crazy moon.

He heard the heavy metal lock of the stage door Exit fall heavily from its bolt slot. It was only a few steps back into the car.

Sam pushed against the spring-resistant door with his shoulder and let Jenn step out first, in case her "boyfriend" was skittishly waiting there. He waited a count, then followed.

Neither he nor Jenn had adjusted their eyes to the reduced light yet, but both could see the man stepping into the passenger seat of the small four door – with Fuong Lee sitting in the back seat behind him.

"Halt!" Sam shouted reflexively, not clear about the reason. "Police!"

"Fuong Lee!" Jenn called out. Would he recognize her from so far away? She stepped out into the alley.

"Head for the river," The Professor commanded Cockney.

"Jesus Christ!" Jenn cried, looking down. Blood had begun seeping out Charlie's nose and ears. He would die any minute now.

Cockney turned the key and the Chevette's ignition cranked reliably to life. He jammed his foot three times hard down on the petal, revving the engine up to strength.

Sam and Jenn pulled out their service revolvers instinctively and began running toward the Chevette, noting only in passing the form of a second body lying in the alley. The car began to pull away.

Sam made a mad grab for the rear passenger door handle under Fuong Lee's face – but was pulled off his feet by the forward motion of the vehicle. The next second he was flung forward with a spinning roll into a pile of residential garbage cans.

The Chevette continued to drive away from the alley but with an unexpected lack of haste.

"Did the concept of 'fast' ever enter into your idea of driving?" The Professor taunted Cockney with agitated pleasure.

The Hong Kong thug pounded on the steering wheel with a violent crack.

"Did the concept of bleedin' bad carburetor! ever enter into your idea when you had me buy this piece a shit!?!"

Jenn kicked off her shoes and ran behind the Chevette. She needed to get close enough to take an effective shot at the car's tires.

Sam found Rodney's body sitting against a wall next to the garbage cans.

Despite its pickup failure, the Chevette's fifteen miles per hour speed was faster than Jenn could keep up with. Reaching the end of the back street, the vehicle turned effortlessly into the flow of North Broadway traffic. The right turn had been made at The Professor's instruction.

"This is the wrong way!" Cockney objected as he made the turn, "I could a got to the river faster turnin' left."

"You could also have invited the lady policeman to join us while we sat waiting for an opportunity to turn left." The Professor closed his eyes to remember the map of Chinatown.

He saw only dead faces. He opened his eyes quickly.

"Sam!"

At the sound of his partner's voice Sam took his fingers away from the carotid artery on Rodney's neck. There was no pulse. He struggled to focus his good eye on the distant street corner, where Jenn stood heaving in great mouthfuls of air for her oxygen-starved lungs.

"SAM!"

"YEAH?" His hands were shaking.

Jenn had caught her breath. She still could not see her partner crouched down next to the garbage cans, but hearing his voice was enough. Whatever happened in the alley, they could not lose sight of the Chevette.

"He headed into traffic – the car's here – gonna try to follow – your end of the street curves up to Broadway – their direction – meet you there!"

Jenn disappeared from Sam's increasingly limited field of vision.

"Yeah. Right," he said bitterly, rising up from his squatting position over the dead body that had once been Officer Rodney Something or Other. Sam's skin ached from the several deep scratches and bruises caused by his fall into the garbage cans. It would hurt worse later. Right now he had to meet Jenn at the opposite end of this back street.

Blinking rapidly to fight back the growing flow of tears into his good eye – the stupid infection was spreading! – Sam could see the traffic edge slowly past the flashing red light of the main street pedestrian intersection. How much time did he have?

Sam began to jog towards Broadway, leaving the alley behind.

The next day's newspapers reported it as a Chinatown gang bang claiming the life of two youths and an heroic police officer. The Chief of Police vowed to crack down on the drug-related gang violence with a new vehemence.

"We're defending our own!" he declared, and promptly ordered his aides to prepare still another application for federal monies.

INDUSTRIAL
CONVERS[AT]ION

I t was a long block.

Traffic moved with sluggish persistence, stopped short by repeated intrusions of celebrators jaywalking across the street. "Hey, I'm a pedestrian!" they shouted self-righteously in English or Chinese (as the mood fitted them). "This is California: the pedestrian is God!" Then they plowed between the impatient bumpers to their unfocussed destinies on the opposite side of the street.

The Professor did not worry about being identified.

The Chevette blended in with a hundred other squat, four-doored Blandmobiles. It was too soon for the police to be alerted. Just to continue moving was enough. The traffic was slow for an automobile, but faster than the woman chasing them could follow.

Fuong Lee did not think about being followed.

That was Lady Jenn who had called to me, he thought blankly, sitting behind the European and his Chinese murderer. The hostage did not feel as lost as he should.

Fuong Lee noticed that the door he leaned against was unlocked. Without thinking he tapped the black rubber protrusion down and secured the door. *I could just as easily open the door and "fall" out – why don't I?*, he wondered.

I could just as easily have picked up a rifle and fought back at Tien An Men – why didn't I?

Fuong Lee knew the answer: it did not make sense to die so immediate and simple a death just to satisfy a passionate urge.

The knowledge was not a revelation. *No, I've known this about myself for some time*, he mused. Not as a speculation... more as a – fact. Who ever imagined they would die at Tien An Men? There was that factor, too.

But, really, it was the control factor that essentially mattered. Fuong Lee understood that, always, he would be in control of the one element over which he could ever hope to dominate without linkage to history, or fate, or luck: he would be in control of himself.

Philippe was pointing the camcorder at him. Fuong Lee knew that he had not displayed open doubt to the video camera.

"This is how you want me to return to China, Philippe?"

The left eye that was not pressed tightly to the view-finder closed shut in response to the question. A sullen expression crossed Philippe's slack features. The left eyelid screwed itself even more tightly closed.

"Yes, Fuong Lee! This is how I keep you from betraying yourself."

The Professor glanced up at the rearview mirror and saw the young Frenchman's image as a faint outline: Cockney had reset the mirror for night driving, angled by a simple tab to refract the harsh glare of headlights from behind into manageable, soulless spots of light in the mirror. Little suns without the reflection, now made into little moons.

"Che pazzo bella luna," The Professor muttered, closing his eyes.

Philippe's petulant aggression turned on The Professor.

"What did you say?! What!?!"

The Professor felt the camcorder's lens brush against his ear. He was tired of Philippe – he felt sorry for the boy – but he was tired of him.

"Put down the camera, Philippe." It was a listless command. Ignored.

They were approaching a legitimate pedestrian crosswalk with a flashing red light. The pulsing circle demanded all cars to stop even though there was no one trying to cross at the moment.

"Whatcher want, guv?" Cockney asked tensely. He was not used to doing anything at such a deliberate pace, particularly when running away from the police. "Want me ta run it?"

The Professor straightened up and twisted around to review the traffic behind: he did not recognize Jenn's car trailing at a distance of ten vehicles in between. She could not announce her pursuit with a flashing light even if she had wanted to: they were using *her* car tonight, their regular unit vehicle was in repair. No flashing lights. No radios. The Professor was a Marxist and did not believe in luck. He should have.

"So? Stop or not?"

"Stop," The Professor decided. "Stop for your required two seconds and then continue on. We do not want another inconvenient traffic ticket."

The camcorder was now in his nose.

"Put down the camera, Philippe." This time the command was definite.

Philippe's response was a repeat of his earlier aggression, made bold by having gotten away with it earlier.

"Non!" he cried, "Je ne vous comprend pas! I don't understand you!"

Cockney wanted to smack Philippe in the head, but the little prick was sitting behind the driver's seat and impossible to reach. He settled for a verbal assault instead:

"Shut up, Frog!"

"Je ne te comprend pas, tu - merde - je ne te comprend pas!"

"The Professor 'ere said ta put down th camera an—"

The black man came hurling out of the back street and across the pedestrian intersection, his eyes screwed almost shut, his face charged with the combined ugliness of fury and exertion.

"STOP! POLICE!" Sam bellowed. He had not expected to reach Broadway simultaneously with the Chevette, there was no time to draw his gun.

And there was no time for The Professor to pull his pistol, either. He stamped his foot down upon Cockney's and sent a surge of gasoline into the fuel line, grabbing the steering wheel and twisting it at the same time. The Chevette's inefficient carburetor coughed once then caught at the rich fuel mixture with a gasp of power.

Sam saw the vehicle charging at him and jumped back to the safety of the curb.

"STOP!" His service revolver was out now –

– and there were too many bystanders to use it.

The Chevette twisted through the opposing lane of traffic and scraped a handful of rubber off a front tire as it skidded away from the pedestrian intersection.

The Professor pulled his pistol out now, too, but he knew it was useless at anything but the closest range. He twisted in his seat to see how close were their pursuers. Cockney was screaming for directions in his ear, Philippe continued to scream "Je ne comprend pas!" in his face, and Fuong Lee sat watching the events without comment, his eyes alive, his body motionless.

Sam could not move, the adrenal power that had given him the strength for this burst of effort had deserted him and he needed to catch his second wind. Numbly he returned his gun to its waistband clip holster. It was not good for civilians to see it out.

"Fuckin' direction, I'm askin' you! Gimme a fuckin' *direction!*" Cocney shouted. "Gimmie!"

The Professor twisted back to a forward position in his seat. Where were they?

"Gimme a fuckin' direction!"

College Street – nothing had changed. The plan held.

"Right," The Professor answered as if he did not notice Cockney's hysteria.

"Here!?!"

"Nothing changes: here. Turn right." To the river.

Jenn saw it happen.

It hurt her to do nothing, sitting helplessly in a car while five short seconds passed like eternities.

Then it was over and she was still stuck behind a half dozen automobiles while Sam stood in the middle of the intersection and the Chevette dodged against oncoming traffic to score a sizeable lead. It hurt her to do nothing.

"Get in!" she shouted a handful of seconds later, pulling up to Sam at the pedestrian intersection amidst a crowd of revelers who apparently thought the near-rundown was a normal occurrence.

Sam shook his head, trying to clear his eyes. Jenn was looking at him. He could see over the line of traffic: the Chevette was turning right down College Street.

The traffic on Broadway was standing still.

"Get in, Sam!"

"N-no –" Procedure. Routine. Think without thinking in an emergency. "Call in –" His second wind was coming, but it was still hard to breath, "– got to call in. Follow him down – down College!"

Jenn was already accelerating forward.

"Two ninety-five George-Larry-Oscar!" she called out.

"Two ninety-five George-Larry-Oscar," Sam repeated, starting to jog again, across the intersection. "2 – 9 – 5 – G – L – O." The Chevette's license number became a short mantra. "295 GLO."

He was heading north along the sidewalk, looking for a pagoda-roofed telephone booth. "295 GLO."

The same direction as Jenn. "295 GLO."

The same direction as the Chevette.

"295 –"

Jenn's car was losing ground, the Chevette was out of sight, heading east now.

"– GLO."

The telephone booth was in an awning-covered corridor of shops connecting Broadway with the next street east.

The pay telephone was broken.

Down the corridor, Sam could see the Chevette heading down College Street. Jenn's car was not in sight. The Chevette was heading towards Spring – if the car turned left there, it could be headed off on foot – if Jenn lost him.

Sam began to run, not jog.

He was not a strong runner, it had not been a skill he enjoyed developing. But Sam had always had strong legs. Weekly bouts on a bicycle kept them strong. He could not run fast, but he had endurance. And there was no phone anyway.

Sam did not want Jenn to see him. He sprinted across College Street and into the maze of apartments on the north side. The two of them had interviewed several residents in this complex once, becoming lost enough times to imprint the unmapped roads on his memory with reasonable clarity. In the daytime.

Sam heard the sound of a familiar engine racing down College Street behind him and turned in time to see Jenn's car speed east in the direction of the unseen Chevette.

Turn left on Spring, he pleaded with the unknown driver of the Chevette, turn left!

"Turn here."

"But this idn't the way to the river?"

"I know."

"But we're almost there!"

"Turn!"

I'll kill the fucker!, thought Cockney as he pulled hard on the steering wheel, turning the Chevette right and into a narrow, unmarked industrial street. *We got to get away, not play games.*

"Left here.

"Left again."

They were on Spring Street.

"We coulda come 'ere straightaway!" Cockney exclaimed, protesting The Professor's stupidity. "Don'cher remember the fuckin' drivin' aroun' we did last night!?"

"I remember," The Professor answered without interest, his eyes glued to the righthand side mirror.

"Then fuckin' make up your fuckin' mind!"

"I also remember where we have to go once we reach the river."

"So who the fuck cares?"

"I can drive."

She thought she'd located them, but now she wasn't sure.

Jenn gripped her fingers tightly on the steering wheel to keep from impulsively making a fist and smashing it down on the dashboard in frustration. Waves of uncertainty swept over her in repeated taunts. Jenn resisted the temptation to stop the car.

She had not made a positive identification of the Chevette going down College – still too many other automobiles on the road between them. Then, a quarter mile ahead, a pair of taillights had veered off from the irregular line of traffic and turned into a small group of industrial warehouses.

Instinct and a vague recollection of the Chevette's silhouette inspired Jenn to follow. If they parked she would drive past, find an unobtrusive observation vantage point, and wait for back-up to arrive. Sam's call would have black-and-whites patrolling the area in numbers fairly soon. This was a good area to cordon off, few civilians to worry about. Only one hostage.

Fuong Lee.

If he was a hostage.

But no car had stopped. Jenn caught a headlight's echoed reflection off the plate glass windows of a squat front office for a furniture retailer and realized that – *whoever* she was following at this point – the vehicle ahead was not stopping. Jenn had a sudden panic that the Chevette would turn around and be waiting for her at the next corner, headlights switched off, the dangerous occupants ready to blast her away with automatic weapons. She'd seen two victims already.

But no sign of guns. Did they use them? Did they have them?

Jenn was familiar enough with Chinese and Japanese crime societies to know that guns were not a necessity. Christ, the Japanese yakuza gangsters used swords!

But Fuong Lee was not Japanese, and he was not a gangster. The gambling and drug gangs were notoriously apolitical.

And there had been a Caucasian getting into the car with Fuong Lee.

Jenn positioned her service revolver ready on the passenger seat. She maintained both hands firmly on the steering wheel as she rounded the corner.

No one was waiting. No distant headlights reflected off plate glass windows.

Fear of ambush was succeeded by dread of failure. With careless panic at that prospect, Jenn gunned the engine up to the point where her car squealed through the industrial street at over sixty miles per hour. She hit Spring Street on the fly and skidded to an unsteady stop in mid-block.

Two distant taillights to the north.

None south.

Sam emerged onto North Spring Street with a push of effort and a lack of coordination. He whacked his shoulder into a telephone pole and felt the fabric on his coat rip. It didn't matter. What mattered was being here first before the Chevette. What mattered was being ready this time. No time yet to find a position, just locate the car and shoot its damn wheels off. He pulled out his service revolver again.

There was no Chevette coming down the road.

I'm here early, Sam convinced himself. Early. The shortcut was good – had it been *that* good? He'd gotten lost at least twice. But he ran fast – "I ran fast – I'm here early!" Sam said it to himself again, out loud this tim, willing himself to believe that he had arrived before the Chevette could, and that the Chevette, of course, had turned north up Spring Street.

Is my gun loaded?, Sam suddenly worried. *Of course it is. Let me check.*

His hands were unsteady as he broke open the chamber. *It would be really* stupid *to get caught out here in the mid-*

dle of a road with my gun apart, Sam thought, clicking the chamber closed with a practised snap. His hands were steadier now, years of experience conquering the weakness of his overworked muscles. He checked his coat pocket and found the small box of spare cartridges. If only he could see better.

His right eye was swollen completely shut now, the infection-carrying mucous gluing the lids together uncomfortably. *Funny,* Sam mused incongruously, *I took off last year with a sprained finger and I'm working tonight with no eyes.* Sam blinked his left eye a rapid dozen and cleared it enough to see down the dark road.

No Chevette was coming up North Spring Street.

Sam knew in the pit of his intestines that the Chevette would not be coming this far up Spring. Not this slow.

Across the street the railroad tracks ran behind the jumbled blocks of factories and lofts where Fuong Lee lived. They would not be going there – to Elmyra Street – but would they be driving through those back streets *parallel* to North Spring?

Or had they already passed by? Were they faster than me?

Sam forced his brain to consider the thoughts hurriedly. There wasn't time for deliberation. *If they're past me they're heading towards the I-5, the Golden State Freeway.* The freeway would escape them out of L.A.

And if they're on the back streets?

He clenched his hands together, the pistol between them. On the back streets – where are they going?

To the freeway.

Or not.

There was no choice for Sam. He began to run up North Spring Street, towards the freeway.

How many are following us?

Have they called for help?

Do they know for certain – anything?

"Turn into this street and make this machine go as fast as it can."

Cockney accepted this order with pleasure and executed the command with an abruptness that almost overturned the ungainly, top-weighted vehicle.

"You are near my home," Fuong Lee said quietly over the roar of the Chevette's small, straining engine. "Did you know that?"

"No," The Professor answered, looking at the surrounding factories with a new interest. What is it like to live in exile here?

"Oh." Fuong Lee turned to face the insistent camera. "Then *you* led them to me, Philippe?"

Cockney guided the Chevette around a series of parked piggyback trailers and over an unpaved intersection crossing an industrial railroad track siding.

"Stop."

Cockney slammed on the brakes in a locking, frustrated gesture of defiance. The little car slid to a halt amidst a stand of temporary cyclone fencing and sidetracked flatcars.

"No lights."

Cockney hit the small black button controlling the headlights and watched the world around them dive into darkness. Within seconds he realized that the overhead street lights were brighter behind them than where they were parked. He could see across the railroad tracks clearly.

The distant headlights stopped at the far end of the lights' perimeter, in the darkness too.

After a moment, the headlights were extinguished.

"I heard her call your name. She knows you, Fuong Lee," The Professor said to the dissident refugee.

"Yes."

"The police?"

A moment of consideration.

"Not all police are my enemy it seems."

A moment of calculation.

"Tell me about what you believe," The Professor asked.

Fuong Lee began to talk: his Eyes recorded him, the European listened – even the disinterested Hong Kong murderer was quiet while he spoke. The exiled student leader gained confidence as he did so, and the words were now for a man who would understand. Fuong Lee did not find it absurd that he was talking to his kidnappers as if they were sympathizers. He was used to converting sceptics. Minutes passed quickly, fully.

He was not finished, though, before the European spoke again.

"Go to the river now," The Professor instructed Cockney, "we are being followed by only one."

Without turning on the Chevette's headlights, Cockney pulled the automatic transmission gear shifter back into Drive and let the car roll away from its surroundings.

Jenn did not turn on her headlights, either, as she drove distantly behind to follow. No converging patrol cars had passed by while she watched the car sitting there. No back-up. But she was not nervous anymore. Nervousness revolved around uncertainty. Jenn was certain now.

She knew it was them. No mistake.

RED RIVER

It was impossible to imagine that there could be so much adrenaline in one's system.

Sam fought back another bout of near-hysteria brought on by the hormonal secretions combining with anticipation of failure. He knew that intense physical activity could provoke heightened emotional responses. He knew it from observation, from reading and from experiences going back eighteen years to Viet Nam. The knowledge did not help very much. It was still a battle to keep from stopping dead still and crying out in frustration.

His legs didn't hurt, that was luck. Sam held onto the thought obsessively as long as it effectively pushed back his emotions, then he groped frantically for a new, more potent focal point.

I am going up North Spring Street, he reminded himself, repeating the vaguely outlined plan of action he had set out upon. *Beat them to the bridge if they're using the back streets for cover.* They had to go over the bridge to get to the freeway.

Or –

– if they were already past the bridge –

Get there fast enough to see them enter the freeway. They would have to drive through a half mile of small streets to make it to the freeway entrance. *I can see them from the bridge. I'll find a phone this time.*

Got the license: 295 G – L – O.

Break into an office if I've got to.

Find a phone.

Find them.

Run up the damn street.

Passing Aurora Street – could they be there? Sam did not slow his pace but turned his head to look down the industrial street, past the factories and warehouses.

Headlights!

Sam swung his body to the right, pulling his gun from the holster without breaking stride, aiming his moving form down Aurora.

I never killed a body, his thoughts panted uncontrollably, *I'll shoot out the tires –*

The headlights were heading up Aurora, towards him!

I'll shoot out the whole window, I don't care!

The low rider blasted his 50s-resonant horn in panic at the sight of the wild-eyed black man charging him with a gun, racing past the threat with a combined thrill of relief and vicarious pleasure at having momentarily shared in some unknown danger.

Sam knew immediately he had been wrong, swung his gun hand down in an angry gesture.

"Oh, damn..." he said without passion, "damn."

The bridge. North Spring Street.

Sam began his dog-tired, hopeless run back to the larger street, then on towards the bridge.

It wasn't far away, even, only around the next corner of parked trucks.

The night freight to Sacramento rolled heavily on the tracks behind Sam as he ran towards the bridge. Both the engineer and the brakeman saw the running figure, and both shared the same relief: he was moving *away* from the tracks. Too many derelicts tried to recapture the hobo myth of hopping a moving train and lost their legs with the dream. Or their lives. This guy was running for some reason, but it did not affect the brakeman and the engineer. Their eyes returned to the tracks ahead and the switching signals that would guide their load north along the river until they crossed the empty concrete channel underneath the Pasadena Freeway.

The bridge was in sight.

For the last hundred yards Sam was aware of the chain-link fence stretched alongside the road, separating pass-ersby from easy reach of the Los Angeles River. He knew that right now, three years into one of the Southland's drought cycles, there was virtually no water down there. Six inches in the center at best. A quarter-mile wide of man-made river-bed, concrete exposed like an abandoned runway. This was below him shortly, as he ran up the hump of the bridge that spanned the river. He stopped here. To see.

Nothing.

The small rush of water below the bridge sounded ridiculously reminiscent of a country brook burbling over pristine stones. Sam had never lived in the country. The only cool streams he could remember were all in Viet Nam. Each one had looked inviting to a boy from Detroit.

The claymore mine shrapnel that had dug into his chest three months into his tour was on the bank of such a perfect stream of water. And almost everyone else had died sooner or later that winter – while "lucky" Sam went home to heal. The healing waters. McMasters would probably not have understood, the hardnosed MP. Mark Cornell had appreciated the irony, though. Mark appreciated any irony, till he started laughing too much and walked away.

We in a Irony Situation now, Cornell?

Sam blinked his left eye the requisite dozen times and cleared it enough to look down on the Los Angeles River.

Damn!, the full moon sparkled on the pathetic trickle of water like a diamond of beauty, giving the river-in-name-only an undeserved grace. *It's a irony, Honky Mark. You can laugh now.*

Sam surveyed the streets below that scattered out toward Glendale to the north and the I-5 Freeway to the northeast. Not even midnight yet... But here, just past the borders of Chinatown, there was no Chinese New Year to celebrate. Dead streets at night. An occasional truck making an overnight run. A couple of cars.

No Chevette.

They had to come this way – or they were not coming at all.

Or Sam's desperate run had been in the wrong direction.

The wrong direction for the wrong decision. An awful lot of wrong decisions. Which one was the first?

Sam heard the engines' echoing roars first, and only when he opened his eye to try to give a direction to the sounds did he realize that it had been closed.

He was not hopeful yet: every idiot gunning his engine within a mile radius cursed the quiet night with echoed noise pollution. It would probably turn out to be a couple of low-end pickups racing between stoplights down on San Fernando Road.

Nobody there to see – yet – and the engines' echoes were growing closer.

Two engines. A pursuit.

Sam turned his head back down to face North Spring Street. Had he been correct about the Chevette using the back streets for cover? And was Jenn catching up to them?

Sam still held his service revolver in his hand, clutched there since the erroneous side trip to Aurora Street. He cocked back the hammer with his thumb, but let his hand hang slack at his side. He would not repeat the overreaction on Aurora. If it was the Chevette coming, he would have time to see it. Time to support his arm and take proper aim. He would shoot at the front tires first, four shots.

And if he missed, if the Chevette stood a good chance of escaping again, then he would shoot at the front window. On the driver's side. Sam was not a great shot, this would not be purposeful murder. Luck, either way. Whoever was in that car with Fuong Lee had killed three people.

The engine sounds grew more intense, though still at a distance. Sam began to doubt the direction. He was facing south down North Spring Street – the sounds were not coming *at* him.

The sounds were coming from *below*!

Sam turned his head to look down from the bridge: two sets of headlights were racing over the riverbed.

It was only a question of choosing the correct opening into the water runoff system.

Cockney was enjoying the mad race to which The Professor had guided them: down into the river bottom, splashing through the shallow trickle of water, dodging the large rocks and debris that littered the concrete plain. He did not care where they were going, there was only one car following them and he would outmaneuver it.

Philippe was recording the chase with intense concentration: the wildly bumping ride allowed him to ignore the cruel thoughts of betrayal that seemed to be flying about in his brain. "Keep the focus on the other car" was the type of self-imposed simple focus he needed now. There was a woman driving the other car.

Fuong Lee recognized Jenn. He had guessed it was her following the Chevette earlier, now he could see her – if not clearly, then... enough.

The Professor watched for the Cat.

He'd found it yesterday, during the long hours of driving back and forth through the area that he had made Cockney endure. L.A.'s underground system of water drainage was firmly in his memory, but he wanted to see the openings. The Professor was surprised to see graffiti faces painted on the huge circular openings, then, immediately, pleased. Such a simple landmark – the face of a cat. The Cat. This was the opening that would lead to the correct underground escape route.

The Cat.

That was where they were headed now, although only he knew it.

Once we have entered the pipe then I will bargain with the single policewoman, he reasoned calmly. *I need only to buy five minutes of her time, her concern for a hostage's safety, and then they will never find us. And no one else will be killed. At least not by my hand.*

Will that make me less a hired murderer?

The Cat was a hundred meters past the bridge.

Jenn felt the steering wheel jolting under her hand and thought idly of the front alignment that would be necessary after tonight.

There was no use now in pretending she was *not* following the Chevette, but even less need to risk her neck by staying hot on its tail and skimming across this treacherous drag racing course. The Chevette had speeded up once it hit the riverbed, and Jenn had goosed her accelerator to do likewise, but the four cylinder car could never hope to outrun her six cylinder powerhorse. Jenn easily cruised at a position parallel and slightly to the rear of the fugitive vehicle.

She had almost pulled close to their rear once – then the Chevette veered radically across the shallow river to cut across her front end.

Jenn eased up on the gas rather than applied the brakes, letting the riverbed's water resistance drag slow her down and not taking the chance of slipping into a skid. Her car was showered by a thick spray of dirty water from the Chevette's passing in front, but no worse happened.

She actually gained on the maroon automobile without trying when it had to veer back to the other side of the riverbed, this time *not* attempting to cut her off.

She saw Fuong Lee clearly then – and she saw him recognize her.

The Cat.

"Pull over here. At the cat," the Professor commanded, "At the Cat!"

"Police is right behind us, guv," Cockney commented. He was not too worried: it was only a woman.

Leaning over the guardrail, Sam clearly saw the Chevette slow down. He began to search the chain-link fence at the foot of the bridge for an opening. Nothing. He started climbing over the fence.

The two cars were separated by the width of the river. Cockney ran the Chevette up almost onto the macadam that fronted the comical cat's face surrounding the pipe opening.

"We goin' in there?!" he called over the noise of the splashing water hitting against the windows as he jammed into a stop.

"Yes!"

"Meetcha there, luvs!" He was out of the door before the last word was finished. Cockney hated getting his shoes wet, but the woman police's car was coming down on them. The Professor had a gun, let him use it.

He *was* using it.

With full knowledge that he had no chance of hitting anything purposely with a small handgun at that range, The Professor stepped out of the Chevette and made a large gesture of taking aim at the approaching vehicle. He contented himself with firing in the general direction – the sudden grinding of brakes was proof enough that his message had been clear. The woman stopped her car two dozen meters away.

"Philippe, Fuong Lee!" The Professor grabbed the Chinese by his upper arm as the hostage emerged from the car, pulling: "You will come with me. Philippe, follow!" He forced the hostage around to the protected side of the Chevette.

Philippe followed them with his lens.

"Philippe!" he heard The Professor call out. "Don't be so stupid. Come!"

Philippe did not like the Professor's tone. He swung the camera back toward their pursuer, to get a clear shot through the open door.

Jenn saw the glint of moonlight reflect off the large barrel. Christ, a shotgun! She swung her door wide, grabbed her pistol, and fired three swift shots at the barrel before diving to the floor. The short scream she heard was muffled from there. Then, crawling across the floor and out the passenger side door, Jenn heard clearly Fuong Lee's wailing exclamation.

"PHILIPPE!"

Jenn hit the silt-covered concrete heavily with her shoulder as she slid to the ground. She rolled sideways through the muck to find cover behind the front wheel.

"JENNIFER! IT WAS PHILIPPE! MY FRIEND!"

Sam, dropping down from the ten-foot high fencetop, heard the plaintive accusation clearly:

"WHY DID YOU SHOOT MY FRIEND!?!"

The Professor pulled Fuong Lee down behind the Chevette and slammed him hard against the fender.

"Shut up!" He put his face against Fuong Lee's and let his green eyes display their fierce emotion. "She did him a favor: now he will never know that he was your Judas!"

And Fuong Lee agreed.

One part of him wanted to cry uncontrollably, to weep at the instant demise of his Eyes – and the other part of him shared the European's opinion. Was more harsh in its judgement, in fact. Philippe had betrayed him. From love, maybe. From weakness of will, certainly. But it had still been betrayal, even if the rich young Frenchman had never understood what he was doing.

Though his body still shook with sobs, Fuong Lee was

discovering within himself that trait which sets leaders apart from the masses, the ability to objectively evaluate others. He continued to sob, but Fuong Lee was uncertain whether it was from true emotion or for subconsciously calculated effect. Would this impress the European? Would the hostage find an advantage from his captor by displaying a sense of loss?

Fuong Lee looked at the European through his tears and believed that the answer was 'yes.' The European might be a leader of sorts, but he was not leader enough. He let belief overpower reason. As if watching one of Philippe's videotapes, Fuong Lee watched the green-eyed terrorist look at his hostage for a brief moment with something akin to loss in his pale eyes.

"Fuong Lee?"

Sam heard Jenn's voice carry faintly across the width of the riverbed. She had never had a strong voice. She was using it to full strength now.

"Fuong Lee!" Jenn leaned her back against the wheel and brought her feet up to her buttocks: she could spring to her feet in an instant if necessary. "Are you all right?"

Rule Number One: Isolate the incident.

Jenn checked her service revolver. It had not been affected by her roll in the slime.

Rule Number Two: Establish the safety of the hostages.

"I said – " Jenn took a deep breath and called out word by word: "Are – you – all – right?"

She had used three bullets. Her spare ammunition was in her handbag, back in the car on the front seat. The white guy had a handgun – what kind?

No one had noticed Sam at the top of the riverbank yet. Perhaps he was impossible to see? Sam only knew that *he* could not see *them* clearly. Their two cars were only half-lit by their interior dome lights and still-glowing headlights that beamed out at unproductive angles. None of the performers could be seen in the sharp contrasts of the shadows in which they hid, at least not at Sam's range.

"Fuong Lee?"

The hostage looked at his kidnapper defiantly: it was time to test his evaluation of the man.

"I know her, I am going to answer her. There is feeling between us."

The European looked down at him without expression, flicked his eyes over at the policewoman's car, then back down at his hostage.

"Do so," The Professor said. "Tell her you will be safe if she lets us go safely to the pipe." There was no sense of threat in his voice, only simple fact.

It was the response Fuong Lee had sought. He understood the full danger of his captor now – and his weakness.

"Jennifer?" Fuong Lee's voice carried clearly across to the other car. Despite his shaken emotions, it was a voice experienced in reaching across distances.

"Fuong Lee!"

"I am safe. I will be safe –" Fuong Lee did not doubt the European's determination on this point, "– if you let us go to the pipe."

Jenn hesitated only long enough to consider the options: Fuong Lee would still be safe – beyond that, she could find no greater advantage to the kidnappers in the drainage pipe than behind the Chevette.

"Done," she called.

The Professor nudged Fuong Lee with his pistol, indicating the cat-faced drainage pipe where Cockney waited safely protected from the policewoman's gunfire.

"Ciao, bambino."

It was clear that the European intended to wait until his hostage was in the pipe before going there himself. Fuong Lee felt uncomfortable about this: from the little he had seen of the two men – the Hong Kong thug and the European "professional" – the hostage understood that his chances for survival would always be better with the European. His reluctance was apparent enough to require a second nudge.

"Ciao, bambino, go," The Professor urged, misreading the young man's hesitation, "I am sorry if your woman police shoots at the first thing that moves, but that is the chance we both take."

The Professor let Fuong Lee see that he was following the other's every movement with the pistol, then leaned comfortably against the side of the Chevette while watching his hostage obey the command. He let his left hand slip into his jacket pocket.

The Professor's fingers caressed the plastique explosive carried there. It was time to eliminate the Chevette as evidence. He was not worried about the policewoman.

Then he saw the black man sliding down the concrete riverbank.

"La grande comedia!" The Professor spat out with disgust at the trap closing in on him. He fired two swift shots at the descending figure to let the fascist police know that their ruse was discovered.

Sam knew that he had been seen. Even as the flashes of light from the gun barrel betrayed the kidnapper's deadly intention, Sam was flattening himself against the cement, an instinctive reaction to a sudden rigidity he had perceived (was it real or intuitive?) in the man's shadowy silhouette. His swollen eye left him with only a one-eyed look at the situation – and no depth perception.

Fortunately, a bullet doesn't need depth perception.

Sam fired back at the flashes of light and threw his body into a roll down the remainder of the riverbank.

It may have saved his life. It most certainly was a mistake from all other angles of consideration.

"Sam!"

He heard Jenn call out his name and follow up the identification with a short barrage of bullets fired at the Chevette. That was all he could make out: the steep concrete riverbank had almost no drag-inducing traction to speak of and he was tumbling down the incline uncontrollably.

Stay relaxed, Sam reminded himself, *pull in your extremities and* stay relaxed!

It was hard advice to follow, especially since the immediate effect of the technique was an increase of speed to his rolling descent. But Sam had lived in cold climates once, Detroit was a hell of ice and snow in the winter, and he knew from a hundred sidewalk spills that to extend an arm or a hand trying to slow down was to invite a broken bone. He was right on that count, but when he hit the bottom of the incline it was with a deadening thud that left him breathless. If the kidnapper wanted an easy target now, Sam had given it to him.

The kidnapper was not interested in easy targets. The Professor quickly stripped off his jacket with its plastique-lined pocket and set it beneath the Chevette. A cheap, sports-store stopwatch was already attached to the detonating device and he gave himself thirty seconds. The policewoman was no longer shooting and the black policeman appeared unconscious from his fall. The Professor dashed for the pipeline.

Jenn saw the white guy making his escape and cursed herself for being out of bullets. She lunged into her car and grabbed up her handbag with its extra ammunition, then sprinted from behind the protective vehicle and across the short distance that separated the two vehicles until she had the kidnappers' own car for cover. The fleeing criminal did not look back as he ran and she made it safely. She began to reload.

"Sam! Sam! Are you all right!"

Through the fog of disorientation following his fall Sam heard himself answer, "OK!" He raised his head and located his partner next to the Chevette.

The Professor hit the cement wall of the pipe with his shoulder and pushed into Fuong Lee and Cockney as he plowed into its shadowed safety. He immediately turned back to face the opening, crouching low in case the policewoman forgot her concern for Fuong Lee. He did not see her immediately.

Then he did.

"La commedia è finita," he whispered in anguish.

The plastique exploded.

It was not a powerful explosive, but The Professor's experience had led him to place it under the Chevette's gas tank. In fact, there were two explosions, separated only by an instant for Jenn to know that she was about to die. Then she was engulfed by the concussion and flame and ceased knowing anything.

The Proffesor allowed himself another moment of regret, then looked over at the remaining danger from the black policeman - and immediately pulled his head back deeply into the shelter of the pipe.

"YOU! *YOU*!" Sam cried savagely, firing wildly at the opening, "I DON'T KNOW WHO YOU ARE! BUT I'M GOING TO KILL YOU! I'M GOING TO KILL YOU!"

He ran out of bullets. With a gesture of disgust, Sam began to reload, still yelling "YOU!" at the top of his lungs and straining to see a face in the pipe opening to shoot at. He did not realize that he had run behind the protection of Jenn's car, but began shooting at the dark mouth of the Cat without major consideration for his own safety.

"I'M GOING TO KILL YOU!"

The Professor realized that it was time to retreat. He made a businesslike evaluation of their situation and addressed Fuong Lee.

"You seem to be worth a lot of death, don't you?"

He turned to Cockney.

"You were right earlier: you are not paid by the hour. Earn it – delay the policeman."

Fuong Lee felt the European pull him deeper into the darkness. And then the pale light of the opening was behind a corner and the policeman's screaming voice was abruptly cut off, lost in the slushing noises of their own footsteps through the echoing passage.

Unexpectedly, the European pushed him against a wall, whispered "Do not move," and abandoned him. Fuong Lee could not tell if the European's footsteps were walking deeper into the passage or not, for the kidnapper was suddenly stepping with quiet care.

Cockney was scared in his gut – and excited. He did not have a gun, but it was dark here, and even a gun would have to be used at the distance of a man's arm. It was no different than a knife at that range. No different than a trained foot. Both could hurt. Both could kill. It was all a question of who was faster. Cockney knew that he was *very* fast.

He had never gone after a police before.

Cockney was scared in his gut – and excited.

Sam stopped yelling: his throat had turned gravelly smooth, the words no longer caught his tongue, lost in the con-vulsions of his neck as he fought back a series of racking sobs. He ran out of bullets again and, without thinking, made a dash for the cover of the burning Chevette, where he squatted down behind its burning hulk and began to reload. He was not actually close to the flames, but they provided him with cover from being seen by anyone in the pipe.

The heat was intense and penetrated Sam's wet, silt-covered clothes. He crab-walked a few yards further away – still using the burning car for cover – and felt his hand come down on something warm.

It was a piece of Jenn's face.

Sam threw his spent cartridges at the torn flesh in a reactive gesture to ward off the horror.

It was a part of her cheek and mouth.

Sam fell back and scrambled away. Sitting in the open space between the two cars, Sam gave in to a series of dry, shuddering heaves that lasted a full minute –

– Until a second, reactive emotion took hold: cold anger.

He stood up with deliberate intention and faced the pipe opening, his pistol held out at arm's length and pointing at the dark hole. If anything moved, anything!, he would empty the chamber. Sam began to walk around the burning Chevette and approach the pipe from the side.

Nothing moved.

Cockney felt The Professor step up behind him.

"You did not think I would desert you entirely, did you, *loov*?" he whispered with reassuring sarcasm. "I will give you an advantage over the policeman."

Sam was almost to the edge of the pipe opening when he heard the voice echo from far within:

"You won't shoot, policeman, or you will kill Fuong Lee."

Cockney smiled at the suggestion and, at the Professor's direction, moved silently closer to the pipe's opening.

"*I* won't shoot him," The Professor continued, "*you* will – if you shoot."

Then, without guile:

"Don't follow: too many are dying."

Harry swallowed hard several times, fighting down the nausea. He was glad that he could not see the details. Harry hated "details." He always tried to imagine they didn't exist.

A mild panic was also squeezing at his guts: he had told them back East to expect some ugliness, but would they accept the cop killings? That was an ugly turn. Nobody's fault really, though. And not a screw-up by any means.

I can clean this up, Harry thought, *it's messy, but not unsalvageable.*

He looked down at the burning automobile and considered options, deciding eventually that the policewoman would have to be an alcoholic, her fiery death an unfortunate result of carrying a gallon of gasoline in her trunk. Stress. Being a woman in a man's profession, a minority to boot. The details began to sort themselves into place. A loose end here or there remained.

Just like in life.

Harry had to admire The Professor. No one could have expected the police to show up, yet the Italian was following through without missing a beat.

And he had picked his cover well. The crackle of small gunfire down in the riverbed was less alarming than the exploding fireworks on the Chinatown streets less than a mile away. Even the car exploding could be mistaken for the spectacular effect of – what was that illegal kind of cherry bomb? An M-80? Yeah, M-80. Timing helped, too – everything went fast. What to do about the black cop down there?

Harry wanted to see how The Professor handled this one.

He could only see the policeman dimly in the fading flames of the burning car.

Sam could barely see the pipe opening. His left eye was almost as clouded with infection now as his right eye and he had to shake his head sharply to clear it. He held his breath and listened for movement.

The Professor let his feet slap heavily in the small stream of water that ran down the pipe as he made his way back into the passage.

Sam knew that he would be silhouetted against the opening if he tried to rush in. He crouched low to the ground and began to edge cautiously around the corner, his gun-carrying hand sliding around the corner first, then half a shoulder.

It saved his life, if not his wrist – Cockney's foot smashed into Sam's gun hand, knocking his arm wide and sending the pistol flying close to the burning Chevette.

A second foot smashed into Sam's shoulder, knocking him up into a standing position.

"'Allo, copper! You ain't got no weapon!" Cockney snapped a double leg kick into the black policeman's chest and pushed Sam into a flying fall onto his back.

This was the time to turn and run. Every instinct in Cockney's ten years of police-dodging experience in Hong Kong, London and Los Angeles told him that.

But he had never been alone with a policeman before. At least not when the policeman was down and he was up. Cockney needed to look closer at his success, enjoy it a moment.

And then the black man spoke:

"You –" Sam's stomach shuddered in a dry heave, "have to kill me."

The idea made sense. Cockney enjoyed the thought.

"Oh, I know that," he said with casual overconfidence, walking over to where Sam laid curled up on the ground. "It's just a question a when, idn' it?"

Cockney pulled back his foot to deliver a few hard kicks to the policeman's ribs – then suddenly had a different thought and stopped in mid-swing. He turned away and walked a few paces back, allowing Sam to struggle to his feet. Cockney whirled back around to face the still-crouched figure.

All those years of fear.

Cockney needed to taunt.

"You're old, I'm young. You're tired, I'm not. I don't 'ave ta kill you – but that's your choice."

"I'm going to kill you," Sam wheezed quietly.

"Yeah," Cockney laughed to himself. To Sam he offered the serious confidence of the professional antagonist: "All my life I'm runnin' from the filth: you're the power, luv, no odds for my kind." He grew more serious still. "I always knew you wanta kill me: they calls it justice, but –" with a wink "– we know wot's wot, right?"

Harry wondered why the stupid little Chink down there was talking to the black cop and regretted listening to the recommendation to take him on as freelance muscle. He was too far away to understand what they were saying.

Then he heard the kiai martial arts yell and saw the small figure of the Chinaman launch itself at the cop. In the flickering illumination of the fire the two ill-defined forms grappled for long seconds, then separated.

Cockney was surprised: he had expected to slam the black's ribs a few times then smash in his face. But without the element of surprise working against him, the cop's two hundred pound frame seemed to absorb the smart kicking blows with less effect than earlier – and the man had even made a successful grab at Cockney's arm when the street thug moved in with his fists. The pulling apart had been by mutual need.

Sam still breathed heavily, but with control. His daily regimen of exercises did not leave him with the obvious fighting skill of the young killer, but his muscles were kicking in with the reserve of strength they always exhibited after the first round of exertion. He knew he had over a fifty pound advantage on the Asian. What other advantages could he find?

Sam realized from the heat that they were standing side-by-side near the burning Chevette.

Without apparent intention, Sam sidled closer to the flames – his opponent edged away – both sizing the other up for the next wave of assault. A few steps. Sam had his second advantage: *he* was the silhouette now, a dark, featureless shape against the bright back-light. The Chinese boxer was fully illuminated, and squinting his eyes against the light. He would have to come in close to find his targets.

And in close was Sam's third advantage.

It took Cockney a badly-executed frontal attack to realize his disadvantage, when the policeman landed a heavy fist against the side of his face as he missed with his first kick and plowed two largely ineffective jabs into the black man's arm.

Up above, Harry wondered who was winning.

Cockney's next attack was from the side, and it was

more effective than the two previous ones – except that the policeman held onto his leg and, despite the fact that Cockney was certain he had broken the black's nose, he found himself floundering in the muck trying to escape the larger man's grip.

As Cockney tried to scramble loose, he looked down and realized that both of the cop's eyes were practically swollen shut: the black couldn't see!

Harry lost sight of the two when they hit the ground and began rolling in the shallow, silt-filled trickle of river. He carefully slid a third of the way down the steep riverbank to find a better observation point. He did not want to be seen yet, but maybe he would hear something of advantage if he got closer. He heard the pathetic crack of a handgun.

There was a second crack, muffled by closeness to two bodies.

One of the figures rose from the muck and stumbled over toward the cat-headed pipe opening. The second figure pulled up to a half-sitting position. Harry could not distinguish details, but he assumed the victor was holding the policeman's gun.

The Chinaman's heavy-breathing voice drifted up from the riverbed.

"Cheers, copper, m'luv."

PIPE DREAMS

It had not been difficult to find the rendezvous spot, not even long. Only dirty.

The Professor led Fuong Lee through the dark passage with such a sense of familiarity that the young man would have been amazed to learn it was the European's first time in the underground drainage system.

In the dark.

The Professor did not carry a flashlight and, in fact, had never considered bringing one. He walked blindly with one hand held loosely in front of his face and the other hovering at waist level, but extended further in front. The Professor knew that the utter darkness would discourage Fuong Lee from any rash ambitions of escape. He let the hostage follow by holding onto his shirttail. A wave of nostalgia embraced him as they made their way towards his chosen destination.

"Marco! Don't leave me, Marco!"

"No, bambino, I told you I would not change my mind and leave you in this labyrinth for the Minotaur to eat."

"I trust you," Fuong Lee said uncertainly.

"You must," Marco told his little cousin, surprised that the boy could be so afraid of the dark. Why, Marco thought in bold strokes of ambition, when I go back to the north after vacation I will tell them how I conquered the Roman catacombs without fire, without candles, without light! He let little Fredo cling to his pants and wended his way through the unknown maze with relish.

"Do you know the way, Marco?"

"Of course," he answered aloud... not. There would be no fun if I knew the way, Marco laughed to himself with a thrill, but I will not tell this to Fredo and set him to crying. I know (how do I know?, I don't know, but I know) that this is the way I faced coming in – this is east – and every turn is in relation to this, and I know where we've been, and – when you are exploring, what more is there to know?! Marco felt a keen kinship with the American frontiersmen he was reading about in school, fearless men like himself who went blindly into the wilderness and discovered greatness. "I will be great," he said aloud. This reassured Fredo.

Too soon, The Professor knew, too soon: we will see the pale light ahead and leave behind our dark world of confidence.

I... can't see, and... would it matter if I could?

The mud-covered figure stumbled blindly through the pipe, exhausted, knowing that even if it were brilliantly lit he would still have no clue where to go.

I... ! ... he scraped his hand roughly against the cement wall of the pipe, almost dropping the pistol into the thick sludge at his feet. *I have to be less stupid*, he thought, changing his walking technique from one of blind groping to a semigraceful attempt at using his free hand as a radar, trying to "feel" the walls and pipe curvings before actually crashing into them with his full weight behind the movement.

I need to find them by hearing them, he suddenly realized, amazed that it had taken him several dozen steps to come to such an obvious conclusion. *I'm too tired, I need to rest...*

And if I do, of course, they'll be gone.

I need to find them.

He listened for sounds

He imagined he could hear the rumble of car wheels overhead. And then a stupid bird chirping up ahead. And then a burbling country brook.

This is shit!, he cursed himself, shaking his head to clear out the false sounds, *I'm city: why'm I dreaming of bein' in country?!* He tried to listen again and heard nothing but his own heavy breath.

He held his breath and listened. He heard his heart beat.

He stopped holding his breath and forced himself to breathe slowly and regularly, quietly.

He listened.

He heard them talking.

They waited under the dim glow of the maintenance light, an orange-tinted lightbulb protected by heavy wire mesh. Iron rungs crawled up the wall from chest height, peppered with surface rust, disappearing up the ten-foot chimney that ended in a dark spot The Professor judged was a manhole cover. Despite the fact that the walls were wet, he leaned against the concave cement structure.

Fuong Lee noted that the European did not appear nervous, though he was definitely tense and – somehow (not physically) – gave the impression of being weary.

A trickle of water roamed around their feet. Fuong Lee did not like this waiting.

"Let us get this over with," he said at last.

"I am waiting for my colleague." The Professor's voice carried a slight echo down the passage.

"He is a criminal, you are not!" Fuong Lee cried, seeking to push his small advantage on the European.

"He is ... tonight ... my colleague."

The Professor let his eyes explore the younger man's face as he explained: "Loyalty is a difficult habit to break. Do you know what I was thinking?"

Fuong Lee's expression indicated clearly that he had no intention of asking.

"I was thinking," The Professor smiled, "that we are lucky this is not Spring, or this pipe would be flooded and we would be drowning like the small animals we are."

He swallowed dryly once before adding:

"And I am thinking about Philippe."

Fuong Lee knew that he had to be emotional for the European.

"You care about Philippe!?" he asked sharply.

The Professor ignored the tone of criticism.

"I had thought he would be more cynical, you know, a typical Frenchman... But he believed – believed in you?"

"He believed in your lies," Fuong Lee answered carefully.

"I did never lie to him – but you did."

The Professor did not want to look at the Chinese student leader.

"You use the word 'democracy' very well, Fuong Lee: you are a 'martyr' for 'democracy.' The 'democratic students' were 'massacred for democracy'." Marco spit into the water, a gesture of contempt.

He was proud to be Italian, sometimes, and filled with human blood instead of politician's bile.

"You, you sided with one faction against another and your side lost. You want democracy as much as I want capitalism: you want your side in power, that's all!"

Fuong Lee was frightened by the words, but needed to test his advantage:

"Why do you not kill me then?"

"Because I... can."

Marco wanted to be The Professor again and know the intricate answers to every dialectic. The Professor longed to be Marco again and be great.

"Do you know," he groped, "I have never ... killed ... anyone – except when I had to? I won't – I don't ... I will not kill you."

It was the right answer for the young leader – almost.

"But you will use me as a shield," Fuong Lee pressed, "and let others kill me."

The Professor understood the little boy's fear of death.

"When our friend the capable Hong Kong Cockney comes, I will let him take you to the end." He smiled and pointed up at the manhole cover. "We are almost there."

Fuong Lee let his eyes search the darkness up above and wondered at what point his advantage over the European would come into play, if ever.

"We can say out good-byes now," he heard the European say.

And he heard the footsteps.

The Professor pushed his body away from the wet cement wall.

"And our Cockney arrives. Let us help him to make the correct turns." He put two fingers to his lips and blew hard, producing a loud, piercing whistle. It was a beautiful whistle, strong and resonant in the dark passage. A beacon. A memory of rallying the football team onto the field for such a clear and perfect day to play the game. It guided the footsteps perfectly.

"All right, my friend, we are down here!"

The footsteps drew closer.

"I would appreciate the courtesy of an answer, my friend!"

The footsteps drew closer still, and then stopped.

With a start, The Professor realized that he had not doubted for a moment that the footsteps belonged to the black policeman.

Instinctively he stepped behind Fuong Lee. He drew his pistol without calling attention to the motion.

"It is not a good idea to come to me this way," he called to the darkness.

Marco could hear Fredo breathing next to him. Fredo was always breathing loudly. Was he afraid? Fredo was a banker now, wasn't he? Marco pushed on his young cousin's shoulder, and Fredo bent his knees obligingly.

Fuong Lee did as he was told.

Marco stood with his gun hand pointing down, waiting to finish a short prayer.

Then, with a snap, The Professor brought it up and fired the pistol. He could see the single bullet spark against the invisible walls down the long passage –

– and then he saw the shower of returning sparks as the black policeman fired every bullet in his gun in response.

He felt the slam in his chest and felt nothing again.

Sam held his breath underwater as long as he could, then raised his head. There had been no return shots fired.

He lifted his body from its prone position in the six inch ooze and tried to focus on the circle of light ahead. It was impossible. His left eye recorded only an orange haze now. If the white guy was still able to shoot, Sam would have to take his chance.

He found two shells still floating around in the soggy debris of his pocket and put them into his service revolver, rotating the cylinder to the proper position by feel. He did not realize that he was walking towards the light until he had almost reached the bodies.

The white guy was a mass of wet clothing, lying heavily on top of a wriggling second mass of sodden material. Sam tried to recognize the face of the dead man, but it was no one familiar.

He pushed the body off of Fuong Lee then squatted back against the sweating cement pipe wall while the refugee sputtered mud out of his mouth and recoiled from the syrup of blood the dead man's body had spilled upon him in its fall. Sam could barely make out the young Chinaman's face.

"Are you really worth so much?" he asked.

Fuong Lee was severely shaken. "I – wouldn't think so," he answered. Almost immediately he did not believe that. Too many people had died for him. He was worth a lot.

Sam found the manhole cover easier to dislodge than he had expected – and harder to slide over.

Twice the heavy iron cover slipped and pinched his fingers painfully. Then he applied an angry shoulder and shoved it almost vertically, not caring that when it came falling down on the street there was a loud, obnoxious clang. He shrugged his shoulders twice to take away the fire from the strain and hauled himself up onto the street. They were somewhere near San Fernando Road, he couldn't guess how far.

"You need any help?" he called down into the manhole, extending an arm.

"No," Sam heard Fuong Lee answer, "it is just slippery."

Sam didn't hear the gunshot.

He felt the bullet hit him, of course. In the small of the back. In the ribs. Just above the kidney. For the first time that night, Sam lost consciousness.

It was only for a few seconds. It had to be only a few seconds, Sam thought hazily, feeling the growing, searing pain in his back and hearing the nearby freeway traffic give off its one-car-per-minute midnight roar. And he must have moved while he was unconscious, Sam quickly realized – or had he been moved? He was not near the manhole anymore, Sam knew that for certain, for he clearly heard Fuong Lee ask in a searching voice –

"Sergeant Williams? Sergeant?"

– and Fuong Lee had to see him if he was still by the manhole cover didn't he?

Then Fuong Lee began to talk in Chinese. Someone else answered. In Chinese.

Sam opened his eyes to see who had come. Or tried to open his eyes: the right one was still swollen shut, the left one little better. Sam could vaguely perceive a shape he figured to be that of Fuong Lee.

And then a Voice began to speak into Sam's ear:

"It's only a rubber bullet, and I'm sorry about that, fella," there was a Midwestern twang to the Voice, "but, hell, a broken rib's better than being dead, isn't it?

"Isn't it?" The Voice carried an insistence with it that demanded an answer. His hand fell heavily on Sam's shoulder and squeezed. Sam's entire back, he was surprised to learn, burned from the touch.

"I need to know if you're hearing me, fella." The Voice became a blurry Face. "Just let me know if you're understanding me."

Fuck you, Sam furiously directed the thought.

The hand squeezed tighter.

"Uh," Sam heard himself grunt.

"Good," the Face continued. "Agree with me on the next few things, then. And listen. Your friend here is listening." The Face waved a hazy arm in the direction of the vague Fuong Lee. "He's listening to an offer he probably won't want to turn down, and – depending upon how he reacts – he may even become a Man of Destiny out of it. Either way, he's going home."

Sam saw the haze that was probably Fuong Lee walking away with other ill-defined figures. He could not tell if the voices were speaking in protest or excitement.

"'Key thing for you," the Face sounded persuasive, "is to remember that the man who killed your partner is dead: you did it. It's over."

"Is he conscious, Harry?" another Voice asked.

"Just barely," the Face with the name of "Harry" moved away from Sam's line of vision. "How's the clean-up going?" he heard Harry ask.

"Professor's no more. Riverbed's set up pretty well. Alley was a breeze from the beginning."

"Fine. Line up a Witness Protection coordinator and our boy here'll be ready to go. We'll get him a medical retirement for stress caused by his partner's death."

The other Voice was reluctant.

"Harry, uh... we don't need him. He's a complication."

Harry was offended.

"You shit!" he hissed through clenched teeth, "you think we're some fucking *terrorists*?! This fella's an American. A policeman. We don't do that crap!"

Harry stomped across the narrow street and back again. His rubber soled shoes made little sound.

"He's one of ours now!" Harry hollered, oblivious to the echo. No one lived on the industrial street to hear them anyway.

"You got this street clean yet?!" he demanded aggressively.

"Yeah, almost," the other Voice answered deferentially, anxious to turn the conversation to other topics. Harry was a high roller: his report could kill a local career.

They began talking about flight schedules and Russians.

Against his expectations, Sam felt numb. His back still burned with pain, but it felt distant. Shock was setting in. He was not hurt seriously, Sam knew, but if he did not receive help soon he would probably die from simple shock and exposure. *Really stupid way to die*, he mused dully, *here I've got full medical coverage!* Sam realized that he was waiting impatiently for Harry to return.

Harry came back after a century.

"You still awake?" he asked.

Sam could not let the bastard know what he was thinking. He willed his eye to stay half open but unmoving.

Harry was persistent.

"You think about what I said? You agree that it's over here?"

Sam wanted to live. He remembered the V. C. standing over him at the bubbling brook that fed into the Mekong River that day when his chest was blown open. Ol' Victor Charlie back then didn't want to be an executioner. Harry here now didn't want to be an executioner.

He said.

"You agree it's over here?!" Harry's Midwest accent grated on Sam's nerves. His eye burned. He refused to blink. He thought of the telephone call:

"Hey, Marie, this Harry's got an edge over Victor Charlie. You'll be happy to hear this: I want to live. Maybe eat a bullet later. Maybe. But live now."

Sam's eye was filling with tears.

"And find out who Harry is. And what happened. And maybe kill Harry. And maybe eat a bullet then."

Sam could not remain motionless much longer.

"I have to live now, Marie. Fuck Harry!"

"I gotta know you're with us," Harry looked at the police I.D., "Sammy".

Sam blinked. "Yeah," he croaked dry-mouthed, "I'm... with."

"Good boy." Harry stood up, relieving his muscles from the uncomfortable squat. "We'll take care of you."

Sam closed his eye. He heard a click. Was it the manhole cover being put back in place, or Marie hanging up?

Sam opened his eye and took a deep breath.

He would never hang up on Marie.

EPILOGUE

"KUNG HAY FAT CHOY!

"No, that's not a Polish obscenity, that's Chinese for 'Hap – py New Year!' And that's what today is here at K – C – A – T, The CAT!"

The sun was bright as it damn well almost always is by eight a.m. in southern California – except for the coastal areas.

"– weather today is all you want it: the morning fog expected to burn off with the morning commuters, bright and pleasant this day. Which should give President Bush something to smile about –"

The street-cleaning machine turned off San Fernando Road and down Albion. It was important to hit the curbs here before the business day started and this industrial street was filled with parked cars.

"– as he announces a new trade agreement with China. Heavy criticism is expected from Congress, but the White House says it expects no major obstacles."

The left side of the street was almost clean and it was still only 8:05, almost another two hours for the No Parking restriction to stay in place.

"That's our one-minute news capsule for this half hour. Stay tuned for a traffic update after this message."

A painful scraping sound etched up from beneath the street cleaning machine.

"Imagine a place where you can dream a dream of luxury – and live it!"

The driver knew what the problem was. He stopped his machine disgustedly and climbed down to the street.

"Imagine a day in the sun, and nights under the clearest stars on earth."

Yep, there it was: some idiot kid had been playing with the manhole cover.

"Imagine a thousand year-old pyramid, a 21st century shopping complex, beds of feathers and restaurants of courtesy."

The driver kicked the heavy metal cover back into place, climbed back up into his cab, and restarted the street cleaning machine.

"Imagine Mexico."

He finished cleaning Albion Street with no further problems.

"Traffic report today is simple: just too many cars on the road! So c'mon, folks!, just stay at home and listen to K – C –A – T, the CAT!"

Eid Al Mubarak

"Sid?"

"Yeah, thanks."

A raised hand, a nod to the East.

"Sid Ecce – to your health, Ian."

"Cheers."

Harry brought the frosty glass to his lips and felt the yeasty liquid attack his taste buds in distressful ways. It was only a momentary discomfort – causing Harry to reflect once again that the Brits would drink anything as long as there was alcohol in it – then the numbing effects of the hundred-proof home brew, "Sid," combined with the ice cubes to produce the desired narcotic effect.

Harry sighed with the contentment of one who's put in a full, productive day.

"How much longer are you with us, Harry?" Ian's soft English accent was delicate and pleasant, almost Southern to Harry's mind. Like a Virginian. Harry had met a lot of Virginians.

He looked out over the oil-sprayed golf course at Ras Tanura and wondered himself about the answer to Ian's question. "How much longer...?" The Persian Gulf rolled quietly up to the edge of the ninth "green,"which here in the Eastern Province was a circle of fine grain sand pounded flat. *No, not the 'Persian' Gulf*, Harry corrected himself, *it's the* Arabian *Gulf here among the Saudis*. And this was only a stop-off trip to remind the field workers that Uncle Sammy back home still loved them.

Or respected them, in Ian's case here. The Iron Lady of Britain, Maggie Thatcher, had her own pride of field workers out here in the desert – beastly hot, even with the A/C turned up full – and it was Harry's not unpleasant duty this summer to visit a few.

Ian was a brick, as the Brits would say, and that made up for the fact that he had lied about his handicap this morning to con Harry out of a cool fifty riyals a hole. Luckily they had had to stop the game at the twelfth hole when the wind set up to gusting and started sucking their balls out to sea. Maybe the wind hadn't been *that* bad, and maybe Harry had sliced a little too deliberately – they *were* Ian's precious few Diamond Gems after all – but the wind had been legitimate and quitting early *had* been Ian's idea.

"I don't know how long I'm here, Ian. What day is it?"

"Almost your July Fourth, Harry. American Rebellion Day."

Harry smiled at the inverted compliment, accepting the implied resentment as natural and impersonal. Ian knew what he was doing and that was fine enough. Better than the assholes in Washington did. Harry contented himself with acceptance of that fact. After all, hadn't the newspaper this morning indicated yet *another* China policy?

I don't know, Harry mused on that thought again, *we go and make a perfect path for quiet diplomacy and then someone has to open his big mouth again.* The L.A. gig six months ago was a perfect example: everything was quiet. Some ugliness, sure, but none pointing our way. The President has everything he wants – so why does he have to go and change his mind?

"We don't need the Chinese as much now that the Soviets are no longer a threat" was the quote by one "unidentified" official.

Yeah, sure!, Harry had snorted over his pancakes and eggs. They made an excellent Golfer's Special at the Ras Tanura Clubhouse. It would be perfect if only the Saudis allowed bacon openly in the country. He could have had some over at Ian's, but the man made notoriously bad coffee. Arabic style. Gone native on the fringes. Brits did that a lot, look at all the Anglo-Indians.

Well, you could never anticipate the President's changes- of-heart. That was life.

"I'm out of here in two days, Ian. On to civilization and legal liquor, not this bootleg brew."

"Bahrain?"

"Better. Baghdad."

"I wanted an assignment there: they've got the best bloody nightclubs out here."

"I like it there, too," Harry agreed, "everything's in order and no raghead fundamentalists spoiling the relaxation."

"I assume you're 'working,' Harry?" Ian had a report to make about his cowboy counterpart; he was getting precious little information from the American so far.

"Just a messenger boy, Ian," Harry could be open about this, it was going to be 'leaked' anyway. "Just have to tell the lady ambassadoring the Embassy this year to let up on Saddam."

"Not a big assignment."

"Not a big message – but I get three weeks R 'n R, then on to Kuwait on August first to fill out the year."

Ian slid his feet into his sandals – Harry noted that they were Saudi 'desert skimmers' – and shuffled across the kitchen floor to extract his bottle of homebrew out of the refrigerator.

"Then I'll be seeing you fairly often, Harry. Kuwait

City's only a couple of hours up the coast, less traffic there than to Bahrain." Ian extended a new ice cube-and-Sid-filled glass to Harry. "Eid al Mubarak!"

"What's that?" Harry responded, dubiously eying the small bits of sediment floating to the bottom of his glass. "You've got a new name for this bootleg stuff?"

"Aw, Harry," Ian moaned with mock petulance, "don't you ever pay attention to the calendar where you are? We are in the Islamic Heijira calendar year fourteen-eleven, the Hajj to Mecca is in full swing –"

"Yeah, I noticed all the pilgrims in the airport."

"And it's a *new* year, Harry: Eid al Mubarak – Happy New Year!"

Preview: HEART OF STONE

Sam Williams from HAPPY NEW YEAR starts his career 17 years earlier as a young G.I. in West Germany, 1972. When his best friend is killed in a terrorist bank robbery, Sam plunges into a maze of student revolt, underground networks and generations-old revenge. Motown meets World War II in

HEART OF STONE

BEHIND THE STORY...

In that odd way that some people call "funny," and others call heartbreaking, Heart of Stone has taken thirty-nine years to earn its 2011 copyright. It started at a Frankfurt youth hostel in 1972 when I went to an impromptu concert where half the Baader-Meinhof Gang turned out to be openly in attendance. Then there was the Polish actress I eventually married in 1977, whose set designer friend disappeared in 1969, found dead months later, after being identified in a certain photo that implicated someone as the kidnapper of a rich man's son. It found its focus in 1984, when an older Jewish movie director I was working with, a man who'd spent six months during 1943 half-dead and hiding in a mausoleum, showed no sympathy for the rich man because he was a suspected Nazi collaborator, and talked about understanding the kidnapper's revenge "like Clint Eastwood." And then, because there was maybe a movie to be made, Heart of Stone languished in development purgatory and litigation hell for money reasons that had nothing to do with revenge, truth, or moral values whatsoever. But, sitting in Russia in 1992, I started writing it anyway - and, when the story finally became free a short while ago (they can own your story, you know, sort of like owning your soul), I talked with the director, now old, and his anger was still alive. This isn't a factual story, then, only true in its heart of stone.

RCF

Just a note about the language: Sorry if some of it is offensive, but that's the way the people talked. The characters and situations, while clearly fictional, are nevertheless based on observations of real people and places mentioned in this book, circa 1972. And the times were different: things were said then that aren't said now. Doesn't make them right, or mean I believe in them, but that's what was going down.

PROLOGUE

The heart of stone. I thought about it a lot. They had it. I had it. The heart of stone.

Didn't have to try very hard to discover the fact: it just sort of presented itself to view with that first choice of emotion over reason. In my case - their story - I chose reason. In their case, they chose murder.

So why did I miss her? Probably a look in the corner of her eyes, a look saying to me that if anyone could be talked to by me - and understood on other than a nodding level - it was her. She held up a mirror and in it I saw myself and her juxtaposed like a surrealistic cliché. Did it reflect that I was as mean-spirited in the end as her? I hope not. I don't know.

The heart of stone. Damn! It was a diamond. And if it happens that the law is glass, then let it shatter like it should.

But, no. A long time ago, before I was thinking about it, I chose to try to keep that glass intact... nostalgia for a decaying old edifice, perhaps. Didn't matter anymore. Just as they did not need any justification for their actions from an outside world that they despised for its softness, so I didn't care whether it was soft or not. I had my own stupid need to be right - and the one or two sparkles in the system were the only guidelines I had left to keep me at least parallel with the rest.

Shoot her for that. She lost that one ounce that gives life any reason. Me, it was only a speck of dust now, lost somewhere in my clothes. And if I stayed dirty, it was just to keep from accidentally washing away that last touch of good with all the rest of the dirt.

Sam Williams

Paris metro, May 1978, Les Halles

Beaches & Bars

Friday night. And the moon cast shadows with a light so bright that one could read by it. In between the shadows stood corners of a small German town. Off to a corner of this *burgermeister's* delight sat a strip joint. Hanau.

Hanau's little corner of suburb rocked with the mellow noise of "Ma Cherie Amour" being sung by Stevie Wonder (until most recently, *Little* Stevie Wonder - time flies and people grow up), played at top volume on a jukebox of Chicago origin, eating up quarters of Washington stamp, fed by a Negro GI of Harlem neighborhood. Volkswagens, Mercedes and U.S. Army Jeeps - a few of each - sat outside the music-producing building, noses pointed toward the brick walls as if their headlights were eyes that could penetrate the solidity (as the sound could) and see inside. A strip joint.

Filled to the gills with G.I.s and townies.

Only -

The West German townies, not a one below the age of thirty, sat on one side of the room, dominating a corner of the bar, trying to look properly bourgeois as they leered at the girls' pasted-over titties and carefully shaved beavers. The American soldier boys, black and white and scarcely a one over twenty-three (only two, actually, both "ranking" corporals) crowded themselves around the runway below the bored stripper of the moment, desperately trying to root themselves into whatever eroticism might be culled from the half spectacle. A few of the soldiers were lucky, having enough money left over from buying beers to purchase a dance with the non-performing strippers. Black private from El-Lay with white ice from Han-au. A cool-eyed, blue-eyed Florida boy gettin' down with the curly-wigged vampette imported all the twenty klicks' distance away from Frankfurt. Havin' fun.

Outside again, the shadows cast by the moon cut even darker than if it had been a cloudy night. Walking down the street, sliding in-light, out-of-light with strobic regularity, various neigh-bors scurried home to their thick, comfortable German beds. They did not look with kindly eye toward the crowded strip joint that muddied their weekend nights with noise and filled the town's coffers with lucre.

"I thought you said it was only five kilometers from base?" a uniformed voice called out across the top of a battered Volks, teenage vocal cords cracking slightly in spite of its owner's attempt to sound adult.

"Five klicks, fifteen - we here, J.C.! Who cares?!"

Well, in fact, *they* did, these two soldier boys. Having made the mistake of coming *together*, this white boy from Long Island and his black Detroit bunkmate belatedly discovered that - in addition to the U.S./German split inside the strip joint - there was a clear color line drawn around certain territories. The dance floor and strippers' runway were still neutral. But the white G.I.s laid claim to the pinball machines, while the black contingent dominated the jukebox slot. Without saying a word of farewell, the bunkmates separated. It could have been a bar in the Midwest.

Except every single fucking beer was German: not even a crap Milwaukee *Blue Ribbon* or Texas *Falstaff* to wipe away loneliness with the proper taste of foamy home. It took a good nine-twelve months to realize that the unpronounceable suds here were better than the American brew - and almost every G.I. in the bar had yet to reach the six-month mark. Instead they got the pleasure of standing in their separate groups - b & w - eyeing one another with an essential hostility that belied their daily training. Covering up their insecurity with a bravado that wavered between good-natured and obnoxious.

The new arrival of chocolate persuasion, tall and sol-idly built, hugged the jukebox and told his loud story with all the relish of homesickness. He did not let his nineteen years stand in the way of assuming an "experienced" point-of-view.

"Well it be Detroit, y'know, Dee-troit, my home. And I be all of maybe 'leven or twelve and it's summer vaca-tion and I don't got no job 'cause even if they was one for a little nigger boy *this* little nigger been told by his Poppa he got to work for his uncle for free. For *free*! No movies for Samuel T. Williams that summer. 'Least not supposed to be.

"But then the brothers they start runnin' in the streets, and the Man he start beatin' on heads - an' *all* kinds a stores just open up to a little nigger kid with big cryin' eyes who just stands outside the right stores an' the Man say:

"'You O.K., son?'

"An' I says: 'No, sir, my daddy's store's getting ripped off and I can't stop them.' And they just go on leavin' me right there and go on to bust other brothers' heads while I do a little 'window shoppin', so to speak."

This last line always brought a burst of familiar laughter from everybody who remembered the news coverage of the Detroit Riots - or who was there - and Sam paused, anticipating the expected response. It came.

Attention successfully captured, he resumed the story with gusto:

" 'Course my Momma was mad when she saw what I got home with, but I figured it was just 'cause she could only get a black and white TV an' I got color!"

Another expected laugh.

"I *did!* I was like a hero, skinny little nigger kid risking his neck while those whitey sticks go beatin' on heads - just so my Dad-dy could watch *Monday Night Football* in color."

Sam was hyper now, rattling on loudly so that the sound of his own voice would keep him and the others laughing. He was not particularly trying for a lot of attention; he was afraid of having nothing to say if he stopped.

And the Detroit story was beginning to tail out. With sud-den inspiration, Sam dropped his own quarter in the jukebox and re-selected the Stevie Wonder disk: he had another surefire joke from high school. As the blind singer's voice echoed through the strip joint, Sam slipped on a pair of sun-glasses and began rolling his head in lip-synced imitation -

"Hey, man! You can't make fun of a brother!"

Sam, apparently, was not the only G.I. pushing for a Stevie Wonder joke: a white kid in sunglasses standing on the dance floor was entertaining his own crowd. The very black Private First Class facing the white boy was not amused.

Which did not stop the performance.

"You can't make fun of a blind brother, man!" the black PFC repeated delicately at the top of his lungs. Sam took advantage of the attention drawn to the dance floor to unobtrusively remove his own shades.

"'Just admiring the music of Stevie Wonder," the white performance artist explained with a smirk. *No way* he would stop now: his audience was growing, he was happy. The jukebox voice of the vocalist in question crooned on, obliviously continuing to fuel the controversy.

A violent shove. "I said stop it!"

"Lay off, private." An ancient, twenty-four year old white corporal stepped onto the dance floor to enforce a sense of discipline in the aggressive colored G.I. His order was immediately challenged by his twenty-six-year-old senior:

"Hey, corp'ral: I a corp'ral, too. You wanta order me aroun'?" The black man stepped between the two privates and the intrusive white non-com.

It was not good Regular Army form to be cowed down. Both corporals knew the routine. They also knew what they valued: their ranks, small shit that it was. A tense, very short moment of nose-to-nose confrontation was followed by the black corporal's statement of fact:

"Hell, I like my stripes." He turned away, pushing the black PFC in front of him, clearing the dance floor.

"Cowardly nigger," a lard-assed Deutschlander noted in loud German from his observation post at the far end of the bar.

"No Nazi can call our niggers 'niggers'!" the white corporal cried, betraying his understanding of the *Deutsche* language. The corporal's temper was louder and faster than his words, shoved out in a wild launch of his body toward the bar, fists first and brain somewhere half-a-room behind.

He even made contact, much to the surprise of himself and a dozen bystanders, each of whom had expected someone else to grab at the American's arms and drag him to a halt. First blood drawn (figuratively - it was a weak connect with a fat-insulated face), within seconds scores of Germans were fighting G.I.s for no particular reason other than the fact that they hated being there together.

It was a lot more fun than watching the bored strippers.

Sam, big and dangerous-looking, was having no particular problem with the situation, his fighting technique being somewhat unique. Lowering his head, football halfback style, he charged into the melee of clanging bodies - emerging on the other side of the room unbeaten and with the probable knowledge of having elbowed a few ribs and stomped on several arches viciously. Sam didn't concern himself with deep inquires as to which side he inflic-ted the most damage on.

Two out of three sorties were successfully executed in this fashion. Sam took a breath at the end of each round, congratulating himself on his acumen, before plunging in once more. The third assault, unfortunately, attracted "blockers" like a magnet: Sam's legs bogged down in a mire of fallen combatants. He sank into a goulash of G.I.s and Germans.

Lady Caroline, the ennui-filled stripper of the mo-ment, calmly looked down from the stage at the tangle of feet and arms struggling below her. She decided then and there to leave work early. "Willy, call my husband and tell him I will meet him at Gerta's apartment," she instructed the bouncer, who remained apart from the fray, guarding the liquor supply room.

"Call him yourself, I'm busy," he answered, distracted: the jukebox was solidly built, no one worried about *its* safety, but there was a glass window…

"Scheisskopf," Lady Caroline (née Hilda Wurst) muttered. Couldn't he see that Armin was using the telephone?! Oh, sure, Armin was the owner, ja, OK - calling the police probably - but did Willy really think that she could tell *Armin* to get off the phone?

"Scheisskopf," she muttered again, resigned to the pros-

pect of having to spend the money herself at a pay telephone outside in order to call her husband to pick her up early, at Gerta's. Gerta had no phone, of course: 'fucking government wired up only the capital-ists and bourgeoisie. Lady Caroline, good socialist that she was, scooted out of the strip joint with quick-clicking high heels and goosebumping titties. Luckily Gerta lived only fifty meters away. Caroline-née-Hilda certainly had no intentions of waiting for the police to come.

Nor did any of the Germans in the strip joint, save owner Armin and bouncer Willy. It was an odd sensation, Sam recalled later: when he disappeared under the pile of fighting bodies, the place had been full of Teutonic faces - soft faces, hard faces, angry faces - faces, anyway, that were not American and whose eyes looked at every uniformed young man through a different language than the one Sam understood. However, when he finally sifted himself out of the scramble of bodies his last football-charge had created, something new immediately became apparent: all of the Germans had somehow melted away - leaving only G.I.s fighting.

Black against white.

Sam shook his head to clear it. He didn't understand the full import of what he was seeing at first. His eyes focused on the nearest skirmish: the two corporals were battling away at one another hard. The white soldier with the sunglasses was stretched out cold at their feet.

The fight had taken on some ugly edges now, too. Three whites ganged up on a single black PFC, pounding him down. A blood from Chi-town edged a jagged piece of glass at a honky private's belly.

Sam decided to join the guys on the outskirts of the dance floor who were pulling out to nurse their wounds. He did not with-draw far enough: a mass of three or four soldiers - color unknown - dropped down upon his back. A lot of chroma-colored fireworks burst behind Sam's eyelids as the side of his head slammed down on the hardwood dance floor.

He did not dive totally into unconsciousness, though. Sam clearly heard the *Ee-Oh, Ee-Oh!* squawk of the German police siren cut through the Hanau night from some dis-tance away outside. So did the majority of the strip joint's combatants: a sudden freeze made play-statues of the scene - accompanied by a concentrated, listening, silence - leaving them all free to hear the gutless Dutch song on the jukebox that had replaced Stevie's wonderful melody.

"La! La-la, la-la, la, la, la -" the lyrics began.

"TURN OFF THAT SHIT!" black and white cried in unison. No one did, but the *Ee-Oh!* sirened loud enough through the just-opened front entrance to distract everyone's attention from matters of pop culture taste.

"Looks like we be rank," the black corporal said to his white counterpart, both emerging from the hurling mass that had recently tackled Sam. "You take it or me?"

The white corporal was still busy dragging himself to his feet. "You go ahead," he grunted.

The assumption of active command required a sufficient volume of voice to shake the rafters. The black corporal shook 'em:

"All right you honky-nigger bastards: BASE!"

He allowed a second for the import of his words to sink in, then bellowed:

"DOUBLE TIME!!!"

Or perhaps it was the white corporal's wickedly-humored addendum - "DON'T LEAVE THE WOUNDED!" - that sent the assembled military forces charging for the exits.

Internecine rivalries were quickly forgotten in the face of a common foe. With a loud whoop of action to counter the ever-louder German police siren, the American army began its disordered retreat. Responsible to their duty, each corporal burdened himself with a fallen body scooped up from the dance floor. J.C., the white boy from Long Island who took the bottom bunk and a Volkswagen for the night, pulled his bunkmate off the floor.

"C'mon, Sam. You don't wanna get caught off-base by the *polizei*," he pulled very hard on Sam's arm at the utterance of the last word. "Don't want that *at all!*"

The color war had not ended for everyone.

The black private holding a jagged piece of glass still wanted his weapon to find a pale belly to lodge in. (It was the same PFC who had earlier been so offended by the white boy's imitation of Stevie Wonder, Sam recalled, uncomfortably remembering his own attempted parody.) The black private cornered a beer-stupored jackass from Alabama by the front entrance and made moves to fulfill his desire. Sam pushed J.C. out the door -

"Go find the Volks, I'm behind."

- and turned to talk to the brother.

He was beaten to the draw by the black corporal, an uncon-scious body slung over his shoulder, who suddenly loomed in front of the PFC. The corporal growled with an angry intimacy, and grab-bed the private's shoulder roughly.

"It sure as hell don't matter if you hate that ofay's guts you about to cut up - you get your asses *together* on getting out of this place FAST!"

A truly inspirational sermon, Sam thought with some panic, taking the corporal's advice before waiting around to see if the black PFC did likewise. Don't want to get caught by the *po-lit-zei*, no!, don't want -

Where's J.C.?

The streets of Hanau were no longer quiet, what with cars peeling out in all directions: some overfilled to the gills with G.I. passengers, others containing but a single cowardly driver leaving too fast to wait for the people who obviously came with them. Sam felt the bitter disappointment of one who in all like-lihood would soon find himself among the latter group. Where was J.C. and the Volks?!

"Hop in, private," the white corporal ordered, pushing Sam into his own Volkswagen, a rusty green variation on the same buglike vehicle Sam had arrived in. Three West German police cars, after driving in circles around the nearby centrum to assemble in force, made their appearance in a honk of sirens, rounding the last corner before the strip joint.

"Sam! *You* got the car keys!"

Even as the corporal's sardine-packed car chugged into life and away from the approaching *polizei* menace, Sam saw J.C. jogging down the street after them, crying desperately. Sam felt his button-flap breast pocket. Sure enough, the car key was there - Sam forgot that *he* had driven from camp: J.C. could borrow a car, but didn't know how to drive a stickshift. Shit!

"We gotta stop!" Sam cried into the driver-corporal's ear. "J.C.'s still back there!"

Apparently the corporal thrived under stress: he answered Sam calmly, without breaking his concentration on the road ahead.

"J.C.'s gonna be black-and-blue, then, 'cause we're not going back for him."

"Why not?!"

"Boy, you're new in this neck of the woods: 'cause he's gonna get caught - not us."

The truth was in the telling. When Sam strained

his neck to peer back through the rusty Volkswagen's cloudy rear window, he saw J.C. running frantically. But J.C. was no longer chasing after his friends - he was running away from the *polizei!* Two of the German police cars swept up next to him, spilling a running, angry policeman each. J.C. disappeared between them.

"They're refighting World War Two," someone in the crowd of bodies surrounding Sam explained, "winning it this time."

"Shit," Sam said, losing sight of his bunkmate's assailants in a haze of pursuing headlights.

"Try being a Yankee in Arkansas: police'll pull the same crap there," the corporal shrugged without animosity.

"I a nigger in Detroit."

"Same thing." Another shrug. "Things don't change. Wherever."

J.C.'s capture apparently slowed down the German pursuit. The corporal's vehicle tore through the outskirts of Hanau into the countryside unimpeded, its nearest posse a good deal behind.

"We're makin' it!" the passengers took turns laughing to themselves.

"Yeah!"

"Oh, Lord - !"

Two German police cars were blocking the road.

"Pull over!" a pale G.I. shrieked. "We're gonna hit!"

"We're not the only ones: lookit!" Sam cried, more obser-vant of the situation than the others: the car ahead of their Volkswagen, a Jeep, jammed on its brakes at the sight of the road block. Too late. Without even swerving, the Jeep screeched to a dead-on stop. A foot deep into the side door of a police car.

Inside the Volks, the corporal stamped his foot down on the gas pedal and turned the stiff steering wheel hard. With a roar of its underpowered engine, the Volkswagen jumped off the narrow road and half into a drainage ditch - swerving *around* the road block. Before a startled cheer could emerged from the passengers' throats, however, German policemen were jumping into the undamaged of their two cars, intent upon pursuit. A cold dread began to pluck at the G.I.s' souls.

"'You think we'll make it?" Sam quietly asked the white corporal, bending into his ear not so much from intimacy as because he was sitting on another soldier's lap in the cramped back seat. For the first time, Sam actually counted how many passengers had fit themselves into the Volkswagen: eight grown men. Not a record, but it was a miracle the corporal could drive; Sam felt himself squeezed behind the steering wheel when he was the only one in a Volks. Then again, there wasn't a lot of shifting going on: the corporal had put the car into third gear within seconds of starting up and had been pushing the gas pedal to goose their speed up past one hundred-twenty klicks ever since.

One hundred-twenty kilometers per hours… Sam mentally converted the number to miles… almost seventy-five miles per hour on a crap road! Oh, fuck this!

"How many klicks to base?" the corporal asked calmly, enjoying the pressure. "Anybody see a sign?"

At one hundred-twenty klicks he did not have to wait long for an answer. "Five."

At one-twenty, there's another kilometer every thirty seconds.

"Four."

Another sign. Safety near.

"Three."

"Two!"

Last sign.

"ONE!"

Push on the brakes for a little home slide to safety in through the back door of camp -

"WE GOT IT!"

- Yeah, *in* the rear door - before the *polizei* get to catch you, and beat your head, and put you in the tank for three days, and turn you over to the MPs for another three days, then a week of shit-work detail, pay cut for the fine paid to the *po-lit-zei* - home *free*, now, just a little turn here -

The gate was closed.

Gates don't get closed on a Friday night at one of the

largest overseas military bases in the U.S. Army. Too much traffic. Especially the rear gates, where supplies are routinely transported - out of sight from the anti-war German groups routinely camped at the front gates, where they protested American presence in Vietnam, in Germany, and (it seemed) just about everywhere in the world, including U.S. presence in the U.S. You needed to have other entrances to the base in order to keep a small city-sized military encampment running smoothly. And they needed to be open.

The gate was closed.

Rather *specifically* closed, so it seemed to the occupants spilling out of the rusty Volkswagen: the high, metal-link double gate was padlocked shut with a thick chain wrapped once, insolently, around the metal bars.

A half-dozen vehicles were parked at skewed angles in front of the sealed entrance, each angle reflecting the astonished moment when the car's driver, having successfully eluded German pursuit, became painfully aware that *he could not get in to safety.*

"I don't believe it," the corporal groaned, slumping back against the curved hood of his Volkswagen.

Sam jumped over to the closed gate, where twenty fellow fugitives stood sullenly staring at the empty darkness behind the chain links.

"Why don't we get over to the front gate?!" he cried, seized with desperate inspiration. He already knew the answer that more than one sullen G.I. spat at him:

"'Cause it's another five klicks away -"

"- and the *po-lit-zei* are comin' -"

"- hot and heavy."

"FUCK!" a voice howled to the moon. "Fuck-fuck-fuck-fuck-fuck-fuck-fuck-fuck-FUCK!" It sounded like a wounded chicken after a while, but Sam shared the sentiment.

The *Ee-Oh! polizei* sirens wailed into hearing range now, chugging along at their legal ninety klicks per hour. The fact that they were still in hot pursuit meant only one thing: the *polizei* had cut a deal with Army brass. The G.I.s standing here, on the wrong side of the gate, had been set-up as sacrificial lambs to military-civilian public relations. Or so one desultory meathead declaimed.

Sam wasn't so certain. Or at least he wasn't prepared to give up trying.

"I'm not gonna sit here like a sardine just waitin'," he said aloud, making his personal resolve into a public challenge. Now he would be too embarrassed to back down. Displaying a visual deliberateness he did not feel, Sam elaborately thrust his hands into his pockets and walked back-and-forth in front of the closed gate, shouting inside in a mock-calm frenzy:

"Mister MPs, Mister MPs! Don't let them bad Germans get to us! Please Mister MPs, please!" He pressed his face into the chain links, shouting to the empty darkness within the camp.

"Good luck, fella," a New York-accented voice behind Sam sarcastically remarked.

Sam chose to explain his "strategy," turning back to face the assembled nineteen and twenty year-olds behind him. "Hey, y'know, maybe they got a heart. Try it with me. C'mon."

For some reason - desperation, silly giddiness - they did. On Sam's count of "One - Two - Three!" they all pleaded like kindergartners:

"Please, Mister MPs! Please!"

His chorus performing as required, Sam turned back to the gate to direct his own voice inward -

To find his nose a scant half-inch away from that of the flat, black face of A. L. McMasters, Military Police, sergeant huge extraordinaire. It was a face crisscrossed by the wires of the chain link fence: MP McMasters was on the safe side of the gate. His dark face scowled at the fugitives opposite him.

All of them, Sam no exception, began to shuffle about uncomfortably, staring at their feet, avoiding the MP sergeant's ferocious eyes.

Those eyes were no longer on the American soldiers. McMasters raised them up a quarter of an inch, to focus down the highway on the approaching, hostile German police. They were pulling their vehicles to a stop, preparatory to descending upon their intended prisoners *en masse* in force.

Sam was as tall and broad as McMasters. He stepped into the MP's line-of-vision and endured the withering glare. "Please, Sergeant, it's not a friendly side of the fence."

McMasters must have unlatched the padlock a moment earlier: with a shove of his arm he opened the gate.

Abandoning their cars to the whims of fate, the crowd of fleeing G.I.s rushed into the gap with a speed that would have made their drill instructors proud and the Charge of the Light Brigade seem lackadaisical. When the last one was safely through, McMasters stepped in front of the gate to stand facing his German police counterparts.

Despite their numbers, in no uncertain terms the *polizei* were intimidated by McMasters' huge bulk planted not three meters away, separating them from the soldier-brawlers, not ten feet behind the gate. Sam could not see a single face: positioned behind the MP's mountainous shoulder, McMaster's head was a haloed silhouette under the multiple-glare stare of the *polizei* headlights focused on the gate. The Germans themselves were framed like scarecrows by the beams beating upon their backs. McMasters did not turn his face away from them as he held a massive paw palm-up behind his back and uttered the single-worded command:

"Keys!"

Three sets of car keys dropped into his hands.

"I left mine in the car, sarge."

"Sergeant!"

"Sergeant, sir!"

"There are *six* cars out there -" McMasters rumbled. No one stepped forward with an explanation for the discrepancy between cars and keys. The MP did not ask again.

Instead, with another shove of his arm, McMasters flung one-half of the chain link gate completely open: wide enough for a car to drive through, which he proceeded to do. Four times. To the G.I.s' roar of approval and laughter. Scornful laughter, aimed at the frustrated German police, left standing helplessly in front of their assembled chase vehicles. As McMasters chugged the fourth car into the compound, abandoning the keyless two remaining outside to *polizei* confiscation, shouts of "Way to go, sergeant!", "What a night!" and "Cavalry to the rescue, weehoo!" resounded through the brisk late-night air -

To be stopped by an overpowering -

"ATTEN-SHUN!"

It was recorded in Sam's mind that no single one of the bedraggled, triumphant, soldier-escapees actually came to Attention upon hearing McMasters' command. He himself most certainly did not assume the ramrod-straight, feet-forty-five, hands-to-pants-crease position. But everyone there, that moment, quite literally froze in his tracks (including a few *polizei,* caught off-guard by the sudden burst of Authority). McMasters did not appear to notice.

Calmly and quietly he began walking among the G.I.s, oozing a deadly superiority in his clear, *basso* declamation:

"Gentlemen, it is one o'clock in the morning, and I fear that there is far too much dirt on this road for me to go to sleep with a contented feeling this night. I need this road to be clean. Push-ups will help attract the dust to your already filthy clothes. And so will sit-ups."

Sam emitted an uncontrollable groan. McMaster's eyes dived in on the source of such unwelcome comment. He strolled over to the open gate, out to the *polizei,* to stand next to his German colleagues and address the American soldiers from there:

"The option is to leave this path and re-enter base through the front gate, thus keeping *my* road clean."

No one exercised the option.

"Le jeux sont fait," McMasters shrugged with French resignation. "Begin. One - two -"

He left his smiling *Deutsche* counterparts to rejoin the American contingent.

"- three - Come, come, only a few hundred more to go! - four, five -"

The *polizei's* laughter dug in deeper than the gravel into their hands. The exercising, half-drunk, half-asleep soldiers under-stood Dante's concept of self-made Hell. Samuel T. Williams tried thinking of anything else in the world. All he could remember was the moldy oldie *My Guy* by Mary Wells.

He got stuck on the words.

Nothin' you can do

Nothin' you can do

Sam knew there was a lot more to the song, but this was how he felt this crappy moment.

* * * * * * * * * *

Saturday. September left a final, lingering hint of summer in the air. It made the beach not half as frigid as it should be. The North Sea, of course, was cold. Braun buried the Uzi among his blankets and laid himself down on the sand. He would watch the others. Sweating profusely from the effort of running across the dunes, not one of the half-dozen university students considered for a moment diving into the salt-icy waves crashing near their ankles with exciting regularity.

Not so Frederick: caution was not his ilk. Maybe because he wasn't a student like the others. Maybe because Frederick believed that, if a ball was thrown, it *had* to be caught, no matter where it flew. Maybe because he was a dog, and a Great Schnauzer to boot.

Or so Braun thought, admiring Frederick's bold, ulti-mately futile leap into the sky after another one of Alex's wild pitches. The tennis ball arced with tempting nearness just beyond the reach of the dog's iron-trap jaws. Frederick twisted his head, neck, entire body in desperate contortion to snatch the small orb from the sky - missed - then seemed to run across the air itself to jump into the whale-grey wave upon whose crest the errant missile chose to rest.

Brrrr-aaah!

Braun uttered an involuntary shudder from the cold that he knew would penetrate even a Great Schnauzer's corkscrew-curled thick fur. Frederick only bounced the faster across the beach, spurred on by his own adrenal impulse, impervious to the ice bath.

The humans all gathered round to congratulate him on his Viking-dog feat, but Frederick held tight to his prize until he could deposit the tennis ball at Birgit's feet. The Great Schnauzer fawned over Birgit with almost as much affection as his love for Braun allowed. Then, of course, he showered the assembly with a nose-to-tail shake of his body that "shared the wealth" from his recent diving expedition. Birgit squealed in delighted horror! Even Jo (and this was an accomplishment Braun took note of) - even that clerically-serious student barked a laugh of surprise.

It could just as easily have been a snarl, Braun reflected appreciatively. Yes, it had been a good idea to bring along Frederick this trip. For a few moments of delicious amnesia he felt that Hamburg - indeed, all of Germany - seemed as far away from their lives as ancient Baghdad and *The Arabian Nights*. Braun was content to lie flat on his dune a hundred meters above the others and let Frederick spread his canine cheer among them.

Though he needed the dog's good-humored hedonism for himself.

"I would love to stop thinking," Braun said aloud to no one present but himself. He had a tendency to repeat himself in his thoughts: "stop thinking." Immediately, Braun dismissed the complaint as a whining, middle-aged version of the students' over-wrought angst. Twenty year-olds could indulge in self-directed tears without too much danger of appearing ridiculous. Fifty year-olds had no such excuse except nostalgia – and Braun would never allow himself to become nostalgic.

"Sit me down in front of a beer stein," he snorted contemptuously at his own attempt at weakness, "and let me cry with the other fat old men!"

Truth and the warm September day that had coaxed Braun into removing his shirt told a different story. He was not a *fat* oldster, and - the issue of birthday aside - Braun's thoughts were as fresh, as radical, as the students' below. His thinking was clearer than theirs, also - but more definitely radical. "More *True*," they said of Braun in Berlin. Where the funding came from. "*True* with a capital 'T'," Braun reflected with a smile, enjoying his hobby of repeating American slang. He was almost certain that no one in Berlin knew what the hell they were talking about. Most certainly they did not know about *his* veracity, as they had not since . . .

When?

Since 1945.

"*Huwhar y'all from?*" *the Kommandant asked. (He was not titled "Kommandant" by the American army he served - but, after three years in the camp before liberation, that habit of addressing anyone in uniform was ingrained in his listener.)*

"*What?*" *the listener asked in German, then added in halting English phrases, "I don't dig your ... jive." And even the Kommandant understood, though he spoke only - in his own words - "hillbilly English".*

"*He does not speak English*" *the translator explained needlessly, his own language skills taxed rather heavily by the polyglot duties thrust upon him since liberation of the camp. The translator was always "rather taxed" with his duties: the smiling skeletons facing the Allied conquerors rattled his confidence. The skeletons seemed to expect* him *to understand* them, *and - and - words were not enough to explain their disassociated smiles, the echoing eyes, the stories they spewed out at him as if he, he alone, could make the camp they stood in, and the memories attached to it, disappear simply by* translating *this atrocity to the American soldiers.*

"*Baked fish,*" *a naked skeleton had solemnly explained on the very first day, pointing to a pile of ash beside the incinerators. The translator just as solemnly converted this into English for the Arkansas captain at his side. For a minute they allowed themselves to believe the lie. Then, of course, the naked skeleton had collapsed in their arms. His veins were too withered, his belly too shriveled to drink in the C-ration soup the Arkansan soldier tried to pour down the skeleton's gullet. They wasted precious time saving the corpse's life - only to be*

ROBERT C. FLEET

repaid by a high command that posted the translator and his captain here permanently until the problem of what to do with this camp's inhabitants was resolved.

What to do with them . . .

"Where - are - you - from?" the Kommandant from Arkansas said in labored German (his three months' in the conquered Reich had not left him totally untutored). The skinny young man in front of him - a third of his weight heavier than when the camp had been liberated - struggled through the American's unruly-accented question to answer simply:

"Breslau. From Breslau."

"Breslau is on the Russian side," the translator explained, "and they say it is now part of Polen - Poland. 'Wrocław' they call it. 'Vrot-swaf'."

The skinny young man shrugged, "Wrocław, I know, that is the old name." He spoke in fluent, non-Teutonic German, his eyes burning ahead to questions unasked by the Kommandant. "The Poles call it 'Wrocław', the Germans 'Breslau'. Who is they who say it is Poland now?"

The translator ignored the man's historical commentary and limited himself to translating only the question.

"Who's they?" the captain repeated, relaxing back in his creaky folding chair to grow expansive. "They sure ain't the Polacks, that's for sure. They is the late, great FDR hisself, plus Churchill and Big Joe Stalin: 'said the Nazi's gotta pay for some a this crap -" He waved his hand at the unseen ex-death camp behind the canvas of his command tent. "So we done took a

34

chunk a Germany 'n give it to the Polacks. Which are ya? Polack 'r Kraut?"

"Śląsk - *Silesian."*

The captain stared blank-eyed back at the young man when the answer was translated to him.

"Yeah… So which is it? German or Polish?"

"Silesian. Not German. Not Polish."

"And I'm not a damn Yankee, but -" The captain hesitated, trying to figure out a way to help the skinny man make a decision. "- but which do you like better, Americans or Russians?"

"It doesn't matter."

"OK, Germans or Polish?"

"It doesn't matter."

"You speak German."

I speak Polish, too."

"So which are you? Polish or German!?"

"Silesian." And now it was time for the young man to ask: "Why does it matter?"

"Because the Ruskies are kickin' the butts a all the Germans outta Wro-, outta there, uh, no offense if you're German," he added hurriedly to placate the large-eyed man in front of him, ignoring the fact that his translation was running half-a-paragraph behind. "Ah mean, if you're German you're no Nazi - being in here 'n all I can figure that out pretty well - but

ya gotta know ya can't go back: only Polacks get to go there."

Braun thought carefully about what he heard the Kommandant say. There had been rumors of all this. Rumors were not the same as hearing it from the American captain's lips. It did not surprise him that no one gave a moment's concern for the Silesians who had lived in Wrocław since before Poles and Germans.

"May I go there to see my city, then decide?"

The Kommandant sighed, "'Fraid it's a one-way ticket, friend: the Ruskies'll let ya in, no telling if they let ya out." This, too, had been one of the rumors.

Braun's dark eyes calculated the odds.

"German," he said at last, "I am German."

"I am German," Braun repeated, mimicking the rhythm of Berlin he had picked up in the twenty-seven years since 1945. "I am German," he said again with a Hamburg accent. He repeated the phrase with the music of an Alsatian and again with the waltz of a Viennese. He wanted to stop repeating the memories, but they would not go away, even when he fell into a near doze upon the sand. His eyes were open, his sight and hearing stuck in thoughts far away.

With the annoyance of a busy man, the farmer stalked away from his open green field to the seclusion of the dunes. "I need a crap!" he called back to his son, knowing full well that nothing useful would get done unless he was there to give instructions.

"Just tell me which rows?" the teenager asked, displaying an unexpected initiative. Of course, when the boy abandoned the tractor to follow his father, the end result was the same: nothing got done.

Still, the boy's gesture pleased the farmer. He almost began to answer in detail which rows need to be plowed for beets - and which for winter cabbage - and which for...

Then he remembered what he was about to do. The farmer waved his son back to the tractor even as he stepped behind a dune to relieve himself.

"You go wait: I'm not talking with my pants pulled down-"

The farmer recognized the dangerous small dark open hole for what it was -

The barrel of a gun.

- and did not move.

Braun pushed the Uzi's barrel a centimeter closer to the man's face. He was angry with himself for dozing, for allowing someone to stumble upon him unaware. He transferred that anger into a productive demand:

"How many are with you?" Brown asked, carefully repli-cating the farmer's rough, North German accent.

"Just my son," was the answer slowly given.

"Tell him to come here."

"You are Black September?" the farmer asked fearfully.

Braun shook his head *No*.

"They are in Munich, we are here." No, he was not allied with the Black September terrorists holding twenty Israeli hostages at the Olympic games.

"Call your son. You will be safe if you don't act stupid."

The farmer reluctantly obeyed the command. As soon as the teenager appeared - and froze at the sight of the Uzi - Braun pursed his lips together and emitted a high-pitched, piercing whistle.

On the beach below, Frederick gave a joyous leap of recognition at his master's call. Jo, Birgit, Alex, Wolf and Karl froze in their places, looking up at the dune expectantly.

Braun put two fingers to his lips and let out a second, stronger whistling call. A moment later Frederick scrambled up the steep sand cliff to join him. The others followed only seconds behind – startled to find Braun holding a farmer and his excited son at bay, Braun's semi-automatic machine pistol sweeping in small arcs between their stomachs.

"Don't move," Braun cautioned the prisoners, as the Great Schnauzer clambered across the dunes and directly to him. Frederick was rewarded with a grasp of affection deep into his fur.

"It is time to leave," Braun explained tersely to

the later-arriving students. They hustled without question toward the van hidden behind yet another dune. Their brief respite from revolution was over.

"You never saw us," Braun cautioned the farmer. He waved the two prisoners back to their field.

"Can I have your autograph?" the farmer's teenage son asked. In West Germany, 1972, knowing a terrorist was almost as good as having sex with a rock star.

Robert C. Fleet was born in Tyler, Texas, where a famous actress was once his babysitter. Never recovering from that experience, he went into show business himself - as an actor with a Chinese theater troupe in New York City. Later marrying into Polish nobility, he taught himself that language while living in Inglewood, California. Meanwhile he paid for the sin of not taking math in college by ghost-writing a mathematics textbook as his first professional writing gig. These experiences have led him to live and work in several countries as either a writer, actor or filmmaker. He has been owned by several animals.

www.ingramcontent.com/pod-product-compliance
Lightning Source LLC
Chambersburg PA
CBHW030617250626
47154CB00006B/1819